RESTLESS SHADOWS

RONALD KELLY

Cover art by Alex McVey

Cover design by Zach McCain

First Edition - 2024

Breathlessly, Hoyt Sawyer directed the beam of his flashlight from one wall of the barn to the other. Several yards to the left he spotted the boy. He was kneeling on the ground in front of a long, narrow box. At first, Hoyt was sure that it was a casket, but the closer he came, the more relieved he was to find that it was only an old-fashioned tool chest.

As he approached the huddled form of the boy, he stepped in several large puddles that washed up over the toes and rawhide laces of his work boots. It was when he shifted the beam of the Maglite downward that he realized that what he walked in was not pure mud and rainwater. The light revealed that the contents of the puddles were dyed a stark crimson.

Feeling his stomach clinch, the lanky farmer continued onward. The closer he went, the stronger the stench of violent death became.

"What is it, boy?" he asked, his voice scarcely a whisper. "What's in there?"

He lifted his flashlight and looked over the teenager's trembling shoulder.

His first impression had been much more correct than he had thought. It *was* a casket that the boy was staring into.

Hoyt Sawyer felt the hot acid of pure bile creep up into the back of his throat as he stumbled away in horror. "Oh dear God in heaven!" he gasped.

Then he turned and ran through the open wall, and away from the death and darkness that pervaded the drafty interior of the old tobacco barn.

For my children,
Reilly, Makenna, & Ryan

PROLOGUE

From the files of Sheriff Taylor White, dated December 27th, 1936:

*I*t is finally over.

    Nearly seven months have passed since three teenage boys—C.J. Potts, Billy Longcreek, and Johnny Biggs—disappeared here in Bedloe County. During that period of time, their mutilated bodies were discovered, hidden in the abandoned tobacco barn of a local farmer named Harvey Brewer, and their murderers were put on trial, found guilty, and sentenced to death.

    The two killers—wandering handymen by the names of Bully Hanson and Claude Darnell—are, indeed, dead now. But they did not die in the Tennessee electric chair as was intended. Instead, they escaped from custody and, later, met horrible fates while terrorizing the family of one of the murder victims. Ironically, both Hanson and Darnell died violently in the very place where they committed their heinous crime—within the walls of the old tobacco barn.

    From all outward appearances, the two seem to have killed one another. But I suspect that there is more to it than that. One of the children present in the barn at the time of their demise, nine-year-old Cindy Ann Biggs, has expressed guilt for somehow "causing" their deaths. I would normally dismiss such a claim, particularly from a frail child who has just recently recovered from a long battle with typhoid fever. But in Cindy's case, I can't. Although some folks would call me crazy, I do believe the child possesses the gift of second sight. After all, it was that amazing ability that helped uncover the bodies of her brother and his two friends, and also revealed the identities of those

1

who were responsible for their murders. And, in an odd way, I am certain that Cindy had a hand in conjuring the deaths of those two evil men, although it was done purely in self-defense.

But that horrible ordeal has passed. Life goes on for the Biggs family, as well as the good folks of the town of Coleman. Everyone believes that Hanson and Darnell turned on one another, striking each other down with shotgun and hatchet. No one suspects that young Cindy Ann had anything to do with their bloody outcome. And no one ever will. I intend to see to that personally.

I've been back to the tobacco barn on the Brewer property twice since the night of Hanson and Darnell's deaths, in order to complete my investigation. I suppose it is natural that the place should give me the creeps, considering what has transpired there. But there is something more. I can't quite put my finger on it, but I still feel terribly uneasy in that old barn.

I know it is downright silly, but it is almost as though the evil has not been eradicated by the deaths of those two murderers. It seems to linger in the dark confines of that rundown structure. Not quite as strong as before, but still there nonetheless.

It is almost as though it is hibernating in the dark shadows and the odors of dank earth and cured tobacco leaves…waiting for an opportunity to awaken once again.

PART ONE

GIFTS AND CURSES

CHAPTER ONE

"Beautiful, ain't it?" said Gordon Elder as he sat on the back steps of his new home.

His wife, Peg, let the screen door swing shut and handed her husband a can of Bud Light, then sat down beside him. She looked to where he nodded. Acre upon acre of high, dense thicket stretched before them, looking as wild and untended as the heart of a jungle. Jutting upward, from the center of the underbrush, was the rusted roof of an old barn. Half of the weathered structure had collapsed due to age and neglect, while the other half barely stood, supported by rotten beams and corroded nails.

The woman brushed a blonde curl from her eyes and, popping the top on a can of Diet Sprite, shrugged her shoulders. "If you say so, dear," she replied, taking a long sip of the soda.

Gordon laughed. He opened his beer and took a swallow. "Oh, I know it's not much to look at now, but with a little hard work, I reckon we might just be able to turn this into a nice farm. And, hopefully, carve a decent living in the process."

Peg snaked her arm around his and squeezed it tight. "A little hard work? I'd say more like a month's worth just to clear away all that thistle, saplings, and blackberry bramble. That and blast all the stumps out of the ground."

"I'm not saying it's going to be easy," he said. Gordon looked over to the big John Deere that was parked a few yards away, next to their white Dodge pickup truck and the U-Haul moving van they had rented in Hopkinsville, Kentucky. The green tractor was twelve years old, but still as powerful and dependable as anything off the assembly line. "But I'm sure I can get it done. With a little help, that is."

"Don't worry," Peg assured him. "We'll all pitch in."

A troubled expression crossed the farmer's sun-burnished face. "Oh, I know you and Michelle will. It's Josh I'm worried about."

"And why would you say that?" she asked, although, deep down inside, she already knew the basis for her husband's concern.

Gordon took another sip of beer. "You know what I'm talking about. That annoying attitude of his. He doesn't have any interest in anything I do. Not farming, not sports...nothing. All he cares about are those damn comic books and video games of his."

Peg reached up and ran the fingers of her left hand gently through her husband's wavy black hair. "He's a thirteen-year-old boy, hon. That's what kids his age are interested in."

A warm spring breeze blew in from the north, bringing the scents of blooming vegetation and fresh country air yet untainted by overpopulation and the fumes of too many gas-guzzlers. "It's just a bunch of nonsense, that's all. Super heroes and movie monsters and crap like that."

"It's just a fascination that he's likely to outgrow in time," Peg told him. "Besides, I don't know why his interests bother you so much. It's healthy to have a good imagination. If he didn't, he'd be a humorless old workhorse like his daddy."

Gordon cut his eyes toward his wife, but couldn't help but chuckle. "Okay, I get your point. I just wish he enjoyed helping me with my farming, instead of seeing it as a bunch of chores to be dreaded and avoided. And no matter what you say, I still don't think it's normal for a kid his age to stay cooped up in his room, doing nothing but reading comics and listening to that godawful racket that passes for music these days."

Peg said nothing else. No matter how hard she tried, she simply couldn't convince Gordon that his son was a normal teenager and not the strange kid he considered him to be. She supposed most of that had to do with Gordon's own upbringing. His father had died when he was nine and had been forced to grow up faster than was customary. By the time he was sixteen, Gordon had pretty much run the family farm on his own. He had not been allowed the frivolous pleasures of being an average teenager. Therefore, he could not see the necessity of allowing his own son to grow up in any manner other than which he had been unwillingly forced to.

She thought of her two children. Josh was upstairs in the attic bedroom of the newly-remodeled farmhouse, unpacking his stuff, while his sixteen-year-old sister, Michelle, was washing the lunch dishes in the kitchen. The two siblings were as different as night and day. Michelle was eternally bright and cheerful, while Josh was as dark and brooding as his father could sometimes be.

Peg hoped this move to the rural community of Coleman in middle Tennessee would remedy that. They had had a hard time of it back in Kentucky with the steady failure of their farm there, mostly due to the plummeting price of tobacco and a list of accumulated debts as long as her arm. Fortunately though, the sale of the Elder farm had paid off those debts and bought this property in Tennessee, and at an amazingly low price. The Elder family was starting over fresh again. Peg prayed to God that the experience would end up pulling them back together as a family and lift them out of the doldrums they had been stuck in for several years now.

Even still, she couldn't help but wonder exactly why the property in southern Bedloe County had been offered to them so very cheaply. The more she thought about it, a hundred and twenty thousand dollars for two hundred acres of land with a remodeled farmhouse thrown in for good measure seemed just too good to be true.

Peg had been meaning to ask her husband about that for a while, but hadn't wanted to do anything to burst the bubble of optimism that seemed to have kept him afloat since their purchase of the property. But now, since they had already moved in and were there to stay, she figured it wouldn't do any harm to ask.

"Gordon, how come this place was such a steal? It should have gone for at least double the amount we paid for it, maybe more." She paused for a moment and took another sip of her soda. "There's nothing wrong with this land, is there?"

The big man shook his head. "Not a thing, except that it's a little run-down. You know I had those tests done before we closed on the deed. The water table is excellent in this part of the county and the soil here is richer than most of the farms in the area."

"Then why hasn't someone snatched it up before now?" she wanted to know. "From what the real estate agent told us, it's just been sitting here going to waste for over eighty years. The fellow who owned it years and years ago, stopped farming this place back in the late 1920s. Now, tell me, have you ever heard of a prime piece of acreage like this laying fallow for so long?"

Gordon smiled. "I know it sounds peculiar, sweetheart, but I'm not about to look a gift horse in the mouth. When I found out this place was for sale and that there wasn't anything wrong with it, I wasn't about to ask stupid questions. Let's just be thankful that we got hold of it before anyone else did."

Peg Elder smiled herself. "I reckon you're right. But it is going to be a big job fixing this place up to look like something."

"It won't take long at all," her husband of eighteen years assured her. "All that stands in our way is a bunch of weeds and wild saplings. That and that rickety old tobacco barn yonder. We'll bushhog that thicket down, put up a brand-new barn, and this'll be a real showplace."

"I'm sure it will be," she said. Seeing the contentment and happiness on Gordon's face filled her own heart with a joy she hadn't experienced in a very long time. She leaned over and kissed him and he kissed back. It wasn't just a quick peck on the lips, but a deep, passionate kiss like those they shared when they were first married. Looking into his eyes, Peg was surprised to find remnants of the old Gordon Elder emerging once again. It had been years since she had seen that sparkle in his dark brown eyes, as well as that easygoing aura she could only identify as peace of mind. The last few years had been so full of worry, doubt, and tension, she had almost been certain that negativity and bitterness had completely buried the loving man she had wed when she was nineteen.

But here he was, sitting next to her, his eyes full of hope and a smile so bright it could nearly blind you. He snaked his muscular arm around her waist and pulled her to him. "Welcome home," he said.

And welcome back, she gratefully thought in reply.

CHAPTER TWO

That evening following supper, Josh Elder sneaked a flashlight from the kitchen drawer and left the farmhouse. Dusk was falling, sending long shadows stretching across the weedy earth and painting the vast canvas of the Tennessee sky a dozen different shades of red, pink, and purple.

Although it was only seven o'clock, the night creatures who occupied the thicket and the dense woods nearby were beginning to make their presence known. As Josh crossed the gravel driveway and slipped, unnoticed, between the moving van and the pickup truck, the reedy chorus of crickets swelled from the tall stands of ragweed, pink-headed thistle, and leafy poke sallet that grew rampant across the flat acreage. To the west, where the clear water branch of Green Creek wound its way through the forest, bullfrogs joined in. They belched and croaked, sounding like a band of rowdy drunkards who had unwisely decided to lend their off-key voices to a finely-tuned church choir.

Josh glanced back at the house. He could tell by the lights of the windows exactly where each and every member of his family was located. His mother was in the kitchen, putting up her cookware and hanging her collection of decorative potholders on the walls. His sister was holed up in the privacy of her bedroom, painting her toenails and yakking on her cell phone to friends left behind in Kentucky. His father was probably stretched out in his easy chair, remote control in hand,

10

flipping between championship wrestling and a fishing show on the local PBS station.

Their preoccupation with other things gave the thirteen-year-old the advantage he had been waiting for. He had been wanting to explore one particular area of their newly-acquired property all day—an area that his father had deemed strictly off-limits, mainly because he considered it to be a death trap on the verge of caving in.

Unlit flashlight in hand, Josh stepped into the deepening shadows of the heavy thicket and slowly made his way toward the dilapidated structure that stood a hundred yards from the farmhouse.

Toward the weathered ruins of the old tobacco barn.

Josh Elder was a lean boy, tall for his age, but still gangly and awkward like most young men his age. He possessed the wiry frame and oval face of his mother, and the black hair, dark brown eyes, and height of his father. His mother claimed that he also shared his father's personality and brooding demeanor, but he refused to believe that. As far as he was concerned, he and Gordon Elder were totally different. Their ways of thinking simply didn't match. Josh knew that his father regarded him with constant disappointment, wishing that he was more into sports, hunting, and fishing, the same as he was. In turn, Josh saw his father as being little short of an uncouth redneck with absolutely no consideration for his son's feelings or interests. Unfortunately, this way of thinking on both their parts had only driven a wedge of estrangement between them. They lived in the same house and ate at the same supper table, but, in reality, existed in two entirely different worlds.

It took him several minutes to battle his way through the barrier of thorny bramble and tangled thicket that stretched between the farmhouse and the object of his fascination. When Josh finally got there, he rested for a moment, his back against the weathered boards of the barn's southernmost wall. Although the spring evening was cool, his face and the small of his back were drenched with sweat. The trip through the underbrush had been much tougher than he figured it would be.

Feeling that he was far enough away from the house to take a chance, Josh snapped on the flashlight. He started along the tobacco barn's western wall, examining it in the pale glow of the beam. The heavy oak boards of the wall were dull gray in color and had been ravaged by termites, dry rot, and the harshness of sun, rain, and frost. Creeping kudzu clung to the rough grain of the wood, snaking its way upward in numerous places. Curiously, he directed the circle of light higher. In the gloom, he could scarcely make out the ashen bundles of old wasp nests tucked away in the shadows just below the eaves of the barn's rusty roof.

He continued onward. The brilliant sunset of fifteen minutes ago was now completely gone. The sky had deepened into a dark blue with a pale fingernail sliver of moon dangling in its midst. The barn and the scrubby landscape around it were pitch black. They were silhouettes without detail and nothing more.

The flashlight helped some, but not all that much. The batteries were nearly dead and the light they generated was sparse. Josh started toward the rear of the tobacco barn. That end of the structure had totally collapsed. All that was there was a jumbled pile of splintered boards, jagged nails encrusted with orange rust, and twisted sheets of corrugated tin that had corroded completely through in spots. The front half of the curing barn was still standing. It leaned forward slightly, like a hungry dog straining against a leash. But, other than that, it appeared to be sturdy enough.

Josh gave the wall an experimental kick, testing it before actually venturing inside. He heard a faint creak echo from somewhere in its dark belly, but the sound was not a very ominous one.

Satisfied that several tons of ancient oak and sheet tin wasn't about to fall on his head, the boy approached a large hole in the western wall. He directed the light through the jagged entranceway, but all it revealed were dust motes drifting lazily from the open loft overhead.

"Well, you waited all day for this," he told himself. "Don't chicken out now."

Josh cast another glance toward the house, then stepped through the hole in the wall. An instant later, he found himself standing within the cavernous interior of the rickety structure. Josh turned slowly, sweeping the beam of the flashlight around, examining his surroundings. There wasn't all that much to see. Only three walls of roughly-hewn lumber held in place by support studs and funny square-headed nails. Some of the boards had dropped away over the years, leaving narrow openings that sprouted lush clumps of kudzu or wicked tangles of blackberry bramble. The thicket was relatively tame on the western side of the tobacco barn, but it literally crowded against the eastern wall.

He directed the flashlight overhead. Twenty or thirty feet above him bowed the heavy beams of the roof, thick with dust and old cobwebs. The mottled sheets of tin that made up the structure's roof were nailed firmly to the sloping beams, but one in the very center had fallen away. Through the rectangular gap, Josh could see the darkening sky. The sliver of moon was there, now accompanied by a scattering of bright stars.

The boy closed his eyes for a moment. He drew in a deep breath and savored it. A mixture of conflicting odors assaulted his senses. Dank earth, rotten wood, and the faint scents of charcoal and long-ago tobacco leaves. And there was something else as well. A much darker scent—one that he couldn't easily identify, but one that was present nevertheless.

The late-evening air seemed to grow even chillier than before. Soon, a rash of goose bumps covered his bare arms. *Something's wrong here,* Josh thought to himself. But, for the life of him, he couldn't figure out what that elusive something might be.

He started forward. The beam of the flashlight picked out a long, narrow box twelve feet to the left. When he got there, he found it to be an old wooden tool chest. Its door lay discarded several feet away. Rusted hinges jutted from its rear wall, while the curve of an iron hasp was attached to the front.

Drawing nearer, he directed the beam inside the long chest. All that he found there was the bare earth of the barn floor, the rusted head of an old ball peen hammer, and a light coating of something that was powdery and white.

Josh crouched and took a pinch of the pale substance between his thumb and forefinger. He brought it to his nose and sniffed. It was incredibly old, but it still held the familiar tang of agricultural lime.

He wiped his hand on a leg of his jeans and stood. The flashlight in his hand grew dimmer. The batteries had just about lost their power.

Josh was about to pick up the rusty hammer head when a sound echoed from behind him. A sound so faint that he barely even heard it.

The soft padding of footsteps on hard-packed earth.

Startled, Josh whirled. "Who's there?" he asked out loud.

But when the faltering beam of the flashlight swung in the direction of the sound, all it revealed was the jumble of collapsed beams and boards, as well as the angling slope of the fallen roof.

There was no one behind him. No one at all.

Josh held his breath and listened carefully. He strained to hear the shuffling of feet across the earthen floor, but it failed to come. All he heard was the chirring of crickets in the thicket outside, as well as the distant call of a whip-poor-will drifting from the direction of the woods.

The flashlight flickered in his hand, then went out. Abruptly, he found himself standing in darkness. He rapped the butt-end of the light against his palm. It flickered a couple of times, then came back on again. He knew it wouldn't remain burning for much longer, though.

Sensing that it was time to leave, he made his way toward the hole in the barn wall. Halfway there, the flashlight betrayed him again. The beam winked out and, this time, no amount of complaining or battery-rattling could bring it back to life.

He stopped in his tracks, allowing his eyes to grow accustomed to the gloom. But, before they did, that peculiar odor curled through his nostrils again. This time he believed he knew what it was. He recalled the one and only time he had helped his father butcher hogs back on their farm in Kentucky. Of all the grisly sights and smells that experience had left with him, the strongest was the awful stench that followed the slitting of the animals' throats.

The rich, coppery smell of blood. That was the mysterious scent that lay, almost hidden, beneath the heavier odor of raw earth and aged lumber.

Again, a chill shuddered throughout him. *Something happened here,* he told himself. *Something really bad.*

A voice suddenly broke his train of thought, causing him to nearly jump out of his skin. A man's voice. But it wasn't there inside the barn with him. Rather, it came from the direction of the farmhouse.

"Josh?" called his father from the back door. "Where are you, son?"

The teenager refrained from answering, aware that he would get into trouble if he revealed his whereabouts. His father had told him and his sister in no uncertain terms that they were to stay away from the rickety, old barn. If he found out that Josh had done otherwise, he would likely take a belt to the boy for his disobedience.

Seeing the dimly-lit opening in the wall a few yards away, Josh hurried toward it. The old barn spooked him, made him feel uneasy and more than a little frightened. But that was part of the reason why it fascinated him so much.

Whether it was creepy or not, Josh knew he would be back to explore it again.

But, preferably, it would be during broad daylight next time.

CHAPTER THREE

"What have we got?" asked Bethany Garrison.

"An eighteen-month-old boy," said one of the paramedics. He and his partner wheeled a gurney into one of the emergency room's partitioned stalls. "He's suffering from internal injuries and multiple broken bones. Possibly a bad skull fracture."

The young doctor with the long red hair and hazel green eyes stepped forward. The tiny body that laid strapped to the padded surface of the collapsible gurney looked utterly lifeless. Massive bruises blotched the toddler's pale skin from head to toe. The thin flesh of his scalp was split open in several places. Blood bathed his small face, causing him to look like an infant at the moment of birth, rather than a child who had lived upon the earth for nearly two years. His left arm was twisted completely around at the shoulder, while a jagged spike of bone protruded from an ugly opening in the upper thigh of his right leg.

"Good Lord!" she said as the members of her trauma team went to work on the child. "What happened to him?"

One of the paramedics—a lean black woman—stared at her grimly, then nodded toward the outer corridor. "He claims the boy fell down the basement stairs."

Beth finished attaching monitor leads to the child's chest and throat. She glanced up and saw a Metro police officer talking to a lanky man wearing oil-stained jeans, a dirty white

17

undershirt, and a red NASCAR baseball cap. He had greasy blond hair that brushed the top of his freckled shoulders, a mustache and goatee that was more peach fuzz than mature whiskers, and a winged Harley-Davidson tattoo on the bicep of his left arm.

"Vital signs?" she asked, returning her attention to the toddler.

"Not good," said Jay Lansing, one of her fellow residents at Nashville's Vanderbilt Medical Center. "His blood pressure is crashing and his respiration is shallow." He gave her the numbers. They weren't very encouraging.

"What's his name?" Beth asked the paramedics.

"Brandon," said the other EMT, an overweight man with a sandy mustache and receding hairline. He turned and eyed the lanky fellow in the hallway with contempt. "That's his daddy out there. Jerry Rucker."

Beth and her team set to the task of stabilizing the youngster. "Where's the mother?"

"She works at a Shoney's on Murfreesboro Road. She's already been notified and should be on her way."

Beth sighed and took a small penlight from the breast pocket of her lab coat. "Hang on, Brandon," she whispered. "We'll pull you out of this mess." Gently, she peeled back the lid of his right eye with the ball of her thumb and directed the narrow beam of the light at the pupil. It was fixed and dilated. Unresponsive.

Beth was about to speak to Doctor Lansing, but she suddenly found that she could not. All that she could do was stare at that tiny, blood-red eye and feel herself growing increasingly light-headed. Abruptly, the sounds of the team at work, as well as the erratic bleeping of the heart and respiration monitors faded into total silence. Then the white brilliance of the halogen lamp overhead dulled into a much more muted glow. The spare light of a sixty-watt bulb.

Uh oh, she thought to herself, that disturbing—yet familiar—loss of control causing her pulse rate to rise. *Here we go again.*

Suddenly, the sensation of dizziness subsided and the silence gave way to noises, muffled at first, then sharpening in clarity. The young ER physician found herself staring up from a peculiar vantage point…within the white picketed enclosure of a crib. The baby bed was in the corner of a dingy bedroom of a low-rent house. Faded wallpaper was peeling from the sheetrock walls and the plaster ceiling overhead was cracked in places. The air of the room was stale. It stank of unwashed linen and feces.

An almost paralyzing flood of emotions engulfed her. Extreme fear and panic were the strongest, along with guilt and shame. She felt her chest heave with sobs and tasted the acidic heat of tears in the back of her throat.

She was utterly terrified. But of *what*?

Beth found out a second later. A tall form loomed over the cradle. It was the man in the hospital corridor, the one named Jerry Rucker. His dark, watery eyes gleamed cruelly, while his lean, unshaven face was contorted into an ugly mask of hatred and disgust.

"Shit on yourself again, didn't you?" he roared. The blistering stench of raw liquor singed the fine hairs of Beth's nostrils. "Well, don't expect me to change your damn diaper again. You can just sleep in it, you hear me, you little bastard? Now shut up!"

Beth attempted to stop her crying, but the emotions were too powerful to quell. If anything, she wept even louder than before.

"Did you hear me?" yelled Jerry Rucker. He moved closer to the crib, his balled fist raised. Then he struck at her, again and again, each word punctuated by the violent smack of hard knuckles against tender flesh. "I said...SHUT...THE...HELL...UP!"

Bursts of pain cascaded across Beth's head and chest. She felt the tiny bones of her face shatter and the flat of her sternum split in half. Then a great, brutal hand reached down and wrenched at her left arm. Ligaments popped like rubber bands and there was an explosion of burning agony as her shoulder dislocated.

Fear suddenly changed into sheer terror. Although her thoughts were those of a young child, one certainty was foremost in her mind. *He's going to kill me,* she thought wildly. Her frantic cries changed into the shrill wails of a tortured animal.

After the damage had been done, the man stood back from the crib, his face slick with the sweat of exertion. For a second, he stared down at her, a startled look crossing his face. Then that cunning cruelty returned to his eyes. "Now look whatcha made me do, you little turd! Well, I ain't gonna get blamed for it." He reached down and grabbed her by the right ankle, then dragged her bodily from the bed, causing the back of her head to strike the crib railing. "Come on and we'll take care of this mistake right now!"

She felt herself falling, then experienced the heavy liquid sensation of her skull bouncing off the hardwood floor. He dragged her like a limp rag doll from the bedroom and down a dark and narrow hall. When they came to a door at the end of the hallway, her mind screamed out in alarm. Her panic increased when he wrenched the door open and she smelled the scent of mildew and dank concrete drifting up from the cool darkness that yawned past the doorframe.

No! she told herself. *This is enough!*

Beth struggled mentally, separating herself from the lingering horror that shown dimly from that injured baby's eyes. Abruptly, she stumbled backward with a loud gasp. She bumped into a rolling table, knocking a tray of instruments onto the tiled floor with a crash.

The other members of the trauma team stared at her for a long moment, startled from their individual duties. "Are you alright, Beth?" asked Lansing, frowning at her pale face and the frightened expression in her eyes.

"No, I'm not," she muttered truthfully. "Can you take over for a minute?"

"Sure," he said. There was something peculiar in his face, something she had seen there before. "We're making progress here. Why don't you step out and get a drink of water or something?"

Beth turned and left the partitioned area. Soon, she was through the emergency room door and into the outer corridor. She stood there unsteadily for a moment, breathing deeply, trying to slow her pulse. Her face and chest felt strangely numb, as if deadened by the flurry of violent blows she had experienced a minute ago.

Her mouth and throat were parched. She turned toward the water fountain at the end of the hallway. The Metro cop was there, getting himself a drink of water. She walked up just as he was turning around.

"Officer?" she called out. "Where is the man who came with the injured child? I believe his name is Jerry Rucker."

"The last I saw of him he was in the waiting room," said the policeman. His hard eyes softened. "How is the little boy doing?"

"We're not sure yet," she said. "We're still trying to get him stabilized. Hopefully, he'll pull through."

The policeman's big hands clenched at his sides, then he shook his head in disgust and turned away. He walked down the adjacent corridor to the men's restroom and disappeared inside.

Beth turned and headed back down the hallway. Soon, she found herself standing in the doorway of the waiting room. Jerry Rucker was at a vending machine, feeding quarters into the slot. He punched a button and a can of Dr. Pepper tumbled into view with a thump.

Just looking at him, Beth felt that familiar quaver of intense fear rush through her. But something else conquered that awful sensation of terror. Rage. That and an underlying knowledge of how events had actually transpired at the Rucker house earlier that night.

She stepped into the room and walked slowly toward him. "Mr. Rucker?" she said, her voice coming out like a harsh whisper.

The man turned with a swagger, popping the top of the soda can. "Yeah? What is it?"

I can't believe the gall of this guy, Beth thought to herself. *He thinks this is the moment he's been waiting for…that I'm here to tell him that Brandon's dead!*

Her hazel eyes burned with rage and a red blush leapt into her freckled cheeks. Beth opened her mouth, but her emotions prevented her from speaking immediately.

Jerry Rucker stared at her, his mouth twisted into a smirky half-grin. "Well, what is it, lady? You got something to tell me, spit it out. I can take it."

Beth's heart thundered in her chest. She swallowed, then finally found her voice. "Brandon's still alive, but there's still a chance that he won't survive. If he doesn't, it'll be because of you."

A wary expression suddenly emerged in Rucker's bloodshot eyes. "You got no right to go blaming me. Oh, sure, I should've made sure the cellar door was locked and all—"

"That's not what I mean and you know it," she said, her voice hissing angrily through her teeth. "You beat the hell out of that poor little baby. Then you tossed him down the basement stairs...just to cover your ass."

The man stared at her for a moment, then backed off a couple of steps and snickered. "You're crazier than hell, lady. That's my son in there. You've got a lot of nerve coming in here and accusing me of a thing like that!"

Beth took a step closer. "You can't lie to me. You see, I already *know*. You got angry because he messed in his diaper. He wouldn't stop crying, so you beat him. When you came to your senses, you took him out of his crib, and flung him down the stairs." She raised her hand and jabbed an accusing finger at him. "And that isn't *all*. You went back to the living room, sat down, and had another drink, you son of a bitch! You finished off that pint of Jim Beam before you went to the phone and called 911."

A glint of pure meanness leapt into his watery eyes. He reached out and grabbed Beth's outstretched hand in his own. "If I were you, bitch, I'd keep my frigging mouth shut. You ain't got no proof. No proof at all."

The man squeezed until Beth was sure that the bones beneath the flesh would break. But she refused to cry out in pain. Instead, she smiled. It was a peculiar smile and not a very nice one at all.

"Do you want to know what it *felt* like, Jerry?" she asked, almost teasingly. "Do you want to experience the terror and the pain Brandon went through? Hey, you can take it. A big bad-ass like yourself."

23

Beth concentrated. She conjured up those horrible impressions passed onto her by the unconscious child and, in turn, sent them jolting into the man who had hold of her. Jerry Rucker stiffened like a man who had grabbed onto a live wire. His face turned ashen and his eyes grew wide with terror and agony.

The man stood like that for several seconds, then released Beth's hand and stumbled backward. He leaned, exhausted and disoriented, against the soda machine, his lips quivering and his eyes brimming with tears.

Beth massaged her hand, attempting to knead the soreness from the muscles and tendons. She took a step closer. "You're going to jail for what you did, Jerry," she told him. "Child abuse isn't treated lightly in this state. And, if Brandon doesn't survive, it'll be cold-blooded murder."

Jerry Rucker attempted to say something in reply, but he couldn't. He simply worked his mouth wordlessly, tears rolling down his unshaven cheeks.

Suddenly, the clearing of a man's voice came from behind. Beth turned to find Richard Miller, the attending physician of Vanderbilt's emergency medicine division, standing there. He glared at her stonily, his beefy face the color of raw meat.

"Doctor Garrison, will you please accompany me to my office?" he said, the anger in his voice barely contained. "There is an important matter that we must discuss in private."

"But I really must get back to—" Beth began in protest.

"*Now*, Doctor!" he said sternly, then stepped aside to let her pass.

Angrily, she glared at Jerry Rucker one more time, then left the waiting room. She was aware that she had probably stepped over the line of professional constraint. But, given the circumstances, she really didn't give a damn.

24

CHAPTER FOUR

A minute later, Beth was sitting directly across from Richard Miller's desk. The chief of emergency medicine leaned back slightly in his black leather swivel chair, his hands tented in front of him. He simply stared at her for a moment. Then he rocked forward, took a form from the center drawer of his desk, and began to fill it out with a pen.

"Doctor Garrison, you are hereby suspended from your duties here at Vanderbilt for a period of two weeks, effective immediately," he informed her.

Beth couldn't believe her ears. "*What?*" she muttered, stunned. "For what reason?"

He looked up. His gray eyes were as hard and expressionless as stones. "For irrational behavior unbefitting a physician of this medical facility," he explained. "That and blatantly accusing the parent of a badly-injured child of physical abuse without tangible proof or a completed investigation by the proper authorities."

Beth felt her temper begin to rise again. "But he *did* it! He beat that poor baby and threw him down the basement stairs to cover his tracks."

"But you have no possible way of knowing that, Doctor Garrison," said Miller. "That is purely speculation on your part."

"No, sir," she told him flatly. "That is not true. I *do* know. I know precisely what happened to that child."

A trace of amusement shown in her superior's eyes. "And exactly how would you be privy to such information?"

Beth opened her mouth, but didn't answer his question. She caught her herself just in time.

"I thought so," said Miller. "One of the strengths of a skilled physician is the ability to refrain from jumping to rash conclusions, Doctor Garrison. You seem to make quite a hobby of it. This is the third such incident that has taken place in the past three months. First there was the gentleman you claimed beat his wife until she suffered a miscarriage. Following that, there was the case of the young lady you accused of poisoning her elderly mother with small doses of strychnine over an extended period of time."

"Both incidents proved to be true, didn't they?" Beth countered.

"Yes, after thorough investigations by the police," said Miller. "Your problem, Doctor, is that you fly off the handle and throw hospital policy completely out the window. You know what our procedure is. If a crime is suspected, you are to discreetly submit your suspicions to the proper authorities and allow them to handle the situation. One doesn't back the patient's family into a corner and openly accuse them...the way you have an annoying habit of doing."

"I may have acted rashly, Doctor Miller," admitted Beth. "But a two-week suspension? Don't you think that's a little harsh?"

"No, I don't. We've discussed this matter before and, each time, you promised to conduct yourself more professionally. What I just witnessed in that waiting room has convinced me that you are incapable of keeping your promises."

"But you only saw the last of it," she told him. "If you'd been there a few minutes earlier, you would have an entirely different opinion."

"I doubt that," said Miller as he laid down his pen. "While the family of patients is on hospital property, they are to be treated with the utmost compassion and courtesy. They are not to be harassed and accused of crimes they may or may not have committed. And they are not to be terrorized by immature doctors with hair-trigger tempers."

"You're just afraid that Vanderbilt might be slapped with a lawsuit, aren't you?" she asked him.

"I won't deny that that possibility hasn't crossed my mind," he admitted. "But that isn't the point." He pushed the form and ink pen across the desk toward her. "If you will, Doctor Garrison, please sign this before you leave. It verifies that you have been advised of your suspension, as well as the hearing that shall follow."

"Hearing?" asked Beth, feeling a little scared. "What sort of hearing?"

"I have decided to request a formal hearing to determine your competency as a productive and stable member of this hospital's staff," said Miller, leaning back in his chair. Again, he tented his hands together and stared at her over the tips of his fingers. "If you cannot provide ample proof that you are deserving of a position here at Vanderbilt Medical Center, your residency here shall be terminated."

"But that could ruin my entire medical career!"

The slight trace of a smile crossed Miller's face. "You should have considered that before you went on the warpath tonight, Doctor Garrison. Now, if you will excuse me, I have some important paperwork to attend to before I go home."

Stunned, Beth signed the form in front of her, then started to leave Miller's office. When she reached the door, she suddenly turned and looked back at him. He had chewed her up, spit her out, and then completely dismissed her. He was now rifling through a desk drawer, looking for a particular file.

Again, Beth's temper got the better of her. *The smug prick,* she thought to herself. She considered something for a moment, then, boldly, walked back to his desk and glared at him.

"Was there something else, Doctor?" he asked impatiently.

Beth said nothing. She simply reached across the attending physician's neatly-organized desktop and took hold of his right hand.

"Just what do you think you're doing, Garrison?" he bellowed, surprised by her action.

Beth held his hand for only a split second before he pulled it away. But that was more than enough time. A self-assured smile of her own crossed Beth's pretty face. She looked down at a framed photograph of Miller's wife that sat on the corner of his desk. She was a thin, bird-like woman with short honey-blonde hair.

"Is this your wife, Doctor Miller?" she asked, picking up the picture and studying it.

"Yes, it is," he said gruffly. "Now put it down and leave my office this instant, before I call security and have you escorted out."

"Does she know?" Beth asked him.

Miller seemed frustrated. "Know *what*?"

"About Tina."

The doctor's eyes widened. He rose in his chair a couple of inches, as though he had been zapped with an electric cattle prod. Then he sank heavily back into his seat. "I...I don't know who you are referring to," he said hoarsely.

"Of course you do," insisted Beth. "That pole dancer in that sleazy strip joint downtown. The one who's half your age. The one you've been having an affair with for the past five months."

Miller swallowed dryly. "That's absurd!"

"You didn't think it was very absurd last night, did you?" Beth asked, leaning over his desk like a cat stalking a mouse.

28

"In Room 417 of the Hampton Inn off Briley Parkway. Just you and her, a bottle of wild cherry body lotion, and that battery-powered contraption you ordered online."

"That's enough!" he croaked. He leaned back in his swivel chair until he was on the verge of toppling over. "Quite enough!"

Beth looked him square in the eyes. His smug expression of superiority was gone now. In its place was shock and fear. "Don't screw around with me, Doctor," she said softly. "I was right about Jerry Rucker, just like I'm right about you and Tina. You have no idea what you are dealing with. Absolutely no idea at all."

Before he could say anything else, Beth turned and left his office. Upon reaching the hallway, the cruel pleasure she had felt at seeing him squirm dissipated. She couldn't help but feel more than a little ashamed. Beth had promised herself long ago that she would never use her hidden ability vindictively, that she would never use it to pressure or manipulate anyone. But she had lost her cool and ended up doing just that.

With a sigh, she went to the doctor's lounge and retrieved her purse from her locker. On her way down the corridor, she spotted Jay Lansing standing in the corridor. His youthful face was weary and sad.

"Jay," she called out, feeling a ball of dread form in the center of her chest. "How is Brandon Rucker doing? Is he out of the woods?"

Jay stared at her for a second, then looked away. "I'm sorry, Beth. We lost him. The poor kid went into cardiac arrest and, no matter how hard we tried, we simply couldn't revive him."

A cold numbness seized Beth. "Oh God...I should've been there."

"There was nothing you could have done for him," Jay assured her.

But she refused to listen. A painful spear of guilt lanced through the young ER physician. They had probably called a Code Blue on the eighteen-month-old about the same time she was confronting his abusive father in the waiting room. True, there was probably nothing she could have done to change the outcome of what had taken place in that emergency room. But, still, she felt as though she should have been there.

Jay reached out to place a comforting hand on her shoulder. But she rejected the gesture. Abruptly, she turned away and started toward the elevator that provided access to the staff parking garage below. As she ran past the waiting room, she spotted Jerry Rucker standing in the center of the room, awkwardly holding a woman dressed in the uniform of a restaurant waitress. She sobbed loudly, expelling the horrible grief of a mother who mourns the loss of her only child.

Beth Garrison had a burning urge to look the murderous father in the face again, but she did not. Instead, she ducked into the waiting elevator, her face pale and pinched with emotion. She waited until the automatic doors had concealed her mercifully from view. Then her own bitter tears broke loose.

She sagged against the elevator wall and wept for what had taken place that night at Vanderbilt Medical Center...to both her and a poor, defenseless child named Brandon Rucker.

CHAPTER FIVE

Josh Elder couldn't believe what he was hearing.

"You're gonna do *what*?" he asked in disbelief.

The other members of the Elder family looked up from their breakfast of scrambled eggs and bacon. They stared at the teenage boy with surprise. Gordon Elder had simply been outlining his plans for the new farm, when the boy's eyes grew wide and he excitedly spoke up. Josh usually ate his meals in total silence, more concerned with his own private thoughts or a comic book laid out next to his eating plate than with casual conversation.

"You heard me," said Gordon. He took a sip of his coffee, then forked a bite of egg into his mouth. "After I get this land cleared completely off, I'm going to tear down that old tobacco barn."

Josh seemed troubled by his father's intentions. "But how come? What's the harm in letting it stay there?"

"Because it's an old eyesore, that's why," his father replied. "Besides, it's standing on its last leg. A good, stiff gust of wind could knock it over any time."

"It's stronger than you think," said Josh.

Gordon looked at his son from across the kitchen table. "How would you know? You haven't been messing around that old barn on the sly, have you?"

The thirteen-year-old thought quickly. "No, sir," he lied. "It just looks pretty sturdy, that's all."

31

"Well, it's not. It's a death trap just waiting to be sprung, that's what it is. You go poking around in there and you could end up being buried alive beneath a pile of boards and tin roofing."

"Aren't you being a little dramatic, Daddy?" Michelle smiled as she mashed grape jelly and butter together with the tines of her fork, then dipped a homemade biscuit into the gooey concoction. "It's just a silly old barn, that's all. Why would Josh want to mess around that place?"

"Yeah," said Josh. He stared at his plate and avoided his father's eyes. "There's nothing I want to see in there."

"And you two keep it that way, too," he warned his son and daughter. "That old building is empty. I've already checked it out, so there's no need to go sticking your noses in where they don't belong."

"Could we please change the subject?" Peg Elder insisted. "Some old shell of a barn isn't the most interesting breakfast conversation, you know." She regarded her two children. "So, are you guys ready for your first day of school this morning?"

"I am," said Michelle brightly. "I can't wait to meet everybody."

"How about you, Josh?"

"Yeah, I guess so," he mumbled, picking at his food. "It's gonna be a pain in the ass getting used to a new school, though."

"Hey!" snapped Gordon, anger leaping into his robust face. "I don't want to hear that kind of talk at the eating table, do you understand me?"

"Gordon," said Peg, a warning in her eyes.

The farmer judged the look on his wife's face for what it was. He sighed and tried to calm down. "So, have you decided to join FFA when the next meeting comes up?"

Josh resisted the urge to roll his eyes in exasperation. In his father's way of thinking, one of the crucial steps toward becoming a man was being a card-carrying member of the Future Farmers of America. He glanced over at his mother. Peg looked back at him and nodded slightly.

"Sure," he said, trying hard to keep the contempt out of his voice. "I reckon I might give it a try."

A big smile crossed Gordon's face. "Well, now, that's more like it. We'll make a sod-buster out of you yet, son."

Josh took a long drink from his milk glass and felt a tiny shudder of revulsion run through him. The thought of having to parade around in one of those dorky blue corduroy jackets with a picture of an owl perched on a plow handle emblazoned across the back was enough to ruin his appetite. But he had discussed it with his mom beforehand and both had agreed it wouldn't hurt to indulge his father this one time. Josh figured it would be worth wearing that funky jacket, if only to keep his old man off his back.

Peg glanced at the sunflower clock that hung on the wall beside the refrigerator. "Well, it's nearly seven-fifteen," she said, getting up from the table. "You two better get ready to go."

"I'll take them to school this morning, hon," Gordon volunteered, cramming the last bite of a biscuit into his mouth and washing it down with the dregs of his coffee. "I've got to run a few errands in town anyway. I'm going to stop by the county CO-OP and rent a Bush Hog to clear this land with." He turned to Michelle and Josh. "I reckon you can ride home on the school bus, can't you?"

"Sure, Daddy," the sixteen-year-old piped happily.

Josh grimaced at her cheerfulness. "Sometimes you make me want to puke, you know that?" he said low enough that his parents wouldn't overhear.

"Aw, why don't you just cut the poor, misunderstood victim routine, Josh," she told him. "It wouldn't hurt you to smile once in a blue moon."

The boy bared his teeth in an exaggerated grin that would have put the Cheshire cat to shame. "How's that, sis?"

"Why don't you just grow up?" she said, helping her mother clear the dishes off the table.

As he waited for his father and sister, Josh stood at the back door and looked through the glass panes at the sea of dewy underbrush that stretched toward the north end of the property. Sitting smack dab in the middle was the weathered structure of the old tobacco barn.

Just looking at it, Josh felt a little sad. He was certain there was more to it than just an empty hull of rotten boards and rusty sheet tin. There was much more to it than that, he was sure of it. But his father was bound and determined to raze the ancient curing barn to make way for a new one.

And, like it or not, there was absolutely nothing he could do to prevent that from happening.

Late that afternoon, a Bedloe County school bus let Josh and his sister out in front of their home. Michelle thanked the driver, while Josh merely gathered his books beneath his arm and hopped down the steel steps to the sun-bleached pavement of the rural road.

When they started down the crushed gravel drive toward the house, the thirteen-year-old suddenly changed direction.

"Hey, where are you going?" demanded Michelle.

"Where do you think?" said Josh with a mischievous grin.

"You're going into that old barn, aren't you?" said his sister with disapproval.

"So what are you gonna do? Snitch on me?"

"Of course not," Michelle replied. She was extremely loyal to her parents, but there was one thing she had never done and that was squeal on her brother. "But if you go in there and the roof falls on your head, I didn't know a thing about it. Okay?"

"Fair enough," said Josh. He laid his textbooks down next to the driveway, then ducked into the dense thicket before anyone could see him.

He heard the slap of the back door as his sister entered the house. From the kitchen, came the sound of country music drifting from the radio next to the sink. Apparently his mother was hard at work, probably waxing the floor or starting preparations for that night's supper. As he started toward the barn, he could detect the sputtering roar of a Bush Hog somewhere in the distance. It sounded as though his father had completed his errand in Coleman and returned in time to begin clearing brush and bramble off the north forty.

The April day was sunny and warm. A breeze like the delicate breath of a baby blew in from the west, shifting the tall weeds and spiky pink thistle gently to and fro. As he fought his way blindly through the thicket, he found himself wondering if the weather was warm enough for snakes to be out of hibernation. The prospect of stepping on a rattler or copperhead certainly didn't appeal to him. Besides, if he ended up getting snakebit, there would be no way to explain why he was stomping around in the underbrush in the first place. His father would know exactly where he had been heading and he would end up madder than a hornet, whether Josh's leg was swollen with rattlesnake venom or not.

After a few minutes, he reached the old barn. It still looked spooky, but not nearly as much as it had in the deepening twilight. He listened to make sure the Bush Hog was still running. It continued to roar several dozen acres to the north. He could imagine his father hard at work, shirtless, wearing work boots, jeans, Wells Lamont gloves, and a sweat-stained John Deere cap. Why his father preferred to break his back every day of the week instead of getting himself a comfortable, air-conditioned job in town was totally beyond Josh's comprehension. Sometimes he simply couldn't understand the man's burning need to farm.

He approached the hole in the wall and cautiously stepped inside. His entrance startled several sparrows from the rafters above, sending them winging through the rectangular opening in the roof. He watched the small birds soar into the pale blue sky, then disappear from view.

Josh stood there for a long moment. Sunlight filtered through the open roof, as well as the cracks of the uneven boards that made up the structure's walls, at least those that remained standing. But even with the addition of daylight, the interior of the old barn was still choked with thick shadows.

He moved on, crossing the earthen floor, starting toward the sagging frame of the old tool chest. It didn't seem half as mysterious as it had last night in the eerie glow of the flashlight's beam. It just looked like a crummy old box and little more.

Josh looked around to make sure that he hadn't missed anything in the gloom of the previous evening. He was disappointed to find that the tool chest was the only point of interest in the entire place. There was a ladder secured to the eastern wall a few yards away, but he wasn't dumb enough to even consider climbing it. He thought his father's concern over the stability of the curing barn was foolish, but he wasn't about to tempt fate, either.

Curiously, Josh stepped into the tool chest and stooped down to examine its interior. He found a couple more tools that he hadn't seen the night before. A pair of pliers and the steel shaft of a screwdriver. Both were lumpy and misshapen with decades of accumulated rust.

He picked up the screwdriver and poked at the earth that made up the bottom of the old chest. Once again, he caught the faint scent of lime, as well as that *other* smell. The metallic odor common of copper pennies...or freshly-let blood.

Josh was rooting through the hard-packed dirt when his digging unearthed something. It was an object that he never expected to find, particularly in such a lonesome and unoccupied place as this.

He pried the hard nub from the dark soil and held it before his eyes. His heart began to race and a peculiar combination of revulsion and fascination filled him.

It was a tooth.

But it was not the elongated tooth of an animal. Rather, it was the stubby molar of a human being.

The scent of blood seemed to hang heavily in his nostrils, growing even more pungent than before. He rolled the tooth between his fingers until the dirt flaked away and it was polished to a smooth luster, or as close to one as he could get.

Something bad did happen here, he thought. A delicious chill ran through him. *Something terrible.*

Josh stood and held his treasure up to the light. It was not the tooth of a child, but that of an adult. It was not perfect, however, amid the bumps and grooves of the molar's crown, he found the deep crack of a cavity. And the enamel of the tooth was stained a nasty shade of brown, whether from age or tobacco juice he had no idea.

Just holding the object made Josh feel uneasy. The only teeth he had actually held in his hand were his own baby teeth and that had been eight or nine years ago. He considered flinging it down in disgust, but he simply couldn't bring himself to do that. Instead, he stared at it for a long moment, then stuck it in his jeans pocket.

Josh sat down on the rear wall of the tool chest and was amazed to find that it was sturdy enough to support his weight. He sat in the shadows for a long time, listening to the distant rumble of the Bush Hog and wondering exactly who that molar had belonged to.

Eventually, the roar of machinery faded until he could no longer hear it. The spring breeze blew through the cracks in the walls, whistling softly, causing dust motes to swirl and dance in the sunlight that shone from the open roof above. Suddenly, a strange coolness seemed to drift through the belly of the partially-collapsed barn and settle upon the thirteen-year-old. It closed around him like a blanket drenched in ice water.

But he didn't get up and leave. Instead, Josh Elder continued to sit there, thinking about the structure that surrounded him, the smell of blood that lingered in the air, and the lone tooth he had discovered in the bottom of the tool chest.

Scarcely a moment had passed when the whistling of the wind took on an entirely different nuance. In fact, the more he listened, the more it seemed to transform from an innocent noise into something much more sinister in nature.

The soft hissing of faint whispers.

Josh was startled at first. *This is so weird!* he thought to himself. But, after a moment, his uneasiness surrendered to curiosity. He leaned forward, forearms resting on his knees, and listened carefully.

What he heard—or *thought* he heard—was not merely a single whisper, but several different ones. They resonated throughout the gloomy interior of the old barn. Fascinated, he concentrated, attempting to understand the message they so urgently seemed to want to convey.

He was unable to distinguish words, however. All he could determine was the individual tones of those mysterious mutterings.

Several rang with confusion, dismay, and a shrill and rising terror.

Those disturbed Josh, but not nearly as much as one in particular. It reverberated through the ancient structure, seeming to cling to the walls and rafters of the old barn, to the very shadows themselves, like the slick residue left by a garden slug.

That particular whisper rippled with dark menace and cruelty...and another emotion as well.

An evil the likes of which Josh Elder had never dreamed existed; one that cherished agony and death like a pair of truly intimate friends.

CHAPTER SIX

It was sunny the morning that Nashville homicide detectives Gerald Hill and Fred Canton turned onto Owl Creek Road and made their way down the winding, wooded road toward Radnor Lake.

The place was a picturesque slice of rural solitude on the outskirts of the Music City, a favorite spot for hikers, bike riders, and bird watchers with its dirt trails winding around the broad, mirror surface of the small lake. But that morning, no one was enjoying what Radnor had to offer. The police had blocked both ends of the road with patrol cars, keeping the public away. The only ones allowed to enter the area were those whose job it was to be there.

The officers at the eastern end of Owl Creek Road waved Hill and Canton past. The detectives drove on to a ranger's station a quarter mile further. They pulled into a gravel lot in front of the park ranger's station and spotted a patrol car waiting there. A beefy officer stood talking to a lanky ranger in a khaki uniform and Smoky Bear hat.

"There's Winters," Canton pointed out. They slid into a spot next to the patrol car and got out.

Officer Winters broke away from his conversation and approached the two detectives as they left their vehicle. "Glad you fellas could get here so quick."

"What have you got?" Hill asked.

Winters' eyes looked tired and haunted. "You know what we have, or they would've sent someone assigned to this precinct."

Canton shook his head and looked over at his partner. "Damn."

"A child?" asked Hill.

The police officer swallowed dryly and nodded. "A little girl. About seven or eight."

Canton stared off into the woods, dreading what was to come. "Where is she?"

"About two hundred yards down that pathway there."

"Who found her?"

"I did," volunteered the park ranger. His eyes were red and moist with tears.

"And you are?" asked Hill, taking a pad and pen from his jacket pocket.

"Henry Jenkins. One of four rangers who work here at Radnor." He stared off down the wooded pathway. "I always walk the bike trail first thing in the morning, just to make sure there aren't any obstacles in the pathway...you know, rocks or fallen branches. Anything that might trip up a biker." He stared down at the toes of his hiking boots for a long moment, looking as though he might throw up. "I saw the bike first. A girl's bike...a Huffy, I think. Hot pink with white streamers hanging out of the ends of the handles, like we had back when we were kids."

"And the victim?"

"Didn't see her at first...then saw something small...pale...off the trail...in a gully." The man sobbed and sagged a little.

Officer Winters steadied the man and steered him toward the ranger's station before he could fall. "Let's go sit down on the porch for a while."

"Is there anyone down there with her?" Canton asked the policeman.

"My partner. Anderson."

Hill sighed. "We're going down."

Winters nodded. "Brace yourselves."

"Why?"

Tears welled in the officer's eyes. He wiped them away with the back of his hand. "This one's the worst yet."

The two detectives passed a sign that read RADNOR LAKE BIKE TRAIL—3 MILE DISTANCE—5 MPH. They continued down the earthen pathway. To their right lay dense stands of maple, oak, and birch, while to their left stretched the quiet expanse of the lake.

They walked for several minutes, dread dogging their heels as they hiked the lonesome, winding length of bike trail. Both men were silent. Each was immersed in their own private thoughts, but both knew that their suspicions and expectations were carbon copies of one another's. They had traveled similar ground before, in other areas identical, as far as seclusion was concerned.

They turned a bend in the trail and, suddenly, Officer Anderson was there, standing in the middle of the path. His hands were planted firmly on his knees and he had heaved up that morning's breakfast. A puddle of vomit pooled on the ground in front of him.

"Anderson," said Canton, "are you alright?"

"Shit, no, I'm not alright!" the officer replied, looking at the plainclothes man like he was the dumbest bastard alive. Then his contempt bled away and his eyes were apologetic. "I'm sorry, sir."

The detective nodded solemnly. "Where is she?"

"Just past the bike there. Off in the hollow on the right."

The two walked past the officer and started down the path toward the overturned bicycle.

"Are you ready for this, Fred?"

"Hell no!" said Hill. "And neither are you."

Canton nodded. Then they were past the bike and standing on the grassy edge of the bike trail, staring into the sloping gully surrounded by tall sugar maples and towering oaks.

Detective Hill gasped, as though someone had physically struck him in the stomach. "Oh God!" was all that he could manage to say.

Canton closed his eyes and breathed in a lungful of crisp morning air, but it did little to settle his nerves. This was the fourth. During the past ninety days, the bodies of other children had been found in the vicinity of various Nashville parks: Percy Warner, Old Hickory, even Centennial, square in the middle of the city. This one was just a stone's throw from the affluent neighborhood of Brentwood. All had fit a concrete pattern: rape and torture, followed by a speedy death.

When the detective opened his eyes, he secretly prayed that all he had investigated during the last three months had merely been a dream. But, instead, it was a nightmare. A very real and terrible nightmare.

"Gerald," he said solemnly. "I think it's time we called the old lady."

"Are we that desperate?" replied Hill.

Fred Canton stared at the small, white body that lay twisted among the spring trees. "I believe so. Don't you?"

Hill's silence was enough to answer his question.

Later that afternoon, the two detectives returned to Radnor Lake.

Canton parked the car near the entrance to the bike trail. The area was still cordoned off with bright yellow crime scene tape. Winters and Anderson's patrol car was gone. The ranger station seemed deserted. Henry Jenkins was nowhere to be found.

"Here we are," said Hill.

They sat there for a long moment. The two could sense her sitting directly behind them, staring at the backs of their heads.

"I know we should have called you sooner—" began Canton.

"Yes," said the old lady sharply. "You should have."

The homicide detective felt a pang of guilt. "Come on and we'll show you where she was found."

Canton and Hill left the car, then opened the rear door and helped her out. The old lady was lean and of average height. She was eighty-six years of age, but looked a good fifteen years younger than that. Graceful lines etched the sides of her mouth and the corners of her hazel eyes, and her face held a healthy, youthful color, as well as a scattering of pale freckles. Her short-cut hair was gray with streaks of natural red throughout, like veins in marble. Her posture was straight and dignified, as though the ravages of age had had little effect on her over the years. She was dressed tastefully in a beige pantsuit, white silk blouse, and brown loafers that had more than likely been purchased at J.C. Penney than one of Nashville's more expensive shops.

Upon leaving the car, she stood quietly and looked past budding greenery at the mirror-like surface of the lake beyond. "Such a beautiful place," she said softly.

"Yes," said Canton. He walked to the strand of barrier tape that closed off the entrance of the trail. "She was found down this pathway here."

"I'd rather go alone," she told them firmly. "I tend to do better when I'm by myself."

"Certainly," he said politely. He wasn't about to argue with someone who had been instrumental in solving twelve major cases during the past twenty years. "The girl's body has been removed from the crime scene, but I have a coroner's photo, if you'd like to see it."

The old lady's eyes were sad. "I'll see her soon enough," she told him. "Do you have anything that belonged to the child?"

Hill took an object from a plastic bag he carried in his jacket pocket. It was a Hello Kitty watch with a pink leatherette band. "This was on her wrist when we found her. It was the only article of clothing she was wearing."

She took the watch and held it tightly in her hand. The lines of the old woman's face seemed to deepen and her complexion began to pale, causing her to age before their eyes.

"How did this child die?" she asked out of the blue.

"After she was raped multiple times and tortured with a cigarette and a pair of needle-nose pliers, she was strangled. She was garroted with a thin filament of some sort. Perhaps wire or fishing line."

Her thin fingers clutched the little girl's watch. "No. It was something else, I believe."

The two detectives were eager to hear what she had to say, but were also patient. They knew from experience that the old lady didn't like to be rushed.

"Her name was Sharon?"

Hill and Canton looked at one another. "Yes. Sharon DeWitt. She was seven years old."

The elderly woman stood there for a moment, then nodded. "I'm ready."

Courteously, Gerald Hill lifted the strand of yellow tape, providing access to the deserted trail. "You'd best take care," he suggested. "The pathway is uneven, it drops off sharply where the body was found. We wouldn't want you to slip and fall."

She turned and stared at him. "I'm not an invalid, Detective Hill."

The cop's face reddened in embarrassment. "No, ma'am," he said apologetically.

"Would you mind holding my purse?" she asked, passing her handbag to Canton. A trace of a smile crossed her thin lips. "I suppose I can trust you."

"Yes, ma'am," said Canton, holding the purse in his right hand.

The old lady turned toward the bike trail. Slowly, she began to walk down the narrow pathway, clutching the Hello Kitty watch firmly in her hand. She blocked out the rustling of wind through the newly-blossomed leaves of the trees, as well as the melody of songbirds that echoed throughout the woods. The old lady slowed her breathing until it grew shallow. She focused on the watch and the peculiar warmth that now seemed to pulse from the object of plastic, steel, and faux leather.

She continued to walk with her eyes almost closed, allowing herself to become immersed by the flood of emotions that radiated from the timepiece and sink into the pores of her skin. Then she let down her guard and surrendered to a unique ability that she had possessed for most of her life.

Suddenly, she was no longer strolling along the pathway in the dappled sun of broad daylight. Instead, she was speeding down the earthen path on a small bike, her youthful hands clutching the white vinyl grips of the handlebars, the equally white streamers fluttering in the breeze, tickling her wrists. It was late in the evening. The forest was choked with lengthening shadows and, to the west, the burning red eye of the setting sun sent shimmering patterns across the surface of Radnor Lake.

The visibility of the wooded trail grew less defined as twilight slowly fell, but, still, she continued to pedal, the draft of her speed rushing through her long honey-blonde hair. In the

46

back of her mind, she knew that she was long overdue for supper and that her mother would be both worried and angry over her absence. But another part of her was having too much fun riding her bike to really care.

Onward, she pedaled down the narrow trail, steering around a bend that began a gradual curve around the lake. She glanced down at her left wrist. The pink hands of the Hello Kitty watch told her that it was nearly seven o'clock. *Just fifteen more minutes and I'll go home,* she promised herself.

Unfortunately, it was a promise she would never be allowed to keep.

Just as she glided past a heavy clump of honeysuckle, she heard the rustle of swift movement over the spinning gears of her bike. She felt a large, strong hand grab her by the upper arm and yank her bodily from the padded seat. As she fell backward, her bicycle continued onward into the deepening gloom, skidding to its side, then hitting a fallen log at the side of the trail, flipping once, tires over handlebars, before finally crashing to a halt.

Now is the crucial moment, the old lady thought to herself. *Now is when I will see the face of her murderer, revealed in the fading rays of sunset.*

She fought off the powerful sensations of confusion and panic that threatened to overcome her. Slowly, she turned her head, prepared to look upon the face of a monster who had brutally molested, tortured, and slain four young children.

But that did not happen. Instead, something entirely unexpected took place. Something that had never happened to the elderly woman before.

The time and location shifted dramatically and without warning. But she did not return to the peaceful lakeside on the sunny afternoon following the heinous murder of seven-year-old Sharon DeWitt. Rather, she found herself huddled in pitch darkness on a rain-drenched night. A wild hysteria filled her mind, just as fatigue and agony invaded her body. Searing pain lanced through her left hip and thigh, the multiple wounds of lead buckshot buried deeply.

Dear God in heaven, she thought to herself. *I don't want to go through this...not again!*

She concentrated hard, but simply couldn't separate herself from what was taking place on that dark and stormy night. Lightning flashed overhead, followed by the throaty boom of thunder a second later. The rain fell harder, pelting the dense thicket heavily, pattering against the huge leaves of the wild tobacco plant that she was hiding beneath.

Somewhere in the distance echoed the sound of someone thrashing through the underbrush. Cussing venomously. Searching for her.

She looked to the west. Through the downpour, she could scarcely see the dark silhouette of the tree line. There, she knew, lay her only hope of salvation from the danger that stalked her. If she could make it into the woods and across the creek, she would be safely home before she knew it.

But that was not destined to happen. She already knew that.

The old lady kept perfectly still within the concealment of the vegetation, listening as the stalker passed right by her hiding place and moved onward. A fleeting sensation of relief filled her as she departed the shadows and, emerging into the driving rain, took a few stumbling steps toward the woods.

Then, from behind, came a low chuckle brimming with sadistic cruelty.

Gotcha...Johnny! rumbled the stalker triumphantly, followed by the deafening roar of twelve-gauge death.

The old lady screamed. The cold pelting of hard rain and harder buckshot against her skin abruptly gave way to the gentle warmth of an early spring afternoon. Disoriented, she stumbled and her foot left the edge of the pathway. Loose earth, twigs, and leaves failed to support her weight and, a second later, she found herself tumbling down the shallow embankment.

She landed on her back in a bed of dry, dead leaves, yellow strands of police barrier tape wrapped around her arms and neck. She suddenly realized that she was lying in the exact spot where Sharon DeWitt's lifeless body had been found. But, oddly enough, the current murder seemed to take a back seat to the awful spectacle she had just witnessed.

"Are you alright, ma'am?" called Fred Canton. She could see both him and Detective Hill running along the bike trail, their faces full of concern.

A second later, they were carefully lifting her to her feet. "No need to fuss over me so," she assured them. "I'm alright."

"But you're hurt, Mrs. Garrison," said Canton.

She looked down to see dirt and grass stains on the knees of her beige slacks and an ugly scrape along the heel of her right hand. "Oh, it's nothing. Only a few scratches and bruises, that's all."

"What happened?" asked Hill. "We heard you scream."

"Something...frightened me," was all she knew to say.

Canton couldn't conceal the hopefulness that sprang into his face. "Did you see him?" he asked. "Did you see who killed the girl?"

"No," the old lady said regretfully. "I'm sorry, but I didn't. Something prevented me from going that far."

The two men helped her back to the bike trail. Once she got there, she found herself dizzy and weak. Her pulse pounded heavily in her temples. "I'd like to sit down for a moment, please," she requested.

"You don't look very well," said Canton. "Should we take you to the hospital?"

"Heavens, no! It's only my blood pressure acting up on me," she assured him. "I tend to forget to take my medication sometimes." She took her purse and fished a prescription vial of pills from the contents.

"Do you need anything to drink?" asked Hill. "I have a bottle of water in the car."

"That would be fine," she said.

As Hill walked to the car, she sat on the fallen log nearby and took a deep breath. "I'm sorry, Detective Canton."

"There's no need to be," he assured her. "It's a real gift, what you've got. We shouldn't expect you to be able to turn it off and on like a water faucet."

"Usually, I can pretty much do just that," she told him. "But something strange happened today. Something frightening."

"Do you think you would like to take another shot at it after you calm down?" he asked, hoping not to sound too anxious.

She was silent for a moment. "No. I know this is important to you, but I don't believe I could make the connection again today if my life depended on it."

Fred Canton simply nodded. She could sense his disappointment and frustration.

As she sat there waiting for Detective Hill to return with the water, Cynthia Garrison reflected on her true reason for not wanting to give the reading of the crime scene another try. It wasn't as much her inability to relive the final terrifying moments of the murdered girl as it was her reluctance to chance another experience like the one she had just endured. The horrifying reenactment of a deadly night many years ago.

Cynthia had provided her special "service" for the Nashville Police Department, as well as law enforcement agencies in the surrounding counties, sometimes even states, on and off, for nearly seventy years now. True, she had been a faithful wife to her husband, Richard, and a loving mother to her five children, but she also used her *gift* when necessary—that precious gift of second sight, or, more precisely, *hindsight*, which allowed her to draw truth from tragedy and, in turn, conjure a complete, and often grisly, picture of events that had taken place in the recent past.

But that afternoon, all had not gone as expected. Something had gone terribly awry. Something had intervened, preventing her from revealing the serial killer who had preyed upon Sharon and three other young girls during the past three months. In a disturbing shifting of time frames, she had relived a horrible experience that she had not encountered for decades, back when she was a shy nine-year-old named Cindy Ann Biggs. That awful moment in the midst of a stormy spring night had happened to her eldest brother, Johnny, but she had experienced every terrifying moment of it as well. Not physically, but mentally.

Why that deadly tableau should have interfered today, Cindy had no earthly idea. What she did know was that she had felt a presence with her that afternoon. A dark and menacing presence she had not known since her youth.

The presence of a murderer who had been dead and buried since the cold, harsh winter of 1936.

CHAPTER SEVEN

That night in the town of Coleman, Sheriff Sam Biggs drove along Main Street and spotted the Elders' white Dodge pickup parked in front of Dixie's Café. He had wanted to talk to Gordon Elder for the past couple of days, so he parked his patrol car beside the truck and walked inside.

He found the Elder family sitting in a back booth of the little restaurant, finishing their meal. He hated to interrupt them, but something had been preying on his mind since he first heard that the old Brewer property had, at long last, been sold. Needless to say, he hadn't been all that pleased by the news. It disturbed Sam to think of anyone living on that cursed patch of land.

"Pardon me," he said as he stepped up to the booth, "I don't mean to bother you folks, but would you be the Elders?"

"That's right," said Gordon. He took a sip of coffee and appraised the man dressed in the tan uniform of a Bedloe County law officer. He looked to be in his late seventies or older, tall and robust with iron-gray hair and a mustache.

"I'm Sam Biggs, the county sheriff," he said, extending his hand. "I just wanted to stop by and officially welcome you to Coleman."

"It's nice meeting you, Sheriff," replied Gordon, shaking the constable's hand. "This is my family. My wife, Peg, and my children, Michelle and Josh."

Hellos were said all around. Of the bunch, young Josh seemed the most subdued. He simply nodded and picked at a piece of pecan pie à la mode with the tines of his fork.

Sam talked pleasantly with the four for a while. Then he knew it was about time to bring up the matter he had come there to discuss. "Uh, Gordon, I was wondering if I might have a word with you for a moment. Alone."

"Certainly," said the farmer. "Hon?"

"We'll go next door to the video store and pick out a movie to watch tonight," said Peg. "Come on, guys."

Michelle left the booth with her mother, but the thirteen-year-old boy continued to sit on the bench seat next to his father. "Aren't you coming with us, Josh?" his sister asked.

"I'd like to finish my pie, okay?" he grumbled moodily.

Peg glanced at her husband. Gordon didn't look at all pleased, but he simply nodded. "Let the boy finish his pie. God knows he needs to put on a little weight. A strong breeze could blow him clear back to Kentucky, as skinny as he is."

The frown on Josh Elder's face deepened at his father's comment, but he said nothing.

When the womenfolk were gone, Sam stood there indecisively for a moment. "Maybe it'd be better if we talked some other time," he suggested.

Gordon waved to the empty seat at the opposite side of the booth. "Anything you want to say, you can say it in front of the boy, Sheriff."

"Please, just call me Sam," said the lawman. "Everybody does hereabouts."

"Okay, Sam," said Gordon. "Now, what is it you want to talk about?"

The sheriff took a pack of Juicy Fruit from his breast pocket, unwrapped a stick, and popped the gum into his mouth.

"Exactly how much do you know about the Brewer property, Gordon?"

The farmer was puzzled. "I know it's prime tobacco land. The soil is grade-A. Even though it's been neglected for years, it has the potential for yielding an excellent crop."

"No, I mean the *history* of the place," clarified Sam. "By any chance did Joe Willoughby at the real estate office tell you what took place there?"

"I don't understand what you're getting at," said Gordon.

Sam looked uncomfortably at the boy. Josh Elder was paying them no attention. He simply sat there and slowly ate his ice cream and pie. Gordon acted as if his son wasn't even present.

"Well," he began a little hesitantly, "I don't mean to cast a shadow over your moving here to Coleman and all, but there's something that happened out on the Brewer property that I believe you deserve to know about."

"And what would that be, Sam?"

"People were murdered on that land," he finally told him. "Brutally and needlessly murdered."

Gordon Elder's thick eyebrows arched in surprise. "Oh, is that so? When did this happen?"

"Not recently," Sam assured him. "It happened way back in the mid-30s." He glanced across the table and was aware that the boy had suddenly forgotten all about his pecan pie. Josh Elder's dark brown eyes were centered squarely on him, full of interest now. Intense interest.

"Tell me about it," said Gordon, taking another sip of his coal-black coffee.

Sam Biggs felt a little self-conscious with the boy staring at him like that, but he continued. "Three teenage boys were lured to that old tobacco barn that sits on your property by the promise of moonshine whiskey. The perpetrators were a couple of wandering handymen by the name of Bully Hanson and Claude Darnell. Once inside the barn, the two demanded money from the boys and, when they resisted, they were murdered in cold blood. Shot down by a sawed-off shotgun and then dismembered by a hatchet, covered with lime, and hidden in an old tool chest in the barn. There they lay for two or three months." The sheriff hesitated for a moment, his eyes seeming to focus on a distant point. "Until several kids went messing around the barn and discovered their remains."

"Were these two handymen ever caught?" asked Gordon.

"Yes. Their identities were revealed, due to unusual circumstances. They were brought to trial. From the way folks saw it back then, Hanson was the true murderer of the bunch. Darnell was mostly a simpleton who participated in the killings either to please Hanson or because he was deathly afraid of him. Even still, the jury found them both guilty and sentenced them to die in the state electric chair. But they escaped before their execution date. That happened in December of '36."

"So, what happened to them?"

"They ended up dying in that exact same tobacco barn where they committed those murders," Sam told him. That distant look in his eyes seemed to almost take on an edge of discomfort and fear. "For some reason, Hanson and Darnell turned on one another. Darnell ended up with his guts blown all over the barn floor, while Hanson died with a hatchet buried in the crown of his head."

"Damn!" said Gordon, probing at his teeth with a wooden toothpick. "That's a helluva story."

"Now you know why I wanted to tell it to you alone," said Sam. He glanced back at the boy. Josh's lean face was flushed with excitement. He seemed to be absolutely fascinated with the sheriff's gruesome tale of rural mass murder.

"Yeah, I do," said Gordon. "I reckon it'd be best if Peg and Michelle were left in the dark about what happened. But why didn't Willoughby tell me about this up front?"

"I guess he thought it might scare you off. He and his father before him have been trying to sell the old Brewer place for over sixty years. No one inside the Bedloe County line would go near the property, let alone lay down cash money for it. You see, a lot of folks here in Coleman and the surrounding towns, they sort of think that old tobacco barn is haunted. That the dead refuse to rest there."

"That's a bunch of bullshit," scoffed Gordon Elder.

The sheriff nodded, but his eyes said that he wasn't entirely convinced of that fact. "Anyway, I just thought I'd tell you about it. I figured you deserved to know the truth, even if Joe believes otherwise."

"I appreciate it, Sam," said Gordon. He stood up and shook the sheriff's hand. "But it doesn't bother me in the least. I mean, it happened a long time ago, right? It doesn't have anything to do with the present. Besides, it won't be long before the folks around here won't have anything to spin ghost stories about anymore."

It was Sam's turn to be baffled. "What do you mean?"

"As soon as I finish clearing that land of thicket, I'm planning on tearing that old barn down," he explained. "I'm going to have the lumber and tin hauled away and then I'm going to build me a brand-new barn on the same spot."

Sam looked over at Josh Elder. The teenager was no longer looking at him. Instead, he glared at his father with an expression Sam could only interpret as resentment. He couldn't understand why the boy should feel that way toward his father. He looked back to Gordon. The burly farmer seemed totally oblivious to his son's reaction.

Personally, Sam felt nothing but relief upon learning of Elder's plans. In his opinion, that old slaughterhouse of a curing barn should have been demolished decades ago and the land around it burned until it was as black as coal. And he wasn't the only one in Coleman who held such an extreme opinion, either.

"Well, I reckon I'd best get back to the office," said the sheriff. "One of my deputies is on vacation this week and I've got a deskload of paperwork to catch up on. It was nice meeting you and your family."

"Thanks for stopping by," Gordon told him. "By the way, Sam…do you do much hunting or fishing?"

Sam couldn't help but grin. "I surely do. I hunt deer and duck in the fall and winter, and fish for bass and crappie over at Willow Lake a few miles from here."

"Maybe we can get together and do a little fishing then," suggested the farmer.

"I'd like that," agreed Sam. He looked at the boy, who sat in the corner of the booth, looking pale and troubled. "See you around, Josh."

The young man looked up. "Uh, yeah. You, too."

As Gordon Elder and his son went to the cash register to pay for their meal, Sam Biggs stepped back into the cool evening air. He climbed into his patrol car and watched as the two left the café and walked down the sidewalk toward Coleman's one and only video store. Sam waved at them through the windshield and Gordon waved back. The boy simply followed his father morosely, his hands stuffed in the front pockets of his jeans.

Sam sat there in his car for a long time. The talk with Gordon Elder had left him feeling uneasy and a little depressed. He normally avoided talking about what happened back in 1936, but he figured the farmer deserved to know the truth, having bought the property and all. Still, it always dredged up a lot of bad memories whenever Sam Biggs talked about—or even *thought* about—the horrible crimes that had taken place in that drafty old curing barn.

After all, he had been there on that winter night when a year's worth of pain, fear, and terror had come to a bloody climax in the dark belly of Harvey Brewer's tobacco barn. Sam had watched in horror as Bully Hanson and Claude Darnell had turned their murderous intentions from others and viciously directed them toward one another. Sam hadn't been the only one there, either. His mother had been present.

And, of course, his sister.

Sam turned on the radio, attempting to drown out those dark and dismal images with music. After a few minutes, those ugly memories had faded. But something still bothered him about his talk with Elder.

It was the way the boy had glared at his father when he had mentioned his plans to demolish the tobacco barn, that expression of an anger bordering on rage that had burned in the boy's dark eyes.

Sam didn't know why that should bother him so much, but it did.

CHAPTER EIGHT

"Are you sure you want to do this?" she asked her grandmother.

"Yes," said the elderly woman. An expression of stern determination shown in her hazel eyes. "I'm going to give it one more try...if only for the sake of those poor children."

Beth Garrison reached out and took the old lady's hand. "Okay, Grandma," she said, squeezing her fingers gently. "But if you get spooked like yesterday, we're leaving. Okay?"

"You've got it," replied Cindy Garrison.

Together, grandmother and granddaughter left the Honda Accord and stepped off the edge of the gravel parking lot onto the earthen pathway of the bike trail. It was mid-morning, a little after ten o'clock. They had passed several joggers as they drove along Otter Creek Road, but the bicycle trail itself appeared to be deserted. The only indication that the wooded spot had been the scene of a heinous crime was a stray yellow ribbon of police barrier tape that clung to the exposed oak tree several yards away.

Beth studied the elderly woman with concern. Her grandmother had been up most of the previous night, agonizing over her failure to expose the identity of the serial killer who stalked Nashville's city parks. But Beth knew that wasn't all that bothered her. Something else had disturbed her, something incredibly frightening that had taken place during her first attempt at a reading. Beth had picked up on her secret fear immediately, but had been unable to identify it. She suspected that her grandmother was purposely shielding herself, not yet prepared to reveal exactly what had terrified her so. Of course, Cindy Garrison was much more powerful and experienced than Beth was, as far as their mutual ability was concerned. Therefore, the younger woman had little chance of breaking through the barrier her grandmother had enclosed herself in.

Concerned about her and the stress that a second attempt might cause, Beth had decided to accompany Cindy to Radnor Lake that morning. It wasn't like she really had anything better to do. Only a couple of days had passed since her suspension from Vanderbilt Medical Center and she hoped that getting out might do her some good. She didn't exactly approve of her grandmother's occupation as a sort of freelance psychic investigator, but she felt it might relieve some of her anxiety if she tagged along. Besides, anything was better than moping around the house, watching old movies on Netflix, and eating entirely too many sweets out of sheer boredom and depression.

The day was overcast with a chance of rain, not at all sunny and beautiful like the day before. The trail looked lonely and foreboding in the absence of sunlight. Beth watched. Her grandmother took a tentative step toward the winding pathway, then hesitated.

"Do you want me to come with you?" she asked.

Cindy turned and looked at her granddaughter. "Only if you want to, dear. This is bound to be more disturbing than those occurrences you've encountered at the hospital."

"I wouldn't be so sure about that, Grandma," Beth told her truthfully. But, even still, she found herself apprehensive. Seeing the brutal beating of a toddler was one thing, while experiencing the torturous rape and murder of a seven-year-old girl was something else entirely. She wasn't sure that she was capable of handling it.

Cindy sensed her reluctance. "You can stay here if you'd like," she said with a gentle smile. "I just thought you might be able to accomplish what I've failed to do so far."

Beth swallowed her nervousness. "I'll go with you."

"All right," replied the old lady. "But just remember...it's only the past. It can't hurt you. Not physically, at least."

The young woman nodded. "Let's go."

Together, the two began to stroll slowly down the pathway.

Cindy went first. She did as she had yesterday, slowing her breathing and closing her eyes until she could barely see through the lashes of her eyelids. She did not have Sharon DeWitt's wristwatch with her that morning, but she no longer needed it. The essence of the girl's last frightening moments was a part of her now. She realized, however, that her granddaughter didn't possess such an advantage.

She reached behind her. "Take my hand," she whispered. "The girl's name was Sharon. You'll know her soon enough."

Cindy felt her granddaughter take her hand. Her fingers trembled within her grasp. As they moved down the trail, she sensed Beth's hand stiffen a little. *She's found her,* she thought. Then she dropped her defenses and allowed herself to do likewise.

Abruptly, the gloomy trail grew even darker. The air around Cindy dropped a good fifteen degrees. She felt herself on the hot pink bike again, gliding along the earthen trail, the breeze blowing through her hair. She turned her head and looked over the peaceful surface of Radnor Lake. The setting sun cast its red glow over the still water and through the dark branches of the tall elms and maples that grew plentifully along the rocky shore.

Let's do it this time, she told herself. *Let's catch this murdering bastard.*

Onward down the shadowy trail she pedaled, part of her enjoying the adrenaline rush of speed and weightlessness, while another part was aware of what awaited her ahead. She glanced down at the Hello Kitty watch, just like before. It was nearly seven o'clock. She experienced fleeting images of Sharon's supper growing cold on the dining room table and her mother looking out the kitchen window, tense with anger and worry.

Soon, she was steering the handlebars of the bike, navigating the gradual bend that encircled the eastern side of Radnor Lake. She spotted the shadowy clump of honeysuckle up ahead and knew what lurked on the other side. But she did not stop. She could not. She continued onward…toward young Sharon's awful destiny.

Suddenly, she was past the underbrush. Again the rustle of quick movement from behind her and the vise-like grip of a strong hand encircling her upper arm. She cried out as she was jerked bodily from the seat of the bike. She landed hard on her back. The wind was knocked from her lungs as the bicycle continued onward several yards, then flipped over a fallen log at the edge of the pathway.

Terror and panic shrilled through Cindy's mind. She opened her mouth to scream, but a hand lashed out, striking her viciously across the side of her face. She looked up as a tall, lanky form loomed over her. She could not make out his facial features at first, but she could certainly see the gleam of cruel pleasure that sparkled in his eyes. Abruptly, she knew—just as poor Sharon had known—exactly what the man wanted, as well as the lengths he was willing to go in order to get it.

Wildly, Cindy scrambled backward across the pathway in a feeble attempt at escape. But her attacker merely laughed in response. He reached down and drew her to him with no effort at all. One hand clutched her tightly by the throat, while the other tore hungrily at her clothing. She began to cry as she felt the chill of dusk against her bare flesh.

Then, as he dragged her toward the side of the trail, toward the private shadows of the hollow beyond, the crimson glow of the setting sun illuminated the murderer's face for an instant. And there was no mistaking those handsome, clean-cut features.

I've got what I came for, thought Cindy. Then, with greater effort than before, she distanced herself from the horrible event that had taken place the evening before last.

Immediately, she was back on the trail, a cloudy morning sky peeking through the canopy of tree branches above her. She breathed in deeply, regaining her composure, assuring herself that she was safe and in no danger. Then, as she fully returned to herself, she was aware that she was still holding her granddaughter's hand.

Grimly, she turned and regarded the young, redheaded woman who stood beside her.

"I know who he is," she said.

Beth stared back at her, tears streaming from stunned eyes.

"Yes," she answered in bewilderment. "So do I."

CHAPTER NINE

Following their visit to Radnor Lake, Cynthia and Beth had lunch at a restaurant in nearby Brentwood.

The elderly woman took a sip of iced tea and studied her granddaughter carefully. Beth still looked pale and shaken from her experience at the murder scene. She had settled down a little, but the fork in her hand trembled as she picked at the greenery of her chef's salad. She had hardly eaten a bite since their food had arrived. But then, Cindy wasn't very hungry herself. Traumatic events such as that which they had both shared had a way of ruining one's appetite.

She reached out and took Beth's free hand. "Are you certain you're okay, sweetheart?" she asked for the fifth time.

Beth forced a half-hearted smile. "Sure, Grandma. It just freaked me out, that's all." The woman stared at the ranch dressing that garnished her salad. "It sort of reminded me of...well, you know..."

Cindy suddenly realized how deeply troubled her granddaughter was. She hadn't even considered the possibility that what they had experienced that morning might dredge up bad childhood memories for her granddaughter. "Yes, dear...I understand. And I'm sorry. I could kick myself for dragging you along with me like that."

Beth laughed. "You didn't drag me anywhere," she assured her. "It was my decision, okay? Besides, I should have gotten over *that* a long time ago."

"Sometimes you never get over a horrible experience like that," she said, thinking of how close Beth had once come to ending up like Sharon DeWitt. Then she considered the horrors she herself had known as a child. "Take it from me. Sometimes it can stay with you for a lifetime."

"Yeah," said Beth. She took a bite of her salad and frowned. "What bugs me the most is the one who has been killing these poor little girls." The killer's face—a familiar and famous face—came back to haunt her, feverish with sexual hunger and bloodlust. "I mean, can you believe who it actually was?"

"It is difficult to believe," admitted Cindy.

"What do you think the police are going to say?" asked Beth. "Better yet, what is the public going to say when they find out?"

"It's bound to cause a stir, that's for certain," said the old lady. "To think that the serial killer who has raped and killed four children here in Nashville during the past few months is actually a well-loved country music star. I mean, he won half a dozen awards at the last CMA show, one for best gospel album." She sat silently for a moment. "A lot of people are going to be shocked and horrified. And, of course, there will be more than a few who will absolutely refuse to believe that he would be capable of doing such a horrendous thing."

Beth took a sip of club soda flavored with a twist of lime. "What bothers me the most is the way he killed those poor kids."

Cindy nodded. "Strangling them with a guitar string. Both horrifying and more than a little ironic, don't you think?"

"I'll say," agreed Beth. She pushed her plate aside and picked up her drink. "Grandma...do you ever hate it sometimes?"

"Do I hate *what*, dear?" replied the old lady.

"You know very well what I'm talking about. This wondrous *gift* of ours. Don't you wish we hadn't been blessed with it sometimes?"

"Certainly," admitted Cynthia. "Sometimes I wish I was blissfully ignorant of things that have happened in the past or shall take place in the future. Believe me, it has made me a nervous wreck over the years. That's the main reason why my blood pressure is so high these days."

"Speaking of your BP, have you taken your medication this morning?"

The elderly woman frowned guiltily. "Oops. I forgot." She took the prescription bottle from her purse and swallowed the tiny pill with a sip of tea. "There. Are you satisfied, Doctor?"

"You need to try and take it on a regular schedule, Grandma," Beth scolded her good naturedly. "If you don't, they might end up wheeling you into my emergency room some day. That is, if I ever get to work in one again."

Cindy reached across the table and patted her granddaughter's hand. "Don't worry, dear. You're a good doctor. Things will work out for the best."

"I just wish I was as confident of that fact as you are," said Beth. She turned back to their original subject, not wishing to discuss the hospital and her suspension from duty. "So, you'd give it all up in a second, huh? Just throw away this precious gift of yours to live like a normal person for a change?"

The elderly woman grinned. "Now, I didn't say that. Oh, it does have its drawbacks sometimes, especially when all you seem to receive is bad news and tragedy. But, when I think back, I remember times when I wouldn't have traded my gift for a million dollars. I'll give you an example. Do you remember that time when you were twelve? Your father was about to take that job working on that oil rig off the coast of Louisiana? I talked him out of going and, a week later, the thing exploded, killing nearly everyone on board."

"Yes, I do remember that. And there was the time when Mom lost her wedding ring and you told her it was in the flower garden, buried beneath the marigolds. Sure enough, she dug them up and found it right where you said it would be."

"There were times when I was a child when it came in handy, too," said Cindy Garrison. She stared out the restaurant window at the gray rain that fell upon the parking lot. "Times when it was the only thing that stood between life and death."

Beth knew what she was referring to. She shuddered just thinking about it.

Cindy pulled her thoughts from the past and smiled at her granddaughter. "Now don't tell me that you haven't had positive experiences with your ability before."

The young doctor thought for a moment. "There was the time when that woman came into the ER to have her finger stitched up. She'd sliced it open with a kitchen knife. I was nearly finished with her when I suddenly knew that she had cancer. I told her and, luckily, she believed me. She went to a specialist and they caught it before it got out of hand. She had a few radiation treatments and now she is doing fine."

"See? In that respect, it turned out to be more of a blessing than a curse."

"Sure, but those times are few and far between," said Beth. "What I can't understand is why *me*? You had six other grandchildren. How come I got stuck with it?"

"I have no idea," her grandmother told her. "But, incidentally, you weren't the only one in the family who had the gift. You probably aren't aware of this, but your Uncle Kenny was blessed with it, too."

Beth was surprised. "You're kidding! Why didn't he ever tell me?"

"Mostly because he didn't want anyone to know. His ability wasn't nearly as strong as yours or mine, but he did have it. Kenny went through his life denying that fact, though. I believe it scared him more than anything else."

"I certainly know how he felt," said Beth.

Cynthia saw the troubled look in her granddaughter's eyes. She had seen it there many times before. "Beth, let me tell you something that an old black gentleman named Jonesy once told me back when I was just a young'un. He told me that the ability I possessed was truly a gift from God, that I should be proud of it, rather than ashamed. He also told me that if I began to fear or mistrust myself because of the gift, then I wouldn't be able to put my trust in anyone else either. And he was right. Sometimes it's difficult to believe that, but it's true."

Beth reached out and took the old woman's hand. "Thanks, Grandma."

Cindy opened her purse and found a business card in one of the inner pockets. "May I borrow your cell phone, dear? I suppose it's time I called Detectives Canton and Hill and told them that there's something we'd like to discuss with them."

Beth fished her iPhone from her purse and handed it to her. "I think maybe you ought to talk to them alone, Grandma."

"You confirmed the identity of the killer as strongly as I did," Cindy told her. "If you think I'm going to take all the credit for exposing this sadistic son of a bitch, you've got another thing coming. You were just as an important part of solving this crime as I was."

"That's not it," said Beth. "Actually, I don't want anyone to know that I even helped you. Doctor Miller already has his sights set on terminating my residency at Vanderbilt. You know as well as I do that the newspapers would have a field day if they found out I was involved in solving this string of murders. And then my career would really be on the line."

The old lady considered it for a moment. "Yes, I understand. Don't worry then. If you don't want the police or anyone else to know that you were out there with me this morning, I'll do my level best to keep you out of the picture. But that doesn't change the fact that you *did* help me today. And you should be proud of that."

The young woman simply nodded and took a sip of her club soda.

"I'm going to step outside to make the call, then I'll be right back."

Beth watched as her grandmother left the table. She thought of the man who wore the masks of both musical entertainer and ruthless butcher, and she knew the woman was right. She should be glad that she possessed the talent to expose such monsters and put an end to the evil that they practiced in secrecy.

But, deep down inside, Beth simply couldn't feel relief or satisfaction over what they had accomplished that day. Instead, she could only recall the awful terror and despair that Sharon DeWitt had experienced before her life had come to such a horrible and tragic conclusion.

What she had experienced on that lonesome bike trail at Radnor Lake had touched entirely too close to home for Beth Garrison. And that, more than anything else, was what frightened her the most.

ı

CHAPTER TEN

Gordon Elder wiped the sweat from the nape of his neck with a blue bandana he kept in his back pocket. He cut the engine on the Bush Hog and admired his handiwork.

The job he had taken on was a difficult one. Only a couple of days had passed and all he had managed to clear was seven acres of land. The thicket that covered the acreage was heavier and much wilder than he had first judged it to be. At the pace he was going now, it would be the end of the summer before he had the land completely cleared off to his satisfaction.

The farmer reached for the water bottle he kept close at hand. There was only an inch of tepid liquid in the bottom. He cussed and downed it in a single swallow, then glanced at this wristwatch. It was already four-thirty in the afternoon, but there was still a good three hours of light to work by. He knew he should take advantage of it, but he also couldn't deny the fact that he was extremely thirsty. He decided to walk back to the house and refill his bottle before starting on another acre.

He left the Bush Hog behind, its engine ticking as it cooled from a long day's work. Gordon realized that he had taken on more than he could manage, but there was only one solution he could think of, and that solution involved his son. If he could teach Josh to run a Bush Hog, he could rent another from the county CO-OP. Josh could help him after school and on weekends. Before long, half of the land would be cleared of weeds and bramble, and ready for disking and plowing.

But Gordon wasn't at all sure that his son could—or even *would*—take on the hot and difficult task of clearing the land. First, there were the boy's physical limitations. He was tall, but painfully skinny. Gordon had watched him perform the few chores he was assigned to do around the house and he always seemed weak and easily winded. And, secondly, there was Josh's attitude. He had absolutely no desire to help out on the farm. That fact had become annoyingly apparent back in Kentucky and even more so since they had moved to Tennessee. He seemed more interested in his silly hobbies and daydreaming than flexing his muscles and doing something truly constructive. Gordon wasn't sure whether the boy's apathy was due to a natural lack of motivation or if it was deliberate. Maybe he refused to lift a finger to help out because he secretly enjoyed watching his father stew in his own juices and end up losing his temper before it was all over and done with.

Gordon felt that familiar mood of frustration and disappointment overtake him. He just couldn't figure out why his son couldn't be more like other boys, more into sports and hunting and fishing the way other kids his age were. Josh seemed more concerned with computers, books, and movies than anything that remotely resembled Gordon's own interests when he was a strapping boy of thirteen. Josh didn't even seem all that interested in girls. That was another thing that worried the farmer. Maybe his son rebelled against manly things because of some other reason. The possibility of Josh being gay alarmed him. He cast the notion quickly from his thoughts, like he had a dozen times before.

He continued on toward the house, stomping his way through the heavy thicket. Gordon decided to bring up the subject of Josh helping out with the bushhogging at the supper table that night. The farmer was aware that the head of the table

71

was one of his strongest soapboxes. He could pretty much bully his family into doing anything he suggested while he sat there sipping his coffee or buttering his cornbread.

Gordon was passing the sagging structure of the old tobacco barn when he heard a noise come from that direction. He stopped and listened. At first, he could detect only silence. Then it came again. The muffled sound of a voice echoing from within the hull of weathered lumber and tin roofing.

"What *is* that?" he grumbled out loud. But he already knew the answer. There was only one member of the Elder family who seemed the faintest bit interested in the old barn.

Feeling his temper rise, Gordon walked to the open wall of the structure and peered inside. In the gloom, he saw his son kneeling before the narrow framework of an old tool chest. He watched as the boy simply stared down into the long box, mumbling something to himself.

Both angry and a little disturbed, Gordon stepped through the opening and started across the barn's earthen floor. "What the hell are you doing in here?" he demanded.

His voice startled the boy. Josh jumped to his feet and turned, his face as pale as a bed sheet. "Uh...nothing," he stammered. "I wasn't doing anything at all."

"What's the matter with you, boy?" Gordon continued, his face growing red with rage. "Do you have wax in your ears? Didn't I tell you this old barn was off-limits?"

Josh said nothing. He simply stood there and stared at him.

"And this ain't the first time you've been out here, is it? You've been out here snooping around before."

The thirteen-year-old swallowed nervously. "Yes, sir."

"You know what happens when you disobey me," Gordon said sternly. He unbuckled his belt and pulled it from the loops of his jeans. "Don't you?"

Suddenly, something happened that Gordon Elder had never seen before. His son's lean face grew rigid with anger and his eyes grew strangely dark, much darker than they normally looked, both in color and mood. "I wouldn't do that if I were you."

"Oh, you wouldn't would you?" Gordon laughed in disbelief. "I'll teach you to sass me, boy." The big man tightened his grip on the belt and started toward the teenager.

Josh began to back away from him, circling slowly until his back was to the opening in the wall. He didn't seem as frightened of his father's intention of discipline as he was wary. If Gordon hadn't known any better, he would have thought his son was squaring off, getting ready to fend off the stinging lashes of the belt.

Gordon closed the gap between them. He grabbed the boy by the arm and jerked him around until the boy's buttocks faced him, the way he had done it since Josh was a toddler. "You shouldn't have backtalked me," he warned, then lifted his hand and let the length of heavy leather fly.

But, before it could find its mark, Josh whirled, causing his father's fingers to slip from his arm. The boy refused to retreat, however. Instead, he grabbed the belt in mid-air. It slapped loudly across his palm and wrapped tightly around his knuckles. Gordon couldn't believe what was happening. He glared at Josh and saw defiance in his eyes unlike any he had ever seen there before.

"Let go!" he demanded.

Josh simply stared at him, the expression on his face stronger than any refusal he might put into words. Gordon jerked on the belt, expecting to pull it from the boy's grasp. But he found that he couldn't. Josh tightened his hold and surprised his father by yanking it clean out of his hand instead. A second

73

later, the teenager flung the belt away. It landed in the jumbled pile of lumber at the collapsed end of the barn.

For a moment, Gordon could say nothing. He simply stood and looked at the boy. Maybe he had underestimated Josh's strength. The lanky young man had shown a resistance that rivaled that of a lot of men Gordon had arm-wrestled back in his younger and wilder days.

"You're not going to do it," Josh told him flatly.

At first, Gordon thought he was talking about the whipping he had nearly been subjected to. Then he wondered if, perhaps, he was referring to something entirely different. "What are you talking about?"

Josh turned his head slowly, admiring the shadows that clung between the rafters, as well as the thin lines of sunlight that shown between the cracks of the weathered boards. "This place," he said. "You're not going to take it away from me."

"What the hell do you mean?" asked Gordon. "This ain't nothing but a pile of rotten lumber and tin held together with spider webs and dust. It's uglier than sin and dangerous, too. And I don't want to see you messing around out here again, do you understand? Now go on up to the house and stay in your room till suppertime." Gordon appraised his son carefully. "Go on now. Do as I say."

The lean boy shrugged and turned to go. He took a couple of steps, then turned around. "Leave this place alone," he warned. "If you don't, you'll regret it."

Gordon expected to feel outrage at the boy's threat, but instead he felt a shiver run down his spine. "Go on, Josh," he said again. "Get your butt on to the house before I grab that belt yonder and tan your hide."

A strange, little grin crossed Josh Elder's face. "Just remember," was all he said in reply. Then he stepped through the jagged opening in the wall and vanished from sight.

Gordon could only stand there and shake his head for a long moment. Sure, Josh had acted insolent and disrespectful toward him at times, but never as defiantly as this. And never as coldly confident, either. That was what disturbed the farmer more than anything else. Never had the boy stood up to him like that, both refusing to take the licking that was coming to him and outright threatening him. In one way, Gordon couldn't help but feel proud of his son. It was the first sign of backbone he had ever seen in the boy.

But, in another way, he also felt a little frightened of what had just taken place. He never believed that he would have backed down as far as one of his children was concerned, but he had. He wondered exactly why he allowed that to happen. Why hadn't he fetched the discarded belt and finished the punishment he had been on the verge of giving? The only reason Gordon could come up with was Josh's strange manner. The steely calm of his words, as well as the cold expression in his eyes; both had unsettled the farmer tremendously, if only for a few critical moments.

Gordon walked over and picked up his belt. As he was threading it back through the loops of his britches, he turned and looked around the empty shell of a barn. What was it about the place that fascinated the kid so? He simply couldn't figure it out.

His attention settled on the old tool chest. That was where he had found Josh upon his arrival. He walked over and looked down into the rectangular box. At first, it looked completely empty, just a narrow frame of warped wood with a floor of dank, black earth at the bottom. Then he noticed that several objects were arranged on the hard-packed dirt. A few objects that hadn't merely been scattered there, but were meticulously arranged.

75

Three wheat pennies, the brass buttons off a pair of overalls, and a human tooth. And, lying in the center of them all, a rusty fragment of a broken tool. The head of an old hatchet.

Gordon wasn't sure why, but just looking at the objects made his blood run cold. Obviously, Josh had put them there, but why? What dark significance did they possess?

He thought of the story Sam Biggs had told him at the café in town and a rash of goose bumps broke out across his bare arms. But the eerie feeling didn't last very long. He scolded himself for being so jumpy, then turned and left the barn.

Once outside, he studied the dilapidated structure and was even more determined to tear it down. Initially, his desire to do so had been simply out of practicality, to rid the farm of a potential death trap and clear a spot for an entirely new building. But now he had an entirely different reason. And that was to eliminate the mysterious and unhealthy obsession his son seemingly had with the old tobacco barn.

CHAPTER ELEVEN

That night, Beth Garrison was six years old again.

It was mid-August, the hottest point of summer. Little rain had fallen that year, leaving the trees and grass of her West Nashville neighborhood brown and tinder dry. The slightest spark from a discarded cigarette could have started an instantaneous blaze. Lawn sprinklers and air conditioners ran day and night, combating the horrible drought, but doing very little to win the war.

Beth was playing in the shade of the concrete culverts that ran beneath an overpass of Interstate 65. The sloping walls of smooth cement were a cool oasis compared to the pavement that radiated mirage-like waves of heat twenty feet above her head. From where she sat in the shade, dressed in denim shorts, a pink t-shirt, and sneakers, Beth could hear the steady swish and roar of cars and semi-trucks traveling the freeway overhead, either heading into the heart of the city or southwestward toward Memphis. The rich and heady aroma of car exhaust and diesel fumes drifted down to her, but not on the wings of a breeze. The air hung heavily around her, as dry as dust and completely void of humidity.

Without her mother's knowledge, Beth had sneaked away from her home on Charlotte Avenue several blocks away. It was stifling and uncomfortable in their back yard and even the steel poles and chains of her swing set were so hot that they burned like the eye of a stove whenever she touched them.

But it was deliciously cool there in the culvert. Beth sat in the shade and played with the Barbie dolls she had brought with her, dressing and undressing them, brushing their long blonde hair. She knew that she wasn't really supposed to be there—that her mother had told her time and time again never to stray from the boundaries of their yard unaccompanied—but it was so hot that she had sort of forgotten. Even an orange Popsicle hadn't been able to do the trick. Only the thought of those great sloping walls of cool concrete three blocks away could satisfy her.

She was sitting there, playing with her Barbies and humming an alphabet song she had heard on Sesame Street the day before, when a noise came from one of the dark openings in the wall opposite her. She stood up and peered into the drainage pipe, but could see nothing.

Beth was about to return to her spot in the shade, when she heard the noise again. It echoed hollowly from the shadows of the pipe. The whistling chirp of a bird.

Curiously, she giggled and walked forward. "Birdie?" she called. "Where are you, birdie?" She wondered what kind it was. Was it a robin or a sparrow? A mockingbird or a blue jay?

The call of the songbird came again, luring her nearer.

It was when she reached the mouth of the drainage pipe that she realized that there was no bird at all. What she had heard had been nothing more than a cruel lie.

Before she could react, large, dirty hands loomed out of the darkness, grabbing her. Suddenly she was pulled into the shadowy pipe, away from the roar of steady traffic and her Barbies sitting in a neat row on the floor of the culvert. Beth attempted to kick and scream, but the hands were much too powerful. They gripped her tightly, bruising the flesh of her arms and scratching her with filthy, cracked fingernails.

"Such a pretty girl," a gravelly voice rasped in her ear. "Such a pretty little thing."

Her heart pounding in fright, Beth peered into the darkness, but could see nothing at first. She could feel the heat of his breath washing over her face, though, blowing through her red hair and stinging her eyes. It stank of onions, bad breath, and liquor. And there were other smells as well. The nasty odors of unwashed clothing, sweat, and urine.

"Let me go," moaned Beth, struggling against the man's iron grasp. "Please! Please let me go!"

Her eyes soon grew accustomed to the gloom and she found herself staring into the man's face. It was an ugly face, wreathed in dirty, uncombed hair and a bushy beard littered with bits of dried food. His teeth were yellow and crooked, and there was a thin, white scar that ran from the bridge of his nose, crossing the right side of his face and disappeared into the thick whiskers that grew along his jawline.

But of all his features, it was his eyes that filled her with terror. They stared at her with a strange hunger. As though he intended to devour her.

She felt her strength diminish as he forced her to the cluttered floor of the big drainage pipe. Soon, hard concrete, pebbles, and crumpled soft drink cans pressed uncomfortably into the flat of her back and between her shoulder blades.

"Be still, child," he whispered, sounding almost out of breath. "Be still and I promise not to hurt you."

In the gloom, Beth heard a sound. It was the metallic buzz of a zipper being disengaged.

Suddenly, she remembered the talk her mother had had with her several months ago. He was one of the bad men she had been warned about, the kind that wanted to hurt her in her private place. Terror ran through her like an electric shock. She began to thrash and kick. "No!" she pleaded. "Please, don't!"

"Shut up, you little bitch!" the man warned gruffly. One of his filthy hands clamped firmly over her mouth, while the other roughly pulled her shorts and panties down around her ankles.

Beth began to cry. It wasn't fair. She had only gone there to escape the heat and play with her Barbies. She sensed him leaning forward, his weight shifting toward her. Beth whimpered as she felt something hard and rubbery brush the flesh of her inner thigh, creeping steadily upward.

Then something strange happened.

A peculiar heat seemed to flow from the dirty palm of the man's hand. As it touched her lips, it turned into a tingling sensation, sort of like the way your foot feels when it falls asleep. Then, all of a sudden, she was no longer frightened. The horror and fear was replaced by something else. A kernel of knowledge concerning her attacker.

Spiders, she thought to herself. *He's afraid of spiders.*

The man above her laughed. It was not a very nice sound. "You're gonna like this, honey. It might hurt at first, but then it'll feel so good."

She felt his weight baring down, pressing against her. She tried to close her legs, but his knees forced them apart.

Then, right when she was sure that nothing could save her, something did. Something from deep inside her head. Something she had never experienced before that hot August afternoon.

A rush of energy seemed to build in the center of her head, then strike swiftly outward, penetrating the palm of the man's hand and traveling up the length of his arm. She heard him gasp loudly and felt him stiffen above her. Then, a second later, he let out a startled cry and was gone.

Dazed, she sat up. In the shadows, she could see him scrambling backward, shuddering and slapping wildly at his arms and legs. His eyes were no longer mean and hungry. Instead, they were bright with hysteria.

"Get 'em off me!" he shrieked. "Good God, get 'em off!"

Beth didn't waste any time. She tugged her shorts back over her hips and scrambled out of the pipe, afraid that he might lunge at her at any moment. But he didn't follow her. He was more concerned with the skittering sensation of thousands of tiny legs scampering back and forth across his body.

Tearfully, Beth stumbled into the culvert, falling and scraping her knees badly on the concrete. Frightened, she rose to her feet and, leaving her dolls behind, ran as fast as her legs could carry her.

She half expected to hear the man's footsteps pounding in pursuit behind her, but she didn't. Instead, all she heard was his awful screams of horror echoing hollowly from the dark mouth of the drainage pipe.

―――――――――

"Beth?"

A door opened, bringing light and mercifully obliterating the pitch darkness around her. The young woman trembled uncontrollably as she huddled in the center of her bed. The last disturbing images of the nightmare failed to fade as easily as they normally did. They seemed to tug at her emotions, anchoring deeply, threatening to pull her back down into the black void of that drainage pipe again.

At first, she felt oddly disoriented. She wasn't sure where she was or whose silhouette stood in the open doorway. Then she regained her bearings. She was in her bedroom in the house she shared with her grandmother. Beth had moved in with her when she was first accepted at Vanderbilt Medical Center, partly to reduce her expenses, but mostly to help take care of the elderly woman and keep her company following the death of Grandpa Garrison.

"Sweetheart?" came Cindy's gentle voice from the open doorway. "Are you alright?"

Beth wiped away her tears with the edge of the bed sheet, but a second hadn't passed before they appeared again, welling up in her frightened eyes. She wanted to tell her grandmother that, yes, she was just fine, but she couldn't. She could only shake her head "no" and burst out crying again.

An instant later, Cindy was sitting on the edge of the bed, holding her close. The old woman pressed her granddaughter's head to her shoulder and felt the damp heat of her tears soak through her flannel nightgown.

For a moment, both were silent. Outside, they could hear a rumble of distant thunder, as well as the drumming of raindrops, falling hard, against the roof overhead. Then Cindy spoke.

"You were dreaming about that man in the pipe again, weren't you?"

That cold feeling of dread resurfaced. Her throat ached with the force of her sobbing, denying her the ability to speak. She nodded wearily and held on to her grandmother, afraid to let go. Soon, the security of the old woman's arms around her provided calm and comfort. But it could not entirely drive away the horror of that sweltering summer day in the culvert beneath Interstate 65.

"It's been twenty-five years since that happened, dear," Cindy assured her soothingly. "It's all in the past. He can't hurt you now."

Beth knew that she was correct. The homeless man who had attempted to rape her when she was six was no longer able to harm her...or anyone else, for that matter.

As far as she knew, he was still committed to a state mental facility, continuing to live out his most mortifying fear. Forever convinced that every inch of his body was covered with poisonous brown recluse and black widow spiders.

CHAPTER TWELVE

A bout the same time Beth Garrison was recovering from her nightmare, Hoyt Sawyer was driving home from Coleman.

The farmer's day had been a particularly full one. He had begun his chores on the Sawyer farm around five-thirty that morning, then did repairs on several stalls of the barn, unable to work outside due to the ceaseless rain that continued to drench the Tennessee countryside. As the afternoon drew on into evening, Hoyt had driven into town to eat supper at Dixie's Café. He had a country fried steak with mashed potatoes and okra, and a sizeable slab of Dixie's pecan pie afterward. He had lingered at the restaurant until closing time, shooting the bull with the cook and flirting with Dixie, who he had taken quite a shine to since his divorce a couple of years earlier.

The spring showers that had saturated Bedloe County all day had, eventually, culminated into a full-blown thunderstorm. The wind howled through the budding branches of trees and jagged bolts of lightning illuminated the dark sky, giving the illusion of broad daylight every few seconds or so.

He was driving along Highway 70, heading toward the rural stretch of Old Newsome Road where his own farm was located, when something suddenly burst from the thicket at the side of the two-lane blacktop and stumbled into his pathway. Hoyt slammed on the brakes of his red Ford pickup, causing the old truck to pitch and slide on the slick asphalt. Fortunately, the vehicle squealed to a jolting halt a second before the front bumper could make contact with the dark form.

"What the hell—?" he blurted out loud, his heart pounding in his chest.

He peered past the sweeping arcs of the windshield wipers. Hoyt half expected it to be a deer that blocked the way. But the truck's headlights revealed something else entirely.

It was a lanky boy of perhaps twelve or thirteen. He was dressed only in pajama bottoms and a white t-shirt, and was soaking wet from head to toe. His black hair was plastered to his skull and his face was as pale as fresh lard. But it was the boy's eyes that disturbed Hoyt the most. They were wide and unblinking, full of mind-numbing shock. But why?

The farmer opened the door of his pickup truck and leaned out. Heavy droplets of cool night rain thumped against the crown and bill of his tan and red Tractor Supply Company cap. "Hey, you!" he called out above the roar of the storm. "What's the matter?"

The boy simply stood there at first, his mouth working wordlessly like a fish drowning in pure oxygen. Hoyt shifted his gaze from the boy's white face to the front of his undershirt. He realized for the first time that it was saturated with blood.

Good Lord! thought Hoyt. *What's happened to him?*

He was about to speak to the boy again, when the teenager finally found his voice. "Come," he croaked, gesturing with blood-stained hands. "Please, come!" Then he turned and plunged back into the wall of dense vegetation that grew tall along the side of the road.

"Wait up!" yelled Hoyt. He shifted the Ford into gear and parked it on the gravel strip beside the highway, then cut the engine. Raindrops hammered on the roof and hood of the pickup truck with the force of hail. The farmer cursed beneath his breath, then grabbed a long, black Maglite from beneath the seat and stepped out into the downpour.

He was soon pushing his way through the thicket that the boy had disappeared into, thinking himself a fool for not calling the Sheriff's office on his cell phone before leaving the truck. It wasn't difficult for Hoyt to follow the kid's trail. A good amount of thistle and blackberry bramble had been shoved aside, as though a bulldozer had bullied its way through, while a good deal still remained, wild and standing nearly head tall in places. The boy was desperate to get back to where he had come from, that was for sure. But given the harrowed look on the teenager's face, Hoyt Sawyer wasn't at all sure that it was a place he himself wanted to go.

The beam of the flashlight revealed frantic motion in the dank darkness ahead, the boy tearing though the underbrush like a madman. Hoyt continued to follow, despite the thorns that tore at his face and hands, and the driving rain that pressed his clothing against his lean body until it was a second skin.

Eventually, the thicket began to thin out. *Where the hell am I?* he wondered. Then a whip-crack of lightning lit up the sky and, abruptly, he knew. He found himself standing next to a tall structure of weathered lumber and rusted tin that had partially collapsed with age.

The dread that filled the farmer grew even stronger. It was the old tobacco barn. He was on the old Brewer property...or, more precisely, the vast stretch of acreage now owned by the Elder family.

Although Hoyt wanted nothing better than to turn back, he clutched the Maglite tighter in his hand and rounded the sagging corner of the old curing barn. "Boy?" he called out. "Where are you?"

"Here!" cried out the young man.

Hoyt turned his flashlight toward the gaping wall of the dilapidated barn. The boy motioned at the jagged opening.

"In here!" he moaned. "They're in here!" The boy looked like a wild animal on the verge of leaping into the jaws of an iron trap.

"Who's in there?" asked Hoyt. But the boy refused to answer. Before the farmer could utter another word, the young man stepped through the hole in the wall and merged with the dense darkness that lay beyond.

Hoyt hesitated, but only for a moment. Then he walked to the open wall, and taking a deep breath, stepped inside. He braced himself for the worst. And, unfortunately, that was exactly what he found.

The first thing that hit him was the stench of death—the high, hot scent of fresh blood and the dark, nasty odor of excrement. Instantly, he knew that something bad had taken place within the shelter of the old barn that night. Something extremely bad.

Breathlessly, he turned, directing the beam of his flashlight from one wall to the other. Several yards to the left he spotted the boy. He was kneeling on the ground in front of a long, narrow box. At first, he was sure that it was a casket, but the closer he came, the more relieved he was to find that it was only an old-fashioned tool chest.

"What's wrong, kid?" Hoyt asked him. His mouth felt as dry as newly-milled cotton. "What's happened here?"

But the boy didn't seem to hear him. He simply stared into the narrow framework of the tool chest, rocking back and forth and emitting low grunts, like someone on the brink of losing their sanity.

Hoyt swallowed nervously and started toward the left wall of the old barn.

As he approached the huddled form of the boy, rain slashed though the open roof of the building at an angle, pattering upon the earthen floor. Hoyt stepped in several large puddles that washed up over the toes and rawhide laces of his work boots. It was when he shifted the beam of the Maglite downward that he realized that what he walked in was not pure mud and rainwater. The light revealed that the contents of the puddles were dyed a stark crimson.

Feeling his stomach clinch, the lanky farmer continued onward. The closer he went, the stronger the stench of violent death became.

"Boy?" he said, nearly to the teenager now.

The young man didn't answer. He merely peered blankly into the shadowy depths of the tool chest. A low moan rose from deep down in his chest. It escaped his pale lips and rose mournfully toward the dripping rafters of the old curing barn.

Hoyt's heartbeat pounded even more forcefully in his chest. "What is it?" he asked, his voice no more than a harsh whisper. "What's in there?"

He lifted his flashlight and looked over the boy's trembling shoulder.

His first impression had been much more correct than he had thought.

It *was* a casket that the boy was staring into.

Hoyt Sawyer felt the hot acid of pure bile creep up into the back of his throat as he stumbled away in horror. "Oh dear God in heaven!" he gasped.

Then he turned and ran, through the open wall and away from the death and darkness that pervaded the drafty interior of the old tobacco barn.

CHAPTER THIRTEEN

"You stay here, Josh," said Sam Biggs.

He stared through the open door of his patrol car. The thirteen-year-old lay on the back seat, his face emotionless. His eyes were strangely empty, as though he were looking inward, rather than outward.

Sam knew the teenager was going nowhere. When he had arrived at the Elder farm after receiving a call from Hoyt Sawyer, he had found the boy lying on the bare boards of the farmhouse's back porch. Hoyt sat next to him. He had fetched an old horse blanket from the lockbox in the bed of his truck and bundled it around the teenager to prevent shock from doing more damage than it already had.

Although he hadn't wanted to return to the ruins of the tobacco barn, Hoyt had gone back and carried young Josh from the drafty structure slung over his shoulder…a mean feat for a man in his late fifties. The poor kid was beyond responding. He merely lay there and shuddered…whether from cold or fear, Sam wasn't sure. The boy was unable to walk on his own or answer any of the sheriff's questions. Apparently, he had suffered some traumatic experience that had caused him to withdraw into himself.

So far, the county sheriff had been unable to determine exactly what might have thrown Josh Elder into such a sorry state. He had questioned Hoyt about what he had discovered inside the old barn, but the old man was strangely hesitant and deliberately vague on details. Sawyer was clearly shaken. Sam had been a friend of Hoyt's for a long time. They had hunted and fished together for more years than he could rightly recall. But never had he seen him as unnerved as he was that stormy spring night.

Sam shut the car door, making sure that it was securely locked. There were no inside locks. The only way the door could be opened was by Sam's keys or a release switch beneath the dashboard. Initially, the sheriff had believed Josh to be a victim of some violent assault. But, upon closer inspection, he had discovered that the boy was uninjured, except for a few minor scratches on his face and hands from running through the heavy thicket. Therefore, Sam couldn't deny the grisly fact that the blood that stained Josh's clothing and hands was not his own, but that of someone else.

The lawman turned to Hoyt. "I'm going up to that barn now," he told him. "Are you coming with me?"

Hoyt stared at him for a long moment, then nodded grimly. Sam reached beneath his rain slicker, took a flashlight from his gun belt, and turned it on. He again peered through the rain-speckled window of the patrol car. Josh hadn't moved an inch. He continued to lie on the cushions of the back seat in that quiet stupor of his.

Together, the two men started through the dense thicket that choked most of the farm's acreage. The storm hadn't settled at all. Rain continued to fall in heavy sheets and thunder rolled loudly overhead. Every now and then, jagged fingers of lightning broke past the dark clouds, illuminating the terrain around them. White light etched the sagging structure of the tobacco barn for an instant. From somewhere far off in his past, Sam remembered the building standing tall and sturdy, as somber as a church, yet as ominous and dreadful as a temple of primitive paganism, a place of dark rituals and bloody sacrifice.

The weather had been much different on that distant night than it was now. Instead of thunder and rain, the old barn had been surrounded by a blanket of newly-fallen snow and an icy December sky that was unnervingly tranquil and as silent as a grave.

The sheriff stopped for a moment, reluctant to enter the structure. Although he had driven by the old Brewer property countless times during his life, he had never set foot inside the barn...not since that cold and terrifying night in the winter of 1936. He had been only four years old then, but the events that had unfolded that night were forever branded into his memory. Sam felt his heart beat faster and he began to sweat profusely beneath the waterproof material of the bright yellow slicker.

But he knew he couldn't give in to those ancient fears. Something horrible had happened in that old barn and it was his responsibility to investigate it. Sam swallowed dryly, then continued onward through the thicket, pushing his way past slashing rain, clinging vines, and the clutching barbs of thorny bramble.

A few minutes later, Sam and Hoyt stood before the western wall of the dilapidated structure. The sheriff glanced back toward the farmhouse. He could see the flashing blue lights of his patrol car, but that was all. His deputy, Gil Meadows, hadn't arrived yet. Sam's other deputy, Joe Wilkins, was on vacation in Florida. He and his family had gone to Disney World. Sam considered the wondrous land of magic, storybook castles, and Mickey Mouse, and knew he was standing on the threshold of a place that was the complete opposite of such goodness and innocence.

Lightning crackled overhead, casting pale light upon the weathered boards of the barn wall, but dispelling none of the darkness that yawned beyond the jagged opening. Sam recalled the same wall, but at a different time. The hand of a young

91

girl—his sister—swinging a loose board aside on its single nail, providing access to musky gloom and horror unimaginable.

He jumped as Hoyt's hand rested on his shoulder.

"Are you okay, Sam?" asked the lanky farmer. His blue eyes were full of grim understanding. "You know, you can wait and let Gil go in first, if you want."

"No, I can't do that," Sam told him. "It's my job and I'm going to do it." He squared his shoulders and unsnapped the retaining strap on his service revolver. Then, flashlight in hand, he stepped though the open wall, into the barn's drafty interior.

Rain dribbled through the cracked seams of the tin roof overhead. Immediately, he smelled the sharp, coppery odor of fresh blood. *Someone has died in here,* he thought to himself. But, strangely enough, the thought did not shock him. Sam could never drive past the old curing barn without instantly associating it with tragedy and death.

Behind him, Hoyt cleared his throat nervously. "The tool chest is—"

"I know where it is," Sam replied. His feet felt as heavy as lead as he crossed the earthen floor and made his way toward the long, narrow box located on the far side of the barn.

The nearer he drew to the tool chest, the harder his pulse pounded in his temples. That old feeling of dread he had experienced as a small child returned, as fresh and as real as it had been those many years ago. The beam of the flashlight wavered as his hand began to tremble. He tried to calm his nerves, but he could not. The fear was there, and there it would stay, until he left that awful place.

Soon, the distance between him and the open tool chest shortened, foot by foot. *Something's in there,* he told himself. A few more steps and he was there.

The glow of the flashlight illuminated a confliction of colors and textures. Waxy paleness and glistening crimson. Flesh and blood arranged almost artistically within the cradle of the old chest. An abstract rendering from the darkest palette of Hell.

Abruptly, Sam turned away, sickened by what he had seen. But as his light shifted from the horrible contents of the tool chest, it settled on another point of reference just as hideous as the first.

It was a round object roughly the size of a bowling ball. A bloodless wad of pale flesh and dark hair resting against the far wall of the tobacco barn.

"Don't, Sam," suggested Hoyt, grabbing a fistful of the sheriff's slicker. "Just stay put until Gil gets here."

But Sam refused to listen. He pulled away and, in a daze, walked over and flipped the grisly thing over with the toe of his boot.

Slowly, a stark, white face rolled into view. It stared up at him blindly. The eyes were dark brown in color. Glassy and totally devoid of life.

Sam stumbled back unsteadily. He clenched his eyes shut and recalled that same face looking at him over a booth table at Dixie's Café, amused by a gruesome tale of mass murder that had taken place on the land he had recently purchased.

But there was no trace of amusement in those features now. There was only an expression of disbelief and dawning terror. He had seen that look before during the war in Korea. It was the expression of someone who knows that he is destined to die...and die badly.

Sam turned away, feeling a wave of nausea wash over him. The flashlight slipped from his fingers, striking the muddy earth with a wet splat and plunging the interior of the old barn into darkness.

God in heaven, help us! he thought to himself. *It's happening again!*

CHAPTER FOURTEEN

I t was after six o'clock the following morning before Sam Biggs returned to his office across the street from the Bedloe County courthouse.

Marge Singleton, the sole dispatcher and receptionist for the sheriff's department, watched as the constable walked in. She was shocked by how ghastly Sam looked. His normally high shoulders were stooped as if in defeat and his face held none of the robust hue it usually did. Instead, it seemed totally blanched of color, as pale as baking flour.

"Good morning, Sheriff," she said, offering a cheery smile.

"Morning, Marge," he said. The lawman hung his hat on the brass coat rack by the door and absently ran his fingers through his iron-gray hair. "I'm going to hole up in my office for a while. Hold all my calls, will you? Unless it's the state police, the Perryville hospital, or the coroner, okay?"

"Sure." Concern shown in the receptionist's eyes. "Are you alright, Sam?"

The sheriff lamely attempted a smile and shook his head "no". Then he walked into his office, shut the door, and closed the blinds.

The swivel chair behind his desk creaked as he sank heavily into its black leather cushions. He sighed deeply and closed his eyes, attempting to drive away the horrible images of the murder scene he had just left. But he knew it would not be nearly that easy. He would undoubtedly carry the bloody massacre of the Elder family around in his head for a very long time, just as he had endured other dark memories of the old tobacco barn over the years.

But at least he could do something to mute the impact of that awful discovery. Sam unlocked a file drawer of his desk and slid it open. He took out a bottle of Jack Daniel's and a large shot glass. He certainly didn't make a habit of drinking on the job, but that morning's indulgence was due to special circumstances. Besides, in his opinion, no one should have to face the investigation of a triple homicide stone-cold sober.

His hands shook as he uncapped the bottle of Tennessee bourbon and poured the glass half-full. He took a long gulp of the liquor. It burned away the nasty taste of vomit that lingered in his mouth and warmed the lining of his stomach, settling his nerves a bit. After that first swallow, he sipped his drink slowly, in no great hurry to pour another.

Sam felt tired, sad, and more than a little scared. He thought of what he had seen in the pale glow of his flashlight upon approaching the open tool chest. The mutilated bodies of Gordon, Peg, and Michelle Elder, their dismembered arms and legs stacked atop their pale, blood-splattered torsos like cord wood. And the thing resting against the far wall, wedged between weathered boards and the earthen floor. Gordon Elder's severed head, slack-jawed and glassy-eyed, staring up at him almost imploringly.

Currently, there was only one suspect and that was Josh Elder. Sam hated to think that the boy was capable of committing such a hideous crime, but, so far, all of the evidence pointed straight at him. His clothing and hands had been covered with blood, and Sam himself had witnessed a trace of the animosity he felt toward his father during his visit to Dixie's diner. If he had known the boy since birth the way he did most of the kids in Coleman, Sam would have had a better idea of whether he was guilty or innocent.

But, unfortunately, Josh Elder was a complete stranger to him. He had only met the thirteen-year-old once before and, even then, he had struck the sheriff as being moody, introverted, and disrespectful. And when Gordon had mentioned tearing down the tobacco barn, the boy had...well, to tell the truth, he had looked mad enough to kill.

The boy was now at the medical center in neighboring Perryville. Josh's condition had rapidly deteriorated following Hoyt Sawyer's discovery of him the night before. He had sunk from unresponsive shock to a state of complete catatonia. When Sam had left him in the care of the Perryville doctors, Josh Elder simply laid in his hospital bed, his eyes half-closed and staring blankly at the ceiling. His heart rate and breathing were normal, but his ability to respond to outside stimuli such as sound, sight, and smell had virtually shut down. One of the physicians had even pricked his finger with a needle, but the boy had given no indication that he had even felt it.

Sam was uncomfortable over the prospect of convicting a thirteen-year-old child of mass murder, whether he was guilty of the crime or not. Of course, the Bedloe County grand jury would be chomping at the bit to take the case directly to trial as soon as the boy recovered from his catatonic state. A lot of folks in Coleman were sick and tired of today's youth getting away with their insolence and apathy with little more than a slap on the wrist. They were more than willing to make an example and show the surrounding counties that they were fed up. And, if that example turned out to be Josh Elder, then so be it.

The sheriff still wasn't one hundred percent certain of the boy's guilt, however. Sure, the evidence was stacked against him, but something told him that all was not as it appeared to be. There was a darker side to this case than some disgruntled kid going off the deep end and butchering his entire family. And there were two points that bothered Sam in particular, two aspects of the gruesome triple-murder that rose more than a few doubts in the back of his mind.

One was the location of the crime. This certainly wasn't the first time that the old tobacco barn on the Elder property had been the site of such depravity and bloodshed. He thought again of the chain of gruesome deaths that had taken place within the barn's weathered structure seventy-seven years ago. The three teenagers lured to the barn, murdered, and dismembered, as well as their killers a few months later, turning on one another in a single violent moment of unexpected fear and mistrust.

The other point that preyed on Sam's mind was the way in which Gordon Elder and his family had perished. It had been almost identical to the way in which the three teenage boys had died. They had first been marched to the barn, shot, then brutally hacked apart. Hud Williams, the county coroner and proprietor of Williams Funeral Home in Coleman, had examined the remains and came to a startling conclusion as far as the murderer's choice of weapon was concerned.

The firearm used had been a twelve-gauge shotgun loaded with double-aught buckshot, the barrels more than likely side-by-side and sawed off short. And the tool by which the bodies had been dismembered had probably been a short-handled axe. A hatchet.

Weapons identical to those used by Bully Hanson and Claude Darnell back in 1936.

But how would Josh Elder have known that?

A cold sensation of dread ran throughout the sheriff's aged frame, conjuring a chill of the soul that no amount of whiskey could hope to smother.

He sat there for a long time, listening to the phone ring in the outer office time and time again. It was probably the editor of the town newspaper, anxious for information, or maybe the TV stations from Nashville. Either that or some of the local gossips. Card-carrying busybodies like Gladys Browne who worked for the county clerk or Myrtle Mae Harris over at the post office.

Sam Biggs knew that, sooner or later, he would have to go back out there and dig up the truth. But he wasn't sure that he was capable of tackling the investigation alone. There was only one person he could think of who could help him separate speculation from factuality, who could see events as they *actually* were and not simply the way they appeared to be.

The question, though, was whether or not she would be willing to.

Sam screwed the top back on the bottle of Jack, then picked up the phone and dialed a number from memory. He drummed his fingertips nervously on the desktop as the call went through. The phone on the other end of the line rang once, twice, three times.

Before the phone could ring a fourth time, someone answered. "Hello?" came a familiar voice.

Sam took a deep breath and hesitated for a second. He thought of the tragedy that had taken place in the old tobacco barn the night before and felt as though some dark evil, long dormant but nonetheless poisonous, had just reawakened.

"Cindy Ann? This is Sam," he said into the receiver. "I need your help."

PART TWO
IMPOSSIBLE SUSPECT

CHAPTER FIFTEEN

Beth yawned as she walked into the kitchen and headed straight for the coffee maker on the counter next to the sink. "Good morning, Grandma," she said sleepily.

"Morning, dear," the old lady said in reply.

Her grandmother sat at the butcher block table in the breakfast nook. The spot was bright and sunny, a pleasant surprise from the stormy weather that had raged across middle Tennessee the night before. Sunlight streamed through the panes of the bay window and lush, hanging ferns dangled from brass hooks in the ceiling overhead. The only thing in the cozy nook that was not cheerful was Cynthia Garrison. The elderly woman sat at her usual place at the table, nursing a cup of creamed coffee and looking weary and troubled.

Beth took her favorite mug from the kitchen cabinet and poured herself some coffee. By the time she reached the table, she knew that something was wrong. Her grandmother was still dressed in her nightgown and robe, and her reddish-gray hair hadn't been brushed. Usually, she had showered and dressed several hours before Beth had even awakened.

Instantly, she sensed that something was bothering her, and bothering her badly. "Grandma," Beth said, sitting down. "Are you alright?"

Cindy looked up from her coffee cup and attempted to smile. "I suppose so. I've just got something on my mind this morning, that's all."

101

"Do you want to talk about it?"

The old lady took a sip of her coffee and finally nodded. "I got a phone call around six-thirty this morning."

"Yeah, I thought I heard the phone ring," said Beth. "So, who was it?"

"It was my brother."

Beth was surprised. "Great-uncle Sam?" She had only met the man once before, at a family reunion when she was sixteen years old. She knew very little about him, except that he still lived in Cindy's hometown of Coleman and was the county sheriff there. "You haven't heard from him in a while, have you?"

"Not for three or four months," agreed Cindy. "Anyway, he called to tell me about a crime that took place there in Coleman last night."

The young woman was intrigued. "Really? Why would he do that?"

Cindy paused for a moment before answering. "He wants me to come down and help him find out exactly what happened."

"Like you've been doing around here? So what's the problem?"

The elderly woman sighed and took another sip of coffee. "The problem is, that this hits a little too close to home for me. I told him that I was sorry, but I couldn't help him."

Beth stared at her grandmother. She was more than a little surprised by Cindy's refusal. The old woman made a point of helping local law enforcement with difficult cases, particularly if they came to her personally asking for assistance. It wasn't like her to flat-out deny someone her special talent for reading the psychic remnants of past events, her "hindsight," as she called it. And it certainly wasn't like Cindy to refuse to help a family member, especially her own brother.

"What's going on, Grandma?" she asked. "Why has this gotten you so down?"

"Is it that obvious?"

"Yes, it is. Now what's the story? You can tell me."

Cindy hesitated, as though she dreaded discussing the case. Then she went ahead. "The crime was a triple homicide. A family by the name of Elder was murdered. A husband and wife and their teenage daughter...shot down and then brutally dismembered. Only one member of the family survived, a thirteen-year-old boy named Josh. Right now, he's the only suspect. He was known to be a little weird and openly resentful of his father. And the boy's hands and clothing were covered with blood when he was found last night."

"It sounds like a cut-and-dried case," said Beth.

"Yes, it does, doesn't it?" agreed Cindy. A peculiar look emerged on her slender face, a *haunted* look. "Except there is one aspect of the crime that casts some doubt on whether or not the boy was actually responsible."

"And that is?"

"Mainly, where the murders were committed," said Cindy. Her eyes suddenly grew bright with emotion. For a second, they looked more like those of a frightened child than of an elderly woman. "The killings took place on a piece of land that has been abandoned for many years. Inside an old, dilapidated tobacco barn."

Suddenly, Beth understood why her grandmother was acting so strangely. "It wasn't *that* tobacco barn, was it?"

The elderly woman nodded grimly. "One and the same."

"But what difference does that make?"

"It's too much of a coincidence," Cindy told her. "That three people would be murdered in that exact same spot again. And, from what Sam told me, that wasn't the only similarity. The method of the killings was almost identical to those back in

1936, along with the way the remains were hacked apart with a hatchet and neatly stacked in an old tool chest at the far side of the barn." The old lady's face turned pale. "It's almost as though—"

Beth waited for her grandmother to continue, but she didn't. "Almost as though *what*?"

"Nothing," replied Cindy, shaking her head. "I'm just being foolish, that's all."

Beth studied the woman sitting across the table from her. She could tell that the early morning call from Coleman had upset her terribly. "Do you remember what you told me last night, Grandma? When I had that dream about the man in the pipe? You told me that it was only the past and that it could no longer harm me. And you were right. It happened twenty-five years ago. But what happened to you and your family back in Coleman happened almost a lifetime ago. I believe you still haven't worked through alot of the anguish and fear that you experienced when you were a little girl." She searched the old woman's face. "Am I right?"

Cindy nodded reluctantly. "Yes, you are. I won't deny that much."

"Then wouldn't it be therapeutic to go back to Coleman and finally confront those fears? Working on this case might help you get a grip on those emotions. Even going back to that old barn again might relieve a lot of your anxiety."

The elderly woman seemed uncomfortable with the idea. "I'm not sure I could do that," she confessed. "I did go there once, a few years after I was married, the year before my father died. But the tobacco barn was just a wooden shell full of bad memories then. It's different now. Blood has been shed upon its earth once again. Innocent people have died there...horribly. I'm afraid it would be too much for me to handle alone."

"Then you won't have to handle it alone," Beth assured her. "I'll be more than happy to go with you." She reached across the table and held her grandmother's hand. "Grandma, since I was just a little girl, I've noticed this shadow on your soul. No one else noticed, but I did. A veil of sadness that's constantly with you, no matter where you are or how happy you appear to be. And it has always bothered me, seeing you suffer that way."

Cindy looked down at the coffee cup in her frail hands and said nothing.

"It's time to lift that veil, Grandma," she urged. "It's time to let in the sunshine and drive away those ugly old shadows. We can do it. Together."

A shimmer of tears shone in Cindy's hazel eyes. "I love you, Beth," she whispered.

Beth squeezed her hand gently. "And I love you, too."

"But I *can't*," Cindy told her regretfully. "I simply can't...not right now. It would be too difficult to go back to Coleman and work on a case like that. I'm afraid Sam will just have to deal with it by himself."

"That's a coward talking. Not my dear, sweet grandmother."

"Then I'm a coward," she told her. The old woman slipped her hand from her granddaughter's grasp, got up from the table, and left the kitchen, looking none too pleased with herself.

Beth sat alone in the breakfast nook, drinking her coffee and contemplating the discussion she had just shared with her grandmother. She wanted to feel annoyed and angry with her for taking the safe way out of a formidable situation by completely ignoring it. But she found that she couldn't.

As she had held her hand, Beth had sensed a fear unlike any she herself had ever experienced, including the one she still carried around inside concerning the attack when she was six years old. It was a fear so dark and deeply-rooted that it was no longer merely an emotion, but very much a part of the person who was Cindy Garrison.

Not only was it like a black stain upon the old woman's soul, but it was as though it were a physical component of her grandmother's aged body, as palpable and true as her flesh, bone, and blood.

CHAPTER SIXTEEN

"Well, good morning, Sam," greeted a familiar voice.

The Bedloe County sheriff stepped off an elevator of the Perryville Medical Center and turned toward the nurse's station of the second floor pediatric unit. Standing at the front desk was John Arnett, one of the medical center's finest physicians and surgeons.

Sam walked over and extended his hand. "Morning, John," he said in reply. "It's nice seeing a familiar face around here for a change. Last night, it just seemed to be a lot of strangers on duty."

Doctor Arnett shook the lawman's hand firmly. The physician was a tall, handsome man in his mid-thirties with wavy blond hair and sky blue eyes. "I take it that they took good care of the boy, though?" he asked.

"They certainly did," agreed Sam. "And they did their best to pull the kid out of that daze he went into after Hoyt Sawyer found him, but there didn't seem to be anything they could do. He just seemed to sink into it deeper and deeper."

"That sometimes happens with victims of emotional trauma."

"Well, we're not exactly sure that Josh Elder is a victim yet," the sheriff told him. "It looks like he could have possibly been responsible for what happened last night."

"Perhaps," said the doctor, "but he's in no condition to confirm whether he is innocent or guilty. I must insist, for the time being, that he be treated as a patient, rather than a murder suspect. Okay?"

"I wouldn't have it any other way. The county D.A. is ready to charge the boy as soon as he regains his senses, but I've barely begun my investigation and, as of right now, I'm not so sure that he was the one who killed the Elders."

John looked intrigued. "Really? Do you have any other suspects?"

"Not presently," said Sam. "But I aim to get to work on it as soon as I leave here. It's just hard to believe that a thirteen-year-old boy would be capable of doing such a thing."

"And yet it happens every day," the doctor reminded him. "Take that news story from Alabama the week before last. That teenager who walked into his high school with a twenty-two rifle and just started shooting. Three people were killed and seven were severely wounded, several of them teachers. From what I hear, the boy was a computer genius and a straight-A student with no history of behavioral problems. They still don't know exactly why the kid went off like that."

Sam knew the incident the doctor was referring to. "I reckon you never know what really goes on inside someone's head, do you?"

Arnett nodded grimly. "You've got that right." He turned and took a clipboard from a rack behind the nurse's station. "I hope you don't mind, but I've specifically asked to be the primary physician in Josh's case."

The sheriff was surprised. "How come? I'm sure you've got your hands full with your practice and your surgery schedule."

"I am," admitted the doctor. "But this tragedy took place in my hometown, Sam. I grew up in Coleman and still live there. It sickens my heart to think that something so horrible could have happened in a sleepy farming town like ours. I'd really feel better if I could do something to help."

Sam clapped his hand appreciatively on the man's shoulder. "I understand, John, and, personally, I'm glad you're taking care of this boy for me. I don't even know the kid that well. He and his family just moved into town last week. If some cold fish was evaluating him, I'd wonder if the kid was truly being given a fair shake, but I've known you since you were born and I know you're an honest and caring man. I have no doubt that you'll do all you can for the boy."

"Well, I'll certainly do my best," the doctor assured him. "Let's walk down to his room and I'll do a preliminary examination."

Together, they walked down a long corridor. Just knowing that John Arnett was in charge of Josh Elder's case made Sam feel a hundred percent better. John was the grandson of Ben Arnett, a lifelong resident of Coleman. Ben was the owner of Arnett's Pharmacy on Main Street and had been an acquaintance of Sam's for as long as he could remember. When John's parents had been killed by a drunk driver in a car wreck when he was eight years old, Ben and his wife, Harriet, had raised him as their own. John could have chosen to move to Nashville when he had attended Vanderbilt University, but when his grandmother passed away, he had decided to continue to live with his grandfather and commute to Nashville and back. Even now, he still lived in Coleman.

Sam had watched John grow up, from a curious youth playing doctor with the girls in his neighborhood to a fine young man with a promising medical career. And he did not dedicate his time and talents solely to the hospital in Perryville. John did more than his share of charity work and community service, spending two weekends out of the month at the Bedloe County clinic, attending to the area's poor and making sure that their children were properly vaccinated and cared for.

Soon, they approached Josh Elder's room. A Perryville police officer was sitting in a folding chair outside the door, just as Sam had requested the night before. The guy was a young, lanky fellow named Joe Ferguson. At first glance, he looked young and inexperienced. But, in reality, he was a veteran of ten years on the Perryville force with several commendations to his credit.

"Hey, Joe," greeted Sam. "How has the boy been this morning?"

"As quiet as a mouse," said the police officer. "I don't think he's moved a muscle all night long." Ferguson left his chair and stretched, causing the bones of his spine to pop in relief. "Do you guys mind if I run down to the cafeteria for a minute and grab myself some coffee and a donut?"

"No, go right ahead, Joe. And take your time."

When the officer had left, John Arnett paused before going into the room. "Is that really necessary, Sam? Having someone standing guard twenty-four hours a day? I honestly think it's a waste of time and manpower. The kid certainly isn't in any condition to make a run for it."

"I know that, John," Sam replied. "But it's merely police procedure, as much to protect Josh as to protect the hospital staff and patients from him, should he suddenly regain consciousness. I'm afraid you'll just have to grin and bear it."

"I suppose so," said Arnett. He still didn't seem to approve of the arrangement made between the Bedloe County Sheriff's Department and the Perryville city police, however.

They opened the door and walked in. The private room was gloomy. The only light was a warm glow that shown from the closed blinds of the room's only window. The doctor walked over and opened the blinds a crack, allowing a little more light to creep in.

Josh Elder lay on his back in the hospital bed. An IV of clear fluid was inserted in the crook of his left arm and he was dressed in a clean white hospital gown. The boy's black hair was still damp from last night's thunderstorm. There were a few pink scratches on his face and arms from where he had run through the thicket, but none of the injuries were all that serious.

Sam stepped up to the bed while John read the boy's admission chart. Josh stared at the ceiling, his eyelids half-closed. He breathed shallowly and a monitor on the wall above his bed showed his vital signs to be steady and normal.

John checked the boy's blood pressure and pulse rate first. Both were satisfactory. He then took a small penlight from the pocket of his white lab coat and, raising the thirteen-year-old's eyelids one after the other, focused the thin beam of light into his pupils.

"Josh," he said loudly. "Josh, can you hear me?"

The boy seemed completely oblivious to their presence. His eyes failed to even twitch when the light hit them.

The doctor then turned down the bed sheets, exposing the teenager's bare legs. He took a small rubber hammer from his pocket and gently tapped at a spot at the base of the boy's right kneecap, then did the same with the left leg. In both instances, Josh's leg jerked only a little.

"His responses are sluggish," said John, not at all pleased with the reaction that had been shown.

When the physician was finished with his examination, Sam stepped closer to the bed. "So what do you think, John?"

Arnett sighed and stared at the young man who lay quietly in the bed. "Well, it doesn't look very good, that's for sure. He is experiencing a state of almost complete catatonia. His reactions to outside stimuli—or rather *lack* of it—are similar to those of someone who is hopelessly brain dead. He is simply not here mentally."

"What's your diagnosis? Or is it too early to make one?"

"I'd say this young man has suffered some form of severe emotional trauma," said the doctor. "He has experienced something so horrendous and unspeakable that he has basically withdrawn into himself. At this point in time, however, I can't honestly say whether he will recover from this state or not. He might snap out of it an hour or so from now, or he could be this way for years. The mind is unpredictable in that way."

"Then this suggests that Josh really was a victim, rather than the perpetrator?"

"I'm not saying that," said John truthfully. "Sometimes someone can perform an act so heinous that, afterward, the awful realization of what they have done can push them completely over the edge. They can react exactly as Josh has, mentally retreating from reality, either to escape insanity or to avoid facing up to the consequences of their criminal actions."

"Looks like I have the right man in my corner," said Sam, impressed.

"I've only dabbled with psychology, Sam. I took a couple of years of it in college. After the boy regains consciousness—if he ever does, that is—then a qualified psychiatrist will have a better chance of giving you the answers you are looking for. I'm just a simple, small-town sawbones, that's all."

"And a damn good one," added the sheriff.

Sam Biggs stood beside the bed and stared at the teenage boy for a while, wondering what was going on behind those glassy, unseeing eyes. Somewhere inside the young man's head, answers were locked away, crucial information that Sam very much needed to be privy to. And as soon as possible.

"Come on and I'll buy you a cup of coffee," suggested John Arnett, laying a reassuring hand on the constable's shoulder.

"Yeah, I could use one right about now," admitted Sam.

When they left the room, they found Joe Ferguson back in his chair, sipping on a cup of black coffee. As the two started down the hospital corridor toward the elevator. John looked over at the sheriff of Bedloe County. "Sam?"

"Yes?"

"Isn't it sort of strange that a triple murder should take place in that barn at the old Brewer place? Again?"

Sam was surprised. "I didn't even think you knew about that."

"Are you kidding?" replied the physician. "My grandfather has told me stories about those killings and the men who were responsible since I was a little boy. He was one of the kids who found your brother in that barn, you know."

Sam felt that familiar tightness in his chest at the mention of his older brother, Johnny. "Yeah, I know." He was silent for a long moment. "And, you're right. It is mighty damn peculiar that this should happen again after all these years."

"I haven't heard all the details yet," said John. "Was it bad?"

"As bad as it can get," the lawman told him. "I'll fill you in when we get our coffee. But I'll just say this up front. The killings were performed in the same way, almost identically, to how those were done back in '36."

"A copycat of some sort?"

"Well, it certainly can't be the original perpetrator," said Sam. "He and his right-hand man have both been dead for decades." Dark images from the distant past played in the back of the sheriff's mind. "I know that firsthand."

"Then who did it?" asked the doctor.

"I have no earthly idea. That's what plants a seed of doubt concerning the guilt of Josh Elder in my brain. I did mention the killings in the tobacco barn when I talked to his father at Dixie's Café the night before last, but I didn't elaborate on the details.

113

There was absolutely no way the boy could have known how to recreate the murders, by the book and with absolutely no mistakes."

"The boy could have researched it on the internet," suggested John. "You can Google any subject nowadays and get an encyclopedia's worth of knowledge."

"That's possible," Sam allowed. "But that's not what my gut tells me."

"Then you're saying that it had to be someone who was familiar with the crime. Someone locally."

"I'm not saying that at all," said Sam. But he couldn't deny that the notion hadn't crossed his mind.

"Well, I'll certainly do what I can to draw Josh out of the state his mind has thrown him into," the doctor assured him. "Then maybe you'll be able to discover the truth about what happened in that tobacco barn last night."

Sam nodded. Privately, he knew that there was a good chance that he could learn the truth concerning the murders of Gordon Elder and his family that very day...if only a certain someone had been willing to help him.

Part of Sam was angry over her refusal to assist him with the murder investigation, while another understood her hesitation. After all, his sister had fought for years to put the horrible events of 1936 behind her. Events that had not only began with the brutal killing of their eldest brother, but had also come dangerously close to destroying her, as well as other members of her family...Sam included.

CHAPTER SEVENTEEN

They had been playing in the woods along Green Creek that sweltering summer day.

There were five of them: Chester Martin, Benny Arnett, the Osborne twins, Sally and Susan.

And, of course, a frail, redheaded child by the name of Cindy Ann.

The oppressive July heat had driven them from the sunny spots where they normally played and into the cool, shadowy depths of the forest. After spending the morning hours wading in the stream and chasing crawdads and tadpoles, they decided to spend their afternoon doing something else...like searching for signs of buried treasure.

Chester led the way, declaring that hidden Confederate gold was somewhere in the woods that grew thick and lush along the winding channel of Green Creek. He had even told them a story his grandpa had spun—a tale of a poor dirt farmer in south Bedloe County who had accidently dug up an iron kettle of gold coins back in the 1920s and instantly become a wealthy man. The talk of gold for the taking and the prospect of becoming rich excited the children. In those desperate, hand-to-mouth days of the Great Depression, the thought of possessing unlimited wealth was as much a childhood fantasy as sword-wielding pirates or fairy tale princesses.

Soon, Chester tired of roaming aimlessly along the creek bed. Before they knew it, the boy was scrambling up a steep hollow toward the sunlight. "Come on, you slowpokes," he called back to them. "I have a good idea where we might find some of that lost treasure."

Reluctant to leave the cool shade of the woods, the others followed their leader up the kudzu-covered grade. A moment later, they were at the edge of a plateau of hot, dusty farmland. But this property had not been properly tended for many years. A dense thicket grew wild across its two hundred acres—an almost impenetrable jungle of pink-headed thistle, honeysuckle vine, and thorny blackberry bramble.

But, despite the scalding heat of the day, Cindy Ann felt a strange chill run throughout her, causing her to shudder. She crossed her thin arms, feeling goose bumps prickle her freckled skin.

The five simply stood there for a while and studied the tall structure of weathered lumber and corrugated tin that dominated the center of the big thicket. It was an old tobacco barn, the largest in Bedloe County. Eighty feet long and forty wide, the building had once been used to smoke cure several crops of harvested tobacco at a single time. And it had also been the site of many a tobacco auction and floor-stomping square dance. But all activity within its gray wood walls had come to a halt following the unexpected death of the owner's wife several years earlier. Overcome by grief, Harvey Brewer had padlocked the barn's double doors and turned his back on the world, allowing both his home and his land to fall into disrepair.

Chester claimed that Brewer had buried gold somewhere inside the old barn and bullied the others into exploring it in hopes of finding out for sure. The last to give in was Cindy. At the very sight of the tobacco barn, she felt a queasy feeling in her stomach. It was the same feeling of agitation and dread she had experienced several weeks before, when she had dreamt of someone unknown fleeing through the darkness of a stormy

116

night, pursued by a dark and dangerous form who had both Death and the Devil on their side.

Carefully, they began to make their way through the heavy underbrush. Halfway to the barn, Cindy Ann paused beside a wild tobacco plant. Suddenly, a frightened combination of conflicting images crowded her mind. Darkness boiling with thunderous fury, the sensation of cold rain pelting her skin, and the sound of swishing footsteps in the high weeds behind her.

*Gotcha…*a voice seemed to utter directly behind her ear.

Swallowing nervously, Cindy turned around and found…nothing. There were only the high weeds of the thicket. No darkness, no thunder and lightning, no raindrops. Only the hot, dry brilliance of the Tennessee summer.

Shaken, Cindy continued to follow her friends. Soon, they were standing at the western wall of the massive barn. Again, Cindy heard a voice, but it was not the one she had experienced a moment ago. *I'm shot!* it proclaimed fearfully. *Oh, God help me, I've been shot!* The voice seemed disturbingly familiar, but she was unable to identify it.

It was at that instant that the girl realized that the mental "gift" she had developed following her long bout with typhoid fever was drawing remnants of a past occurrence to her, like metal filings to a magnet. But who had been shot? And who had been the one responsible?

Unable to enter the barn by the front doors, Chester found a way nonetheless. Sliding aside a loose board, he ushered the others inside. A second later, they stood in dusty darkness, the only light coming from the slits between the unleveled boards of the barn walls. The floor beneath their feet was bare earth scattered with old charcoal. As their eyes grew accustomed to the gloom, they found that, other than a broken-down old plow, there was really only one thing of interest in the entire building.

It was a long, wooden box at the far side of the barn, an old chest once used for storing tools and farming implements.

Benny began to get cold feet. "There ain't no gold in here," he said. "I think we oughta get outta here. We're trespassing and, besides, this joint gives me the willies."

Chester ignored him, his eyes settling on the tool chest. "There...there's where I'd stash my gold if I was Old Man Brewer." He walked over and examined the box closely. A rusty padlock was snapped securely through its iron hasp.

"What're you gonna do?"

A mischievous grin crossed Chester's face. "I'm gonna bust that lock and take a look inside."

As the other children joined Chester at the wooden chest, Cindy Ann stood as still as a stone, afraid to even move. Unexpectedly, the girl found herself surrounded by dark images and voices that rang strangely familiar in her young mind. Helplessly, she watched a frightening tableau take place before her *inner* eyes.

What the hell's going on here? A cocky, little fellow was standing with two others of the same age.

You've been suckered. A big, burly man stood holding an object wrapped in burlap in one hand. The bag fell away, revealing the stubby length of a sawed-off shotgun.

Now, wait a minute...

Just shut up! This from a gawky scarecrow of a man who set a coal oil lantern on the lid of the tool chest.

We want what money you're toting.

I'm getting outta here. I ain't gonna take this anymore.

A cruel grin split the big man's face. *No, not anymore.* Then came the deafening roar of a shotgun blast.

The little fellow laid on the ground, dying, his blood-drenched hands attempting to keep his innards from spilling out.

A shrill scream. One of the remaining two—a dark-haired young man with the blood of an Indian—ran for a ladder that was nailed to a nearby wall.

Stop him!

The lanky man took a rusty hatchet off the lid of the tool chest and, laughing, swung it downward. The young man reeled backward, his hand severed from its wrist. Then the hatchet descended again, slicing past hair and flesh, splitting the teenager's skull cleanly in half.

The awful phenomena faltered for an instant. Cindy Ann watched in dread as Chester picked up an old hammer and began to batter at the rusty padlock on the tool chest. "I've gotta get out of here," she muttered to herself. "Before it's too late."

Then, abruptly, she was back again, in the nighttime darkness of the barn with rain drumming heavily on the tin roof overhead. She regarded the last boy to fall victim. The one with the easygoing face of a young Will Rogers. In panic, he turned and ran as the big fellow quickly reloaded his twelve-gauge.

Cindy Ann stumbled backward, away from the children gathered around the tool chest. A second later, she found herself back at the wall.

Where is it? Where the hell is the loose one? They were not her thoughts, however, but those of the frightened young man.

The voice rang hauntingly in her mind. Slowly, a sinking fear pressed in on Cindy as she realized who the one in the thicket really was—the one who had been mercilessly hunted in the dark, disturbing depths of her nightmare.

Momentarily, she forgot about the loose board in the wall. Something caught her attention—a dark object tucked away in the dank shadows near the old plow. Frightened, but unable to stop herself, she walked over and picked it up.

It was a hat. A gray fedora with a band of tanned snakeskin around its crown.

Gotcha…Johnny! Rasped the same gravelly voice in her ears. It was the one that had preceded the thunderous discharge of a sawed-off shotgun.

Cindy whirled, her heart pounding and tears welling in her eyes, just as the padlock burst apart beneath a mighty swing of the ball peen hammer. Chester grinned in triumph as he freed the broken lock from the clasp and lifted the lid.

"DON'T OPEN THAT BOX!" screamed Cindy at the top her lungs.

But it was too late to stop him.

Cindy turned, grappled for the loose board, and then squeezed through the narrow opening into the scorching sunlight. Behind her in the dusty shadows, the barn was suddenly filled with the shrieks of frightened children, as well as the hideous sights and smells of death revealed.

―――――――

Cindy Garrison lurched upward into the darkness that surrounded her bed, her eyes wide open, her throat raw with the force of her screams. Terrified, she felt for the lamp on the nightstand, yearning for light. The elderly woman became entangled in the bed sheets and lost her balance. Soon, she was on the floor, still wailing, attempting to escape the horrible dream she had just emerged from.

Then the bedroom door opened and light spilled in from the outer hallway. "Grandma!" cried Beth in alarm. A second later, she was there on the floor beside her. "What's the matter? Are you alright?"

Cindy shivered violently. Her screams subsided, giving way to heaving sobs. "Oh God, why won't it end?" she wept. "Why can't I get it out of my head?"

A few minutes passed, Beth's comforting words and caresses continued to settle her nerves, until, exhausted, the old woman simply laid there in her granddaughter's arms. Slowly, the horror of the nightmare dulled, leaving only fading images.

"What did you dream of, Grandma?" Beth asked gently.

"That day in the tobacco barn," Cindy told her hoarsely. "When we found Johnny."

The two remained quietly on the floor for a while. Beth softly stroked her grandmother's brow, causing the old lady's heart to beat slower and her breathing to grow normal again.

"I'm going to do it," said Cindy after several minutes of saying nothing at all.

"Do what?" asked Beth.

"I'm going to Coleman and help Sam," she said, her voice trembling. "And I'm going back to that old barn, too. I've got to try and put this behind me. I thought I'd done it once before, but obviously I haven't." She looked up at her granddaughter anxiously. "Will you come with me?"

"Of course I will," Beth assured her. "Now let's get you back to bed. You can call your brother in the morning."

Cindy nodded and allowed the young woman to help her back into bed. Beth went to the bathroom across the hall and returned with a glass of water. The old woman took a long swallow without protest, then settled back into the soft folds of her feather mattress and pillows. The fear of returning to the nightmare she had just left did not concern her. She felt utterly exhausted and knew that she would sleep the remainder of the night restfully, unhampered by dark dreams of the past.

And she was right. Scarcely a minute had passed before sleep reclaimed her. Her slumber was so deep and complete, in fact, that she was unaware of the moment when Beth left her bedside and silently closed the bedroom door behind her.

CHAPTER EIGHTEEN

I t was the same as she last remembered.

The rural town of Coleman, Tennessee, had added several dozen new residents to its population and boasted a number of new businesses, including an auto parts store, a Piggly Wiggly supermarket, a Redbox DVD kiosk, and a modern bank with a drive-through window and automatic teller machine. But other than those few changes, the farming community was pretty much the same as it had always been.

Highway 70 North cut smack dab through the center of the town, changing into the picturesque thoroughfare of Main Street. The town square consisted of an ancient two-story courthouse of red brick and immaculate white trim, surrounded by a lush green lawn of shady oak trees, a park bench or two, and a tarnished statue of the town founder, Cordell Coleman. Running along the opposite side of Main was a row of privately-owned businesses, most of which had been in operation for the past thirty years or even longer. Among them were Bramm's Tobacco Shop, the Coleman Five & Dime, Dixie's Café, the Dress Boutique, and Arnett's Pharmacy. As Main Street exited the square, it passed through a residential section of old homes and several white, steepled churches of different denominations. Then the street changed into Highway 70 South and gave way to open countryside again. There, down a dusty rural track called Old Newsome Road, was where

Cindy and her kin had lived, along with a number of other poor farming families.

"This sure is a pretty place," said Beth as she slowed her Honda Accord and braked to a halt at Coleman's one and only traffic light.

"It always was," Cindy told her. "But don't let that fool you. There was always a fair amount of ugliness underneath it all. Tragedy and prejudice. Greed and evil." She considered the shadowy hull of weathered lumber and rusty tin that stood seven miles south of Coleman. Yes, even the most destructive and horrifying of evils had existed in that peaceful, God-fearing town. Evils she had hoped had been banished forever, but apparently not.

"You're in an awful cheerful mood today, Grandma," said her granddaughter. "Lighten up, will you?"

"I'll certainly try, for your sake." But, still, Cindy couldn't help but feel a sensation of dread that had settled deep down in the pit of her stomach. True, she had decided to come to Coleman and assist with the investigation of the Elder murders following her frightening dream of the night before. But, upon arriving in her hometown, the elderly woman couldn't help but feel a twinge of regret and, yes, even fear. She would have much rather been back at her comfortable little house in Nashville, with her plants and flowers, her soap operas on TV, and her rocking chair and cross-stitching in the warm sunlight on the front porch.

But she knew there was no use in brooding over her decision. She was there now and all she could do was try to make the best of her rare visit home.

The light turned green and Beth drove forward, toward the southwestern side of town square.

"The sheriff's department is over yonder on that side street," Cindy instructed. "See it? The tan brick building across from the courthouse."

Beth nodded and then engaged her turning signal. A moment later, they pulled into the small parking lot in front of the police station. "Well, here we are," she said, looking over at her grandmother. "Are you ready to go in?"

Cindy sat there for a long moment, then sighed deeply. "Yes," she replied. "I suppose so."

"Come on, Grandma," Beth scolded good-naturedly. "You're treating this reunion like a dose of bad-tasting medicine."

"Seeing Sam again isn't what concerns me," she told her. "It's dredging up all those old memories that is going to be the difficult part."

Beth leaned over and kissed her grandmother on the cheek. "Well, you're not going to have to face it alone, remember? I'm here with you."

Cindy couldn't help but smile. "And you don't realize what a comfort that is to me, either. Come on, let's go see your great-uncle Sam."

They left the Accord and entered the sheriff's office. Upon entering the cedar-paneled lobby, they found a squat, black-haired woman sitting behind the front desk. She wore a loud, flower-print dress and pink-framed eyeglasses on a delicate gold chain around her neck.

"May I help you ladies?" she asked sweetly, looking up from a stack of paperwork on her desk.

"Now, you haven't forgotten me that easily, have you, Marge?" asked Cindy with an expression of mock hurt on her lean face.

Marge Singleton fished her glasses up by the chain and slipped them on. Suddenly, a huge smile brightened her plump face. "Miss Cindy! Lord have mercy, I haven't seen you in a coon's age!"

A moment later, the receptionist was around the desk and clutching the older woman in a warm embrace. "My, you're looking as healthy and chipper as ever. City life must agree with you."

"I've just been keeping busy, that's all," she told her as the two parted. "Oh, Marge, this is my granddaughter, Beth."

"The youngest? Why, the last time I saw her, she was barely sixteen. And look at her now! So beautiful and grown up!"

"And a doctor to boot," Cindy boasted proudly. "She's on the staff at Vanderbilt."

The middle-aged woman with the coal-black hair nodded adamantly. "I know the place well. That's where my Harold had his prostate operation and both my grandbabies were born there, too." She turned to the young woman with the long red hair. "It must be pretty exciting to work in a place like that."

Beth recalled her last night on duty—the death of Brandon Rucker, followed by her heated confrontation with Doctor Miller. "Yes," she replied. "A little *too* exciting sometimes."

Marge turned back to the old lady. "It is so good to see you again, Cindy." She went around her desk and spoke into the intercom. "Sheriff, would you come out here, please? There's someone here who'd like to see you."

A moment later, the door to the sheriff's office opened and Sam Biggs stepped out. He paused in the doorway, a broad smile slowly crossing his beefy face. "Cindy Ann," he said softly.

"Hi, Sam," she said, her voice breaking. "It's good to see you again."

They stood there, stone still, for a moment. Then the two meet in an embrace that made Marge's seem tame in comparison. "Thanks for coming down and helping me with this, sis," he said, stepping back.

Cindy avoided looking him square in the eyes. "Well, I should've said yes in the first place. Turning you down was a shameful thing to do. I'm sorry."

Sam reached out and gently lifted his sister's chin until their eyes met. "Heaven knows you had your reasons," he assured her. "That's all water under the bridge now. The important thing is that you're here." The county sheriff suddenly seemed to notice Beth for the first time. "And who is this pretty young lady here? One of your friends?"

"I declare, Sam!" Cindy said laughing. "You wouldn't know your own kin if they ran over you with a truck full of bricks!"

Sam stepped closer and grinned. "Naw! This isn't little Bethany, is it?"

"Hi, Uncle Sam," Beth said, returning his smile.

The constable soon had the young woman in a hug similar to the one he had subjected his sister to. "Well, now, take a look at you! All grown up and as pretty as a summer peach! And a big-city doctor, too. How have you been, girl?'

"Just fine, Uncle Sam" she said, struggling to breathe as his thick arms tightened around her.

"Please, you make me feel like some skinny fella with a striped top hat and white chin whiskers calling me that," he chuckled. "Just call me plain old Sam from now on, if you want."

"Okay," said Beth, feeling a little like a chipmunk being hugged by an affectionate grizzly bear.

The elderly lawman released his grand-niece and then regarded his sister. "So, where do you want to start, Cindy Ann?"

Cindy considered it for a moment. "Why don't we go to the hospital in Perryville and see the boy first?" she suggested. "If

I can read him successfully, there may be no need to even go to the murder scene. I may be able to find out exactly what took place in that old barn, right there at his bedside."

The sheriff nodded. He understood his sister's reluctance to return to the place that had caused the Biggs family so much grief so many years ago. And, to tell the truth, he wasn't exactly chomping at the bit to go back there himself.

A startled look crossed Marge Singleton's face. "So, you're here to help out with the murder case?" she asked Cindy. "I always thought those stories I heard about you having the gift of second sight was a bunch of nonsense. But it isn't, is it?"

"No," the old lady admitted. "It's true, although sometimes I'd rather it wasn't."

"Marge, I'd really appreciate it if you kept this under your hat," Sam told her. "I don't want the newspaper knowing what Cindy Ann is here for, and I certainly don't want the town gossips getting wind of it, that's for sure. If Gladys Browne or Myrtle Mae Harris send this through that grapevine of theirs, the whole town will be breathing down our necks, wanting to see a real, honest-to-goodness psychic at work, and I don't need that kind of headache. Not with such a delicate case as this."

"Don't worry about me," vowed Marge. "They couldn't pry it out of me with a crowbar and one of their homemade pecan pies."

"Then I know we're in good hands," chuckled the lawman.

Soon, they were in the sheriff's patrol car and backing into the street. Sam turned and looked lovingly at the woman sitting next to him. "Dammit, Cindy Ann. It *is* good to see you."

She reached out and took his hand. "It's good to see you, too, little brother. I'm sorry I stayed away so long. I reckon I haven't been the best sister in the world to you. Particularly since Mama and Pappy passed away."

A warm gleam formed in the sheriff's aged eyes. "You know I always thought you hung the moon. And I always will. Nothing could ever change that."

Cindy squeezed his hand, then let go. She breathed deeply and relaxed a little. She didn't fully feel as though she was truly home again, but she did feel a little closer to that sensation than when she had first entered the Coleman town limits.

CHAPTER NINETEEN

"Here he is," said Sam.

The two women followed the sheriff into the private room. Cynthia and Beth approached the hospital bed and stared at the boy who laid there. He was pale, except for a few pink welts on his face and arms, and his eyes peered sightlessly from beneath lids that were partially closed.

"Poor child," said Cindy. She reached out and tenderly brushed a strand of black hair off his forehead.

"You might be a little premature in your pity, sis," Sam reminded her. "We've got to keep in mind that this poor boy could have very well shot and hacked up his own family."

"Well, we'll see about that," said the elderly woman. She cast a glance toward the door, which stood partially open. The Perryville police officer named Ferguson was seated outside, reading a copy of *Field & Stream.* He seemed totally oblivious to what was going on inside the hospital room.

"Then go ahead and give it a try," her brother suggested. Sam seemed anxious, as well as a little nervous.

Cindy nodded. She pulled a chair up to the side of the bed and sat down. The old lady took the boy's right hand in her own. It was limp and cool to the touch.

"Just take your time, Grandma," Beth told her. The young woman stood behind the chair, far enough away to give her grandmother plenty of space, but close enough to be there for

129

her if the reading should become difficult or too disturbing for the old woman.

Cindy took a deep breath and closed her eyes. Then she tightened her hold on the boy's listless hand and began to concentrate.

A couple of minutes passed. Then Cindy opened her eyes and shook her head. "Nothing."

"Huh?" asked Sam, afraid that he might have misunderstood. "What do you mean?"

"I mean absolutely nothing," said Cindy. "I don't understand it. I can usually tap right into a person's feelings, particularly traumatic ones. But I can't read this boy at all. There's just a blank space where his thoughts ought to be."

"Well, I'll be damned," said Sam, obviously disappointed. "Has that ever happened to you before, Cindy Ann?"

"No," she said. "Not since I was a young child, before I suffered the typhoid when I was eight."

"Do you mind if I give it a try, Grandma?" asked Beth.

Sam looked puzzled. "What do you mean 'give it a try'? Don't tell me that..."

Cindy smiled as she left the chair. "That's right, Sam. Beth possesses the gift, too. I reckon I neglected to tell you that, didn't I?"

"Apparently so," said the county sheriff in bewilderment.

The elderly woman turned to her granddaughter. "Give it your best shot, dear. It could be that I'm subconsciously blocking myself off from him...because of where those killings took place. Maybe, deep down inside, I really don't want to know what happened in that old tobacco barn."

Beth nodded. She could understand her grandmother's reluctance to relive the horrors that had been committed in the abandoned barn. But she had no such prejudices. Beth sat down in the chair that the old woman had occupied a moment before.

She took hold of Josh Elder's hand, closed her eyes, and concentrated, shutting out everything else in the room: the sound of Sam and Cindy's breathing, the low beeping of the heart monitor, the steady drip of the IV...everything.

She sat there, motionless, for several minutes. Then she released the boy's hand in frustration. "It's just no good, Grandma. I drew a blank, just like you."

"But how come?" asked Sam.

Beth shrugged. "I don't know. Maybe what this kid experienced was so horrible that he has completely shut himself off mentally. He's put up a barrier in his own mind, one so strong that we're unable to penetrate it."

"Did you sense anything at all?" asked Cindy, walking over and placing her hands on the young woman's shoulders.

Beth shook her head. "For a second I thought maybe I did, but it was very faint. Like a dark gray mist with dark forms milling around inside. Restless shadows. But that's all, I'm afraid."

"Did the boy react to you in any way?" asked Cindy curiously.

"Not that I could tell." Beth lifted Josh Elder's wrist and checked his pulse. "His pulse is steady with no indication of agitation. It's as though he is totally unaware that we're even in the room with him."

The sound of someone clearing their voice drew their attention. Sam glanced over and, seeing John Arnett standing in the doorway, suddenly looked guilty. "Hey, John. How are you doing today?"

"Just fine," said the doctor. He appraised the two women as he entered the room and approached the boy's bed. "So, what's going on here, Sam?"

"I know I should've okayed it with you first," said Sam, "but I didn't think it would do any harm for us to stop by and visit with the boy for a few minutes."

"Just an innocent visit, huh?" said John. He smiled at Beth. "Then why was this lovely lady checking Josh's vital signs? And quite professionally, I might add."

"This is my grand-niece, Beth Garrison," Sam said in introduction. "She's a doctor, too."

"Ah," nodded John, taking Beth's hand. "I'm John Arnett, a physician here at Perryville MC. It's always a pleasure to meet a fellow doctor. Do you have your own practice, Ms. Garrison?'

"No, not quite." A slight blush colored Beth's cheeks. "I'm a resident at Vanderbilt in Nashville. Emergency medicine."

"Ah, my old alma mater!" He raised his eyebrows, intrigued. "A thrill-seeker, huh? I suppose you see some hair-raising things up there in the big city, don't you? Shootings, stabbings, things like that?"

"Yes, I've seen my share of stab wounds and bullet holes."

It was Sam's turn to clear his throat, for it seemed like the only way to pry Arnett's attention away from the young lady. "Uh, John, do you remember my sister Cindy?"

A big smile broke across the doctor's handsome face. "Of course I do. How have you been, Miss Cindy?"

"Fit as a fiddle," she replied.

John studied the elderly woman for a long moment. Then his smile faded a little. "You know, I used to hear some pretty wild stories about you when I was a boy. About how you had psychic powers and could tell what folks were thinking. Even their most secret fears."

"Oh, you did, did you?" said Cindy, looking a bit uncomfortable.

"Yes. But I always figured them to be a bunch of old wives' tales," he told her. "Or was I mistaken?"

132

The other three in the room said nothing.

"Is this what this is all about, Sam?" John Arnett asked him. "You brought your sister in here to read Josh's mind?" There was a hint of sarcasm in the physician's voice, as though he believed that such a thing was utterly impossible.

"Well, to tell the truth, John...yes," Sam admitted. "That was exactly what she was trying to do."

"Come on, Sam," the doctor said, shaking his head. "You're not that desperate yet, are you?"

Anger suddenly blazed in the old woman's hazel green eyes. "No matter what you believe, young man, I do possess the gift of second sight. And it's not some silly parlor trick, either. It's for real."

An apologetic look suddenly replaced the expression of skepticism that had filled the doctor's face a second before. "I didn't mean to insult you, Miss Cindy. You must understand...I'm a man of science and medicine. It's difficult for me to believe in such abilities, that's all."

"I'm of the same profession as you, Doctor," stated Beth, appearing as angry as her grandmother. "And I do believe that such abilities exist."

A stricken look crossed John Arnett's face. "Yikes! I certainly didn't intend to raise the ire of two redheaded women in a single day. Please, forgive me. I certainly didn't mean to offend either one of you ladies."

Cindy and Beth looked at one another and laughed. "Charming young fellow, isn't he?" asked the elderly woman. "Especially for a disbeliever."

"So, did it work?" asked John. "Did you find out anything, Miss Cindy?"

"No, I'm afraid I drew a blank," admitted Cindy. She looked over at her granddaughter and saw tenseness in her face. Obviously, she didn't wish for it to be known that she possessed the same gift that her grandmother did. At least, she didn't want the handsome, young physician to be privy to that fact. "It's as though he has locked his mind away in a protective cocoon."

John nodded. "Yes, that would certainly concur with my own assessment of the boy's current mental capacity. I've witnessed the effects of severe trauma before, but never have I encountered a case where someone has shut themselves off from the outside world so completely. He doesn't even respond to outside stimuli in the same manner that comatose patients do. It is extremely perplexing, to say the least."

"Have you noticed any evidence that he dreams, Doctor Arnett?" Beth asked curiously.

"Please, don't be so formal," the man suggested. "I'd rather you call me John. And, to tell the truth, I have kept a close watch on him to see if he has emerged into an actual dream state. Despite the fact that his eyes remain partially open at all times, there still should be some indication of rapid eye movement. But there has been none whatsoever. His eyes remain completely still and fixed, as though he is staring at one particular point in space and nothing else."

They talked for a while longer, then John Arnett prepared to continue his rounds. He said his goodbyes to Cindy Garrison and then smiled at Beth one last time. "It was certainly nice meeting *you*, Doctor Garrison," he said, then tucked his clipboard beneath his arm and left the room.

The young woman held her breath for a long moment, then exhaled slowly. "What a hunk," she said, more to herself than anyone else.

"I believe young Dr. Arnett has made quite an impression on Beth," said Cindy with a wink.

"He was very professional and well-mannered, that's all," said Beth, her face growing red with embarrassment.

"Of course," said Sam, breaking out in a big grin. "And, for your information, he's also extremely single."

Beth tried not to look too pleased. "Oh, really? That's interesting."

Sam checked his watch. "It's about eleven-thirty. Why don't we grab a bite to eat and then we'll head back to Coleman." He turned to his sister. "Once we get there, we can go on to the Elder farm. If you're ready, that is."

"I'm as ready as I'll ever be," Cindy replied with a sigh of resignation. "We might as well go ahead and get it over with." She turned and took Josh Elder's hand once again. "Sleep well, young man," she said softly. "Hopefully, we'll be able to pull you out of this mess yet."

The thirteen-year-old's face remained impassive. His eyes continued to stare sightlessly toward the ceiling, failing to even blink.

As they left the room, Beth noticed the worried look on her grandmother's face. "Maybe it won't be as bad as you think, Grandma," she said encouragingly, taking the elderly woman by the arm.

Cindy Garrison turned and looked at her granddaughter. Beth saw something more than apprehension in those wise, old eyes. She saw a dark fear that was linked more to concrete knowledge than unfounded paranoia.

"Yes, perhaps you're right," she allowed. "But, on the other hand, maybe it will. Or, heaven forbid, it might be worse. Much worse than even I could imagine."

CHAPTER TWENTY

The last time Cindy had set foot in the old tobacco barn was on Thanksgiving Day of 1956.

She had been twenty-nine during that visit home—a young woman with a husband and two small sons. But she did not recall feeling the same sense of anxiety and apprehension upon entering the ramshackle structure back then that she did now. True, there had been sadness and a little uneasiness, but that was all. She had picked up faint traces of the horrible incidents that had taken place there in the year of 1936, but they had lost much of their impact. As far as she could remember, they had not been overwhelming or even threatening. Instead, the thing Cindy remembered most about that lonely Thanksgiving evening was the distinct feeling that someone's spirit—or the *essence* of their spirit—lingered in the empty hull of rotten lumber and rusted tin.

The spirit of her lost brother, Johnny.

But now, standing at the open wall of the same barn at the age of eighty-six, Cindy experienced none of the bittersweet memories of her elder sibling. Instead, the original horror of the summer of 1936 had seemingly returned, even stronger than before. Death and mutilation, cruelty and rampant evil...they saturated every board and beam of the old tobacco barn like a stain that could never be sponged away or a stench that could never quite be eradicated.

Cindy considered that timeworn myth connected to old age—how the elderly reverted to a childlike state during the declining years of their lives. She wondered if that might be the extent of what she was now experiencing—the horrible impressions of that awful massacre she had sensed in the broiling summer of '36, when Chester Martin had busted the padlock on the tool chest and exposed the dismembered and lime-covered remains of three unfortunate young men.

But, as she stood there hesitantly on the threshold of the open wall, Cindy knew that that was not the case. This was not the revitalized remnants of an old transgression, but, instead, an evil that was entirely fresh and new. One that had been committed within the drafty shelter of the old barn only a short time ago.

"Are you okay, Cindy Ann?" asked Sam. Her brother reached out and laid a concerned hand upon her shoulder.

The old lady swallowed dryly and nodded. "I'm alright." She turned toward Beth. "Do you feel it, dear?"

The young woman with the fiery red hair had to take a couple of steps back from the opening in the wall before she could reply. "I feel it," she whispered. "God help me, I *do*."

Beth rubbed her arms absently, attempting to drive away the chill that seemed to sink clear down to the marrow of her bones. She understood what her grandmother was referring to, but the flood of raw emotion and unobscured evil she now felt was entirely different from the ugly images she had witnessed at the site of young Sharon's death several days ago. It was much more potent in nature, like a poison that was not diluted, but lethally pure.

"Do you want to go in with me?" Cindy asked her. "Or would you rather wait outside?"

"I'll go in," she told her.

137

"If you're sure that you're up to it. I can protect myself, but I'm afraid you're on your own."

Beth understood what she was talking about. Her grandmother had once explained that she was able to protect herself from overwhelming psychic residue such as that which they now faced. She had spent a lifetime forging a sort of "mental armor" in order to insulate herself from poisonous emotions such as hatred, sadism, and evil. But, unfortunately, Beth possessed no such defenses. She could manage to block such disturbing feelings for a short period of time, but, sooner or later, they managed to seep into her mind and, eventually, overwhelm her.

"Don't worry about me, Grandma. I'll be okay." Beth took a deep breath and braced herself. "Come on. Let's see if we can solve this thing and get it over and done with."

"Amen to that," agreed Cindy.

"Do you want me to stay out here?" asked Sam.

"It might be better if you do," said his sister. "You have strong emotions concerning this place, Sam. It's possible that they could interfere with what we're about to do."

The sheriff nodded. He looked relieved that he wouldn't have to enter the old barn. "Good luck," he said. "To you both."

Cindy and Beth looked at one another. Then, together, the women stepped through the jagged hole in the barn wall. A second later, they were standing within the gloomy hollow of the ancient structure.

Abruptly, an icy chill engulfed Cindy. Deep down inside, she knew that it had no real physical bearing. Rather, it was a chilling of the soul that she experienced. For a long moment, nothing happened. Then the shadows of the barn seemed to thicken and converge, and somewhere, beyond the human ability to hear, she sensed whispers. Some were frantic with fear, while others snickered cruelly, anticipating violence and the hot, quick rush of blood released.

The old woman turned her head slightly and saw her granddaughter standing no more than a couple of feet away. Beth stood, rigidly, her eyes closed, absorbing the dark emotions that swirled through the structure, reading them like the printed words of some obscene book.

Cindy relaxed, lowered her guard, and did the same. But the images she expected to see did not appear. Instead of the picture-clear sense of place and time that she had experienced on the bike trail at Radnor Lake, she found herself existing amid a murky mist of muted light and dark shadows. The forms were blurry and without definite form. They were human, but, for the life of her, she simply couldn't determine whether they were male or female, adult or child.

Why the hell have you brought us here? This from a man, or so the deepness of this voice suggested. Cindy could feel his confusion and his outrage, as well as slowly mounting terror.

One stood apart from three others—the perpetrator of the horrid crime. They simply laughed. It was a low, dry rasping like the coarse rubbing of a snake's hide as the reptile slithered beneath the wooden boarding of a hen house wall. Then something black and stubby was lifted from their side, followed by a crisp, metallic click. The cocking of a shotgun's hammer.

No! Please! The shrill pleading of someone who knows that death is imminent. A woman's voice.

We'll give you anything! The male victim, his bravado gone now. *Anything you want!*

That sinister chuckle again. *This is what I want.*

Then the thunderous explosion of the first shotgun blast.

Cindy stumbled backward a couple of steps, as though feeling the stinging bite of the pellets herself. Then the murky tableau before her grew even more obscure and, once again, she found herself standing in the shadowy structure. Slashes of raw sunlight shone brightly through the cracks between the weathered boards, causing her to blink.

The old lady closed her eyes again and attempted to return to the spectacle she had just witnessed, but found that she was unable to. It was almost as though something was actually *preventing* her from doing so.

Cindy opened her eyes and sighed. She turned and looked through the open wall into Sam's anxious face. "I'm sorry, little brother," she said regretfully. "I had something for a moment, but not very much I'm afraid."

"Same here," admitted Beth. Her face was blanched and bewildered. "I think I saw four people here. I believe three were the Elder family, while the other was the murderer. But other than that, I couldn't tell exactly what was going on."

Cindy related the murky images of her own experience. They pretty much matched Beth's down to the fatal first shot.

"I already know that Gordon, Peg, and Michelle Elder were awakened and marched out here by someone," Sam told them, his eyes full of disappointment. "I was hoping you could tell me something more, like who actually did the killing. Do you think it was Josh Elder? Was there any way you could possibly tell?"

"I'm afraid not," Cindy said. "I heard the voice of the murderer, but couldn't determine whether it was male or female."

Beth shook her head. "I'm sorry, Sam, but I couldn't either."

Cindy stood there for a long moment, turning something over in her mind. "Sam...were the Elders asleep before they were brought out here?"

"Yes, they were. We checked the farmhouse and it appeared as though they were roused from their beds and marched out here at gunpoint."

"Then how come the murderer didn't take Josh as well?"

Sam scratched his head. "The only thing I can figure out is that the bastard didn't know exactly where Josh was. The boy's bedroom was located in the attic upstairs, not downstairs with the others. And the stairs to the attic is kind of hard to find if you don't know where to look. Maybe the killer searched for Josh. When he couldn't find him, he decided to go ahead and take the other members of the family to the barn without the boy."

"Maybe," said Beth. "Or maybe Josh was actually the killer."

"I really don't want to believe that," said Sam, "but I might just be acting like a stubborn, old jackass. Could be that you're right."

As Cindy and Beth left the old barn and emerged into the warm, spring sunshine, the elderly woman turned to her granddaughter. "Beth, when we were in there a moment ago…did you experience an *obstruction* of some sort. A strong sensation of resistance, as though something deliberately stepped in and interrupted what you were sensing?"

"Yes," admitted Beth. "I certainly did. But it was different than what I felt when we tried to read Josh."

Cindy nodded. "I agree. It was more than just a barrier. It was like an actual consciousness of some sort. Thwarting our attempts to see the truth and blinding us before we could even go that far."

Beth crossed her arms and shivered. Despite the warmth of the day, goose bumps began to prickle her skin. "What are you driving at, Grandma?"

An uneasiness shown in the old woman's hazel eyes. "Some folks here in Coleman believe this old place is haunted. Who knows? Maybe they're right."

Sam laughed uncomfortably. "Come on, Cindy Ann! You're not trying to say that some sort of ghost interfered with you, are you?"

"I don't know exactly what I'm trying to say, Sam. But I do know one thing. Just before I lost sight of what had taken place here, I sensed a presence. A presence I haven't sensed for a very long time. The most evil presence I've ever known in my life."

The sheriff's jaw dropped an inch. "Good Lord, Cindy, you're not talking about—"

Before he could utter the name out loud, Cindy's eyes sharpened, as though warning him to remain silent.

Beth sensed the uneasiness they shared and considered asking them exactly who they were referring to. But she didn't. She had a feeling that they didn't wish to discuss the matter.

Especially not there, next to the half-fallen structure in the center of the weedy thicket.

CHAPTER TWENTY-ONE

They ate supper at Dixie's Café. It was shortly after six that evening and the place was packed. Those in the town of Coleman who didn't prepare their meals at home normally congregated at the little restaurant just off Main Street, hungry for the delicious Southern cooking that Dixie Knox and her cook, Dale Shanks, were known for throughout Bedloe County.

Sam ordered chopped steak smothered in mushroom gravy with French fries on the side, while Cindy and Beth each ordered a salad and a jumbo baked potato with the works. They were sipping on sweet iced tea, waiting for their food to arrive, when Beth broke the silence that stretched between the three—an uncomfortable silence that had plagued them since they had left the Elder farm.

"I know you may not want to talk about it, Grandma," she began, choosing her words carefully, "but I'd really like to know what happened here back in 1936. I've heard bits and pieces over the years, but, to tell the truth, the story is still a little hazy to me. Dad never talked about it much, that's for sure."

Cindy looked across the table at Sam, then sighed. "That's probably because I never told him very much about what happened way back then. The whole business was so sordid—and painful—that I chose to keep it in the dark. Like a skeleton in the family closet, you might say."

Sam nodded in agreement. "I did the same with my wife, Betsy, God rest her soul. There just didn't seem to be any reason in dredging up things that were better left alone."

"I understand that," said Beth. "But if I'm going to assist you with this case, I think maybe it would help to understand exactly what took place in that old barn seventy-seven years ago."

"You're right, of course," said Cindy, reaching out and patting her granddaughter's hand. "And not because of what we're here to do. You have a right to know everything about your family, even the tragedies we've had to endure. I'm sorry if you've felt left out concerning that part of the Biggs family history."

"That's okay," said the young woman. "I've just been curious about this deep, dark secret that's been hidden away all these years, that's all."

"Then it's time for you to know the truth," the elderly woman said. "And, after I'm through, maybe you'll have a better understanding of exactly why that broken-down old barn holds such a dark place in our hearts."

Cindy was quiet for a moment. Then she began to tell the story.

"I was nine years old that year. Sam was no more than four. I was a frail, sickly child who had just recovered from a bad bout with typhoid fever. My illness had placed a lot of strain on the family, both emotionally and financially. I ended up staying in a Nashville hospital for several months and my father eventually had to sell off most of his tobacco land to pay the bill. He was a proud man who couldn't stand owing anything to anyone. Times were hard as it was. The country was several years into the Great Depression and the local bank was repossessing farms in Bedloe County left and right. We barely had enough to keep our bellies full and a dry roof over our heads, and Pappy was even considering traveling up North to find steady work. Thankfully, my mother talked him out of it and he stayed here in Coleman, doing mechanic work and odd jobs for a few dollars a week.

"Anyway, that spring, as soon as school came to a close, my oldest brother, Johnny, decided to go off to work in a CCC camp in east Tennessee, along with his friends C.J. Potts and Billy Longcreek." The old lady's eyes softened at the memory of her brother. "Johnny was a handsome boy. Tall and lanky like Pappy, but always with a smile on his face and a joke to tell. He was talented, too. He could play the guitar and sing like a mockingbird. He had a dream of traveling to Nashville and playing on the Grand Ole Opry, but he never got to live out that dream. What happened on the night of his death deprived him of the chance."

Cindy took a long sip of iced tea and then continued. "A couple of months passed and no one had heard from Johnny or his pals. Not even a letter or postcard to let us know that they were faring well. Around the middle of that summer, Pappy went to Nashville to sell some wild ginseng he'd dug up in the woods and dried. He was passing a pawn shop on Broadway when he spied Johnny's flattop guitar hanging in the window. He knew then that something bad had happened to my brother. That guitar was Johnny's pride and joy; he'd just as soon cut off his right arm as part with it. Well, a few days later, me and some of the other children who lived in Coleman were out roaming the woods, trying to beat the summer heat, when we came upon the Brewer property. The leader of the bunch, a bully of a boy named Chester Martin, headed for that old tobacco barn in the center of the thicket, claiming there was gold hidden inside. We tagged along, although I had a bad feeling that we were headed straight for disaster. To make a long story short, Chester opened that old tool chest in the barn and revealed the decaying bodies of three young men who had been brutally murdered and dismembered…the remains of my brother, Johnny, and his two buddies. From what Sheriff Taylor White could tell, the three had been tricked into going there by the promise of moonshine whiskey made by someone the boys had met at a local honky-tonk called the Bloody Bucket. When they got inside, away from prying eyes, they found themselves facing a couple of bad apples, one armed with a sawed-off shotgun. Money was demanded of them and, when C.J. Potts gave the robbers some gruff, all hell broke loose. He and Billy Longcreek were killed inside the barn, while Johnny was chased through a thunderstorm and finally shot down at the far edge of the thicket, scarcely a stone's throw from his own home. The killers took a hatchet and chopped up the bodies, then dumped quicklime on the remains and locked them in that chest. If we kids hadn't shown up and opened the box, we might have never known what had become of Johnny and the others."

Beth noticed her grandmother's flushed complexion. "Grandma, if you'd rather not continue—"

Cindy shook her head and took another drink of tea. "But I do. I want to tell it all." She was silent for a moment before she began talking again. "Sheriff White tried to find out who had committed the murders, but his efforts were in vain. Nobody had a clue as to who had killed those poor boys…until the autumn of that year. That was when the gift I possessed unexpectedly revealed their identities.

"Pappy and I were at Woody's General Store down at the forks when I heard someone talking at the front counter. The man's voice frightened me for some strange reason, so I went outside. A moment later, two men left the store. They were traveling handymen from Kentucky named Bully Hanson and Claude Darnell. Bully was a big, beefy fellow with blond hair cut close to his scalp and the coldest, cruelest eyes I've ever known. Claude was a skinny scarecrow of a guy with buckteeth and greasy black hair. He was a simpleton, but a mean one, and would do most anything Bully told him to. Even if it involved killing someone.

"Well, it wasn't long before I knew, without a doubt, that Bully was the man who killed my brother and I said as much. He threatened me right there in front of that store, told me that he would kill me and my family if I told anyone what I knew. On the way home, however, I broke down and told Pappy all about it. That night he went after Bully and was nearly shot for it. But, luckily, the sheriff showed up and took Bully into custody, having heard him admit to killing Johnny and the others.

"After that came the trial. It was the most sensational murder trial the state of Tennessee had seen up until that time. A lawyer named Willard Shaw prosecuted Hanson and Darnell, and got them the death penalty. They were sentenced to die in the electric chair at the state pen." She looked at her brother. "But that wasn't how they died...was it, Sam?"

A haunted look crossed the sheriff's face. "No, it wasn't."

Dixie brought their food and set it on the table before them. Cindy waited until the waitress was gone before she continued her story.

"On around Christmas of that year, Bully and Claude were being transferred to the penitentiary to be executed, when they overpowered and killed the two guards who were transporting them. They escaped into the worst snowfall that Tennessee had seen in a long while. They armed themselves with a shotgun and a hatchet, then came back here to Coleman. You see, Bully had revenge on his mind. Revenge against *me*. He aimed to make good on his promise. He intended to kill me and my family because I'd defied his earlier threats and turned him in."

"My God," Beth muttered, shaken.

147

"Pappy was off hauling firewood to someone in town, leaving me, Mama, and Sam alone at home that night. I heard a car pull up outside and immediately knew that we were in trouble. I had Mama put out the lamps and we managed to escape out the back door. We'd hardly gotten across the back yard to the woods when we heard Bully and Claude break into the house and shoot the place up. We kept right on running, heading through the woods, across Green Creek, to the Brewer property. We could hear them behind us, crashing through the trees, gaining ground. We picked our way through the thicket and found that there was only one place where we could possibly hide from them."

"The tobacco barn," said Beth.

"That's right," continued Cindy. "We squeezed past a loose board in the wall and hid behind the same tool chest that Johnny's body had been stashed in. A minute later, we heard Bully and Claude enter the barn and start toward us. Then, suddenly, they turned on one another. Bully shot Claude with his shotgun, while Claude cleaved Bully's skull in half with a hand axe. They both died instantly."

Beth's eyes widened. "But why? Why did they end up killing one another?"

Sam stared at his sister for a long moment and then turned his eyes toward his plate. Cindy did the same, avoiding the curious expression on her granddaughter's face. "I'd rather not talk about this anymore, dear," she said, her voice sounding strangely regretful. "Okay?"

Beth couldn't understand her grandmother's sudden change of mood, but didn't press the matter. "Sure, Grandma. Thanks for telling me the story."

"You're welcome," said Cindy, but her thoughts seemed to be elsewhere.

They were nearly finished with their meal, when a voice came from the aisle between the tables. "Hey there, Sam. How's it going today?"

"Just fine, I reckon," said Sam. "How're you doing, Ben?"

"I can't complain. I'm hungry as a winter bear right now."

Beth glanced up from a slice of spiced apple pie to see a short, elderly man about the same age as her grandmother. He was lean and balding, with a salt-and-pepper beard and wire-rimmed glasses. But the old man wasn't the one who sent the young woman's heart racing in sudden shock. Standing directly behind him was John Arnett, the handsome young doctor she had met at the hospital in Perryville.

The elderly man looked over at the two women who sat opposite Sam and a smile crept across his face. "Well, I'll be damned. Cindy Ann."

Cindy returned the smile. "Hi, Ben. It's been a while."

"A while is right," he said, leaning down and giving her a hug. "It's mighty good to see you again, Cindy. And who is this pretty young lady?"

"Ben, this is my granddaughter, Beth Garrison," she said in introduction. "Beth, this is Ben Arnett, the town pharmacist." A sly grin crossed her face. "And I believe you've already met his grandson."

John Arnett smiled at the young woman. "It's nice seeing you again, Doctor Garrison."

"Same here, Doctor Arnett," Beth said, wondering if the man could detect the pounding of her heart. *Calm down, Beth,* she told herself. *You're acting like some silly twelve-year-old girl, instead of a grown woman!*

"Well, it's a small world, ain't it?" proclaimed Ben Arnett.

"We'd invite you to join us, but we're nearly through here," Sam told him.

"Aw, we'll grab us a booth in the back over yonder," said Ben. His good-natured face suddenly turned grimly serious. "Had any luck finding out who killed those poor folks who moved out on the old Brewer place?"

"Not yet, but I'm hoping for a breakthrough soon," said Sam, picking at a dish of peach cobbler with the tines of his fork.

Ben cut his eyes toward Cindy. "Is that why you're here in Coleman, Cindy Ann? To help Sam with this mess?"

"I'm just here for a visit, Ben, that's all," she replied. Apparently his grandson had neglected to tell him about their meeting in Josh Elder's hospital room earlier that morning.

Ben winked at his childhood friend. "Okay. Whatever you say, Cindy. But if anyone could find out what really happened out there in that old barn, it'd be you." He looked over at Beth. "Your granny could sure spook the hell out of us kids way back when we were growing up. Why once, when Chester Martin was bullying Cindy on the school playground, she played some sort of trick on his mind. Made him think he was surrounded by snakes. Lordy Mercy, you should have seen that boy running into trees, trying to get away from those things. Do you remember that, Cindy Ann?"

The old woman looked uncomfortable. "Yes, I do. But that was a long time ago, Ben."

The pharmacist nodded. "It surely was. I suppose you've probably lost that weird talent of yours over the years, haven't you?"

Cindy said nothing. She simply sipped at her cup of after-supper coffee and avoided looking at him.

"Well, I reckon we'd best get to our booth and place our order," said Ben. "If you get a chance, Cindy Ann, stop by the drugstore and visit for a spell before you leave town. I've still got that soda fountain set up along the back wall and I

150

remember how you used to love those Coca-Cola floats of mine. I'll make one for you, on the house, if you stop by."

Cindy smiled. "Then I'll certainly try to make time, Ben. Thanks."

As they moved toward the rear of the restaurant, John Arnett turned and smiled at the woman with the long red hair. "It was nice bumping into you again, Beth," he said.

"Yes, it was...John," she replied, smiling self-consciously. "Maybe we'll run into each other again, before I head back to Nashville."

"I'd like that," said the doctor. "I really would."

After the Arnetts had left, Sam grinned across the table at Beth. "You know, I believe that boy has got a crush on you."

"Oh really, Sam!" Beth scoffed. "He's just showing a little professional courtesy, that's all."

"Professional courtesy my big toe!" laughed the sheriff. "He's got the hots for you, little lady."

"I certainly didn't know you were going to end up hooking a boyfriend when I asked you to come down here with me," said Cindy, adding fuel to the fire.

"Aw, Grandma! Stop your teasing!"

She felt her face grow warm with embarrassment as she finished her dessert. But, deep down inside, Beth couldn't help but hope that they were right. It had been a long time since Beth had felt so strongly about someone after such a brief encounter and it excited her to think that, perhaps, John Arnett felt similarly attracted to her as well.

CHAPTER TWENTY-TWO

"I really wish you'd reconsider staying with me, Cindy." Sam looked a little peeved as he pulled off the rural stretch of Old Newsome Road and parked in a long dirt driveway. "Since Betsy passed, I've got that big old house in town to myself. You and Beth would be more than welcome."

Cindy smiled at him. "I know that, Sam, and I appreciate the offer. But I'd really rather stay here. Who knows, it might put my mind at ease and make me a little more receptive to what took place in that old barn. After all, this is where it all started…for both of us."

Sam cut the engine and sat there quietly, staring through the windshield. An old, single-story farmhouse stood a few yards away, surrounded by scrubby brush and high weeds. Harsh weather had stripped every last bit of paint from the slatted walls and the tarpaper shingles of the roof had needed replacing long ago. But, given the fact that no one had actually lived there for going on twenty-five years, the old place was in remarkably good condition. The glass panes of all the windows were still intact and, as far as Sam knew, there were no leaks in the roof to damage the furnished rooms inside. In fact, except for a few plastic painting tarps that he had thrown over the furniture, the old Biggs house was exactly as it had been when their mother, Maudie, had passed away in the summer of 1988.

The sheriff shook his head, irked by his sister's stubbornness. "Well, it sure isn't going to be very comfortable.

I had the electricity cut off years ago and this place hasn't been cleaned in a coon's age. It's dark and dusty, and as drafty as it was when we were young'uns."

"I still want to stay." Cindy leaned over and kissed her brother on the jaw. "But thanks for trying to talk me out of it anyway."

"You're just as mule-headed as Pappy was," Sam grumbled. He glanced in the rearview mirror of the Bedloe County patrol car and watched as Beth parked her Honda in the drive behind him. "Come on and I'll carry your bags in for you."

Sam climbed out of the patrol car and walked back to Beth's car. The young woman already had the trunk open and was setting their luggage on the dusty, red clay driveway that cut across the front half of the Biggs property. "Can't you talk some sense into your grandmother?" he asked her, keeping his voice low.

"I tried," assured Beth, "but she's bound and determined to stay here while we're in Coleman." She looked toward the rickety farmhouse that stood surrounded by weeds and undergrowth. "I think she has missed this place something awful."

Sam looked back at the patrol car. Cindy stood next to the vehicle, staring longingly at the old house. "Yeah, I guess I know what she's feeling. I've just lived around here so long that I've kind of taken the old homeplace for granted."

He picked up the two bags and accompanied Beth down the rutted driveway. The sun was setting to the west, casting a soft, golden glow upon the house, causing it to resemble the sepia-toned image of a faded, but cherished, photograph.

Beth noticed a peculiar frown on the old woman's face. "What's the matter, Grandma?"

At first, Cindy looked as though she were at a loss for words. "I don't know," she said softly. "Something's wrong. I've felt it ever since we got to Coleman."

Sam and Beth looked at one another, wondering what was troubling the elderly lady. Then, without warning, Cindy slipped off her shoes and stockings. Barefooted, she stood in the powdery dust of the driveway, wiggling her toes in the dirt. At the same time, the tense expression that etched her wrinkled features softened and she let out a long sigh of relief.

Sam smiled and put his arm around her. "Welcome home, Cindy Ann."

"It feels good to be back," she admitted. "But in another way, I can't help but feel a little sad."

"I wouldn't doubt it, as much misery as we grew up with here on this place," said her brother, leading the way toward the front of the house.

"Sure, there were hard times. But there were good times, too." She looked around at the weedy yard and the sagging platform of the front porch. Cindy smiled to herself, remembering treasured moments from the distant past: Johnny sitting in the porch swing, playing his guitar and singing old-time gospel hymns for their mother; munching on waxed-lip suckers bought from Old Jonesy, the black peddler who came along every day or so with his mule-drawn wagon of household wares and spruced-up junk; and awakening on Christmas morning, overjoyed to find a single candy cane and a navel orange in the stockings they had hung on the kitchen wall next to the pot-bellied stove.

"Maybe you have fond memories of this old dump," said Sam. "But about all I remember is being hungry and poor and not much more than that."

"Stop being such a cynic. Don't you have any nostalgia in you at all?"

"I'm sorry, sis," apologized Sam. "I reckon this damn murder case has me kind of down."

Cindy slipped her hand through the crook of Sam's arm as they mounted the porch steps. The wooden risers creaked noisily beneath their feet. "Don't worry, little brother. I haven't given up yet. We'll give it another try tomorrow. Who knows, maybe things will be different next time and I'll be able to tell you what you need to know. Or, if I can't, maybe Beth can."

Sam took an old skeleton key from his pants pocket and unlocked the front door. It squealed on its hinges as he pushed it open. "Well, here you go," he said, peering into the gloom of the narrow hallway that ran past the parlor and three bedrooms and ended at the kitchen at the rear of the house. "I'll stick around and get you settled in, but I've got a lot of work to catch up on at the office. And the state lab is supposed to call tonight and give me the results of some tests we made at the tobacco barn following the murders."

"I appreciate you indulging an old woman and not putting up too much of a fuss about all this," Cindy told him.

"Well, I'm not too happy about it. Especially since there could be a killer on the loose out there somewhere." He turned back toward the front yard. "I'll go out to the car and fetch that kerosene lantern and camp stove I picked up on the way over here. If you can't do anything else, at least you'll be able to heat you up a hot cup of coffee before I pick you up in the morning."

The two women stood on the porch and watched as Sam made his way back to the patrol car. Beth turned to her grandmother. "Grandma, what was your real reason for wanting to stay out here tonight? This isn't exactly the Hilton, you know."

"I can't say for sure, dear," she told her. "I suppose it was just something I had to do. I guess I just felt like maybe this would help me get back in touch with myself."

"What do you mean?"

"Well, it's sort of hard to explain, but I feel like I've lost my true self. When I was growing up, my entire world was Bedloe County. I walked its back roads barefoot, climbed apple trees like a tomboy, and swam in every creek and cow pond between here and Perryville. But I lost a big part of that when I got married and moved to Nashville. Sometimes living in the city can sap the spirit of a country upbringing plumb out of you and, lately, I've gotten the feeling that has happened to me over the years. I miss simple things like seeing the stars in the sky at night without the glare of streetlights getting in the way. Or just smelling the scent of honeysuckle and hearing a whippoorwill's lonesome cry at twilight. Maybe all I want to do out here where I was born and raised is to find the old Cindy Ann that's bound to be deep down inside me somewhere. That little redheaded young'un who cut paper dolls from the Sears & Roebuck catalog and flew June bugs at the end of her mama's sewing thread. That same little girl who feared and respected the wondrous gift God blessed her with, instead of taking it for granted the way I tend to do from time to time."

"I'll sure help in any way I can," Beth offered, taking her grandmother's gaunt hand in her own."

"Just being here with me helps," said Cindy. She stared into Beth's face for a long moment. "Believe it or not, I see a lot of that little girl in you, too. Much more than I would have ever thought I'd find."

Beth squeezed the old woman's hand gently. "I'm glad. I really am."

Together, they turned and watched as Sam unloaded the trunk and brought a few things that would undoubtedly make their stay in the old house a little more comfortable.

Shortly past midnight, Beth awoke from a deep sleep.

At first, she was disoriented. She had no idea where she was. Then she felt the cool air of the spring night around her and smelled the musky scent of mildew and old furniture and realized that she was in the farmhouse her grandmother had grown up in as a child.

But what had startled her from her sleep? She listened carefully. The steady chorus of crickets came from the high weeds outside the house, but that hadn't been the noise that had disturbed her. Instead, it was the low rumbling of a muffler, along with the metallic chittering of an engine, the type of engine Beth had only heard in old black-and-white movies.

"Grandma?" she whispered. She reached out to the other side of the big king-size bed that had once belonged to her great-grandparents, Clayburn and Maudie Biggs. But the old lady wasn't there. The mattress was still warm, but the covers had been turned down and there was no one there.

Alarmed, she sat up in bed. "Grandma?" she called out loud.

"I'm here, child," came Cindy's voice from the far side of the room.

Once Beth's eyes grew accustomed to the gloom of the bedroom, she saw the elderly woman standing next to the window that faced the front porch. Her grandmother had the edge of the curtain peeled back and was peering out into the night.

"What's wrong?" Beth asked uneasily.

She could barely see the pale oval of her grandmother's face in the darkness. "Someone's out there," she said softly.

Beth left the bed and joined her. She peered through the gap in the curtains.

There, parked a yard or so behind the Accord, was a truck. But it was no ordinary truck. Instead, it was a very old pickup truck, painted a dull primer gray in color. If Beth had to guess, she would say that it was of early 1930s vintage.

"Who is it?" she whispered.

"I don't know," said Cindy. "But they've been there for five minutes now. Just sitting there, letting the motor idle."

Beth moved closer to the window until the tip of her nose nearly pressed against the glass. The form sitting behind the steering wheel of the old truck was no more than that...a dark, indistinguishable form and little more. That night's moon was hidden behind a heavy mat of spring storm clouds. Beth hoped that the cover would break and shed some revealing light on the trespasser. But, unfortunately, the pitch darkness of night persisted and the one in the truck remained unidentified.

"What do you think they're doing out there?" she asked her grandmother.

Cindy was silent for a moment. When she finally spoke, Beth detected a trace of fear in her voice. "I believe they're trying to scare us."

Beth felt a chill run through her, from the top of her head to the soles of her bare feet. "Well, they're sure doing a good job of it." She felt her way back through the darkness of the room, toward the nightstand next to the bed.

"Where are you going?"

"I'm going to call Sam on my cell phone." Beth's face was illuminated as the screen of her iPhone came on. "Crap! No service!"

"We're out in the boonies, dear," her grandmother told her. "I doubt if there's a cell tower within thirty miles of here."

Beth accompanied her at the window again and they watched the truck for a few minutes longer. Then the coarse grinding of shifting gears came from the vehicle and it slowly began to back down the driveway. A moment later, it had swung back onto the cracked asphalt of Old Newsome Road and, with a roar of its ancient motor, headed in the direction of town.

"Who was that?" Beth wondered.

"I don't know," said Cindy, her face grim and pale in the gloom. "But I've seen a truck like that before. A long, long time ago."

Beth didn't ask her grandmother to elaborate on her statement. She was almost afraid to. As she looked at the old woman, she felt the fine hairs on the back of her neck begin to tingle. For a fleeting second, Beth saw the same expression of dread that had possessed Cindy's face after they had departed the shadowy hollow of the old tobacco barn.

During that moment when she claimed to have sensed a dark and malevolent presence from her past.

CHAPTER TWENTY-THREE

"Now you see? If you'd been somewhere where your phone would pick up, you could've called me," Sam said over ham and eggs at Dixie's the following morning. "I'd have been there in five or ten minutes."

"They would have been long gone by then," Cindy told her brother. "Besides, they didn't really do anything. Just parked in the driveway and let the motor run for a while, then backed out into the road again."

"And they headed in the direction of town?"

"That's right," said Beth.

The sheriff shrugged. "Who knows? It could've been some teenagers out parking or some boys trying to find some out-of-the-way place to drink a six-pack. Something innocent like that."

"I would've thought so, too," said the elderly woman. She sopped a bite of pancake in maple syrup and forked it into her mouth. "But Beth's car was parked right there in the driveway. There's no way kids would stick around with the chance of being caught. No, whoever it was, they were there intentionally. They knew that we were there in the house and I believe they knew exactly who we were, too."

"Well, that settles it then," Sam told them. "You two are getting the hell out of that old house and staying at my place tonight."

Beth felt relief at the sheriff's ultimatum. Spending the night at the old Biggs house had been a lot like camping in the wilderness and she had found herself missing simple conveniences like electricity, running water, and a functional toilet more than once during her stay.

But her grandmother wasn't about to give in. "I'll do nothing of the kind. I intend to stay there till it's time to go home. Beth, on the other hand, can stay at your place, if she wants to."

"Aw, come on, Grandma," Beth laughed. "You know I wouldn't leave you out there all by yourself. If you can tough it out, so can I."

"Danged stubborn females!" rumbled Sam, looking none too pleased. "It must by some kind of infernal gene that shows up in the Biggs women." He ate in silence for a minute, then sighed. "Okay, I reckon I'll give in this time, despite my better judgment."

Cindy smiled to herself, pleased by her victory. "I'm glad you saw fit to see it my way, little brother. You remember how fiery my redheaded temper can be sometimes."

"Lord have mercy, yes!" Sam replied, unable to suppress a smile of his own. "I know better than to get you riled up, Cindy Ann."

The old lady took a sip from her coffee cup, then looked across the table at the sheriff. "There was something peculiar about that truck, Sam."

"Oh, yeah? And what was that?"

"It was an old truck," she told him. "A very old Ford pickup. It was primer gray and, if I were to take a guess, I'd say it was an early thirties model."

Sam seemed startled. "You're kidding."

"No," said Cindy. "I'm serious."

"But you know whose truck that sounds like, don't you?"

Beth was about to ask them to explain, when the answer suddenly struck her. "*He* had a truck like that way back in '36, didn't he? That fellow named Bully Hanson?"

Sam and Cindy said nothing. They simply nodded and kept on eating.

"Well, there has to be some other explanation," she suggested. "There has to be someone living here in Bedloe County who owns a truck like that."

The sheriff thought about it for a moment. "Come to think of it, there is. Chester Martin and his son have a hobby of fixing up old cars and trucks, when they're not up to more shady dealings. And I'm pretty sure they've been restoring an old Ford truck lately. A '31 model, from what I recall. But the last time I drove out to Chester's place, it was up on blocks in the front yard with the engine yanked clean out of it."

"Chester Martin," repeated Beth. "Grandma, wasn't that the boy that opened the tool chest in that old barn?"

"That was him, all right," Cindy admitted. "Come to think of it, I haven't seen him since I first left Coleman. From what I hear, he pretty much stays out on his place like some sort of hermit and rarely goes into town."

"That's about right," said Sam. "But his boy, Bud, sure gets around. I've had to run him in more times than I can remember. Most of the trouble he's been in has been for fighting or getting drunk and disorderly at the Bloody Bucket across the railroad tracks. It's a respectable place now—a country dance club—but some of the local rednecks treat it like it's still the sleazy roadhouse it was years ago. Bud's been convicted for possession of meth and car theft before, too. He spent a year in the state pen for stealing a car, but that's been a while ago. He's still on probation, though. That's the only reason I know for going all the way out to their place in the backwoods—to make sure Bud Martin is still walking the straight and narrow."

"Do you think Chester and his boy could've been involved in what happened last night?" asked Cindy.

"I don't see why in the world they would want to drive out to Old Newsome Road and scare two women half out of their wits," Sam said. He looked at his sister closely. "And don't you dare get it into your head to go out there and talk to Chester about it, either. If anyone goes and pays him a visit, it'll be me. Those Martins aren't exactly the hospitable type. They'd just as soon shoot at you for trespassing than give you the time of day."

"Okay, Sam," said Cindy turning her attention back to the breakfast plate on the table before her. "We hear you."

Sam emptied his coffee cup and stood up, adjusting his gun belt beneath the swell of his belly. "Well, I'm sorry that I've got to run, ladies, but I've got some business to attend to in Perryville this morning. You two can go shopping or visit old friends or do whatever you have a mind to do. I'll be back around noon. Then we'll go to the Elder family's funeral together." An uneasiness shown in his eyes. "God knows I don't really want to go, but it wouldn't be fitting for the county sheriff not to show up and at least pay his respects."

Cindy understood her brother's dislike for funerals. He had pretty much shied away from burial services since her brother Johnny's funeral seventy-seven years ago. But, despite his feelings, he had been forced to make exceptions. During the past sixty years, Sam and Cindy had had to bid farewell to most of their immediate family: their brother, Joshua, who had died in the Normandy invasion; their older sister, Polly, who had perished in a car crash twenty years ago; and their mother and father, both whom had died of cancer. And, earlier that year, Sam's wife of fifty-seven years, Betsy, had died of a fatal stroke. Given that, Cindy supposed she couldn't blame her brother for being so skittish about funerals and death in general.

"We'll see you at the office around twelve then," Cindy assured him.

When he had paid the check at the register and left the café, Beth turned to her grandmother. "So, what *are* we going to do this morning?"

A mischievous grin crossed Cindy's wrinkled face as she brought her left hand from where it had lain in her lap beneath the table. The middle and index fingers were crossed, as though secretly canceling a promise that had been made.

"I believe we ought to pay Chester Martin a visit," she said. "Whether Sam likes it or not."

The Martin place was located halfway between Coleman and the forks that split Highway 70 into Old Newsome Road. Nothing of the property could be seen from the highway, except for a rutted dirt road that disappeared into a heavy stand of pine forest. The only thing that gave them a clue that it was actually the place they were looking for was a battered metal mailbox sitting atop a weathered wooden post. The name MARTIN was crudely painted across the side of the box and nothing more.

"It looks sort of spooky in here," Beth said as she drove down the winding road. The pine grove that surrounded them was so dense that the thick boughs of one tree seemingly merged with those of the next, forming an impenetrable wall of lush greenery.

"Don't let what Sam said frighten you, dear," Cindy assured her. "Chester's bark was always worse than his bite. He acts tough, but he's basically a coward beneath all the bluff. I reckon I know that better than most folks."

Beth recalled the incident Ben Arnett had mentioned, how her grandmother had once manipulated Chester Martin's emotions, bringing the boy's worst fear to the surface and causing him to imagine a multitude of serpents around him. At first, the thought of a young Cindy Ann terrorizing the school bully with visions of rattlesnakes, copperheads, and water moccasins seemed unthinkable; she simply couldn't imagine her sweet little grandmother doing such a thing. But then Beth considered her own ability to influence and the way she had used it to give the child-abuser Jerry Rucker a taste of his own brutal medicine, and she realized that her grandmother's willingness to strike back in such a way wasn't so far-fetched after all.

"I'm not as worried about Chester as I am his son," she confided. "The one who's been in so much trouble."

"I don't believe I've ever laid eyes on the boy," said Cindy. "He must be in his late fifties now. But if he's anything like his papa, I don't think we'll have anything to worry about."

As Beth drove onward, the pine forest seemed to grow even deeper and darker than it had appeared from the highway. "I sure hope you're right, Grandma."

A few minutes later, they rounded a bend in the road and found themselves in a large clearing. A rickety house of weathered wood slats and a rusty tin roof stood amid the hulls of several dozen automobiles, most of which were missing their wheels, doors, and engines. To the right stood a tall oak bearing a chain and pulley affixed to its sturdiest limb, from which a greasy transmission dangled. Out back of the house stood a huge barn and several outbuildings a few loose nails short of total collapse.

As they parked the Accord next to the oak and left the car, Cindy nodded toward the front porch. It was bowed in the middle due to the amount of junk and trash that crowded the boarded floor: heavy steel truck wheels, a pyramid of old car batteries, and a stack of oil-blackened concrete blocks that were used for propping up the various vehicles the Martins did repairs on.

Sitting in the center of it all, reared back in a kitchen chair with a woven cane seat, was an overweight elderly man dressed in grungy denim overalls and a greasy white undershirt. The old man's face and arms were tanned as brown as leather, but his hair and beard were as white as virgin snow.

Cindy stopped short, a little intimidated by the cold blue eyes that glared at her from beneath bushy white brows. Then she stood straight and tall and approached the front porch. "Howdy, Chester," she called out.

The old man simply stared at her for a long moment. Then he spat a stream of tobacco juice off the porch and into the crabgrass at her feet. "Who the hell are you?"

"You know who I am."

Chester Martin chewed on his wad of tobacco a while longer, searching her face for some clue to her identity. Then, all of a sudden, he knew. The image of a shy, red-haired girl in a faded flower-print dress came to him.

"Well, I'll be double-dog damned!" he cursed, an ugly scowl crossing his even uglier face. "If it ain't Cindy Ann Biggs of all people!"

"Cynthia Garrison now," she told him. "I have been since the Fifties." She studied his face, trying to detect the least hint of cordiality and good humor. She wasn't surprised to find nothing but contempt and animosity instead. "So, how have you been?"

"That sure as shit ain't no concern of yours, Cindy Ann," he growled. "And you ain't got no right to come visiting without an invitation, either. This here's private property. Now get off before I sic my dogs on you and that little gal over there."

The two women turned their eyes to the dogs Chester was referring to. They were a couple of mangy redbone coonhounds who lounged in the shade beneath the far end of the porch. Each wore a length of rusty chain clipped to their collars, but the restraints seemed to be unnecessary. Both dogs were sleeping peacefully and looked completely unconcerned with the strangers who stood only a few feet from their elderly master.

"I just thought I'd stop by and say hi, Chester, that's all," said Cindy. "And maybe ask you a couple of questions."

Chester took a sardine saturated in hot mustard sauce from an open tin balanced on one of his threadbare knees, then chased it down with a gulp of chocolate Yoo-hoo. "Questions? What kind of questions?"

"I heard that you've been working on an old Ford truck lately," she said, seeming much calmer and in control than her granddaughter felt. "An old gray one that's early 1930s in make. Is that true?"

"So what if it is?" snapped Chester, wiping his mouth on the back of his hairy forearm. "Ain't none of your affair anyhow."

Cindy looked around the junky front yard. The only vehicle that was sitting up on blocks was a Mustang GT that was in the process of being stripped and repainted. The gray Ford pickup was nowhere to be seen.

"Well, to be honest with you, Chester, my granddaughter and I were staying out at my old place last night and we woke up in the middle of the night to find an old Ford truck parked in the driveway. I was told that you were working on such a truck and was curious as to whether it was one and the same, that's all."

"I reckon you found that out from that nosey-ass brother of yours, didn't you?" Chester asked with a sneer. "Well, if it'll make you happy, yeah, I do have an old '31 Ford I'm working on. But it ain't been nowheres. It's been parked out back in the barn for the past two months."

"Do you mind if we take a look at it?" Cindy asked.

"Hell, yeah, we mind!" said someone from the front doorway of the house.

Cindy and Beth turned their eyes from the old man in the kitchen chair. The screen door opened and a tall, chubby man in his mid-fifties stepped out onto the porch. He was dressed in tan work boots, oil-stained jeans, and a Budweiser ball cap. He wore no shirt, exposing a flabby chest and bulging beer belly, both covered with wiry hair. His face was just as mean and ugly as his father's, the only difference being that his whiskers were dirty blond in color, rather than snow white.

The two women found themselves stepping back a couple of paces. But it wasn't the physical presence of the big man that frightened them. Rather, it was the 30-caliber Winchester deer rifle that he held fisted in one hand, the muzzle aimed haphazardly toward them.

"Who the hell do you think you are anyway, coming out here and asking questions?" he demanded. He grinned hatefully, showing off a mouthful of rotten, tobacco-stained teeth. "Now y'all clear off our land, before I let loose with this thing and end up taking you back home to ol' Sheriff Biggs, tied to the fender of your Jap car."

"This here's my son, Bud," Chester said, beaming with pride.

"A chip off the old block," said Cindy. She stared at the gun in the man's hand. It lifted an inch or so, centering on the old woman's chest. Whether it was done by chance or intentionally, she couldn't be sure. But she would have picked the latter over the former, given the hostility that burned in his muddy brown eyes.

"Now ya'll git!" he warned. "And don't come snooping around and bothering my papa no more…you hear?"

"We're leaving," Cindy said. She turned to her granddaughter, who looked pale and upset. "Come on, dear."

As they reached the Honda, they heard Chester Martin's coarse laughter, thick with arrogance and phlegm. "I recommend that you heed what my boy says and stay clear of this place, Cindy Ann. He's so ornery, I wouldn't put it past him to shoot a woman or two. He's come close enough to drilling a couple of his girlfriends already, for giving him too much lip and not enough tail."

Cindy and Beth said nothing. They climbed into the car and, a minute later, were driving back down the dirt road, toward the highway at the far side of the pine woods.

When they reached the stretch of two-lane blacktop, Beth released a sigh of relief. "Good Lord, Grandma…why did we do such a stupid thing like that?"

"I don't know exactly," her grandmother admitted. "Maybe I wanted to see if I could get a look at that gray truck. Or maybe I just wanted to get a glimpse of Chester after all these years. Him and that boy of his."

"Well, I don't know what sort of impression they made on you, but they both scared the crap out of me!"

"Oh, Chester was about the same as I remember," Cindy told her. "He was just as full of bull as when we were young'uns." A troubled look crossed her wrinkled face. "But that boy of his…Bud…he was different. That man is dangerous. Crazy dangerous. I could see it in his eyes."

Beth laughed nervously. "No kidding."

"If I were you, dear, I wouldn't say anything about this to Sam. If he knew we went out there on our own, he'd pitch a fit."

"Don't worry," her granddaughter assured her. "I intend on putting that little trip completely out of my mind. If I can."

She glanced at the digital clock on the dashboard. The time was 11:40. Beth turned north up Highway 70 and headed for

Coleman, aware that they were supposed to meet the sheriff at his office in twenty minutes. She pressed down on the gas pedal, half of her intending to make their appointment, while the other half was anxious to put as much distance between them and the Martin place as possible.

CHAPTER TWENTY-FOUR

F ollowing the autopsies of Gordon, Peg, and Michelle Elder, their remains were claimed by their kinfolk in Kentucky. No official funeral of the three was held in the town of Coleman, but, out of respect for the unfortunate family, a memorial service was held at the Coleman First Baptist Church.

Very few of those who attended had actually known the Elders or had even had the chance to meet them, but that didn't matter. A crowd of total strangers lined the pews, to gaze solemnly at the proceedings and even shed a few tears of grief. They felt badly that the Elders had become victims in their community after pulling up stakes and moving all the way from Kentucky. Obviously, they had considered the town of Coleman to be a safe haven in a world of violence and crime, just like all the other residents believed. But, as it had turned out, the certainty of a small-town paradise had merely been a cruel illusion. The Elders had paid a horrible price learning that truth, while the citizens of Bedloe County found themselves living with the chilling reality that a deadly evil had invaded a place that they had once believed to be peaceful and perfectly safe.

Following the service, Cindy and Beth were walking across the parking lot to find Sam when someone called out.

"Cindy Ann?"

They turned to find two elderly women walking toward them. At first, Beth thought her eyes were playing tricks on her. The two old ladies looked identical. They possessed the same gaunt face, pale green eyes, and curly gray hair. The two were even dressed similarly, from their black dresses and pillbox hats, to the tortoiseshell frames of their eyeglasses. Both smelled of mothballs and Rolaids antacid, as well as the dusty scent of kitty litter.

Her grandmother seemed just as surprised to see them as she was, although she appeared to recognize them immediately. A slight smile crossed her face, but it was a guarded smile. "Hi Sally," she said politely. "Susan...it's nice seeing you both again."

"Why it is you, isn't it, Cindy?" said the old woman named Sally. "Didn't I tell you she was here in town, sister?"

"You certainly did," the other replied. "I didn't believe it, but here she is, in the flesh."

"This is my granddaughter, Beth Garrison," Cindy said in introduction. "Beth, this is a couple of childhood acquaintances of mine, Sally and Susan Osborne."

The significance of the two didn't dawn on Beth at first. Then she remembered. The Osborne twins had been two of the children present in the old tobacco barn the day the bodies of Johnny Biggs and his two friends had been discovered.

Susan Osborne studied Beth through the thick lenses of her spectacles. "I do declare, Cindy Ann, she's the spitting image of you when you were her age!"

Beth was pleased by the compliment. "Really?"

"That's right, dear," confirmed Sally. "Your grandmother was a real beauty back then. She was downright beautiful...a far cry from that homely, freckle-faced young'un she was when we grew up together."

"It was nice seeing you two again," said Cindy, taking her granddaughter by the elbow and turning to leave.

"Now don't you run off so fast, Cindy Ann," said Sally Osborne. She reached out and hooked the strap of Cindy's purse with her bony fingers. "We haven't seen you in a month of Sundays!"

"I really would like to stay and talk," Cindy apologized, although Beth was certain that that was far from the truth. "But we've got to find Sam and head back to town. I really do wish we had the chance to stick around and visit a while longer."

"Then you'll simply have to stop by the house and have coffee with us before you start back to Nashville," suggested Susan.

"Yes, please do," agreed Sally. "Promise us that you'll come over one afternoon, Cindy Ann. We'll have a bite to eat and talk about old times. And bring your lovely granddaughter with you."

"We'll see if we can't do that," said Cindy, forcing a smile.

The old lady and her granddaughter were turning away, when Susan Osborne stopped them once again. "Oh, Cindy?"

Cindy looked around, the smile on her face held in place by sheer willpower. "Yes, Susan?"

"It is sort of peculiar, you showing up out of the blue like this," she said, her eyes searching Cindy's face. "I mean, right after that horrible tragedy in Harvey Brewer's old tobacco barn and all."

"Yes," echoed her sister. "Very peculiar."

"It's only a coincidence, that's all," Cindy insisted. "Now, if you'll excuse us, we really have to go."

"Don't forget," Sally called after them as they ducked through the crowd. "Coffee at our place. Just give a call when you have some free time. We're in the phone book."

"What a couple of strange, old ladies," Beth said when they were out of earshot.

"Strange isn't the word for them," said Cindy, looking relieved to be away from them. "The Osborne twins have been inseparable since they were born. They always dressed alike, acted alike, and have lived in the same house off State Street ever since I could remember. They're lifelong spinsters; neither one of them ever married. I guess neither one could bear to be apart from the other long enough for the honeymoon."

"You don't seem to be very fond of them, Grandma."

"No, and they were certainly never all that fond of me, either," Cindy told her. "Especially after that summer of '36. They've gone their entire lives snubbing me and my family, thinking they were better than we were. And now they have the gall to invite me to their house for coffee!"

"But you're still going to see them, aren't you?" Beth asked.

Cindy couldn't help but smile. "Yes, I suppose I will before we leave…out of curiosity, if nothing else. Those two old ladies are extremely eccentric. As far as I know, no one in Coleman has ever set foot in that old house of theirs, let alone been invited to visit. I'd be a genuine fool to pass up the opportunity to at least go over there and snoop around a little, now wouldn't I?"

"Remember, they invited me, too," Beth reminded her.

"Why, of course," said Cindy, taking her granddaughter's arm. "You don't think I'd dare go in that creepy old house of theirs alone, do you?"

The two laughed and, seeing Sam standing a few yards away, went to talk to him before they left the church parking lot.

CHAPTER TWENTY-FIVE

"Are you sure you want to do this?" asked Beth.

Cindy nodded. She stared at the sagging hull of the tobacco barn through the Accord's windshield. The fading light of sunset cast a crimson glow upon the structure of roughly-hewn lumber and rusted tin sheeting, causing it to appear as though it was bathed in blood.

"I didn't give it my best yesterday," she confessed to her granddaughter. "I was scared and I shielded myself too much. I want to try again, this time with my mind completely open."

Beth regarded the old barn reluctantly. "Then come on and we'll—"

"No," said Cindy flatly. "Not *we*. I'd like to go in alone this time…by myself."

"Do you think you ought to? I mean, all the horrible things that you've gone through in there—"

"Yes, but that was in the past," Cindy told her. "No matter what I experience in there, it's simply that—the past. I keep telling you that the remnants of past events can't harm you. Well, it's about time that I believe my own advice."

"What do you expect to find in there? We tried before and could only uncover so much."

"But it's there," claimed Cindy. "I know it is. Something may be interfering, trying to prevent us from seeing more. But I believe I can break past that barrier if I put all I have into it."

Beth took her grandmother's hand, concerned. "Don't put yourself in danger, though. Remember your blood pressure."

Cindy smiled. "I know...I'm no spring chicken, dear. But it's important that I at least try again. This horrible mystery must be resolved, no matter what. I realized that when we attended that memorial this afternoon. If I do it for anyone, it will be for those poor folks who lost their lives here a few days ago."

"Well, if you're certain you want to do this —"

"I am," the elderly woman assured her. "I'd be grateful if you'd wait for me outside, though. Just knowing you're nearby will make me feel a lot better."

"Sure, Grandma. Anything you want."

The two left the car and trudged through the high weeds, to the western wall of the tobacco barn. As they neared a stand of thistle, several quail were spooked from the undergrowth. The birds took wing and flew into the darkening Tennessee sky, soon disappearing from sight.

"Good luck," Beth told her when they reached the opening in the wall.

"Thanks." Cindy took a deep breath, then stepped through the jagged portal of rotten boards.

She soon found herself surrounded by the dark, dusty shadows of the barn's interior. The last ebbing rays of the sun shone through the cracks between the boards, casting slashes of red light across the earthen floor. Cindy gathered her nerve and started toward the narrow framework of the old tool chest several yards away.

When she got there, she stared at the narrow box where the bodies of so many dead and mutilated had ended up. Amid the dank, earthy odor of the dirt floor beneath her, Cindy could smell the coppery stench of blood, both incredibly old and freshly let. And she detected that dark and disturbing undercurrent as well—the presence of a lingering evil that was, at least, partially responsible for what had taken place there several nights ago.

She turned and looked toward the opening in the wall. Beth stood there, watching silently. She gave her granddaughter a smile of reassurance, then turned back to the grisly task at hand.

Cindy crouched and stared at the earth that lined the bottom of the tool chest. She noticed traces of lime around the corners and realized that it was remnants of the substance that Hanson and Darnell had poured over the bodies of Johnny, C.J. Potts, and Billy Longcreek seventy-seven years ago, in hopes of stifling the stench of decay. Cindy felt a queasiness threaten to overcome her, but she managed to suppress it. She had no time for petty weaknesses at that moment. There was important work to be done that evening.

She breathed in deeply, drawing in the scent of earth and slaughter, and, casting away all defenses, opened her mind completely. She reached out and gathered up a fistful of dirt—earth damp with humidity and congealed blood.

Cindy stood up and concentrated. For a few moments, the interior of the barn remained as it was. Then, slowly, the environment around her began to change. The glow of sunset faded, until only darkness shown between the cracks of the boards. Then, within the old building, a soft, flickering glow began to illuminate the ground and walls around her. She saw the source of the light a second later. It originated from a Coleman lantern that hung from a crooked nail in a support post several feet away.

She retreated a yard or so, providing a better view of what was about to transpire. Abruptly, voices sounded behind her, coming from the direction of the open wall. She fought the urge to turn and look, afraid that, to do so, might break the spell and send her faltering back to the present. She stood her ground and continued to stare at the area surrounding the wooden tool chest.

It wasn't long before three forms stumbled into view, appearing frightened and confused. One was a tall, husky man with wavy black hair and dark brown eyes, dressed in boxer shorts and a white undershirt. She knew immediately that he was Gordon Elder. The farmer's face was flushed with anger and defiance, but Cindy could detect the stronger emotion of raw fear sparkling in his eyes.

The other two were both women. One was in her late thirties, while the other was sixteen or seventeen years of age. Both were blonde and possessed similar facial features, identifying them as mother and daughter. The older woman wore a flannel gown, while the teenager was dressed in a Barbie nightshirt.

Both were crying and were visibly terrified. Cindy knew at once that they were Peg and Michelle.

Why the hell have you brought us here? demanded Gordon, standing protectively in front of his wife and daughter.

Suddenly, a fourth form stepped into the picture. But, unlike the crystal-clear images of the Elder family, this one remained shadowy and vague. It was definitely human, but not distinctly so. Cindy couldn't tell whether the culprit was large or small, male or female. They were simply there.

The only reply they expressed at Gordon's frantic demand was a low, dry laughter. It was a laughter brimming with contempt and cruelty, and tinged with an amusement that could only be described as sadistic. Then they lifted their right arm slowly. Fisted in one featureless hand was the stubby length of a sawed-off shotgun, a twelve-gauge with double barrels from the size and shape of it. And, apparently, it was an antique model of firearm, the type with a separate hammer set along each breech. The abductor's thumb crisply cocked back one hammer and then the other.

No! cried Peg Elder, her hands outstretched. *Please!*

Gordon retreated a couple of steps, his face growing ghastly pale in the lantern light. *Come on...don't do this. We'll give you anything!* he said, his voice pleading. *Anything you want!*

Again the laughter, sinister and utterly without compassion. *This* is *what I want.*

This time the horrible event did not fade with the roar of the first shotgun blast. A dark crater appeared in the center of Gordon Elder's chest as a load of double-aught buckshot slammed into him. The force of the blast was so violent that it pitched him completely off his feet. He flew backwards, knocking his daughter off balance. Both slammed to the earthen floor next to the tool chest, Gordon deathly still, while Michelle screamed and fought to escape. But she could not. She was trapped beneath the weight of her father's body.

Peg Elder let out a shriek and darted toward the western wall, as though hoping to reach the jagged opening. The second barrel of the shotgun belched flame and thunder. Lead pellets ripped through the back of Peg's nightgown, burrowing deeply past her shoulder blades. She hit the ground on her face, rolled over once, then came to rest in a limp bundle a few feet away.

The shrill screams of the teenage girl drew the murderer's attention. Leisurely, they turned and slowly walked toward her, opening the twin breeches of the shotgun and expelling the empty loads. Two fresh shells were taken from a pocket and slipped into the smoking chambers, then the barrels were snapped back into place with a flip of the wrist.

Oh please! wailed Michelle, her face an agonized mask of terror and tears. *God help me—*

Her plea was drowned out by a third shotgun blast. Cindy watched, horrified, as the girl's head rocked backward on her narrow shoulders, her face completely obliterated. Then Michelle Elder slumped lifelessly to the ground, joining her mother and father in death.

Cindy expected the hideous spectacle to end there. But it didn't.

Before the lantern-lit images began to fade into darkness, she saw the murky form of the killer turn and stare directly at her. As the dark muzzles of the shotgun—one smoking, the other as black as the eye socket of the Grim Reaper himself—swung toward her, that harsh and horrible laughter sounded in her ears again, this time like a death knell.

But, strangely enough, the voice was much clearer than the one the Elders had heard prior to their grisly deaths. This one was coarse and unrefined, brimming with rural ignorance and cruelty.

It was a voice Cindy had known before, nearly a lifetime ago.

Gotcha...Cindy Ann!

A swirl of darkness and disorientation gripped the elderly woman. With a cry of alarm, she stumbled backward and fell to the earthen floor. She soon found herself back in the place where she had first started—in the center of the old tobacco barn with the colorful rays of the setting sun peeking through the cracks of the walls.

Beth was beside her in an instant. "Grandma! Are you alright?"

"Yes, dear," she replied, her heart pounding in her chest. "I just lost my balance, that's all." She closed her eyes and breathed in deeply, attempting to drive those devastating images of cold-blooded murder from her mind, as well as the dark, but vaguely familiar form that had just confronted her.

"Did you see more this time?" Beth asked her after a few moments.

Cindy nodded. "I saw the Elders die here in this barn. But I still couldn't tell who was responsible. Lord knows I tried, but it just wouldn't come to me."

"Come on." The young woman looked around the barn uncomfortably. "Let's get out of here."

Cindy was as anxious to leave the place as her granddaughter was. She placed her left hand on the ground to push herself up and, suddenly, felt something hard press against the flesh of her palm. She closed her fingers around the narrow object as Beth helped her to her feet.

They were outside the barn before Cindy looked down at the thing she held in her hand. She was surprised to find that it was a fishing lure. It was long and oval in shape, painted silver with one tiny red eye. The hook was missing at the end and it was caked with dirt, as though it had lain there upon the dirt floor of the barn for a very long time.

"What have you got there?" Beth asked.

"It looks like a fishing lure," she told her. "I found it when you were helping me up."

"What would a thing like that be doing in there?"

"I don't know," said Cindy, looking distracted. She opened her purse and found a Wal-Mart receipt lying loose among the contents. After studying the dirt-caked lure for a moment, she wrapped it in the scrap of paper and tucked it into her hand bag.

"Why are you keeping that filthy old thing?" Beth asked.

Cindy shrugged. "Your Uncle Sam is a big fisherman. I thought maybe he might be interested in it."

Beth frowned at the lack of color in her grandmother's lean face. "Let's get you to the house," she suggested. "You don't look like you feel very well."

"You're right," admitted the elderly woman. "I believe my nerves are up. And maybe my blood pressure, too."

181

As Beth helped Cindy back to the car, the old lady considered the true reason why she had held onto the old fishing lure, a reason she wasn't yet prepared to reveal to her granddaughter. Not until she knew for sure.

For, when she had held that simple object between her fingers, it had given off the same dark emanations that she had sensed upon grasping the fistful of bloody earth. But, oddly enough, it had varied somehow, as though it was connected to an entirely different period in time.

But a period that was, undoubtedly, every bit as bloody and fatal as that which she had just witnessed several minutes ago.

CHAPTER TWENTY-SIX

That night, Cindy and Beth were again awakened by a sound. But this time it was not the rumbling of a truck engine that roused them from their sleep.

"Grandma?" Beth whispered in the darkness. "Did you hear that?"

"Yes," replied the old woman softly.

The two were silent for a long moment, listening. Then it came again. The creaking of footsteps at the far end of the front porch.

Both lay in the four-poster bed and peered at the square of pale light that distinguished the front window from the rest of the bedroom wall. At first, the moonlight that shown through the sheer curtains remained constant and undisturbed. Then, abruptly, a dark shadow moved past it. A shadow that was distinctively human in form.

Neither woman moved. They simply lay there and waited. The footsteps continued across the porch, the weight of each pressing against the ancient boards, causing them to creak every so often.

"They're going to the front door," said Cindy. Quietly, she threw back the covers and climbed out of bed.

"Grandma!" hissed Beth. "Don't!"

But Cindy refused to listen. Barefooted, she felt her way through the darkness, moving around the bed, toward the bedroom doorway. The door was open, providing access to the shadowy hallway beyond.

Beth kicked the covers off herself and, cursing beneath her breath, also left the bed. As she passed her great-grandmother's antique dresser, she reached into the suitcase that lay open on the stool. Blindly, she felt past the clothing she had packed for the trip, searching for something that was concealed at the bottom. She found the object nestled beneath her spare panties and bras. It was a small canister of pepper spray that she had bought last year when a rapist was on the loose in a neighborhood near Vanderbilt Medical Center.

Clutching the weapon tightly in her fist, she stepped through the open doorway into the hallway. The corridor was dimly lit by the pale glow of moonlight that shone through the single pane of the front door. Her grandmother stood several feet away from the entrance, her face more grim than frightened in the gloom.

Beth was about to say something when her grandmother raised a wrinkled hand, motioning for silence.

Immediately, the young woman understood why. The footsteps outside suddenly came to an abrupt halt and a broad and imposing shadow was cast across the door's upper pane as well as the dusty curtains that covered the window from the inside.

Neither Beth nor Cindy said anything. They scarcely breathed as the shadow remained there, motionless, for a long moment. Then they watched as the door's brass knob turned slightly.

Beth frantically looked toward the metal plate beneath the knob. The skeleton key that Sam had left with them was in the keyhole, turned securely to the right. But that didn't make her feel any better. The door and its lock were old and nowhere as sturdy as a modern deadbolt. If the one outside had a notion to come in, all they would have to do would be to give the door a good swift kick. More than likely, the door would pop right open with no trouble at all.

She thought about her iPhone on the nightstand next to the bed. Even if it did cooperate and pick up a signal this time, Sam would never be able to get there in time. Beth snaked her thumbnail beneath the safety cap of the spray's canister and released it with a snap. If the intruder did decide to break in, she intended to empty the contents into their eyes, then make a run for the back door.

The doorknob rattled a couple of times, then grew still and silent. The shadow on the opposite side of the curtained windowpane simply stood there for a moment, as though attempting to stare through the drapes at what might be in the hallway beyond.

What are they waiting for? wondered Beth. She looked over at her grandmother. Cindy stood there, as motionless as a statue, her hazel eyes centered on that shadow at the window. Suddenly, a thought came to the young woman. *She knows who it is. Or thinks she knows.*

Outside the door, they could hear the coarse rasp of the trespasser's breathing. There came a small thud on the floorboards of the porch, as though something had been deliberately dropped. Then the shadow moved away. The two women stood there and listened as the footsteps retreated down the porch steps and swished through the high grass and weeds of the front yard.

Quickly, Cindy stepped forward and opened the curtains enough to peek out. The yard appeared to be completely empty, except for what should have been there: the magnolia tree to the right, a plaster birdbath full of stagnant green water, and a lilac bush at the edge of the road. She searched for some sign of a dark form in the moonlight, but there was none.

Both waited a moment longer. Soon, their patience was rewarded. It wasn't long before they heard the cranking of a truck engine. It kicked into life a second later and then faded as the vehicle drove off in the direction of town.

"It was the same one as last time," said Beth, her voice shaky. "It had to be."

Cindy said nothing. She turned the key in the lock and opened the front door. Stepping out onto the porch, she looked down. Something lay on the boards of the floor, just as she expected. Slowly, the old woman bent down and picked it up.

"What is it?" Beth asked.

Cindy held it up in the moonlight.

At first, Beth couldn't make out what it was. Then she recognized its shape, as well as the gleam of polished metal, and an icy chill ran throughout her.

It was a shotgun shell. But not a modern cartridge constructed of colored plastic and alloy metal. This one was made of cardboard tubing connected to a brass casing, like those from an entirely different era. And that wasn't all. The shell had been recently fired. The end of the tube was frayed and scorched. And, in the crisp night air, the sulfurous scent of burnt powder could be detected.

"It's a warning," Cindy said. Her voice sounded strangely detached, as though she was speaking from the far reaches of a dream.

"But a warning from *who*?" Beth wanted to know. Again, she got the impression that her grandmother knew the identity of the one who was terrorizing them.

Silently, Cindy closed the door and locked it. Then she returned to the room adjoining the hall and sat down heavily on the bed.

Alarmed by the peculiar way her grandmother was acting, Beth lit the kerosene lantern that sat on the nightstand. In the flickering glow of the lamp, she was shocked to see a look of bewilderment and severe fright on the old woman's face. It was an expression of conflicting emotions, stark realization at odds with total disbelief.

She reached out and cradled her grandmother's hand in her own. It trembled, more from some secret terror than from the chill of the night. "Who was it, Grandma?" she asked. "Who was out there?"

"It couldn't have been," muttered Cindy. "It's impossible."

"What's impossible?"

The elderly woman took a shuddering breath and stared at the shotgun shell she held between her fingers. "Everything inside me, every instinct my gift has blessed me with, tells me that the one who stood on the other side of that door a couple of minutes ago was—" She shut her eyes and shook her head in denial. "No, it couldn't have been!"

Beth felt her blood run cold. "Who?" she asked. But, deep down inside, she already knew who her grandmother was referring to.

When Cindy spoke again, she sounded not so much like a mature and sensible woman, but like a frightened child who still believed unfalteringly in the boogeyman.

"It was *him*, Beth," she said, her voice scarcely more than a whisper. "It was Bully Hanson."

CHAPTER TWENTY-SEVEN

The following day, Cindy and Beth returned to Perryville Medical Center to check on Josh Elder.

As they rode the elevator to the second floor, Beth glanced over at her grandmother. The elderly woman looked as though she hadn't slept at all the previous night, or at least not after the frightening incident that had roused them from their sleep. Cindy's face was pale and drawn, and Beth had noticed her hands shake that morning as she ate her breakfast at Dixie's. Apparently, the shadow at the front door had unnerved her even more than Beth had realized. And, although the old woman hadn't said so, it was apparent that she still had that crazy idea in her head, that a psychopathic killer who had died decades ago was, again, roaming the rural back roads of Bedloe County.

Beth didn't know what to say to her. To believe such nonsense was insane, but her grandmother was convinced that her instincts were correct. Beth had never believed in ghosts, but she did believe that truly evil people existed. The one who killed the Elders in the tobacco barn was most certainly that, but Beth wasn't sure that the one who had terrorized them last night was even one and the same. It could be some idiot pulling a cruel prank on her grandmother.

Or it could be someone hired by the killer, someone who was trying their damnedest to scare them off. And, in Beth's opinion, they were doing a pretty good job of it so far.

When the elevator door opened, Beth spotted John Arnett at the nurse's station. He had his back to them, studying a patient's chart. When she saw the doctor standing there, Beth couldn't help but feel a jolt of adrenaline shoot through her. Again, she was surprised that he affected her in such a way. For the past few years, Beth had focused solely on her medical career, leaving little time or desire for romantic relationships. But now, away from Nashville and Vanderbilt, she found herself suddenly smitten, or so it genuinely felt that way.

After the elevator door had closed behind her and her grandmother, Beth stepped forward and cleared her throat. "John?"

The doctor turned and smiled when he saw her. "Beth! Hi."

Beth couldn't help but smile back. "Hi."

John nodded courteously at the elderly woman. "Good morning, Miss Cindy. How are you doing today?"

Cindy attempted a sunny smile, but failed miserably. "Okay, I reckon. We just thought we'd stop by and see how Josh Elder was doing."

"I just checked on him a couple minutes ago," John told them. "There have been signs that he may be emerging from his comatose state...very, very slowly. A nurse heard him muttering in his sleep last night, but that's about all."

"But that's encouraging," said Beth.

"Of course it is. Any sort of response after such a total departure from consciousness is extremely encouraging. I just hope he continues to show progress and doesn't slip back into the void again."

"All we can do is hope and pray, I suppose," said Cindy.

"Yes, ma'am, you're right about that," he replied. He glanced at the clock on the wall. It was a little after twelve-thirty. "It's already past lunchtime. Have you two ladies eaten yet?"

"No, we haven't," said Beth, trying hard to conceal the hopeful look in her eyes.

"Well, why don't you join me for lunch then?" John suggested. "There's a nice Chinese restaurant across the street. They have a great lunch buffet."

"I'm not very hungry," confessed Cindy. "But why don't you two go on."

Beth felt a pang of guilt. "Are you sure, Grandma? I can stay with you if you like and we can grab a bite later."

"No," the old lady told her firmly. She gently turned John and Beth toward the elevator. "You two have a good time. I'll just visit with Josh for a while."

"Alright," said Beth, "if you're certain."

"Please, dear," laughed Cindy, shaking her head. "I'm eighty-six years old. I don't need a babysitter every moment of the day. So go on and eat. And don't fret over me."

"You heard the lady," John told her. "Besides, your face is too lovely for worry lines." He held out his arm like a gentleman. "Are you ready, ma'am?"

Beth giggled, feeling silly for doing so, but not really caring. "Yes, sir." She slipped her hand in the crook of his arm and, together, they stepped into the elevator.

Before the door closed, she glanced back at her grandmother. She knew why Cindy had wanted to come to Perryville that day, as well as her reason for wanting to see Josh Elder again. *Be careful,* her eyes warned.

Cindy smiled slightly. *I will,* she promised. Then the steel doors shut and the two young doctors began their awkward, yet pleasant, journey to the ground floor and their lunch date at the restaurant across the street.

The room was dark, the blinds drawn. Cindy shut the door,

until only a crack of outer light remained.

Josh Elder lay in the hospital bed. His eyes were partially closed and his breathing was shallow. He seemed as pale as a mushroom in the gloom. An unsettling thought came to Cindy—that the boy looked more dead than alive.

She pulled a chair up to the side of the bed and sat down. A sterile smell filled the room—disinfectant and purified air. The only natural scent that she could detect was the faint fragrance of a flower arrangement that sat on a small table in the corner of the room. The plant had probably been sent by a relative from Kentucky, or perhaps one of the few citizens of Coleman who didn't believe the boy was guilty of murdering his parents and sister.

"You've had such a hard time of it, haven't you, dear?" whispered Cindy. She bent forward and swept strands of dark hair off his forehead, arranging them back in place. She wished she had a comb, but she didn't.

Josh failed to respond to either her touch or her voice. He simply stared at a point on the opposite wall between the floor and the ceiling. His breath rasped through his nostrils, steadily, with no variation whatsoever.

"Well, no matter what all the others think," she told him, "I believe you're innocent. I don't think you had anything to do with what happened in that horrible old barn."

He continued to stare into space, his lungs breathing and his heart beating. He was there, but that was about all.

"Shall we try it again?" she asked. Cindy set her purse next to her chair, then reached out and took the boy's right hand. His fingers were limp and heavy in her grasp, the palm cool and clammy. "And this time let me in, okay? If you stay hidden behind that wall of yours, I won't be able to help you at all."

The boy's face remained slack and emotionless. He gave absolutely no indication of having heard her, or that he was even aware of her presence in the room.

Cindy tightened her grip on his hand and closed her eyes. She could feel the slow rhythm of his pulse and she breathed deeply, relaxing her own heartbeat until her pulse matched his. Gradually, the noises of the outer world—the sound of cars in the parking lot outside, the steady beeping of the heart monitor, and the sound of a doctor being paged—began to grow more distant and muffled, until they faded completely. Soon, total silence insulated the old lady from her immediate surroundings.

Again, she found herself in that indistinct pall of swirling grayness, a place without earth and without air, without time, space, or palatable substance. She attempted to move forward, to venture toward the center of the boy's consciousness. But it was as though she was trudging through black tar. A resistance pressed against her, nearly halting her in her mental tracks. She found her attempts to go further suddenly hampered, which frustrated her to no end.

Come on, Josh, she urged. *Don't resist me any longer. I'm your only hope. The only one who can really tell the world what happened to your family in that evil place.*

Suddenly, she felt the gray mist around her begin to thin a little. It seemed almost imperceptible at first, but gradually the murky darkness started to lift and distinct images began to form before her.

That's it, child, she encouraged, her inner voice steady, not too pleased and not too excited. *Work with me and we'll solve this thing together.*

Somewhere in the distance, she heard a low, hoarse moan. The boy responding subconsciously.

Cindy waited patiently. The grayness remained constant for a moment longer, then was gone, like a heavy fog burned away by the sun. Abruptly she found herself not in the featureless place she had ventured before, but in a definite place in a definite frame of time.

She sat up in the darkness, the pliant support of a mattress beneath her and the light veil of bed sheets draped over her waist and legs. Startled, she stared into the darkness. A small four-paned window hung in the blackness. It was the only window of Josh Elder's attic bedroom, set in the wall at the far end of the house's upper eaves.

Thunder rumbled outside, followed by a brittle whip-crack of lightning. The window was illuminated by a brilliant flash for a split second, then returned to the eerie glow that distinguished the natural light of night from complete darkness. As her eyes focused, she saw that raindrops streamed across the outer surface of the glass. And the steady drumming she heard was the noise of rainfall pelting the tin roof overhead, mercilessly with no indication of letting up anytime soon.

A sensation of intense unease filled her. She couldn't figure out exactly why, but a cold stone of dread sat heavily in the pit of her stomach. In one way, she wanted to toss the bedclothes aside and leave the bed, while in another, she wished nothing more than to pull the covers up over her head and ignore the awful feeling of disquiet and impending disaster that haunted her.

But she found that the latter was impossible. Restlessly, she slipped from beneath the sheets and stood up. The wooden boards of the attic floor were cool against the soles of her feet. Blindly, she felt through the gloom, until she found the brass knob of the door. She took a deep breath, as though bracing herself, then opened the door and stepped out onto a small landing.

Below, the faint glow of the microwave oven's digital display shown from the kitchen at the base of the narrow wooden stairs. She strained her ears and listened. All that she could hear was the steady ticking of an old German cuckoo clock in the connecting hallway downstairs. That and the commotion of the violent thunderstorm that assaulted the rural countryside on that dark, rain-drenched night.

Slowly, she descended the staircase, that awful feeling of dread growing with each step she took. She didn't know why, but the house felt empty, as though nary a living soul occupied the farmhouse. Just herself and no one else.

Cindy felt her heartbeat quicken as she reached the ground floor. She turned and started down the hallway that ran through the center of the house. She stopped in front of one of the bedrooms. The door stood open. Only darkness could be seen inside.

"Mom?" she whispered. Then she spoke again, her voice a little louder. "Dad?"

A flash of lightning shown beyond the bedroom window, illuminating the room for an instant. She found the king-size bed empty. The bed sheets and wedding ring quilt were in a tangle on the floor, as though flung there in the midst of some wild struggle.

Frightened, she turned and went to the only other bedroom that was located on the ground floor. The door of that one stood open as well. She found the room in similar condition—the sheets twisted and in disarray, a stuffed pink teddy bear won at the Kentucky State Fair lying face down on the floor next to a pair of teenager's slipper socks.

Where is everyone? she found herself wondering. A shrill sensation of mounting panic ran through her like an electric current, but she managed to calm herself. She couldn't quell another feeling that gripped her, however. A feeling of inexplicable loss and abandonment.

She reached up and ran a hand through her hair. She found that it was the short, lank hair of a teenage boy, instead of the thin gray curls of an elderly woman. Her heart grew heavy in her chest, the thudding pressure of each heartbeat becoming almost painful in its intensity. Quickly, she ran down the hallway to the kitchen. For some strange reason, she wasn't at all surprised to find the back door standing wide open.

Almost afraid to proceed, Cindy walked across the newly-installed linoleum of the kitchen floor. The door grew nearer and nearer, until she stood directly within its wooden frame. Only the screen door stood between her and the boarded platform of the back porch. Through the wire mesh, the dank mist of the pounding rain drifted, along with the earthy smell of water striking the dusty ground.

And there was another odor as well. A hot, coppery scent that was both familiar and dreadful at the same time. A smell she had known before. Intimately.

With a trembling hand, she opened the screen door and stepped out onto the porch. Cold rain blew past the overhang, dampening her face and arms, causing her to shiver. *Could they have come out here?* she wondered.

Then she looked out across the dark tangle of thicket that covered acre upon acre of prime tobacco land. Amid the undergrowth jutted the sloping roof of the half-fallen tobacco barn. Lightning crackled overhead, streaking across the sodden sky like a white-hot finger. The brilliance of that thunderclap illuminated the weathered structure of the old barn for an instant, then vanished just as swiftly.

But it was at that moment, when darkness closed in once again, that she noticed that a light was coming from the interior of the sagging barn. A muted glow seeped from the cracks between the uneven boards of the walls. The flickering luminance of a kerosene lantern turned to its highest setting.

They're out there, she realized. *They must be. But why?*

She stood there, hesitant, for a moment longer. Then she stepped off the porch into the downpour.

Abruptly and without prior warning, Cindy found herself back in the hospital room, crouched forward in the chair next to Josh Elder's bed. She had to hold onto the railing of the bed for a second in order to steady herself. Her head swam dizzily and a throbbing pain seized the base of her skull, as though a vise had been clamped there. The rest of her body also suffered from the drastic transfer from subconscious thought to stark physical reality. Her stomach rolled and she tasted hot bile as it crept into the back of her throat. She was certain that she was about to vomit, then the sick feeling retreated and was gone.

Feeling strangely weak and drained, Cindy released the boy's hand and sat back in the chair. She stared at his face and saw a frown crease his pallid features. His lips parted a little, emitting a string of unintelligible sounds. He mumbled for a moment longer, then grew silent.

"Well, at least we got further than we did before," she said, as much to herself as to the boy who lay listlessly in the bed next to her. "But there's still one important place we have to go before we can call it quits. And that's the old tobacco barn."

But Cindy wasn't in any hurry to go there. Just the thought of reconnecting with the boy's hidden thoughts and making that horrifying journey into the lair of the beast mortified her. She knew that she wasn't up to it now, and neither was the thirteen-year-old. She could tell that by the soft murmurings that rose from down deep in his throat, as well as the twitching of his eyeballs beneath the lids, which were now firmly closed.

Josh Elder was dreaming…but of what?

Cindy Garrison thought that she knew.

He was visiting the same nightmarish temple of death and depravity that she herself had visited many a troubled night. A temple of weathered lumber, rusty sheet tin, and an earthen floor on which the flood of innocence had been brutally spilt, upon more occasions than one.

CHAPTER TWENTY-EIGHT

B eth Garrison gazed across the table as she ate her last bite of sweet and sour pork. John Arnett smiled back at her, looking relaxed and completely comfortable.

She wished she felt the same. She took a drink of water, willing the kinetic sensation in her stomach to go away. But it ignored her. It seemed that since she first met the handsome, young doctor and one of Perryville Medical Center's most skilled surgeons, she had felt as though she were in a constant state of nervous agitation. She hadn't felt so giddy since Tony Hutchison had written a love poem in her high school annual when she was sixteen years old.

"Do you mind if I ask you a question, Beth?" he asked.

"No," she replied. "Go ahead." So far, their conversation had been mostly about their personal lives and various interests. Surprisingly, they had neglected to discuss the medical profession at all, which was fine with Beth.

John hesitated for a moment, as though debating whether or not he should actually ask the question. Then he took a drink of iced green tea and blotted his mouth with his napkin. "Does your grandmother really possess the gift of second sight?"

Beth had been expecting him to bring that up sooner or later. "Yes, she does. But you don't believe in such nonsense, do you?"

"Well, I didn't at first," he admitted. "But I'm beginning to question my own unwavering opinion. I talked to my grandfather last night. He seems to be totally convinced that Miss Cindy possesses some incredible talent, that she can predict the future, as well as see events that have happened in the past. He claims that she's like a human divining rod when it comes to sensing people's emotions, whether they're alive or dead."

"That's true," said Beth. "She can do just that. It's not generally known, John, but my grandmother has helped the Nashville police solve numerous crimes, some that were cold cases."

"Name one for example," challenged the doctor, testing her playfully.

"The case that was just solved in Nashville, for instance," she said. "The one where those children were murdered in several of the city parks."

John's jaw dropped an inch. "You mean the one where the country music star has been accused and arrested? Your sweet, innocent grandmother was responsible for bringing that ugly business to light?"

"That's right. But don't let Grandma fool you. She's not as sweet and innocent as you'd think. She's seen alot of death and misery in her time."

"She started out young from what I've heard," said John, growing more serious. "Nine years old, I believe. That's when she and my grandpa and the other kids found those bodies in that old barn just off Highway 70."

"Yes, that seems to have been the worst of what she has experienced," Beth said. "At least, until a couple days ago."

John nodded. "Yes, of course, what happened at the Elder place. It must seem to her that that horrible business back in the mid-Thirties has started up all over again."

"Yes." She recalled how disturbed her grandmother had been late last night. "More than you would believe."

"But she's not tackling this investigation alone, is she? You're helping her, aren't you?"

Beth stared at the sly look on his face, feeling as though she had just stepped into a trap. "What do you mean?"

"Well, let's put it this way," he said, smiling slightly. "If your grandmother does possess this incredible ability, it's probable that it is an inherited trait of some sort. More than likely her mother or grandmother was blessed with the same unique powers. And that means that out of her own children and grandchildren, odds are that at least one inherited the ability from her."

Beth tried to laugh it off, but was unsuccessful. "And you're suggesting that that lucky one of the brood is me?"

"Well, isn't it?" asked John, seemingly genuinely interested. "You're the most likely candidate, I'd say. You're intelligent, compassionate, and very intuitive, just like your grandmother. And you have her red hair and hazel eyes. In fact, Grandpa claims that you're the spitting image of Miss Cindy when she was your age."

"Yes, somebody else just told me that yesterday," admitted Beth. She searched the man's handsome features, looking for some sign of suspicion or growing distrust toward her. But he continued to smile at her with the same degree of warmth and interest that he had shown since they first entered the restaurant.

"Well, are you going to fess up or what?" he asked.

Beth sighed and shrugged her shoulders. "Okay. I do have the gift, just like Grandma. It's not quite as strong or developed as hers, but it's getting there." She looked at him closely. "That doesn't make me a freak, does it? It doesn't change your opinion of me?"

John let out a laugh. But, fortunately for Beth, it was one of respect, rather than of arrogant amusement. "Of course not!" he assured her. "In my eyes, you're still the lovely, wonderful person I met only a couple of days ago." His eyes suddenly held an expression that caused Beth's heart to skip a beat. "A person, I might add, that I just can't seem to get out of my mind lately."

Beth's face reddened, but strangely enough, she felt pleasure rather than embarrassment. "I like you too, John," she said softly.

The doctor's smile broadened. " 'Like' is a good starting place. But I wouldn't mind if your assessment of me went a little further than that. Mine is certainly heading in that direction."

Beth laughed nervously, feeling incredibly warm in the face. For a second, she felt as though things were going a little too fast for her, as though the relationship between her and the young country doctor was spinning out of control.

She pulled her eyes from his and immediately spotted the jade green bowl of fortune cookies sitting on the table between them. "Hey! We haven't read our fortunes yet." She took one of the hollow cookies from the top of the stack and pitched it across the table to him. "There. Read yours first."

John chuckled and, picking up the cookie, broke it in half. He unfurled the narrow strip of paper hidden within and read it out loud. "A vision of beauty and wisdom shall make itself known to you." He looked across the table at the pretty young woman with the long red hair. "How's that for a prophecy come true? Now read yours."

"Okay," said Beth. She cracked her cookie in half and read the fortune that was inside, but to herself rather than aloud.

Do not let love blind you to the darkest side of human nature.

Beth stared at the slip of paper, not knowing whether to laugh or not. For some reason, the words disturbed her, as though they were speaking directly to *her*, rather than any customer who might open the same fortune cookie by chance.

"Well?" urged John. "What does it say?"

201

She hesitated for a second, then made up something off the top of her head. "It says 'You will be blessed with untold treasures, both of gold and of the heart' ". Or, at least, she wished that was what it had said, instead of the eerie warning she had actually received.

"Hey, that sounds encouraging to me," said John. "You can't have too many untold treasures these days, that's for sure."

Beth folded up the slip of paper and stuck it in the pocket of her jacket. She didn't know why she had lied to John about the fortune. She supposed it really didn't matter, though. It was just a few silly words on a piece of paper, that was all.

The man across the table glanced at his wristwatch. "Yikes! It's past two. I have afternoon rounds to make. I guess they're right after all. Time does fly when you're having fun."

"Yes," said Beth with a smile. "It sure does."

"Not that I want this fun to end," said John. He reached across the table and took Beth's hand in his. "Not anytime soon."

Beth felt as though her breath had been completely sucked out her lungs. "Neither do I."

"I'm glad to hear that," John said, pleased. He gave her hand a gentle squeeze, then released it. "Come on and we'll walk back to the hospital together. We wouldn't want the staff or your grandmother to wonder whatever became of the two of us."

"Yeah," she said, feeling oddly unbalanced as she rose from her chair. "We wouldn't want them to start gossiping. It might create a scandal of some sort."

John shrugged his shoulders. "Hey, let them talk. I don't mind."

As they started toward the entrance, Beth looked at the handsome doctor next to her and found herself feeling a little uneasy. She couldn't fully understand why she should feel that way, given the encouraging way their first date together had turned out. But she felt a sensation of disquiet nevertheless.

Considering the peculiar mood that had stricken her, Beth wondered what could have possibly brought it on. Had it been the ominous message in her fortune cookie? Or could it have been the confusing sensation that had seized her the instant John Arnett's hand had touched hers?

A sensation of underlying darkness, as well as one of great rage. A sensation that had passed just as quickly as it had appeared.

She considered the warning in the fortune cookie and couldn't help but shiver in the warmth of the sunny spring afternoon.

CHAPTER TWENTY-NINE

"So you don't think Josh Elder had anything to do with the deaths of his family?" Beth asked. She drove the lonesome stretch of Old Newsome Road, heading back to the Biggs house.

"That's right," Cindy told her. "From what I experienced, he woke up in the middle of the night and found no one in the house. Then he went to the back door and spotted a light coming from the tobacco barn. He was stepping off the porch to go look for his parents and sister when I hit another snag. Maybe he'll allow me to go further next time." A troubled look shown in her eyes. "Whatever he saw when he went inside that barn must have been horrifying."

"But we still have to find *physical* proof that he didn't do it," Beth reminded her. "The Bedloe County grand jury isn't going to take your word for what happened out there. They're going to demand cold, hard facts. And, unfortunately for Josh, most of the circumstantial evidence points straight at him."

"Then we'll just have to find our own evidence," declared the old lady. "That boy is innocent. He didn't kill his folks and I refuse to allow him to pay for it, while the true murderer walks away scot-free."

It was already well after dark. Following their trip to the hospital that afternoon, Cindy and Beth had done some shopping in Perryville, then drove back to Coleman and had supper with Sam at the café. All in all, it had been a long, but eventful day—what with Beth's lunch with John Arnett and Cindy's breakthrough with Josh—and both women were more than ready to get a good night's sleep.

They were silent for a moment, listening to the peppy rhythm of a country song on the car radio. Then Cindy turned and smiled at her granddaughter. "You know, I'm glad that you and John hit it off so well," she said. "You've been alone so long that I was beginning to worry about you. A sweet girl like you should have someone important in her life. And, besides, I wouldn't mind having me a great-grandchild or two."

Beth laughed in disbelief. "Grandma! We just had lunch together, that's all. It wasn't even an actual date."

"Did he kiss you?"

"No, he didn't!" replied the young woman, feeling the heat of a blush rise in her freckled cheeks. "But he did hold my hand."

The approval in Cindy's face suddenly turned into solemn curiosity. "Did you *connect* with him?" she asked. "Did you get a feel for what the man was inside?"

Beth considered what she had experienced the instant John had taken her hand in his. She recalled the puzzling feeling of an intense but concealed anger, as well as something that she could only describe as a shadow across his soul. A pall of darkness down deep inside him that hid something important. Something that he did not want her to know about. At least, not yet.

But she didn't tell her grandmother that she had sensed such emotions in the handsome, young physician. John was one of the nicest guys she had met in a very long time and she certainly didn't want a slip of the tongue to turn her grandmother against him. Cindy was awfully protective of Beth—sometimes a little *too* protective—and if she were to show any reservations about John Arnett, her grandmother would immediately see him as a potential threat to her granddaughter's well-being. In fact, she would more than likely trick the doctor into shaking her hand, just so she could see for herself what truly lurked within him.

Beth looked over and saw Cindy staring at her, waiting for an answer to her questions. "He's fine, Grandma. He's a really great guy. The nicest one I've met in years."

The elderly woman seemed to relax a little. "That's wonderful, dear," she said. "Take it slow and don't rush things, and you might just end up with something that could last a lifetime. Your grandfather and I courted for three years before we tied the knot. And we ended up being married for over forty years."

"We'll see what happens," Beth told her.

"Just let me know if he gives you a diamond-studded stethoscope or something like that, okay?"

The pretty doctor laughed. "You'll be the first to know."

They were a mile from the house, crossing a small concrete bridge that spanned the rural channel of Green Creek, when the roar of an engine sounded from directly behind them. Beth glanced in the rearview mirror and was nearly blinded. There was a vehicle a couple of yards from the Accord's rear bumper with its headlights on high beam.

"Where the hell did they come from?" she asked.

"There's a gravel turn-off back on the other side of the bridge," Cindy said grimly. "They must have been parked back there. Waiting for us."

"Waiting for us?" At first, Beth couldn't understand why someone would be sitting in the dark, waiting until they drove past. Then she glanced in her sideview mirror and spotted the vehicle's body past the glare of its headlights. She caught a glimpse of dull gray paint on an oddly-shaped fender. "Oh my God! It's *him*!" She thought of the ancient Ford pickup idling in the gravel driveway, as well as the hulking shadow that had been cast upon the window the night before.

"Speed up," Cindy suggested. "Maybe we can outrun them."

Beth did as she said. She pressed the gas pedal and, slowly, began to outdistance the gray truck. But their advantage didn't last for long. The engine of the old Ford roared loudly and, soon, it had closed the gap between them. It wasn't long before the interior of the Honda was completely illuminated by the glare of the truck's lights.

"What are we going to do?" asked Beth.

Cindy fished her granddaughter's iPhone from the front pocket of her purse. She unlocked the keypad and began to dial a number from memory. "I'll give Sam a call and maybe he'll—"

Her sentence was interrupted by a jarring concussion that rocked the car, propelling it forward a few feet. "He rammed us!" Beth cried out in alarm. "The bastard rammed us from behind!"

She stamped on the accelerator, but the truck matched her increased speed and then some. It slammed into her back bumper again, harder than the time before. So forceful was the impact that Beth had to wrestle with the steering wheel to keep the Accord on her side of the road.

Beth looked over at her grandmother. The old woman was bent forward in her seat. She sagged against the restraints of the seat belt, her head almost beneath the dashboard.

"Grandma!" she yelled out. "Are you alright?"

Cindy lifted her head a little. Beth was relieved to see annoyance on her wrinkled face, rather than the searing pain of a heart attack or stroke. "I dropped the phone during that last bump," she explained. "It must have slid beneath the seat."

Beth looked at the speedometer. The needle was wavering between seventy-five and eighty. Abruptly, the truck slammed into them again. This time she heard the plastic of her taillights crackle and the clang of metal. She glanced in her sideview mirror in time to see her license plate bounce off the asphalt of the country road and spin off into the bordering darkness.

"I'm getting sick of this shit!" Beth hissed between her teeth, her green eyes flaring with anger.

Cindy looked over at her. "What are you going to do, dear?"

"I'm going to turn the tables, that's what!"

Beth squinted and stared into the rearview mirror. Past the glare of the truck's headlights, she could barely see the dark form of someone sitting on the driver's side of the cab. Beth narrowed her eyes a little more and concentrated. *Turn it,* she urged, projecting with all her might. *Turn it to the right...now!*

Cindy turned in her seat and watched, startled, as the driver of the gray truck suddenly, and quite unexpectedly, jerked his steering wheel sharply to the right. The tires of the vehicle squealed against the paved road, then the old Ford shot past the gravel shoulder and landed, nose first, in a deep drainage ditch.

Beth sighed and, slowly, began to brake to a halt. "Now why don't you find that phone and —"

The elderly woman was still peering out the rear window. "Back up," she said.

At first, Beth couldn't believe her ears. "What?"

"I said to stop and back up," instructed her grandmother. "I want to get a good look at the jackass who tried to run us off the road. Quick...before he can make a run for it!" Beth didn't think it was very wise to go back and confront the one who had terrorized them, but she did as her grandmother requested. She stopped in the road, then shifted into reverse and began to back the car up. A few seconds later, she saw a cloud of gravel dust still hanging in the night air, tinted red by the glow of the truck's taillights.

She stopped the car and waited. All she could see of the truck was its back end sticking up out of the ditch. "Now what?"

"Now we go take a look at the weasel who's been trying to scare us off." Without warning, Cindy opened the passenger door and stepped out of the car.

"Grandma!" called Beth, wrestling with the buckle of her seatbelt. "Come back here!"

When she finally left the car herself, Beth found her grandmother halfway to the wrecked truck. There was an angry determination in her stride and her aged hands were balled into fists at her sides. It was clear to see that Cindy's redheaded temper was in full bloom.

Beth was about to call out to the old woman when she heard a commotion coming from the drainage ditch. In the darkness came the noise of a truck door opening with a creak, followed by angry swearing. Then she heard the sound of someone clawing their way up through the brittle weeds, toward the edge of the road.

"Grandma!" she said, frightened. "Come on!"

"No," the old woman said flatly. Calmly, she stood on the rural roadway, head held high, her jaw tightly clenched.

Then, from out of the darkness of the ditch, came the huge form of a man dressed in a denim jacket, white t-shirt, and grungy jeans. Beth recognized him as he stepped into the crimson glow of the truck's taillights.

It was Bud Martin, the ex-con son of Chester. The man's face was livid with disgust and rage, and he clutched a jack handle in his right fist.

Beth reached into her jacket pocket and closed her hand around the vial of pepper spray. "Grandma, get back to the car!"

Cindy ignored her granddaughter. She simply remained where she was and stood her ground.

Lord help us, Beth thought as the man tightened his grip on the tire iron and started toward them. *He's going to kill us both!*

She took a deep breath, released the safety on the pepper spray, and started forward, hoping that she could get between him and her grandmother before he started swinging.

But Cindy Garrison was not nearly as helpless as her granddaughter assumed she was.

Far from it.

"Stupid bitches!" snarled Bud, walking toward the old lady who stood twenty feet away. "I don't know what you did back there, but you're sure as hell gonna pay for it."

Cindy stared at him coldly. "I don't think so."

Bud laughed cruelly, then choked up on the jack handle and lifted it over his head. A couple more steps and he would be within reach of the old woman.

He was almost there, when a peculiar little smile crept across Cindy's face. "I know what you fear, Bud Martin," she said.

The big man couldn't help but slow his pace a little. "Huh?"

"What have you got in your hand, Bud?" she asked. Her eyes twinkled with a strange amusement. "I'd put it down if I were you. Handling something like that could be downright dangerous."

"What the shit are you talking about?" he growled. Then he glanced over at the length of iron in his right hand. But, oddly enough, it was no longer a tire tool that he held.

Instead, it was a rattlesnake. The serpent was about four feet in length, from its flat brown head to the tip of its buttoned rattler. The squirming diamondback wrapped its body around Bud's wrist and forearm, then its head arched back on its slender neck, as though on the verge of striking.

Bud screamed and flung the snake away from him. The second it hit the road it changed back into the jack handle. The length of iron struck the hardtop with a clang, then bounced off into the shadows.

"Damn!" the man cussed, clearly shaken. "What the hell are you? Some kind of witch?"

Cindy's eyes narrowed with a fresh burst of anger. In the back of her mind, a childhood memory emerged. Chester Martin on a school playground, taunting her with a cruel rhyme he had made up out of his head. *Witch, witch, the red-haired bitch! Set her on fire and roll her in a ditch!*

A vindictive grin crossed the old woman's face. "That wasn't the only one, Bud. Look…there's more."

The redneck's eyes bulged as narrow shapes began to emerge from out of the surrounding darkness. He watched in horror as dozens of rattlers, copperheads, and cottonmouths slithered across the pavement toward him.

Bud cried out and turned to run. But, unfortunately, he was much too close to the drainage ditch. He lost his balance and fell, head over heels, down the glassy slope to the bottom of the trench. He landed on his back in the high weeds and stared up at the clear night sky. A second later, the old woman appeared at the edge of the ditch.

"Who sent you?" she asked. "Who hired you to scare me off?"

"Screw you, lady!" he snapped, struggling to his elbows. "I ain't telling you jack shit!"

"You should show more respect for your elders," she warned him. "Listen."

Bud Martin froze. The weeds around him began to shift and rustle. He could hear *them* slithering through the tall grass toward him. The snakes.

"Tell me and I'll make them go away," she offered.

"I can't!" he yelled, then leapt to his feet. In the moonlight, he could see the patterned bodies of poisonous snakes winding their way through the weeds at the bottom of the ditch. A moment longer and they would converge, directly where he was standing.

Frantically, he began to scramble up the opposite side of the ditch. He could hear the sinister hissing of the snakes at his heels as his shoes slipped on the dewy grass, unable to take hold. Then, finally, he made it to the edge of the ditch. Nearly in tears, he dragged himself out.

"Stay away from us, Bud," Cindy warned from the opposite side of the ditch. "And don't bother us again. If you do, *they'll* know where to find you."

Bud glanced back into the trench he had just escaped from. His heart thundered wildly in his chest. The entire length and breadth of the drainage ditch was alive with squirming, slithering snakes.

The man said nothing. All the spit dried up in his mouth and throat, and he found it impossible to speak. Without a second thought, he turned tail and ran. Bud jumped a barbed wire fence that ran along the far side of the ditch and disappeared into the night.

Bewildered, Beth joined her grandmother. She looked down into the ditch, but could see only weeds and a few discarded aluminum beer cans. "What did you do to him, Grandma?"

"Just played with that feeble mind of his a little," she said, staring off into the darkness. "His father and grandfather both had the same fear that he does. Funny how those Martins are horrified of a silly little thing like a snake."

"Come on," said Beth. "Why don't we go now? Who knows, he might change his mind and come back."

Cindy smiled to herself. "No, I don't believe he'll be coming back anytime soon."

"He could have killed us," Beth said, putting her pepper spray back in her pocket. "Bashed our skulls in and left us by the side of the road."

The old woman didn't answer. She turned toward the car, looking disappointed. "I was hoping to get close enough to him to find out who sent him, but I couldn't."

"What now?" asked Beth as they walked back to the car.

"We'll find that confounded cell phone of yours and call Sam," said Cindy. "Maybe he can pick up Bud and question him. And, hopefully, find out what I was unable to."

CHAPTER THIRTY

"Come on and finish that drink, will you, Bud?" urged Vince Schofield impatiently. "It's already past midnight. I should've closed up twenty minutes ago."

Bud Martin took another swallow of beer and grimaced. "Just let me polish this longneck off and I'll get outta your hair."

As Vince took a rag and began to mop the water rings off the bar top, Bud caught a glimpse of the tavern owner's snakeskin belt. He couldn't help but shudder at the sight of it.

"What's got you so rattled tonight anyway?" Vince asked him.

"Ain't none of your business," grumbled Bud. He took another drink, then retreated into the dark mood he had possessed since first walking into the bar around nine-thirty.

Vince could tell that the big man was troubled about something or other, but he didn't really care. All he wanted at that moment was to lock up, get his tills counted, and get into bed before two. "Hurry it. You finished off those first seven bottles fast enough. Now do the same with this one and get on home."

"All right, dammit!" The ex-con chugged the rest of his Budweiser, banged the bottle down on the bar, and belched loudly.

Schofield took his keys from his pants pocket and started around the far end of the bar. "Now don't go giving me any shit or I'll call the sheriff to come pick you up."

A nervous look crossed Bud Martin's face. "I'm going! No need to drag old man Biggs outta bed on my account."

Together, the two walked through the building, toward the front door. The Bloody Bucket Saloon was utterly deserted. The long drinking bar had been abandoned an hour ago, the circular dance floor was empty, and all the chairs had already been flipped over and sat on top of their tables, legs pointed skyward. The big wagon wheel chandelier that hung overhead was dark now. The only source of light in the place was a dozen neon beer signs that hung along the walls, casting a muted, but colorful glow throughout the main room. The big jukebox between the restrooms—which were labeled BULLS and HEIFERS—played an old George Jones tune.

Vince unlocked the door and held it open for his last customer. "Goodnight, Bud," he said, although his eyes said *good riddance* instead.

"I didn't see your Bronco in the parking lot, Bud," called Janet Cantrell. The blonde waitress crouched between two bar room tables, sweeping up peanut shells into a dust pan. "If you want to wait outside for me, I'll be glad to drive you home."

"No thanks, sweet-thang," slurred Bud. He stared hard at the three doorways that wavered in front of his eyes, picked the one in the middle, and stumbled toward it. "I need to walk this booze off anyhow."

"Well, be careful," she said. "Don't end up falling into some ditch along the way."

Uncomfortably, Bud recalled the drainage ditch full of squirming snakes. "I'll sure do my best, Janet," he said, then stepped reluctantly into the night.

Despite his intoxication, his nerves were still on edge. He nearly jumped out of his skin when the saloon door slammed shut behind him.

"Damn!" he muttered. "How'd I ever get into this mess?"

Bud thought of the events leading up to his present situation. It had begun innocently at first. He and his father had been hired to restore an old 1931 Ford pickup for someone several weeks ago. Then, a couple of days ago, someone had called Bud out of the blue. They had offered him a proposition—throw a scare into Cindy and Beth Garrison out at the old Biggs place in exchange for five hundred easy bucks. Although the caller's voice had been muffled, Bud was almost certain that it had belonged to the same one who had discreetly hired him and Chester to fix up the old truck. He was sure of it when they had called back several hours later and requested that the truck be used for the purpose of unnerving the old woman and her granddaughter, although Bud couldn't figure out what possible significance that old rust bucket might have.

But tonight he had royally screwed up. Both his father and his grandfather had told him stories about the spooky things Cindy Garrison had done as a child, but he had always figured them to be more tall tales than actual fact. But he had found out earlier that evening that his assumption had been wrong.

Bud was crossing the parking lot and heading in the direction of the railroad tracks when he heard something rattle behind him. At first, the thought of those confounded snakes creeping up on him came to mind. Then he realized what he had heard. No, it had sounded more like the crackle of crushed gravel beneath the weight of someone's footsteps.

He whirled and peered into the shadows that stretched along the northern wall of the honky-tonk. "Who's there?" he demanded. "Is that you, Vince? Janet?"

But he already knew that it wasn't them. The waitress was still inside cleaning up, while Schofield was probably holed away in his office, totaling that night's receipts.

Bud stood there for a long moment and listened. He heard nothing but the reedy noise of crickets in the darkness. With disgust he turned and started back toward the road. He hadn't gotten ten feet before he heard the crunch of footsteps again.

He looked around. This time the one who followed him was no longer hidden. They stood away from the shadows, in plain sight.

"Oh," said Bud in relief. "It's you." Then he saw the look on their face and found himself wishing that it wasn't.

"You betrayed me, didn't you?" came a voice as cold as a winter grave. "You told her who I was."

"No!" Bud stammered. "I didn't say anything. I swear to God!"

"I think you're lying."

"I'm not!" insisted the ex-con, almost pleadingly. "You've gotta believe me. I didn't tell the old bitch nothing!"

The form at the edge of the darkness said nothing, just stood there and stared at him for a long moment. Then, without another word, they simply faded into the shadows again.

Bud felt his pulse rate begin to settle. He turned and started toward the edge of the parking lot, walking a little faster than before. It was good that he hadn't mentioned the wrecked truck. Then they would have really been pissed.

"Bud?"

He turned at the sound of his name and was shocked to find the barrels of a sawed-off shotgun protruding from the darkness. They were aimed directly at him.

"Hey now, come on!" he started, retreating a couple of steps.

Bud Martin knew he was in trouble when he heard the metallic click of a gun's hammer being cocked. He was on the verge of turning to run, when a single shot exploded in his ears.

The impact of the shotgun blast struck him an instant later. Bud felt something akin to a cannonball hitting him in the stomach and, abruptly, he was knocked completely off his feet.

He landed on his back in the gravel lot, fifteen feet from where he had stood before.

With the report of the gunshot still ringing in his ears, Bud laid a trembling hand on his belly and found that most of it was gone. In its place was a deep and bloody crater.

"Oh God!" he groaned. Blood, along with bits of torn flesh and shotgun pellets, rushed into his throat and filled his mouth. At first, his abdomen was strangely numb, but it wasn't long before that deceptive lack of sensitivity was replaced by sharp, dancing pangs of agony.

A second later, he looked up and saw them standing over him. "Why?" he croaked, blood bubbling over his lips.

The look in those cold eyes gave him the answer. No slip ups would be tolerated, especially like the one Bud had made that night. Their identity must be protected...at any cost.

"Please," he implored. Bud raised a blood-stained hand, as though to ward off the next shot, although he knew his attempt to do so was futile.

When the shotgun was lowered toward his face, Bud clenched his eyes shut and prayed that he wouldn't hear the shot that ended his life.

At least, in that respect, he succeeded. Other than the cocking of the twelve-gauge's other hammer, he heard absolutely nothing. Mercifully, silence and darkness swallowed him whole and he knew nothing else.

PART THREE
DARK SOULMATES

CHAPTER THIRTY-ONE

"I'm sorry, Miss Cindy," said Marge Singleton, "but Sheriff Biggs hasn't even been in the office this morning."

Cindy looked at Beth. She had known that something was wrong when they had arrived at the county courthouse and found the patrol car missing from its usual parking place out front. "I don't understand," said the elderly woman. "Sam was supposed to meet us here. We were planning on having breakfast together."

"Well, I reckon he just forgot to call you," the dispatcher assured her. "He's been pretty busy since early this morning, with what happened over at the honky-tonk last night and all."

Cindy and Beth simply stood there and stared at her.

"Dear me," said Marge, aware that they had no idea what she was talking about. "Then you haven't heard yet?"

"Heard about what?" asked Beth.

"Someone was killed in the parking lot of the Bloody Bucket around twelve-thirty this morning. Got most of their head blown off by a shotgun, from what I've heard."

Cindy's face paled a little. "Who was it, Marge?"

"I'm afraid I'm not at liberty to say, Miss Cindy," the dispatcher told her. "The sheriff wanted me to keep quiet about it till after he's finished going over the crime scene." She lowered her voice. "Just let me put it this way…the victim was someone who won't likely be missed very much in the community, and that's the God's honest truth."

"Thanks for letting us know what's going on, Marge," said Cindy.

The old woman and her granddaughter left and walked out to the Accord. "The Bloody Bucket?" asked Beth. "Isn't that where your father went looking for Bully Hanson? After you told him who was responsible for Johnny's death?"

"That's right. But it's far from being the same cutthroat roadhouse it was back in the Thirties and Forties. It was owned by a shady character named Otis Schofield back then, but now it's operated by his grandson, Vince. He fixed it up real nice. Put in a dance floor and everything."

When they got to the car, Beth turned to her grandmother. "So, what do you want to do? Go on to breakfast by ourselves?"

"Let's drive over to the Bloody Bucket and see Sam first," suggested Cindy. "I have a hunch this killing is more than a mere coincidence. I believe it has some connection to what happened at the Elder farm."

"You know, I believe you're right," agreed the redhead.

It took no more than a couple of minutes to make their way around town square and cross the railroad tracks that ran along Coleman's eastern side. When they got to the nightclub known as the Bloody Bucket Saloon, they found the entire property cordoned off with long strands of yellow barrier tape. The words **POLICE LINE—DO NOT CROSS!** were printed across the tape in bold black letters.

Beth parked the car at the side of the road and, together, she and Cindy walked to the barrier that blocked the entranceway. From their vantage point, they could see Sam crouched at a certain spot in the center of the parking lot, discussing something with a couple of state policemen.

When he spotted them, he excused himself and walked over. "What are you two doing here?"

Cindy looked a little peeved. "Well, I thought we were supposed to meet you for breakfast, before Marge told us otherwise."

"I'm sorry, sis," the sheriff apologized. "I guess I've been so busy the last few hours that I plumb forgot to call you and cancel." He looked back toward the place he had been examining. The crushed gravel and gray dust of that particular spot had been stained an ugly reddish brown. "It was a mess, I'm telling you. A damn awful mess."

"Who was it, Sam?" asked Cindy.

"Well, I really shouldn't say anything, but I reckon you've got a right to know, considering he nearly ran you two down last night."

Beth's eyes widened. "You mean to tell us that it was—"

Sam nodded. "Bud Martin." The sheriff looked disturbed, as though he partially blamed himself for what had happened to the ex-con. "After you called me last night, I went out looking for him. Searched both Old Newsome Road and Highway 70, then went over to his place. Chester swore up and down that he had no idea where his boy was. After that, I checked a couple more places I figured he might be. I hoped he might be visiting one of his buddies or maybe sinking some balls over at Taylor's Pool Hall next to Parnell's Texaco. But I couldn't find hide or hair of the guy. I should've figured he would come here to do some drinking, but this hasn't exactly been one of Bud's favorite watering holes since Vince changed things around in there and put in that hardwood floor for line dancing. So I kind of overlooked it."

"Where's Bud's body now?" asked Cindy.

"Hud Williams has already taken him to the funeral home," Sam told her.

"So, exactly what happened?"

"Well, according to Vince, he herded Bud out the front door a little before twelve-thirty. He went back to his office to count last night's money and it wasn't long before he heard a gunshot. One of his waitresses, Janet Cantrell, ran back and fetched him. They were halfway to the door when they heard the second shot. By the time they got outside, the one who did the shooting was long gone. They found ol' Bud lying on his back over yonder in the parking lot. He'd been shot twice—once in the stomach and once in the face." A sick expression crossed the lawman's face. "Needless to say, there wasn't much left of his head. Whoever the killer was, they used a twelve-gauge shotgun with its barrels sawed short."

"Like the one that was used on the Elder family?" asked Beth.

"The wounds were similar," agreed Sam, "but I can't say for sure that the two incidents are definitely connected."

"Aw, come on, Sam!" said his sister. "You know very well the one who killed Bud Martin was the one responsible for murdering the Elders. In fact, they probably hired Bud to frighten us off."

"Why would they go to all that trouble?" asked Sam. "Unless it was someone who knew what you were capable of. Someone who knew that you could end up posing a threat to them."

"That's what I believe," said Cindy. "And I also think that old truck Bud and his daddy were fixing up belongs to the murderer. What do you think?"

"I believe you're probably right, although I haven't been able to prove it yet. After I got your call last night, I drove out and examined that old Ford in the ditch. It didn't have any sort of identification at all. No license plate and of course vehicles that old have no VIN number like today's models. There's a number stamped on the engine block, but that didn't help none.

According to Chester, Bud bought a replacement engine at a junkyard in Perryville and put it in that old truck more than a week ago.

"Doesn't Chester know who the truck belongs to?"

"He claims Bud showed up with it out of the blue and wouldn't tell him exactly who it belonged to," said Sam. "If he's lying, he's doing a mighty good job of it."

"Sam, have you noticed how much that truck resembles—"

The sheriff nodded grimly. "Bully Hanson's old Ford pickup? You bet I have, sis. It bugs the hell out of me, too. It's as though someone has deliberately fixed it up to look like that bastard's truck. It's the spittin' image of it, right down to the patched tires and the rust spots on the fenders." He attempted a smile. "But don't fret. I've got Marge checking around, trying to find a trace of it in the state records. Hopefully something will turn up before long and we'll find out who the rightful owner is."

Cindy stared at the bloody spot in the gravel lot. "Sam, did you find anything of interest near Bud's body?"

"Matter of fact, we did. For some crazy reason, the killer ejected his empty shotgun shells before he left. We found them lying near the north corner of the building. But, the funny thing is, they're not your normal, run-of-the-mill shells."

The old lady nodded solemnly. "They were the old-fashioned kind, weren't they? With cardboard tubing and brass casings?"

Sam looked stunned. "That's right. But how did you know?"

Cindy opened her purse and took out the shotgun shell that had been left on the front porch of the Biggs house a couple of nights before. "It was left as a warning, Sam. Just like the ones you found here. Whoever the murderer is, they're cocky and arrogant. In a way, this is their calling card."

"Do you mind if I take that shell off your hands for a while?" Sam asked. "So I can see if it matches up with the two found this morning?"

She handed him the empty shotgun shell. "Sure. But they'll match perfectly, I'm betting. And I don't believe the killer cares whether you know that or not, either."

Sam placed the shell in a small plastic bag and stuck it in his jacket pocket. "So, other than going to breakfast without yours truly, what do you ladies have planned for today?"

Cindy frowned. "Well, to tell the truth, we've been invited to have coffee and cookies with the Osborne sisters this afternoon."

The sheriff laughed. "You wouldn't want to miss out on that, would you?"

"Surely not. After that, we thought we might drive over to the hospital and see how Josh Elder is doing."

As the two women turned to go, Sam spoke again. "By the way, try and be extra careful, okay? If this psycho does have some sort of vendetta against you, they might leave you with more than an empty shotgun shell next time."

"Don't worry about us," Cindy assured him. "We can take care of ourselves. Isn't that right, dear?"

"Uh, sure, Grandma," said Beth, although the look on her face suggested that she wasn't nearly as confident of that fact as her elderly grandmother seemed to be.

CHAPTER THIRTY-TWO

The Osborne sisters were obviously cat lovers.

As Cindy and Beth sat in the downstairs parlor of the big Victorian house on Beechwood Drive, they couldn't help but notice that the room had a distinctly feline motif. Cat portraits in gold-painted frames decorated the walls, while all manner of porcelain, brass, and jade knickknacks—all in the forms of cats—sat on the antique tables, bookshelves, and even on the ornate mantle of the white marble fireplace.

But what struck them the most was the number of actual cats that occupied the parlor. There had to be at least nine of the animals, perhaps even as many as twelve. Persians, yellow tabbies, Siamese, coal black shorthairs—seemingly one of every breed imaginable. And when they had entered the spacious foyer upon their arrival, the two women had spotted at least three or four more lounging on the carpeted steps of the elegantly-curbed staircase that led to the upper floor.

Beth didn't have anything against cats. She thought they were beautiful and mysterious creatures. But her allergies were not quite as tolerant. She sneezed for the sixth time since they first entered the parlor, nearly losing the cup and saucer that was balanced precariously on her right knee.

"Bless you, dear," said Sally Osborne. She stared at the young woman through her thick eyeglasses. "Are you catching a cold?"

Beth sniffed. "It must be my hay fever kicking in."

"Pollen is extremely bothersome here in Bedloe County," said Susan Osborne. "Particularly in the spring of the year. You know, with the trees budding and the flowers blooming and all."

"Yes, I know," agreed the redhead. She avoided looking at the cats that congregated around the sofa and took another sip of coffee.

"We are so pleased that you decided to take us up on our invitation," Sally told them. "At first, we were sure you would head back to Nashville before we had the opportunity to chat, Cindy Ann. Then we'd have to wait another ten or fifteen years before we would even see you again."

Susan turned to Beth. "We do miss your grandmother something terrible. She was quite a fixture here in Coleman, especially when she was a child. Why she wanted to move all the way to Nashville and leave her hometown and her family behind, I'll never know."

Cindy ignored the remark. She ate one of the frosted shortbread cookies perched on the rim of her saucer and washed it down with a swallow of creamed coffee. "You've kept this old place up very well over the years," she said.

"Well, Papa left us with ample means following his death," said Sally Osborne. "So much so that we've never wanted for anything, or even had to resort to marriage in order to provide for ourselves." She turned to Beth. "He was the mayor of Coleman and the owner of the textile mill just outside of town, you know. And what was your father again, Cindy Ann? I seem to have forgotten exactly what his livelihood was."

"He was a tobacco farmer," she replied, her voice steady.

"Oh, yes. So he was."

The snide expression of social distaste on Sally's wrinkled face was as clear as the nose on Cindy's face. The elderly woman bit her tongue and began to think that their visit to the

Osborne residence had been a big mistake. "Of course, we were brought up on separate sides of the track, so to speak."

"Oh, but did it really matter? We did have our good times together, remember?" said Susan. She stroked the back of a fluffy white Burmese with one spidery hand, while daintily lifting her coffee cup to her lips with the other.

"Yes," agreed Sally. "We were practically as close as sisters back when we were nine or ten, weren't we, Cindy Ann?"

Cindy simply smiled politely. Her memories of the Osborne sisters differed greatly from theirs. From what she could recall, there had only been a brief period of a month when the twins had actually treated her halfway decent. Before then, they had been two of Chester Martin's most loyal allies, taunting her viciously following that tragic incident concerning the Holt baby.

Thinking about Vera Mae Holt and her unfortunate child still saddened Cindy. She remembered it as though it had happened yesterday. She, along with her mother and four-year-old Sam, had attended a baby shower for the expectant mother one sunny spring day. It had started pleasantly at first, with talk common of married ladies and opening of humble gifts. Then Vera Mae had felt the baby kick and called Cindy over. When the girl had pressed the palm of her hand against Vera Mae's swollen belly, she had experienced the full force of her newly-acquired ability for the first time.

Cindy had suddenly found herself surrounded by liquid darkness, as though cradled within the walls of the expectant woman's womb. Then the comforting sensation of warmth and nurturing had turned into sudden horror. She felt something long and pliant loop around her throat and grow tight, strangling her. Before she could black out, Cindy had emerged from the disturbing spectacle with the knowledge that Vera Mae's baby was dead. She had said as much and had received a whipping for her insolence. But her terrible premonition had come true several days later. After a long and painful labor, Vera Mae Holt had given birth to a stillborn baby boy. Afterward, practically the entire town thought Cindy had somehow jinxed the infant. The cruelest were her classmates at Coleman Elementary.

After the suspicions had died down, Cindy had spent the first part of her ninth summer playing and roaming the county with several of the more well-to-do children in town. Susan and Sally had been among them. But their friendship had been a short one. It had ended abruptly on that sweltering July day when they had wandered into Harvey Brewer's abandoned tobacco barn and unexpectedly discovered the bodies of three murdered and mutilated teenagers.

"So, Cindy Ann," said Susan, breaking her train of thought. "What have you discovered so far?"

"Pardon me?" asked Cindy, acting as though she had no idea what they were referring to.

"Oh, come now, dear, you mustn't put us off any longer," replied Sally. "Everyone in town knows your real reason for coming to Coleman. Why don't you tell us what you've found out concerning that nasty business out at the Elder farm."

"Yes," urged Susan. "Tell the truth. It was Josh Elder, wasn't it? The whole town knows it was the boy who killed his family. There's simply no doubt about it."

"You want to hear every juicy tidbit, don't you?" Cindy asked them. There was an edge to her voice, a definite hint of angry impatience.

"Of course we do," said the sisters in unison, leaning forward eagerly.

"Uh, maybe you shouldn't, Grandma," Beth started to warn.

"No, dear, if that's the only reason they invited us here— and I believe it is—then I think it would only be proper to tell them precisely what they want to know."

The two twin sisters grinned and leaned forward even more, so much so that they seemed on the verge of falling completely out of their chairs.

"Well, if you really want to know, I believe that I've discovered who the true murderer actually was."

"And who might that be?" asked Sally Osborne almost breathlessly.

Cindy smiled slyly. "Why the one who committed the original murders, of course. As it turns out, he's come back after all these years to wreak havoc on Coleman all over again."

The smiles vanished from the Osborne's lean faces, leaving an appalled expression there instead. "Huh?" muttered Susan.

"Yes, that's right," said the elderly woman, enjoying their bewilderment. "It's Bully Hanson. Apparently, his ghost has come back from the grave to haunt us all."

Beth closed her eyes. "Oh boy."

At first, the Osborne sisters were speechless. Then the paleness of their identical faces abruptly blossomed into a flushed red. "Well, I do declare! What do you take us for, Cindy Ann? A couple of senile fools?"

"No," said Cindy, finishing her coffee. "More like a couple of meddling, old busybodies."

Sally gasped. "Well, I've never! How rude!"

"Not as rude as inviting me here for the sole purpose of trying to dig up some dirt on what happened to those poor people in that blasted barn," she retorted. She set her cup and saucer on the coffee table and stood up. "Now if you'll excuse me, we have more important places to be this afternoon."

"By all means!" sniffed Susan indignantly. "I believe you know the way out."

"Yes, I do…if I can manage to step around all these damn, flea-bitten cats of yours!"

As Cindy grabbed her purse and headed for the parlor door, Beth nodded apologetically at the two spinsters. "Uh, it was nice meeting you both."

They simply glowered at her and said nothing.

A moment later, Beth caught up to her grandmother as she marched down the sidewalk toward the Accord. "Don't you think you were kind of rough on them, Grandma?"

"Maybe," she admitted, "but I reckon it was about time somebody found the nerve to knock those two old biddies down a notch or two. All they did when they were spoiled brats in the Thirties was turn up their powdered noses at us poor kids and act like we were nothing more than trash. And, as far as I can see, they haven't changed a bit. They're still the same self-centered snobs they were back when we were young'uns."

"But what you told them," said Beth, frowning. "I mean that nonsense about Bully Hanson…they'll have a field day telling the whole town about that."

"I'm not so sure," Cindy told her. "I believe they knew that I was just pulling their leg."

Beth looked over at the old lady. "Pulling their leg, Grandma? The last I understood, you were actually beginning to believe that Bully Hanson had something to do with those murders."

As they climbed into the car, the satisfaction that had shown in Cindy's face changed into uneasiness. "Well, let me put it this way, dear. I know that the actual killings were performed by a flesh and blood person, and not some vengeful ghost. But I can't seem to shake the feeling that Bully had *something* to do with the murders. It's almost as though, if nothing else, the essence of his evil spirit had reenacted the massacre that he and Claude Darnell were responsible for seventy-seven years ago."

Beth shuddered. "Come on, Grandma! You're starting to sound like some silly horror novel!"

Cindy sat there for a long moment, thinking to herself. "Okay, how about this? Why don't we do our best to discover the truth concerning this ugly matter once and for all?"

"What do you have in mind?" asked the young redhead.

"Let's use our powers of hindsight and attempt another reading with Josh Elder," the old woman suggested. "We'll give it our very best shot...but, this time, we'll do it together."

CHAPTER THIRTY-THREE

"How is he doing today?" asked Cindy.

The nurse was changing the IV needle in Josh Elder's arm when they walked into the hospital room. "He seems to be a little more responsive today, but he still hasn't regained consciousness." As she smoothed down the tape on his forearm, she looked over at the two women. "Are you relatives of Josh?"

"Just friends," Cindy told her.

"Well, I'll leave you folks alone and let you visit awhile."

After the nurse had left, they positioned two chairs on opposite sides of the bed. Cindy closed the window blinds and shut the door, then took the chair to the right. Beth took the other.

They sat and stared at the thirteen-year-old for a moment. He laid where he had for the past several days, his eyes partially closed, his breathing slow and steady. As before, the boy seemed completely oblivious to their presence in the room.

"Are you ready?" Cindy asked her granddaughter. She took Josh's right hand, entwining her fingers with his.

Beth nodded. She held the boy's left hand in hers.

The elderly woman leaned forward. Her lips were only a few inches from his ear as she spoke. "Josh, it's me again. You've had time to rest. Now it's time to go on. To the barn."

The boy's forehead creased with a trace of a frown and a low groan sounded down deep in his throat.

"I know, son," whispered Cindy. "I'd rather not go either. But we must. We've got to find out exactly what happened there. You owe it to your family, as well as yourself."

The teenager murmured something unintelligible.

"Please, Josh," she continued. "We've got to break past this barrier you've erected between yourself and reality. If not, you'll be lost. Either you'll wither away, hooked up to some cock-eyed machine, or you'll end up spending the rest of your life in prison. Let's prove that they're wrong about you. Prove that you had nothing to do with the deaths of your family." Cindy stared intently at the young man. "If you understand, squeeze my hand."

At first, the boy's hand remained motionless. Then, gradually, his fingers tightened around hers.

Cindy looked across the bed at Beth. "This is bound to be difficult, dear. More than likely it'll be a dozen times worse than what you experienced at Radnor Lake."

Beth's face was pale, but her hazel eyes were steady. "I'll be with you all the way, Grandma."

Cindy nodded. She regarded the boy once again. "Okay, Josh, we're ready. Now take us there. Take us to the tobacco barn."

A moment passed. Slowly, the gloom of the hospital room began to darken. The furnishings began to grow less distinct, until they faded completely. The restrictions of their physical surroundings soon followed. Walls, ceiling, and floor dissolved, leaving a swirling void of murky dark grayness around them.

Beth held onto the boy's hand tightly as a disorienting sensation of shifting gripped her. Somewhere, beyond the complete silence of the gray mist, she could hear a roaring sound, like static on the unresponsive channel of a television set.

Or, rather, more like the earthward rush of a heavy rainfall.

———————————

Josh Elder stepped off the back porch and started through the wet darkness toward the old barn.

He hadn't gotten past the gravel driveway before he was drenched. He began to regret not bringing an umbrella with him, or at least a newspaper to hold over his head. But he knew the latter would have offered little protection. He would have only ended up with a couple of handfuls of soggy paper by the time he reached the weathered structure.

A feeling of mounting dread filled him as he picked his way through the thicket. He still couldn't understand why his father, mother, and sister would be out there in that old barn in the middle of the night. It simply wasn't normal. He and the rest of his family had a nightly routine that was rarely deviated from: supper at six, television until ten, and then on to bed. Why they would be outside messing around in a violent thunderstorm was beyond him.

Lightning crackled overhead, illuminating the thicket for a split second. Then pitch blackness closed around him again. Blindly, he pushed through the high weeds, making his way slowly in the direction of the barn. Through the driving rain, Josh could see the flickering glow radiating though the uneven cracks between the boards, as well as through the big hole in the western wall.

As he grew nearer, he heard a noise that he couldn't identify.

Thud…thud…crack…thud…crack…

The sound was chillingly sinister in nature. Josh didn't know why, but it tied his stomach into knots just listening to it.

What's going on in there? he wondered. In one way he didn't want to know, but in another he knew that he *had* to.

Finally, he reached the opening in the wall. Josh's heart thundered in his chest as he stepped inside and escaped the fury of the storm. But he found no comfort there whatsoever. Instead, he found himself caught in the midst of the worst nightmare imaginable.

The first thing that struck him was the smell. It was a hot, cloying stench like copper heated in a furnace. He recognized it immediately.

It was the odor of freshly-let blood. A lot of it.

He squinted against the glare of a kerosene lamp as he took a couple of steps inside. As his eyes grew accustomed to the light, Josh saw a narrow shadow flashing across the rough boarding of the inner walls. One shadowy arm rose and fell in time with the sickening rhythm of fleshy *thuds* and brittle *cracks*.

Dazed, he stumbled toward the end of the barn that was still standing, where the lantern hung from a crooked nail on a support beam. He turned toward the long, coffin-sized tool chest, but couldn't see it clearly. Something blocked his view, or rather *someone*. A dark, human form wielding a hatchet.

Suddenly, Josh realized that something fiendishly horrible was taking place. Something that involved the missing members of his family. He got an almost overwhelming urge to turn and run, but he found that he couldn't. He could only stand there, rooted to the spot, and stare at the unthinkable act that was being committed before his eyes.

Past the crouching form, Josh caught a glimpse of the open tool chest. It was filled to capacity with things that were long and pale, the ends glistening with gore and jagged, splintered bone. It took him several seconds before his stunned mind allowed him to see the objects for what they actually were.

A neatly-arranged stack of dismembered arms and legs.

"No," he gasped. "Oh, God, no!"

He turned his eyes from the awful contents of the tool chest to the one who was responsible for the carnage. As the form hacked steadily, allowing the steel wedge of the axe head to fall again and again, Josh looked at the torn mass of flesh and clothing that was being labored over.

His heart leapt wildly in his chest. A pale and slack-jawed face stared past the left knee of the murderer, its dark brown eyes glazed and totally devoid of life.

It was the face of his father.

The hatchet ascended with a mighty swing, landing just below the face's left ear. A jet of crimson shot high into the air. It landed across Josh's face and T-shirt in a thick red spray. The boy choked and stumbled backward, frantically attempting to wipe the lukewarm dampness away. He stared down at his hands in horror and found them covered with blood.

Another *thud* rang out, along with the crackle of shattering vertebrae. He watched as the head of Gordon Elder separated from the body and rolled lopsidedly along the blood-soaked earth toward the far wall.

Suddenly, Josh's terror could no longer remain silent. A shriek of fear and anguish tore out of his throat, surpassing the roar of the storm outside.

The dark form stood and whirled, alerted by the teen's hysterical screams. It stood in dark relief against the yellow glow of the kerosene lantern, more of a featureless silhouette than anything else.

Aware that he had betrayed himself, Josh began to back away from the horrid scene of murder and mutilation that he had unwittingly stumbled upon. Terrified, he watched as the killer flung the bloody hatchet aside and, stooping to the earth, picked up something else.

Josh recognized the object at once. It was an old-fashioned twelve-gauge shotgun with most of its twin barrels and wooden stock sawed away.

Run! a voice inside him screamed. *Run as fast as you can!*

An instant later, he was past the open wall of the barn and into the downpour again. He plunged headlong into the wet darkness and began to run. He glanced back only once and saw the form of the murderer standing in the opening, weapon raised.

Josh cried out and dropped to his hands and knees. A loud boom roared in his ears, drowning out the thunder that roared from the storm clouds overhead for a split second. The swarm of double-aught buckshot missed him, but severed a small mimosa sapling completely in half, five feet away.

Quickly, he began to scramble through the underbrush, trying to put as much distance between him and the old barn as possible. He listened, trying to hear the sound of the murderer coming for him. But he could hear nothing. The rumbling of thunder and the steady rush of the rainfall completely drowned out any lesser noises.

He began to crawl, heading into the dense heart of the thicket. Vines and thorns pulled and ripped at him, but he dared not cry out in pain. Eventually he reached a spiny clump of blackberry bramble and huddled in the middle of it, praying that it would conceal him from his stalker.

Josh shivered as the cool spring rain pelted him, drumming heavily across his head and shoulders. A violent clap of thunder exploded overhead. He looked up in time to see a dark form step into view. It stood no more than eight feet away, staring into the night and clutching the stubby shotgun in one hand.

Josh remained perfectly still, afraid to even breathe. If they spotted him, he would die as horribly as the rest of his family had.

A brilliant whip-crack of lightning split the stormy sky. Abruptly, the face of the murderer was revealed, but only for an instant. Then it was cloaked in darkness once again.

When the form had moved on, the boy continued to crouch in the bramble, afraid to move. He breathed shallowly and closed his eyes. He couldn't bear to keep them shut for very long. In the darkness behind his eyelids played the grisly images he had witnessed only a few minutes before in the sagging hull of the old tobacco barn.

He squatted there, shivering and wet, for what seemed to be a very long time. Then, when he was certain the murderer was gone, he left the tangle of thorny blackberry bramble and, carefully, made his way through the thicket, toward the highway.

CHAPTER THIRTY-FOUR

Cindy let go of Josh Elder and opened her eyes. As she breathed deeply and willed her heartbeat to settle down, she looked across the bed at Beth. Her granddaughter sat rigidly in her chair. Beads of perspiration glistened on her forehead and her eyes were clamped tightly shut.

"Let go, Beth," she said firmly. "Let go of his hand."

Slowly, the redhead's fingers uncurled, releasing their hold. As the boy's hand slipped from her grasp, Beth opened her eyes. They were damp with tears. "Sweet Lord in heaven!" she muttered, clearly shaken. "How awful. How terribly awful."

"Yes," said Cindy grimly. "It certainly was. But at least what we saw answered some important questions. At least now we know, without a shadow of a doubt, that Josh had absolutely nothing to do with those murders."

Beth reached over with a trembling hand and brushed a strand of dark hair from the boy's sweaty forehead. "Poor guy. No wonder he shut everything out and withdrew. His mind just couldn't deal with what he saw in that old barn."

A startled expression suddenly crossed Cindy's aged face. "Beth...*look!*"

Puzzled, Beth turned her gaze from her grandmother to the thirteen-year-old. She was astonished to find that the boy's eyes were completely open. And they no longer possessed the glazed and unresponsive expression that had been there before.

Instead, they were fully alert and brimming with mental anguish.

"Oh," he said, struggling to sit up. "Oh my God!"

Beth stood and gently pushed him back down to the mattress. "Just try to remain calm, Josh," she said, utilizing her best bedside manner. "You're okay and you're safe. Completely safe."

"But my mom and dad," he rasped hoarsely. Tears began to well up in his dark brown eyes. "And my sister...they're dead. Worse than dead."

Cindy took the boy's hand again. "Josh, do you know who I am?"

Josh Elder looked up into the old woman's face and nodded. "You're the one in my dreams. The one who showed me the way out." He turned and looked at the young woman to his left. "And you, too."

"Yes," said Beth. She took the boy's wrist between her thumb and forefinger and checked his pulse. It was almost normal, no longer the sluggish, subdued heart rate that he had exhibited for the past several days.

He looked around the darkened room. "Where am I?" he asked, seeming a little frightened.

"You're in a hospital, Josh," said Beth. "Perryville Medical Center."

That look of absolute grief and inner torment resurfaced as he began to sort out his thoughts. "And my family...they *are* dead, aren't they?"

Beth looked at her grandmother. Cindy laid a wrinkled hand on his forehead and stroked it soothingly. "Yes," she told him softly. "They are."

The boy broke down. He wailed and cried, his face contorting into a grievous mask streaming with tears. As Cindy leaned over and embraced Josh, drawing him to her and comforting him, Beth reached up to the panel of electrical outlets and buttons that was set into the wall over the bed and called for a nurse.

Thirty minutes later, the two women stood in the hospital corridor, waiting for word about Josh. John Arnett had gently ushered them out of the room twenty minutes earlier and was currently in the process of examining the newly-awakened boy.

Cindy paced the floor nervously, while Beth stood with her back to the wall and her arms crossed. "What's taking him so dadblasted long?" asked the elderly woman.

"Chill out, Grandma," Beth told her. "Nothing's wrong. John just has to make a thorough examination, that's all. You know, checking vital signs and reflexes, as well as testing for signs of disorientation or memory loss. Josh has been through a horrible ordeal. And he's practically been in a coma for the past four days. I don't blame John for being overly cautious. I would do the same if I were in his position."

The old lady was about to answer, when the door opened. John Arnett walked out with a big grin on his face. Immediately, the worried look on Cindy's face changed into one of relief. "How is he, Doctor?"

"Considering everything he's been through, I'd say he is doing incredibly well," he assured her. "Physically, he's as fit as a fiddle. A little weak, but that's all. Mentally, he is still very distraught over his family, but that is to be expected. All in all, he has seemingly come out of the coma unscathed. If he has suffered any detrimental effects, I haven't been able to detect them yet."

"May we see him?" asked the elderly woman.

"I'm afraid not, Miss Cindy," he said respectfully. "Josh was so upset, I had to give him a mild sedative to help him relax. I'd prefer that he get a little rest before seeing visitors again. Especially, the two of you." He smiled at them. "Honestly, I didn't mean that the way it sounded. It's just that you helped him face reality again and I believe it would be best if he wasn't reminded of that awful experience again for the time being. At least not until he regains his bearings."

"We understand, John," Beth agreed. "Watching what happened to his family in that creepy old barn was bad enough for an outsider like me. I can imagine how traumatic it was for Josh."

The doctor nodded. "Yes, it's difficult to comprehend the type of horror the poor kid must have endured. In any case, I would prefer that he be isolated for the next day or so, if only to allow him the freedom to deal with his family's deaths on his own terms. A counselor will be available to help him in that respect, of course."

Beth searched the man's face. "You're not angry with us, are you?"

"For attempting that mind-reading act of yours without consulting me first?" The expression of mock sternness on his handsome face vanished with a broad smile. "I suppose I should be. But considering how things turned out, I guess I have no complaints. Of course, you'd better thank your lucky stars that I'm totally lacking when it comes to the overblown ego of most doctors. Most physicians would have considered it a personal insult against their God-like abilities that you brought him out of that where they couldn't. But me? Well, I'd just like to say 'thanks'."

"Didn't I tell you he was a nice man, Grandma?" said Beth with a smile.

"Yes," replied Cindy. "That and more."

"I'll tell you what," said John. "Why don't we celebrate? I've got to work until eleven tonight, but tomorrow is my day off. Why don't the three of us make a day of it? We'll go out and have dinner or something. How about it?"

"I have some things I need to do tomorrow," Cindy told him. "But I'm sure Beth would enjoy spending the day with you. I suspect her nerves are a little frazzled, considering what she's experienced since coming to Coleman with me."

"I could use a little R&R," admitted Beth. "But are you sure, Grandma? I hate for you to spend the day all by yourself."

"I'm a grown woman, remember?" said the elderly woman. "Just leave the Accord and your phone with me and I'll be fine. Besides, there are a few old friends I might just look up tomorrow. And I don't mean the Osborne sisters, either."

Beth laughed. "Well, okay then." She turned to John. "So where would you like to meet?"

"How about Dixie's Café for breakfast?" he suggested. "Then, after that, I'll take you around Bedloe County and show you the sights, what little of them there are. We might even have a picnic. How does that sound?"

"Fabulous," said the young redhead. "So, I guess I'll see you tomorrow then?"

"I'll be looking forward to it," said John Arnett.

"Me, too."

The doctor glanced self-consciously over at Cindy, then laughed. "Aw, what the hell." He leaned forward and kissed Beth on the cheek. "See you around eight in the morning at Dixie's."

"I'll be there," said Beth. Her face was red, but with pleasure rather than embarrassment. "Bye."

When John had left to continue his rounds, Cindy walked up behind her granddaughter and laid her hands upon her shoulders. "You're really falling for him hard, aren't you?"

Beth swallowed dryly. "Yeah, I guess I am. But do you think he feels the same way about me?"

"Without a doubt," her grandmother assured her, giving her an affectionate hug. "Remember what I said before, though. Be careful and take your time. There's no need to rush things."

"But what if some big-boobed nurse comes along and snaps him up first?"

Cindy chuckled as they turned toward the elevator. "What, with a beautiful, redheaded doctor like you around? He'd be a damn fool."

"Thanks for the vote of confidence," Beth said, taking her arm.

"That's what grandmothers are for, dear," Cindy told her as the elevator doors opened and they stepped inside.

As they approached the ground floor, the old woman turned to her granddaughter. "Beth...I know we got sidetracked with Josh waking up and all, but there was something I meant to ask you...after the reading."

Beth knew precisely what she was referring to. "You want to know if I saw the killer's face?"

"Yes," said Cindy. "But you didn't, did you?"

"No," admitted Beth. "I remember the lightning flash illuminating their face, but I can't seem to recall any of their features. It's really weird."

"And terribly frustrating," the old woman added. "I didn't see it either." A troubled look crossed her gaunt face. "It's almost as though something was purposely blocking out that part of the incident, preventing us from seeing who actually murdered the Elder family."

CHAPTER THIRTY-FIVE

That night, she again found herself in the youthful body of a nine-year-old.

It was a blustery day in late September. Cindy Ann sat on the seat of the Biggs' rattletrap pickup truck. Her father, Clayburn, turned and winked at her as he drove. Clay Biggs was a tall, lanky man with jet black hair, a homely, hang-dog face, and a talent for farming, mechanic work, and rolling homemade cigarettes singlehandedly.

Happily, Cindy smiled back. In the past, she and her father had never been very close, particularly after her long illness had forced him to sell the tobacco land that his father and grandfather had farmed before him. But, thankfully, all of that had changed. Following the harrowing discovery of Johnny's body in Harvey Brewer's tobacco barn, a renewed affection had blossomed between the girl and her father. It was just unfortunate that it had taken a terrible tragedy to bring them both together.

They pulled off the lonesome stretch of Old Newsome Road and onto the dirt shoulder that fronted Woody's General Store. The mercantile looked like a picture postcard—a weathered, tin-roofed structure wreathed by oaks and maples that were already beginning to show their autumn colors.

When the truck jerked to a halt, Cindy was the first one out. The girl preferred to go barefoot, but the ground had grown chilly after the first hard frost and she had reluctantly worn her new winter shoes that afternoon.

Hand in hand, she and her father passed the rusty gas pumps and climbed the two-by-four steps of the store's lengthy porch. Halfway up, they met Jasper Loftis, an elderly gentleman with iron-gray hair and wire-rimmed spectacles. He and Clay exchanged pleasantries, after which Loftis gave Cindy a coin to buy herself a penny candy. She shyly thanked him for his generosity, then accompanied her father inside.

The long, single room of the country store was dark and drafty, and smelled of chewing tobacco, cider vinegar, and peppermint sticks. The proprietor, Woody Sadler, greeted them as they walked in. Clay waved to several men who gathered around a potbelly stove in the back, then handed Woody a grocery list. He went over to talk to his friends while the storekeeper gathered the items from the wooden shelves behind the counter.

Cindy Ann bought herself several jawbreakers with her newly-acquired penny. Cramming all three into her mouth, the girl with the fiery red hair went directly to her favorite shelf in the entire store. On it was a collection of toys: a couple of baby dolls, a wind-up tin toy or two, and a cast-iron hook and ladder fire engine with a little speckled Dalmatian sitting on the driver's seat. Cindy knew she would never have the money to buy any of those treasures, but they sure were fun to look at.

The copper cow bell over the front door jangled as two men strolled in. Woody glanced up from Clay's grocery list and spoke to them. He called the two by name—Hanson and Darnell. Cindy had never heard their names before that day.

One asked where the shotgun shells were located and Woody told him. As they headed down the aisle for the ammunition shelf, a husky fellow in a plaid wool coat and hunting cap brushed past Cindy as she coveted a pretty china doll dressed in a blue calico dress. She would have paid the two no attention, except that something strange happened. A peculiar feeling washed over her, an abrupt sensation of cold contempt and fear combined. She stared up at the big man, a shiver running throughout her lean body.

"What's the matter, girl?" asked the man named Hanson. "Did a possum walk across your grave?"

The two continued on. Shaken, Cindy turned from them and walked back down the aisle. "Pappy," she called, "I'm going on back out to the truck."

Clay leaned back in his chair next to the iron stove. "I'll be out directly, pumpkin," he said as he took a drag on a hand-rolled cigarette.

She let the door slam behind her, then ran to her father's pickup. She sat on the running board on the passenger side, her eyes staring absently at the flattened bottle caps on the hard-packed earth. She tried to shake the awful feeling that had gripped her inside the store, but found that she couldn't. The broad, ugly face of the big man loomed in her mind's eye—the sandy blond crewcut, the nose that had been twice broken, and those eyes…those cold gray eyes as cunning and humorless as those of a ravenous wolf. She had seen something bad in those eyes and heard something evil in that gravelly voice of his.

The slap of the screen door and the heavy clumping of boots on the porch steps roused Cindy from her thoughts. She sat perfectly still on the running board, hoping the two wouldn't notice her as they passed. But Hanson caught her out of the corner of his eye and, nudging the man named Darnell, couldn't resist stopping to tease the nine-year-old.

"Now I hope I didn't go and scare you none back in there," he rumbled loudly, stooping to her level. "Surely wouldn't want you to fear me, girl. It's plumb bad luck to have a redheaded woman peeved at you."

"Yeah," put in Darnell. "You oughta know, Bully. As many redheads that have jilted you."

Hanson gave his partner a withering glare, then turned back to Cindy. "You're a cute, little heifer. All fire-red hair and freckles. And that nose…why I believe I'll steal that for myself." And, with that, he brought his massive hand close to her face, then drew it away with a snap.

"Gotcha!" he said laughing, his thumb protruding between the index and middle fingers, giving the illusion of a captured nose.

Cindy could only stare in saddened horror, so much so that she swallowed her jawbreakers. But it wasn't the childish prank that disturbed her. Rather, it was the man's voice. It seemed to somehow alter, growing more menacing as it grated in the far reaches of her subconscious. *Gotcha*…it reverberated over and over again, until frightening images soon accompanied the word. A murky figure of a man in the driving rain, the brittle click of a shotgun's hammer being cocked, and a skeletal grin in the darkness.

Gotcha…Johnny!

Cindy gasped, her hazel eyes widening in shock. Terrified, she recoiled until the back of her head bumped against the truck door.

Hanson roared with laughter. He opened his hand and released his reddened thumb. "I was just funning you…see?"

Cindy could only stare at him. Her lips quivered as she looked Bully squarely in his cold gray eyes. "You're the one," she breathed. "You're the one who done it."

"Done what, little missy?" he asked, chuckling.

"You're…the one…who killed…Johnny."

Bully's laughter choked off into silence. Claude Darnell stood there with the frightened eyes of a rabbit, looking as if he had seen a ghost. "Shit, Bully! Let's get the hell outta here!"

"Shut up!" the big man growled. Then he turned back to Cindy Ann. "What kinda foolishness are you talking, girl? You know we ain't the ones who done that terrible thing."

"Yes, you did!" said Cindy, her eyes defiant. "You killed them all in that old tobacco barn, then buried them there. You both had a hand in it!"

Suddenly, she sensed what Bully Hanson truly was. Past those small stone-gray eyes, Cindy detected the cold heart of the killer within. It was the same face her brother Johnny and his two traveling buddies had seen before their brutal deaths— a face totally lacking in conscience.

For a second, she was certain that he was going to react violently. That he was on the verge of reaching out and snapping her neck like a stick of dry kindling.

But whatever Bully had in mind, it was lost to the sudden slam of the mercantile door as Clay Biggs crossed the porch with his groceries.

For a long, lingering moment, the murderer and his young accuser remained face to face. An evil like none Cindy Ann had ever known exuded from the man as his eyes bore deeply into her own.

"You tell your folks—you tell *anyone* at all," warned Bully Hanson. "And I will surely *kill* you!"

"Grandma!" came Beth's voice from out of the darkness. "Calm down!"

Cindy woke up to find herself lying flat on her back on the floor, the bedcovers tangled around her legs and ankles. "What happened?"

"You screamed and fell out of bed," her granddaughter explained. "You must have had another nightmare."

"Yes," said the old woman with a sigh. "I remember now."

Beth helped her back into bed and lit the kerosene lamp on the nightstand. A pale glow filled the room, casting long, black shadows upon the plaster walls.

She studied the elderly woman carefully. "Good Lord, Grandma! Your face is blood red. I bet your blood pressure is through the roof."

"Oh, I'm alright," Cindy insisted.

"I'd better check it anyway, just to be on the safe side."

Beth went to her suitcase and came back with a blood pressure cuff. After wrapping it around her grandmother's lean arm and pumping it up, she checked the gauge. "Just like I thought. One-eighty over ninety-six." Suspicion suddenly shown in her eyes. "Did you take your medicine before you went to bed tonight?"

Cindy frowned guiltily. "Honey...I have a confession to make."

"Yeah? What's that?"

"For some reason, Hydrochlorothiazide seems to inhibit my abilities." She raised a bony finger and tapped her forehead. "I can't seem to *see* what I need to...up *here*...if I take it on a regular basis."

"Grandma!" Beth said, shocked. "Exactly when was the last time that you took a dose?"

Cindy dropped her eyes. "Three days ago."

"Well, abilities or no abilities, you're taking your medicine before you end up suffering a stroke." Beth poured Cindy a cup of water from a thermos, then took the prescription vial from the old lady's purse. When she opened the container, she found only two of the white pills left. "You're almost out. You really need to get it refilled as soon as possible."

"I'll take it to the pharmacy in town tomorrow," promised Cindy as she swallowed one of the pills with a sip of water.

Beth stared at her grandmother with concern. "You were dreaming about Bully Hanson again, weren't you?"

"How did you know?"

"You cried out his name in your sleep," Beth told her. "You sounded like a frightened, little girl."

"In that dream, I was." Cindy settled back into her pillows and tried to relax. "I just don't understand it. I don't understand why Bully Hanson keeps coming to mind. It seems to be a constant thing with me lately."

"Well, I suppose it's understandable, what with all the bad memories returning here to Coleman must have dredged up."

"But that isn't it," Cindy told her. "You know me well enough. There's not much that can rattle me. I don't suffer from a wild imagination and I'm not senile...yet. No, something's causing these nightmares and strange premonitions, something that feels very *real*."

She thought of the dense woods that stretched behind the Biggs house. Beyond it lay the winding brook of Green Creek and, amid the heavy thicket of the Elder farm, stood the old tobacco barn. Although she didn't say it out loud, Cindy had a feeling that, somehow, Bully Hanson was, indeed, playing a part in what was going on in Bedloe County. If not directly, then he was watching over the atrocities of the present murderer with gloating approval.

CHAPTER THIRTY-SIX

"Well, good morning, Cindy Ann," greeted Ben Arnett as the elderly woman walked into the drugstore. "I was hoping that you'd stop in sooner or later."

"I just thought I'd come in and say hello." Cindy walked over to the elevated pharmacy counter and handed him her prescription vial. "And I need this refilled, please."

The pharmacist put on his reading glasses and studied the printed label on the front of the amber container. "High blood pressure, huh? I've got a touch of that myself. Give me your insurance card and I'll have this ready for you in a jiffy."

While Cindy waited, she looked around the small-town drugstore. It appeared nearly the same as it had when Ben's father had operated it sixty years ago. The packaging of the merchandise had changed, but the narrow aisles were laid out exactly the same, except for a large display of Hallmark greeting cards near the front door. To the right was the pharmacy counter fronted by shelves of vitamins and diet aids, while a long eating counter ran along the entire length of the left wall. It pretty much looked the same as it had when Cindy was growing up, except that the menu board over the soda fountain showed that Ben served mostly ice cream floats, milkshakes, and hot fudge sundaes now. Gone were the sandwich platters garnished with potato chips and kosher dills that the pharmacist's father had once offered. She supposed Dixie's

Café got all of the lunch business anyway. Besides, most people had an aversion to eating inside drugstores these days.

"So, where is your sidekick today?" asked Ben as he typed up the label for her prescription.

Cindy smiled. "Beth is spending the day with your grandson. We all had breakfast at the café and then they left together. I think they're planning to have a picnic out at Newsome Mill Park."

"Well, it sure is a fine day for it," said Ben. He set the blood pressure medication on the counter and then rang up the purchase on the cash register. "You know, John thinks mighty highly of your granddaughter."

"Yes, I know," said Cindy. "I think they make a cute couple."

"That's true. I sure wouldn't mind having the girl for a granddaughter-in-law, that's for sure. And I wouldn't mind having me a passel of redheaded great-grandchildren, either."

"Now you just hold on, Ben," Cindy told him. "If you go making requests like that right off the bat, you're liable to scare the two away from one another."

"Then I reckon I'd best keep it to myself…at least for the time being." Ben Arnett opened a swinging door and stepped down from the pharmacy counter. "Now before you run off, let me fix you that Coca-Cola float I promised you before."

"I don't know, Ben. I just had a big breakfast."

"You'll just have to find room for it," insisted the pharmacist. Resisting further protest, he ushered her toward the soda fountain.

A few minutes later, Cindy was seated on one of the padded counter stools, sipping on a float in a tall glass. The delicacy was a winning combination of Coca-Cola, vanilla ice cream, and whipped cream with a single maraschino cherry on its foamy top. "This is delicious, Ben! In fact, I believe it's better than what your daddy used to make."

Ben beamed at the praise. "Well, thank you, Cindy. I admit I do my best to keep it as close to the original as possible." He took a wooden toothpick from a dispenser on the counter and stuck it between his false teeth. "I reckon you must be mighty proud of Beth, practicing medicine at a big city hospital like Vanderbilt and all."

Cindy neglected to tell him that her granddaughter was currently on suspension. She was certain Beth hadn't mentioned it to John, either. "Proud as a peacock. But then you must know the feeling. John seems like a wonderful doctor."

Ben nodded. "And he's a right fine surgeon, too. Most of the folks here in Coleman who need surgery depend on him. I reckon they feel it's more comforting to have a hometown boy cutting at them than some stranger."

"I'd say so."

The pharmacist was quiet for a moment. "You know, I wanted to be a doctor myself at one time."

Cindy was genuinely surprised. "Is that right?"

"Yep. I even started out in medical school and everything. But do you know what ruined it for me? A weak stomach. I simply couldn't stand the sight of blood. Every time I started dissecting a frog or making an incision in a cadaver, my head would swim and my hands would begin to shake. I even passed out cold a couple of times. I finally had to give up that dream, no matter how much I wanted it. I enrolled in pharmacy school after that. Studied all that Latin and decided to make my living dealing in pills and cough syrups instead."

"You know," said Cindy, "your weakness might have had something to do with what we saw in Harvey Brewer's barn back when we were young'uns. What we found in that old tool chest could turn anyone's stomach for life."

"You're right," agreed Ben. "It's certainly crossed my mind before. It could've very well been psychological. I'm just glad that John has a stronger constitution for such things than I did."

It wasn't long before Cindy reached the bottom of her soda with a loud, gurgling slurp. "That was wonderful, Ben." She glanced at her wristwatch. It was a quarter until eleven. "I've enjoyed our visit, but I really must be going."

"Before you do, could you answer me one question? And, believe me, I'm not trying to be a busybody like most of the jaw-flappers in town."

"Go ahead, Ben. What's on your mind?"

"Well, I was wondering if you've found out who murdered those poor folks out on Highway 70? The Elders? John mentioned that you'd been working with Sam on the case."

The old woman considered it for a moment, then decided that it wouldn't do any harm to tell him. "I found out that Josh Elder was definitely not involved. He was simply an innocent bystander. But, for some strange reason, I can't identify exactly who *was* responsible. I can see them committing the murders and chasing the Elder boy through the thicket, but their face is a total blank. It simply won't come to me, no matter how hard I try."

"Well, I do declare," said Ben. An expression of concern shown in his wrinkled face. "Has it been a hard road for you, Cindy Ann? Putting up with this talent of yours all these years?"

"In a way, I suppose," she admitted. "But in other ways, it has given me as much joy as it has pain. So I reckon I can't complain."

Cindy bid her old friend goodbye and left the drugstore. As she reached into her purse for the Accord's keys, her hand brushed something wrapped in a handkerchief. She took it out and unfolded it. It was the fishing lure she had found on the earthen floor of the tobacco barn. She had completely forgotten about it until that moment.

For a long moment, she studied the object. Why had the lure been there in the ancient structure to begin with? It was certainly not an antique. In fact, it looked relatively new to her. If she were to make a guess, she would say it was no more than ten years old, maybe even less than that. It certainly wasn't a relic from the days when Harvey Brewer owned the place, that was for sure.

But it wasn't entirely the mystery of how the lure had come to be in the tobacco barn that bothered her most. Rather, it was the distinct feeling of dark despair and raw fear that she sensed every time she held the object between her fingers. The emotional turmoil of someone who considered themselves beyond hope. Someone who had, unfortunately, been at the wrong place at the wrong time.

The sensation was faint, but it was definitely there.

Cindy stared at the fishing lure for a moment longer and then an idea suddenly came to her. Without a second thought, she hopped into the Honda, started the car, and pulled away from the curb. Soon, she was heading southward out of town.

For the most part, there was only one true fishing spot in Bedloe County. A place where local fishermen and out-of-town sportsmen alike armed themselves with reels and tackle, and went in search of bass, trout, and perch.

And that place was Cherokee Lake.

CHAPTER THIRTY-SEVEN

"What a beautiful place."

Beth stood beside a stone wall that ran along the widening channel of Green Creek. On the far side of the stream stood the Old Newsome Mill, a picturesque structure also constructed of gray stone and topped with a sagging roof of cedar shingles. The big paddlewheel of dark pine turned slowly, kept constantly in motion by the gentle current of the rural creek.

"Yes," agreed John Arnett. "It certainly is." The young doctor stood at the stone wall next to her. He was dressed casually that afternoon: white polo shirt, khaki slacks, and tennis shoes. "This was one of my favorite places when I was a kid." He looked at her quizzically. "You mean to tell me that your grandmother has never brought you here before?"

"No," said Beth. "But then I've only been to Coleman once or twice. The last time was at a Biggs family reunion back before my great-grandmother Maudie passed away. I believe I was sixteen then."

"So you weren't all that close to your father's side of the family?"

"Well, sure. It was just that Grandma sort of kept her distance from Bedloe County. I suppose it had something to do with that sordid business she was involved in when she was a child."

John nodded in understanding. "Those murders in that old tobacco barn. And those two psychos…what were their names?"

"Bully Hanson and Claude Darnell." Beth stared absently into the clear blue sky. "They still haunt her, you know. She had a nightmare about them last night. I think that it's Bully who bothers her most of all."

"Even though he's been dead all these years?"

"Yes. She even has this crazy idea that he's still around somehow," she confided. "Not physically, of course, but in spirit."

"She doesn't actually believe that Bully Hanson is responsible for what happened at the Elder farm, does she?" asked John.

The redhead shrugged. "I don't know. In one way she does, but in another she realizes that it's impossible. To tell the truth, about the only thing Grandma and I are really sure of is Josh's innocence. His only crime was being unfortunate enough to stumble upon the killer while they were in the process of disposing of his family's bodies. He himself had absolutely nothing to do with those murders." The grave expression on Beth's face bloomed into a smile. "So, how is Josh doing?"

"I called the hospital and checked earlier this morning," John told her. "He's fully alert now, the same as when you last saw him. But the attending nurse says that he is severely depressed and refuses to eat. I guess you really can't blame him for reacting in such a way, considering what he's been through. Anyway, a psychiatric counselor will be spending some time with him today. Maybe they will be able to help him work things out."

"I certainly hope so."

John reached out and took Beth's hand. "Hey, we didn't come out here to talk about stuff like this, did we? Do you want to go over and see the mill?"

"Okay," replied Beth. As they started along the rock wall to a narrow footbridge that spanned Green Creek, Beth tightened her hold on the man's hand. She expected to feel that confusing sensation of anger and emotional darkness that she had experienced at the Chinese restaurant a couple of days ago. But she didn't. Pleasantly enough, the only emotions she could pick up on were positive ones—happiness and enjoyment, as well as an affection that was stronger than mere friendship.

Beth told herself not to get her hopes up, but she couldn't help it. After years of loneliness and concentrating solely on her medical career, it seemed that a genuine romance was imminent. And, deep down inside, she found herself wishing that it would turn out to be a lasting one as well.

As they started across the bridge, Beth looked back at the wicker basket and checkered tablecloth that was spread out beneath a weeping willow tree—the spot where they had enjoyed a picnic of chicken salad sandwiches, potato chips, and apple pie from Dixie's. "Shouldn't we take that stuff back to the car first?" she suggested.

"It'll be alright," he assured her. "This is Coleman, remember? Not Nashville. Folks around here can go to sleep at night with their doors unlocked." A troubled look crossed his handsome face. "Well, at least I thought so until those murders at the Elder place."

Beth tugged playfully at his hand. "Hey, I thought we weren't going to talk about that? Come on. Let's explore that creepy old mill."

A minute later, they were across the creek and standing at the threshold of the ancient structure. Beth's enthusiasm faltered a little as she peered through the open doorway. All

261

that she could see were shadowy rafters and plenty of cobwebs. "Are you sure that this place is safe?"

"The floor might creak a little, but it's sturdy enough," promised the doctor. "The state wouldn't have made this a historical landmark if it were on the verge of caving in. Follow me."

Beth clutched his hand as they stepped inside. The interior of the mill was cool and drafty, and smelled of dank stone and pine tar. The big wheel on the outer side of the wall turned steadily, causing the inner network of revolving shafts and cogs to squeak and grind. "What a racket!" she said.

"Needs oiling," joked John. "I'll show you where the old millstone used to be. They took it out years ago, when this place turned from a functional mill into a tourist attraction. I guess they didn't want some little kid falling in and getting ground to paste."

"John!" Beth laughed at his stab at black humor, then followed him down a narrow staircase to the lower regions of the old building. The wooden steps beneath their feet groaned loudly, but seemed to be solid enough to support them.

It wasn't long before they reached the cellar. A circular railing wound around a deep pit where the grinding of corn and wheat had once produced sack upon sack of flour and meal. John had been right. The millstone was gone. Only the nub of the main shaft spun a foot or so from the surface of the grinding platform.

"Hmmm," said Beth. "Interesting."

John chuckled. "Yeah, about as interesting as watching grass grow, huh?" The man moved closer and placed his hands around Beth's waist. "Believe it or not, I didn't exactly bring you down here to show you where some stupid millstone used to be."

Beth smiled shyly. She leaned nearer and put her arms around his neck. "I should have known you had an ulterior motive."

"Are you disappointed?"

She breathed in the scent of his cologne and felt the warmth of his body against hers. "Matter of fact...not at all."

John smiled in the gloom. "Good." Then he leaned down and kissed her.

Beth closed her eyes and savored the sensation of his mouth pressing softly against her own. When the kiss grew longer than was normally customary, she knew that he was as serious about the two of them as she was. She snaked her fingers through his blond hair, drew his face a little closer, and opened her mouth. A second later, their tongues met. The last time Beth had shared a French kiss was when she was in college. But she didn't find the act immature or inappropriate at all. In fact, it seemed to ease her anxiety a little and, in turn, awaken a sexuality that she had practically denied for the past four years of her life.

When they finally parted, Beth stared up into John Arnett's face. An expression—part dreamy, part serious—shown in his handsome features. She knew the words he was about to speak before he even said them.

"I...I think I'm in love with you, Beth."

Beth's heart began to beat faster. "I'm starting to feel the same way about you, too, John."

They stared at one another a moment longer, then kissed again, this time much more passionately than before.

Beth focused on the wondrous feeling that engulfed her, a feeling of being cherished and cared for, totally and without reservations of any kind. *So this is what love is like,* she told herself. She realized at that moment that all the times before had only been teenage crushes or wild infatuations and nothing more.

But, unfortunately, that comforting emotion didn't last for very long.

Beth felt her head spin dizzily, changing her pleasure into startled bewilderment. Without warning, her heart began to race and she felt an inexplicable sensation of sheer panic. Although she was in the arms of a man who she obviously cared for a great deal, she felt no sense of safety whatsoever. Instead, she felt as though she was being pursued by some horrible, yet unknown, menace. In fact, she felt very much like she had that sweltering summer afternoon when she had nearly been raped in the culvert beneath the interstate when she was six years old.

She tried to shake off the unpleasant feeling, but found that she couldn't. For a long moment, Beth felt as though she were drowning in a cold, dark pool of conflicting emotions. Oppressive emotions that both terrified and repulsed her. Suddenly, a disturbing thought came to her. She felt almost as though she were embracing a dead man. Or a man who knew death intimately.

Beth cried out and pushed away. As she stumbled back from John Arnett, she felt the confusing sensation of soul-chilling dread fade. She gulped in deep breaths of cool air, trying to clear her head and slow her erratic heartbeat.

The doctor stared at her, puzzled. "What's the matter?"

Beth didn't know what to say at first. "Uh, just give me a moment, will you?"

The two stood there in silence for what seemed like an eternity, although it couldn't have been over thirty seconds at the most. "Are you alright, Beth?" John asked, concern showing in his eyes.

"Uh, sure," she managed. "I just think maybe we're going a little too fast, that's all."

The man's face reddened in embarrassment. "Oh, Beth, I'm sorry if I rushed things…"

"No," she said, forcing a smile. "I wanted it to happen as much as you did. I care for you very much, John. I really do. It's just been so long since I've involved with someone. *Seriously* involved. I'd rather just take it slowly, if you don't mind."

"Of course," John agreed. "I understand completely." He reached out to her. "It's just that you're so beautiful and I care for you so much...well, it's difficult to not show you how I feel."

Beth allowed him to take her hand. Again, she detected only sincerity and love being directed toward her. "Maybe I'm just being silly," she told him.

"No, you're not," he assured her. "In fact, I think you're right. I believe this is too important and too precious to simply jump into. If you want to take it easy, then so do I."

"Thanks," she said, still feeling shaken and off-balance.

The two left the cellar and started back up the stairs to the upper floor of the old mill. As Beth emerged from the gloom and stepped back into the cheerful spring sunlight once again, she couldn't help but recall the combination of dark emotions that had engulfed her—emotions that were diverse, yet joined together like the lengths of a single chain. They remained with her, clinging to her subconscious like a bad aftertaste that could not be driven away.

Rage, nervousness, anticipation, and excitement.

And, strangely enough, shame.

Shame most of all.

CHAPTER THIRTY-EIGHT

Cindy stood at the edge of Cherokee Lake, staring across its still, mirror-like surface. From the opposite side, she heard a mockingbird sing. But, as far as she could tell, she was the only human present.

Her father had told her the history of the lake's namesake when she was a youngster. It was said that a small tribe of Cherokee Indians had lived on the northern bank of the lake in the early 1800s. They had kept to themselves, bothering no one, but had been driven from their camp when most of the Cherokee Nation had been exiled from North Carolina and Tennessee in 1838. They had joined the 18,000 of their kind on that long and tragic march known as the Trail of Tears, but Bedloe County's single natural reservoir had remained known as Cherokee Lake. Flint arrowheads and shards of clay pottery could still be found on the northern bank where those proud people had lived and hunted centuries before the white man had even shown his face in the Tennessee Valley.

Cindy breathed in deeply and looked around her. The thick stands of maple, oak, and birch that grew plentiful around the perimeter of the lake were budding with fresh, green life and bouquets of yellow daffodil were already in bloom. On the way from the car, she had spotted the tracks of a whitetail buck in the soft earth of the pathway. The prints had led toward the water's edge, where the animal had gone to drink its fill in the misty light of dawn.

She remembered back when she was a child, during the months following that difficult year of 1936. Her father and mother would take her and her siblings to Cherokee Lake on a Sunday afternoon. There they would have a picnic beneath the shade of the trees, after which they would take a swim. As they played and wrestled in the cool water, Clay Biggs would sit alone on a nearby bank. There he would fish with a cane pole and stare silently across the lake. Although he would smile at their antics every now and then, she knew that he had Johnny on his mind. In fact, the tragic death of his eldest son was a wound of the soul that her father never quite recovered from.

"Well, enough of this daydreaming," Cindy told herself. "Time to get down to business." She opened her purse and took out the fishing lure.

Holding the lure firmly in her right hand, the elderly woman began to walk, clockwise, around the lake. She didn't know exactly what she was searching for, or if she would even find anything at all. Truthfully, she was grasping at straws and nothing more. But she had a feeling that the fishing lure she had found in the tobacco barn had something to do with the elusive murderer of the Elder family. And, so, she figured it would do no harm to act on her hunch and explore the county's most popular fishing hole on the remote chance of discovering something of importance.

Leisurely, she circled Cherokee Lake, keeping her breath steady and her mind focused on the object in her hand. The banks of the lake varied. Sometimes they were steep and high, while occasionally they sloped gently to the level of the water. In several places, dirt tracks led to the lake's edge, providing access for fishing boats.

It wasn't long before she was halfway around the lake. Cindy was beginning to think that her hunch was merely the inaccurate intuition of a foolish old woman, when she approached one of the boat ramps. Almost immediately, she knew that something crucial was about to take place. The lure in her hand began to give off the same sensations of deep despair and hopelessness that she had experienced upon picking it up from the barn's earthen floor. And that was not all. The warm spring air around her seemed to drop twenty degrees, taking on the cool dampness of an early morning hour, rather than that of mid-afternoon.

Cautiously, she left the bank and started down the graveled ramp to the water's edge. The moment she set foot on the rocky border between dry land and lake, an overwhelming attack of *hindsight* seized her, quickly sweeping her away like the rushing waters of a flood. She felt like turning and running, leaving the approaching vision behind. But she knew that she couldn't do that. She had spent most of her life fleeing the evil that had plagued the town of Coleman that tragic year during the Great Depression. But the time for running had ended. Whether she actually wanted to or not, she knew that she must remain where she was and take in everything that came to her. She had to do it, for the sake of Josh Elder and his murdered family, if for no one else.

She closed her eyes and let go. Instantly, the sense of time and place grew less vague and more pronounced. A moment later, she opened her eyes and found herself standing on the western shore of Cherokee Lake. But it was no longer a spring afternoon. Instead, it was a cool autumn morning, perhaps at three or four o'clock AM. The sky was pitch dark overhead and the air was dank and cool with pre-dawn moisture. Crickets chirred, unseen, in the darkness of the trees behind her.

In the faint glow of a 6-volt flashlight, she found that she was in the process of readying a small johnboat for a morning of fishing. The boat was filled with equipment: an expensive rod and reel, tackle box, fishing net, and an Igloo cooler packed with ice for keeping the catch cold. As she began to push the boat into the water, she looked down and found her hands to be those of a middle-aged man. Curiously, she studied herself. Her torso was heavy, the belly flabby, clad in a checkered flannel shirt and khaki fishing vest. Upon her head was a cloth crusher hat adorned with various fishing lures. Among them was the lure that she had held in her hand only seconds ago.

She was on the verge of stepping into the boat when she heard the sound of footsteps behind her. She turned and squinted as a brilliant light shown in her eyes. Blinded, she spoke out. "What the hell—?" she protested in the gruff voice of a man. That was the only thing she had a chance to say, however.

A dark form beyond the light moved in quickly, closing the distance between them. There was a blur of motion as the assailant lashed out. She cried out as something hard crashed against the side of her head. Startled, she fell backward. Her skull throbbed and the warm wetness of blood trickled down her scalp and across her face.

Again, the bludgeon descended. It hung in dark relief against the glare of the light for a split second—the slim length of a jack handle. Feebly, Cindy lifted her arm in defense. The tire tool struck viciously, shattering the bones of her forearm. With a groan of pain, she staggered away from the attacker. Dazed and bleeding, her right arm utterly useless, she found herself lying in shallow water. A rush of panic and fear swept through her mind and she knew she must escape. But her attacker did not intend to give her that chance. They went into the water after her.

The jack handle lashed out again, this time striking her heavily on top of the head. The blow was a devastating one, severely fracturing her skull. A gorge of blood rose from out of the wound, saturating the inner lining of the fishing cap and plastering it to the crown of her head.

Dizzily, she felt consciousness begin to slip away. She found herself lying in the cold water, staring up at the dark and indistinctive form of the one who had assaulted her. They stood over her, breathing hard, but from excitement rather than exertion. Then, as they waded closer, everything plunged into darkness.

Cindy gasped out loud and, opening her hand, flung the fishing lure toward dry land. Disoriented, she found herself standing knee-deep in the chilly water of Cherokee Lake. Her heart beat so strongly that it felt as though someone's fist was pounding against her breastbone from the inside.

Feeling weak and shaken, she pulled herself from the water and sat down heavily on the bank. She spotted the lure on the rocky ground at her feet and, taking the handkerchief from her purse, picked it up with the cloth. Cindy didn't dare retrieve it with her bare hands. She certainly didn't wish to experience the terror of what had happened to the early morning fisherman again. One time was enough for her.

"Dear Lord in heaven," she breathed. "What's going on here?"

But, deep down inside, Cindy Garrison knew what had taken place. Whoever the unfortunate fisherman had been, they had fallen victim to the same fiend who had massacred the Elder family. The attack at the lake may have taken place months before the triple-murder, or perhaps even years. But it had most definitely happened, there was no denying that.

And there was something else that Cindy was certain of.

She didn't understand exactly how or why, but the victim whose consciousness she had just shared had, for some dark and unknown reason, ultimately ended up in the drafty structure of the old, abandoned tobacco barn.

It was several minutes before Cindy could summon the strength to make the long walk to the opposite side of the lake. By the time she reached the Accord, she was exhausted. She sat behind the wheel for a long time, breathing deeply, trying to calm her nerves. When she realized that she was feeling no better, she opened her purse and took out the vial of blood pressure medicine. She shook one of the pills into her palm and swallowed it with a sip of fountain drink she had purchased at Woody's General Store on her way to the lake. She had only been there a few minutes. She had talked to Janie Sadler—the granddaughter and current owner of the store—for several minutes, then paid for her drink and left.

It wasn't long before her heart rate began to return to normal. Wanting to leave Cherokee Lake as fast as possible, she started the car and was soon back on the two-lane blacktop of Highway 70 again. She headed north toward Coleman.

Cindy was driving along a curvy stretch when she suddenly realized that something was wrong. Her vision began to blur and distort. She felt her arms and legs grow alarmingly heavy and, soon, found it difficult to steer the car. The length of highway was a treacherous one—to the left were rocky limestone bluffs, while to the right was a deep embankment lined with steel guardrails.

What's the matter with me? she wondered. *Why do I feel this way?* She fought against the sluggishness, but couldn't break free from its leaden grip. A horrifying thought came to mind. *Am I suffering a stroke?*

Beth's iPhone was lying in the passenger seat. She reached for it several times before finally getting hold of it. Slowly, she punched in Sam's office number, while desperately trying to hold the car in the center of the right lane.

A second later, a voice came through the receiver. "Bedloe County Sheriff's Department. How may I help you?"

"Marge…this is Cindy…Garrison." The elderly woman tried to talk clearly, but found that her speech was slurred. "I…I'm sick. I think I'm going to…pass out."

"Just a second, hon!" piped Marge.

Cindy heard the receptionist yelling in the background and then Sam was on the line. "Cindy Ann? Are you okay?"

"No," she croaked. She stared through the windshield, saw the rock wall of the bluff rushing toward her, and jerked sharply on the steering wheel, pulling the car back into the roadway.

"Where are you?"

"Highway 70," she managed. Her eyelids began to close, as though being dragged down by lead anchors. "A few miles…north of Cherokee Lake."

Sam said something else, but it came to her as distant gibberish and nothing more. The cell phone grew so heavy in her hand that she dropped it. It bounced off the center console and fell onto the floorboard of the passenger side, out of reach.

A pall of swirling grayness obscured her vision. *Lord, help me,* she prayed, then felt the car drift swiftly toward the right. With a tremendous amount of effort, she forced her eyes open. Seeing that disaster was imminent, she tried to turn the steering wheel again. But she couldn't. She simply didn't have the strength.

Then, an instant later, the car struck the guardrail. She was aware of the jar of the impact and the shrill wrenching of tortured metal. Then, just before she blacked out, she found herself staring into the open space of a fifty-foot ravine.

CHAPTER THIRTY-NINE

It was a little past four that afternoon when Beth and John returned to Coleman.

"I wonder what Grandma's been up to today?" she wondered. "I feel kind of guilty leaving her all to herself."

"We did invite her along, you know," reminded the doctor.

"I know, but the only reason she refused was so that we could have some time alone together."

"Well, that wasn't so bad, was it?"

Beth smiled. "No, it wasn't. I really enjoyed myself." She thought about their day of picnicking and sightseeing. The only sour moment had been that one awkward instance in the cellar of the old mill. Beth wanted to forget the incident, but found that she couldn't. She still recalled those disturbing feelings of anger and shame she had experienced as she and John had kissed.

"If you're so worried about your grandmother, why don't you call her?" He took his cell phone off the console of his BMW and handed it to her.

"I believe I will." Beth took the phone and dialed her own cell number. But when the call went through, she was surprised to find that it wasn't her grandmother who answered.

"Hello? Sam Biggs speaking."

Beth felt her stomach sink. "Uh, Sam...this is Beth. Where's Grandma?"

A tense silence stretched on the other end of the line. Then the sheriff answered. "She's on the way to the hospital."

"To the hospital? What happened?"

"She was on her way back from Cherokee Lake when she had some sort of attack," he explained. "She ended up running off the road."

"Oh God!" Beth took a deep breath and tried to compose herself. "Is she alright?"

"As far as I could see, she only suffered a bruise or two. She was unconscious when I found her, though. The paramedics managed to bring her around before they left for Perryville." He paused again, then continued. "It was a close shave, Beth. She nearly went through a guardrail and over a steep embankment. If the back wheels of your car hadn't snagged the rail...well, she probably wouldn't have made it."

The awful realization that her grandmother had nearly died on some lonely country road struck the young woman like a blow to the gut. "Damn! I should have been with her. Then none of this would have happened. And, anyway, what was she doing way out at Cherokee Lake all by herself?"

"I haven't figured that out myself."

Beth's mind raced. "But what caused her to run off the road like that?" She felt a lump of emotion lodge in her throat. "She didn't have a heart attack, did she? Or a stroke?"

"We're not certain yet," Sam thought, "She blacked out. If she hadn't, she might have been dangling over the side of that embankment for no telling how long."

"I'll tell you what, Sam...we'll meet you there, okay?"

The man on the other end of the line attempted to reassure her, although he didn't sound very confident of what he was saying. "Don't worry, Beth. She'll be okay. I know she will."

Beth ended the call. For a long moment, she simply sat there staring through the windshield, her face deathly pale.

"What's wrong, sweetheart?" John asked. Seeing that Beth was upset, he pulled into the courthouse parking lot and let the engine idle.

"It's Grandma," she said numbly. "She's had an accident. They're taking her to the hospital right now."

"Then we're on our way, too."

John began to swing his car around town square, heading north toward Perryville. He wasn't halfway around the block when his cell phone received a text, alerting him of an emergency.

Two hours later, Beth and Sam sat in a waiting room near the emergency ward of Perryville Medical Center. The young woman had bought a soda from a vending machine to help settle her nerves, but she had only drunk a few swallows, allowing the beverage to grow warm in her hand.

"What's taking them so long?" she asked sharply.

Sam reached over and patted her arm. "Now, just calm down, girl. You're an ER doctor yourself. You should know it takes time to touch all the bases with a thing like this. You know, they have to examine her and do tests and such."

Beth nodded. "I know. It's just driving me crazy, that's all…not knowing exactly what happened to her." An image of her grandmother crept into Beth's mind for the umpteenth time—the elderly woman lying in a bed in a nursing home, small and drawn-up, more of a vegetable than a vibrant human being. "I just don't think I could stand it if something bad happened to her."

"Come on," said Sam. "Stop beating yourself up over this. She probably would have still had the attack, even if you'd been with her. It wasn't a crime for you to be away from her for a while."

"But her blood pressure has been sky high lately. I should have kept a closer eye on her, and not been out on some stupid date."

A somber look crossed Sam's ruddy face. "To tell the truth, Beth, if anyone's to blame for this, it's me. If I hadn't insisted that she come down here and help me with this murder case, she wouldn't be so all-fired nervous and her blood pressure wouldn't be acting up."

Beth smiled slightly. "Now who's beating themself up?"

The two lapsed into silence for a while. It wasn't ten minutes later when John showed up in the hallway. "Hey, guys," he called, his face more relaxed than it had been when he had donned a lab coat and accompanied Cindy and the paramedics into the emergency room an hour and a half ago.

Beth was out of her chair in a flash. "So what's the verdict? Is she okay?"

"She's just fine," he assured her. "I examined her thoroughly. There was absolutely no sign of cardiac arrest or a stroke. Not even a mild one."

"Was it her BP?"

A peculiar look crossed John's face. "No, her pressure is rock steady. We did do some blood work on her, however." He stared at the redhead. "Is your grandmother on any medication other than her blood pressure pills?"

"No," Beth replied. "Why?"

"Well, this is really strange, but there were traces of a strong barbiturate in her bloodstream. Enough, in fact, to put a good-sized horse down for the count, let alone an eighty-six year old woman."

"But how did it get there?"

"I have no idea," admitted John. "I sent her BP prescription down to the hospital pharmacy to have it checked out. It turned out to be plain old Hydrochlorothiazide, 25 milligrams, just like she's been taking all along. So there wasn't a mistake made in that respect."

"Then she must have gotten hold of it sometime before she left Cherokee Lake," said Beth. She recalled Sam mentioning that a fountain drink was found in one of the Accord's cup holders. Had someone drugged it while Cindy was walking around the lake? And had that someone been the killer?

She turned to the sheriff. "There was soda in the car. Can we have that tested? To see if something was put there without her knowing it?"

"Sure," agreed Sam. "I had your car towed to Parnell's Texaco in town. I'll have my deputy pick the drink up and bring it over. Is that okay, Doc?"

"No problem," said John. "If we can pinpoint where the barbiturate originated from, we can determine whether she ingested it accidently, or if it were slipped to her intentionally."

Beth looked at the doctor anxiously. "So, can we see her?"

John smiled. "Better than that. You can take her home if you like."

"Is that wise? Shouldn't you keep her overnight, for observation?"

"Well, I don't really think that's necessary," he told her. "We gave her some fluids to help dilute the drug in her system and, presently, she's feeling a lot better. She's a little sluggish and weak, but that's to be expected. What she needs most is a good night's sleep, but she can get that just as well at home as here." A smile of amusement crossed his face. "Besides, from talking to her, I've gathered that she doesn't exactly cotton to hospitals for some reason."

Sam nodded. "It comes from when she was a child. She spent the better part of a year cooped up in a hospital ward, fighting typhoid fever."

Beth looked toward the ER, appearing a bit worried. "Well, if you think it's safe to release her—"

"Well, you could seek a second opinion if you want," suggested John.

She stared at the doctor, then blushed and laughed out loud. "That's not necessary. I trust your judgment."

"Then I'll sign the release papers and turn her over to your expert care," he said, starting back toward the emergency room.

Beth turned to her great-uncle. "Sam, do you know why Grandma drove out to Cherokee Lake all by herself?"

The sheriff shrugged. "I'm not exactly sure. She was a little out of her head when the paramedics loaded her into the ambulance, but she told me that she went there to check out a suspicion of hers. And, from what I understood, she found out what she needed to know."

CHAPTER FORTY

"I don't know why I'm in this confounded wheelchair," grumbled the elderly woman. "I feel just fine now."

"It's just a legal formality we have to go by, Miss Cindy," John explained. "Until your ride gets here and we escort you to the sidewalk, you'll just have to humor us and stay put."

"Well, it's a bunch of nonsense, that's what it is."

Beth turned from the entrance of the hospital lobby. "Aw, stop griping, Grandma. You'd better thank your lucky stars that you came out of that accident in one piece. If the car had gone over that embankment, you'd likely be laid up in intensive care right now...or even worse." The hospital morgue came immediately to mind, but she didn't dare say it out loud. It terrified her to think that her grandmother had come so close to death.

"Yes, I suppose so," Cindy allowed with a sigh. "I'm just sorry that I wrecked your car, darling."

Beth laughed and gave the elderly lady a hug. "Oh, it's just an old car. You're the one that really matters."

Sam seemed irritated as he checked his wristwatch. "I'm sorry that you're having to wait so long, Cindy Ann. Gil should have been here fifteen minutes ago. I'd drive you back to Coleman myself, but I've got some business to take care of here in Perryville this evening." He looked over at John and winked. "Right, Doc?"

John smiled back. "Right."

Beth eyed the physician suspiciously. "Now what's that supposed to mean?"

"Oh, nothing. But don't be too surprised if you have an unexpected visitor later tonight."

As Beth and John moved toward one of the front windows to watch for Gil Meadows' patrol car, Cindy motioned to her brother. When the sheriff had drawn closer, the elderly woman spoke softly. "I reckon you've been wondering exactly what I was doing out there at Cherokee Lake, haven't you?"

"You said something before about going out there to look for something," he replied. "But you were a little out of your head then."

"Well, I'm as clear as crystal now. Actually, I went out to the lake to do a reading on something I found at the tobacco barn the other day." She reached into her purse, took out the handkerchief, and unwrapped it. "This."

Sam took the object from the folds of the cloth. "An old fishing lure? What in tarnation was that doing in that old barn?"

"I couldn't figure it out myself," admitted Cindy. "But seemed like every time I held it in my hand, I got the most awful sensation of fear and misfortune. So, on a hunch, I drove out there and took a walk around the lake. I figured if I was going to find out anything, it would be there, where most of the area fishermen hang out."

"And what happened?"

"I was halfway around the lake when it hit me," she said. A dark look shown in her hazel eyes. "I found myself in the place of a fisherman shortly before dawn on a fall morning. I was about to launch my boat when somebody came out of the darkness and pretty much beat the living daylights out of me. It wasn't long before I blacked out completely...or, rather, the poor soul whose shoes I stepped into. I couldn't read anything more after that. But I got the distinct impression that that

280

fisherman was abducted by someone and taken across Bedloe County to the tobacco barn. And it could very well be that his attacker was the same one who killed both the Elder family and Bud Martin."

Sam considered what she had told him. "Do you have any earthly idea when this happened?"

"It wasn't recently. I'd say two or three years ago at the least. Maybe longer than that."

"Well, after I leave Perryville, I've got to stop by the office. I'll look through the files and see if anything jogs my memory. Seems that Gil had some trouble out at Cherokee Lake several years ago, but I was at that law enforcement convention in Atlanta round about that time."

"See what you can find out, okay?" she asked. "I think it'd be well worth looking into."

"Then I'll do it," he assured his sister. "God knows, you've never steered me wrong before."

———————

At the front window, Beth and John stood closely, staring out into the hospital parking lot. The sky overhead was choked with dark clouds that promised a heavy rainfall before the night was over.

"I want to thank you, John," said Beth. "For taking such good care of Grandma."

He dismissed her gratitude with a shake of his head. "Don't mention it. I'm just glad that she's leaving here with only a few bumps and bruises. It could have been a lot worse, you know."

"Yes, I realize that. It's been on my mind all afternoon."

John put his arm around her. "Well, just breathe easy, okay? It's over with and she's just fine." A worried look crossed his face. "Uh, Beth, what happened to your grandmother today…well, it has me a little concerned."

"What do you mean?"

"Let's say that someone did give Miss Cindy that barbiturate somehow. It's safe to assume that that someone is the one who murdered the Elders. If that's the case, then who knows? They might decide to take a more direct approach against her next time. And against *you*, too."

"Aw, don't worry about us, John—"

"I can't help but worry, Beth." An expression akin to fear shown in his eyes. "It's just that the thought of you being stalked by some butchering lunatic…well, frankly, it scares the hell out of me. I'm not trying to tell you what to do—either one of you—but I really believe it would be best if you just forgot this psychic investigation of yours and went back to Nashville."

"A couple of days ago, I might have agreed with you," the redhead told him. "But, considering what happened today, I really think we ought to stay and find a solution. Besides, you'd have a better chance at winning the lottery than talking Grandma into leaving now. Someone tried to kill her and it's gotten her temper up. She'll find an answer to these crimes or die trying."

"Then, more than likely, all you'll end up doing is stepping on this bastard's toes. He'll see you and Miss Cindy as a threat and he'll have no other choice than to shut you two up…permanently." The frightened look on John's face intensified. "I don't want to see you get hurt, Beth. Please, try to talk some sense into your grandmother. Convince her to leave this ugly business alone. Sam and the state police can handle it. They'll find out who killed those poor people sooner or later."

"I know, John, but we can find out *quicker*," explained Beth. "Grandma already told me that she wants to go back to the tobacco barn tomorrow for another reading. She believes that our third try there will be the charm, and I think she's right."

282

Beth raised a hand to the doctor's face. "But I appreciate your concern, sweetheart. I really do."

"Just be extra careful," he warned. "For me."

"Of course."

John glanced toward Cindy and Sam, then ushered Beth to the other side of a potted fichus, out of sight of her family. An awkward smile crossed his handsome face. "I, uh, have something for you." He reached into his pants pocket and brought out a black velvet jewelry case. "I intended to give it to you earlier, when we got back to Coleman, but things sort of got sidetracked."

Beth's face grew flushed. "Oh, John...you shouldn't have."

"No, I insist," he said, handing her the case. "It's just a little something to let you know how much I care for you."

Her hands trembled as she opened the case. Inside was a silver pendant on a delicate chain of the same precious metal. The article of jewelry was star-shaped, adorned with diamond chips and a gleaming black onyx set in the very center.

"It's gorgeous!" she breathed. "It looks old."

"It's an antique, to be sure," he told her. "I've had it for a while. Just holding onto it, waiting for the right girl to come along. And she has."

All of Beth's misgivings vanished as she looked up into the man's eyes. "I really do love you, you know that."

"I love you, too."

The doctor lowered his face to hers and, soon, the two were sharing their third kiss of the day. This one was less impetuous than their last, but, for Beth, it was much more satisfying. She no longer felt the disturbing emotions that she had experienced during their previous moments of intimacy. All she sensed now was love, pure and simple.

Someone cleared their voice, drawing their attention from one another. Embarrassed, they turned to find Sam standing a few feet away. He had his hands buried in his pockets and his eyes directed the other way.

"Uh, don't mean to interrupt, but Gil is here with the car," he said, seeming as embarrassed as they were.

"Thanks, Sam," said Beth. She marveled at the pendant one last time, then closed the case with a snap and stuck it in her purse. "Well, I've got to go. Thanks again...for everything."

"I'll give you a call later on tonight," he suggested.

"Yes, please do." She gave him another quick kiss before leaving. "I'll be waiting."

A moment later, they were outside, wheeling Cindy to the edge of the sidewalk, where the Bedloe County patrol car was parked.

"I'm sorry that I was late," apologized Gil Meadows. "I got held up at the office a little longer than I expected. Hope you're feeling okay, Miss Cindy."

The elderly woman smiled. "I'm doing much better, Gil. Now could you please help me out of this dadblamed contraption?"

"Yes, ma'am."

"I'll try to stop by and check on you sometime tonight," Sam assured her.

"You do that, little brother. And see if you can dig up that information we were discussing, will you?"

"I'll do my best."

As Cindy climbed into the back of the patrol car, Beth turned toward the hospital entrance. She waved at John. He smiled cheerfully and waved back, then turned and started for the bank of elevators at the far side of the lobby.

Deputy Meadows held out his hand, to help her off the curb and into the back of the car. Suddenly, an unexpected feeling of dark dread and impending disaster gripped her deep down inside. She tried to shrug off the unsettling sensation, but found that it was impossible to do so. And, no matter how hard she tried, she couldn't determine exactly where it had originated from, either.

The low rumble of thunder drew their eyes toward the turbulent sky overhead.

"Looks like there's a storm brewing," said Gil.

"Yes," said Beth uneasily. "It certainly does."

CHAPTER FORTY-ONE

The old German cuckoo clock in the hallway struck the hour of eight.

Cindy and Beth sat in the kitchen of the Biggs house, drinking coffee that had been brewed on the Coleman camp stove. The only source of light was the kerosene lantern. It cast a pale glow upon the walls of faded, flowered paper, but was scarcely able to reach the shadowy, cobwebbed corners of the water-stained ceiling.

Rain fell steadily in the darkness outside. The downpour drummed loudly on the tin roof overhead. The two women reacted differently to the noise. Cindy found it comforting, remembering how a good rainstorm had always lulled her to sleep as a child. But the relentless pounding of the thundershower made Beth feel nervous and on edge, as though it were a prelude to something more sinister in nature. Something that she was yet unable to put her finger on.

"So you definitely want to go back to that old barn tomorrow and give it another try?" she asked her grandmother.

The elderly woman took a sip of coffee and nodded. "I do. We've gradually made progress since we've been here. I have a feeling that tomorrow will be the crucial point. If we put all we've got into it, we'll finally see the face of the killer. We'll know exactly who it is."

Beth tried to possess her grandmother's confidence, but, for some reason, all she felt was uncertainty. Her opinion had matched Cindy's earlier that day, when she had talked to John in the hospital lobby. But, upon stepping foot outside and seeing the black blanket of storm clouds that crowded the sky overhead, her feelings had changed. A dread she could only describe as ominous had settled within her—one that she had, so far, been unable to shake. If anything, the actual arrival of the storm had *heightened* the peculiar sensation.

Cindy eyed her granddaughter curiously. "What's the matter, dear? You seem a little distant tonight. As though you're worried about something."

"It's nothing, Grandma." She sipped her coffee and sat back in the cane-backed chair. "I guess what happened to you today just threw a scare into me, that's all."

"No, that's not it. Something else is wrong. It's as though you're waiting for something to happen."

"Yeah, sort of. But, for the life of me, I can't figure out what it might be." She searched her grandmother's lean face. "Have you ever felt that way before?"

Cindy nodded grimly. "More times than I could honestly remember."

Beth opened her purse and took out the jewelry case, hoping that it would take her mind off that dreaded cloud that hung over her head.

"What is that?" asked Cindy.

"John gave it to me just before we left the hospital." Beth opened the lid and showed her grandmother the silver pendant.

"It's beautiful." Cindy smiled warmly. "This is really turning into something special, isn't it?"

"Yes," she said, though there seemed to be a hint of uncertainty in her voice. "He told me that he loved me today, and I told him the same."

"Then why don't you seem happier?"

Beth frowned. "I don't know. I can't understand why I feel so down." She took the star pendant between her fingertips, wanting more than anything to feel joy at having received such a wonderful gift. But it seemed that the longer she held it, the worse she felt.

A knock at the back door caused her to jump violently.

"Relax," Cindy told her. "It's probably just Sam."

She left her chair and opened the door. Sure enough, it was the county sheriff. He was dressed in a yellow rain slicker and was holding a copy of that day's newspaper over his head.

"Lordy Mercy! The bottom has plumb dropped out of the barrel out there." He stepped into the kitchen quickly, but didn't allow the screen door to slam shut. "I brought someone with me. Someone who insisted on stopping by and saying howdy."

Both women were surprised to find that the one who accompanied him was Josh Elder. The thirteen-year-old stepped out of the rain, discarding his soggy newspaper on the kitchen floor next to Sam's. "Hi," he said. There was a thin smile—partly shy and partly guarded—on his lean face.

"Josh," said Cindy warmly. She walked over and took his hand. "How are you doing?"

"I'm feeling okay, I guess," he said with a shrug of his shoulders.

"Sit down a spell," insisted the elderly woman. "Both of you."

"We can't stay long, Cindy Ann," Sam told her. "Josh's aunt is coming down from Kentucky to pick him up tomorrow morning. I talked to the county district attorney this morning and we agreed that there was no cause to take the boy to the grand jury, since the murder of Bud Martin proved that the killer was still on the loose while Josh was laid up in the hospital. And John figured that he was doing well enough to be released, so I decided to spring him from that joint early. He'll be staying over at my place tonight."

A loud crack of lightning outside caused the boy to flinch. He turned troubled eyes toward the rain-speckled panes of the kitchen window. The three adults knew what was on his mind—the stormy weather was bringing back uncomfortable memories for the boy. Memories of that tragic night at the tobacco barn.

"Josh, you hounded me about coming over here to talk to these ladies and now you act like the cat got your tongue," joked Sam good-naturedly. "Isn't there something you wanted to say to them?"

"Yeah," said the teenager. Self-consciously, he turned to Cindy and Beth. "I just wanted to say thanks again…for what you did for me. You know, working so hard to bring me back like you did. If you hadn't broken through and made me face…what happened to my folks…well, I'd probably still be in that coma. I just wanted to say that I appreciate it…you saving my life the way you did."

Cindy nodded and sat back down at the table. "You're welcome, son, but we really didn't do all that much. You had the courage to face it yourself. We just sort of helped you find the right pathway home, that's all."

"Well, anyway, thanks." Having said what he had come to say, Josh lapsed into silence. He stuck his hands in his jacket pockets and looked down at the muddy toes of his sneakers.

Cindy turned to her brother. "Did you find out anything, Sam? About that fisherman?"

"Matter of fact, I believe I did," he replied. "I talked to Gil and, with the help of a couple of files, he refreshed my memory. Seems that back in 2003, a guy by the name of Kenneth Hutchinson upped and disappeared during a fishing trip to Bedloe County. He was a Nashville businessman and came down every other weekend or so to do some bass fishing. Well, Gil handled that one, just like I thought, and it appeared that the guy just vanished into thin air. His Bronco and trailer were found, along with his boat and fishing gear, but neither hide nor hair of him ever turned up. Back when Gil did the investigation, he discovered that Hutchison was on the verge of a nasty divorce and figured maybe he'd pulled a disappearing act on purpose, to keep from paying alimony and child support. But I'm beginning to think we were dead wrong about that."

"Yes, I believe so," Cindy agreed.

As the two talked, Beth took the pendant from the velvet box and unfastened the clasp of the silver chain. *What's the matter with me?* she wondered as she swept her long red hair to the side and began to put the chain around her neck. *Why am I feeling so jittery tonight?*

"Incidentally," continued Sam, his face somber. "Hutchison wasn't the only unsolved missing person case we remembered."

Cindy felt her stomach sink. "There was *another*?"

"Yes, back in the summer of '89. A woman named Sarah Vandusen. She was an antique dealer from Chattanooga. Her car was found abandoned on Highway 70, not far from here, but there was no trace of her at all. It was as though she stepped out of her car and the ground just swallowed her up."

Beth fastened the clasp of the silver necklace and then removed her hands from the nape of her neck. Almost immediately, a frightened shift of reality took place. The sensation of dread intensified, causing her heartbeat to quicken and her mouth to grow paper dry. The lantern-lit kitchen of the old house grew dimmer and dimmer, until pitch darkness surrounded her. Then the sounds around her faded—Cindy and Sam's voices, as well as the pounding rush of the downpour on the roof overhead.

She found herself suspended in blackness, waiting. Then a peculiar smell began to fill her nasal passages. It was faint at first, but soon grew cloyingly pungent.

At first, she had difficulty identifying the odor. Then it hit her.

It was the potent scent of ether.

Alarmed, Beth watched as the darkness lifted and a silvery veil of moonlight revealed her surroundings. She was in a shadowy building of some sort. Initially, she thought it was the Old Newsome Mill, but soon realized that it wasn't. The structure around her was much more spacious and lacked the cool dankness of the creek-side mill. Instead, the air was much warmer and humid, like that of a balmy summer night.

Beth felt a restrictive tightness around her wrists and ankles, almost as though they were bound and secured. She struggled and felt something coarse bite into her skin. Rope. Movement was impossible, and the smothering fumes of the ether that was being pressed forcefully against her mouth and nostrils wasn't helping matters any. She felt the strength begin to drain from her body and her thoughts soon grew murky and unfocused.

Blackness began to close around her once again. A darkness she was certain that she would never escape. As unconsciousness threatened to overtake her, she stared up at the one who crouched above her. The roof of the structure was open at one point and, in the night sky beyond, she could see the source of the nocturnal light. A full, round moon the color of pale butter.

Standing in relief against the moon was the lean head, neck, and shoulders of a young man. He extended a hand toward her, pressing down hard with the ether-soaked cloth.

Hold still! demanded a frustrated voice. *Hold still, you bitch!*

An instant later, the crude anesthesia had done its job. Beth felt listless and unable to move a muscle. She saw one last thing before she began to black out completely.

The assailant's right hand hovered into view. Clutched between the shadowy fingers was a narrow object. An object that betrayed its lethal sharpness with a flash of moonlight upon honed steel.

Then, just before a thin line of pain slashed across her nerve endings, the voice rang out again. This time it was gleefully triumphant…as well as darkly oppressive.

Do it! Do it now, dammit!

Beth cried out. She tightened her fist around something and pulled. The delicate links of the silver chain broke, severing the bridge between her and that awful moment from the past. A moment of panic and pain that had forever been preserved within a starburst of diamonds and onyx.

Horrified, she flung the pendant away from her. It slid across the wooden surface of the kitchen table and stopped in the very center. Bewildered, Beth stared at it, aware that its previous owner had now been dead for nearly twenty-four years.

For a long moment, the other three in the room simply stared at her, startled by her abrupt outburst. "Beth?" said Cindy softly, starting to leave her chair. "What's wrong?"

Beth's mouth worked, but at first she couldn't find her voice. When she finally regained the ability to speak, the full horror of what she had just experienced came to her. As well as dark truths that she would have just as soon been ignorant of.

"Oh, dear God!" she whispered. Tears formed in her hazel eyes. "No! Please, God, not—"

It was at that instant that she looked past Cindy and Sam. Beyond the rain-speckled panes of the kitchen window, she suddenly saw a shadowy form revealed in a fleeting flash of lightning.

"Look out!" she screamed shrilly.

But, before either of them had time to react, the window exploded with a deafening roar that was much louder—and much more deadly—than the rumbling of heavenly thunder.

CHAPTER FORTY-TWO

A blast of shotgun pellets obliterated the window, showering the kitchen with shards of glass. Sam had been standing between Cindy and Josh and the window, so he took the brunt of the blast. He yelled out as double-aught buckshot struck him, spinning him around and knocking him completely off his feet.

Cindy dropped to the kitchen floor, then crawled on hands and knees to the counter where the lantern stood. Reaching up, she turned the wick of the lantern down to its lowest setting. Soon, darkness filled the room.

"Sam?" Frightened, Cindy felt her way across the floor, cutting her palm on a sliver of glass as she went. She ignored the pain in her hand and spotted her brother's form in the gloom. "Sam...are you alright?"

"Not really," he replied grimly. The sheriff grunted and placed a hand to his left shoulder, which was totally numb. His palm came away slick and warm with blood. "I'm bleeding badly."

A second later, Beth was beside him. Her hands roamed in the darkness, attempting to assess the damage. "Damn it, I can't see a thing!"

Wind bellowed through the open window, blowing a fine mist of cool rain into the kitchen. Another gunshot roared only a yard or so away. This time the blast shattered the framework of the backdoor screen and blew a hole the size of a softball in the center panel of the kitchen door. Splinters and buckshot fanned across the room like shrapnel. Shards of wood pierced the opposite wall, while lead pellets careened off the old iron cook stove in the far corner.

The two women huddled together, shielding themselves, then rose and continued tending to the injured man. "There's a penlight in my purse, Grandma," Beth told her as she began to loosen Sam's clothing.

Carefully, Cindy reached over the edge of the table and located her granddaughter's purse. She rummaged blindly through its contents, until she found the tiny flashlight. "Here it is."

Beth switched on the light and studied the sheriff's wounds. He had been hit by seven or eight shotgun pellets, but the extent of the damage seemed to be confined to his left shoulder and the upper half of his left arm. Fortunately, none of the pellets had struck him in his head or neck. If that had been the case, Beth knew that he would have probably bled to death. Either that or been killed instantly.

"Pretty bad, huh?" asked Sam. His face was pale and pasty in the dim glow of the penlight.

"Not as bad as it could have been," assured Beth. The shoulder wound was what worried her the most. Three pellets had punched through flesh and muscle, leaving ragged holes the size of a nickel. The projectiles hadn't severed an artery, but it looked as though they might have nicked one. The wound bled steadily, with no sign of letting up.

Cindy read the concern in her granddaughter's face. She removed the white cotton sweater that she was wearing, bundled it up, and handed it to Beth. The young woman took it and pressed the garment tightly against the hole in Sam's shoulder. Almost immediately the white sweater turned dark crimson as it became saturated with blood.

"How are you feeling, Sam?" she asked.

The constable stared up at her. "Sort of lightheaded...and my shoulder is starting to hurt like hell." His eyes shifted, full of alarm. "Where's Josh?"

Startled, Cindy and Beth looked at one another, suddenly remembering the thirteen-year-old.

"Josh?" Cindy called as she turned. "Josh...where are you?"

Somewhere outside, in the distance, came a shrill cry. It cut through the fury of the storm, full of grief and anguish.

"Hand me that light for a second," the old woman requested. She took the penlight from Beth and directed it toward the spot where Josh had stood several minutes ago. The boy was nowhere to be found.

Cindy moved to the open doorway that led out onto the back porch. She peered past the driving rain and, in a split-second flash of lightning, saw a form running through the night, heading for the dense woods that stretched along the rear of the Biggs property.

"Good Lord! Josh!" she uttered beneath her breath. "Where are you going?"

She was turning from the door, when she noticed something. It was a tatter of dark material that was snagged on a jagged edge of the doorframe. She reached out and pulled it away. It was a fragment of the navy windbreaker that the boy was wearing. The jacket had undoubtedly snagged on the splintered wood and ripped as he left the kitchen.

But it was the flood of strong emotions that Cindy derived from handling the strip of nylon that struck her the hardest. Frightened, she turned to Beth. "He's gone," she said. "Those gunshots...they've triggered something in him...caused him to freak out."

"But where is he going?" asked the young doctor as she continued to work on Sam's wounds.

The feelings that Cindy drew from the piece of torn jacket were unmistakable. "He's going back to the last place he saw his family. Don't ask me why, but he is."

Beth's eyes widened. "Then that means that he's—"

"Going back *there*," said Cindy. "To the tobacco barn."

The throaty boom of a shotgun echoed from somewhere off in the distance.

"Lord have mercy! The killer has already seen him!"

Sam looked up at the two women. "You've got to go after him."

"We'll call Gil and get him over here," suggested Cindy. She dialed the number for the sheriff's office, but the phone bleeped as the call tried to go through. "Confound it! No service!"

"If we wait for someone to hear the shots and call the office, Josh will already be dead." He stared pleadingly up into his sister's face. "You've got to try to find him, Cindy Ann. You and Beth. There's only one eyewitness to that triple murder and the killer knows it. He'll do his best to shoot the boy down if he can."

Cindy and Beth looked at one another. They knew that Sam was right. If they didn't act immediately, there was no doubt that Josh Elder would end up like the rest of his family.

"Keep that sweater pressed firmly against your shoulder," Beth instructed. "If you don't, you could end up bleeding to death." She took the iPhone from her grandmother's hand. "If I can get a signal on the way, I'll send help."

Sam nodded. "Before you go, take my gun with you."

"I don't think that's necessary—" she began to protest.

"The hell it ain't!" snapped the law officer. "Now don't give me any lip about it, girl. Take the damn gun!"

Beth reached down to the sheriff's waist. Unsnapping the retaining strap on his black leather holster, she withdrew the

Smith & Wesson revolver. The .38 felt incredibly heavy in her hand. "Okay, but—"

"No buts about it! If you can get the bastard in your sights, unload into him. He sure isn't going to think twice about shooting at you, that's for sure."

Beth looked at the blue steel revolver for a hesitant moment, then stuck it in the side pocket of her jacket. "Remember what I said about applying pressure to that wound."

"I heard you the first time, Doctor," said Sam. "Now get going!"

Beth stood up and joined her grandmother at the kitchen door. The storm had increased in ferocity. Heavy sheets of rain slashed downward from the dark heavens, which boiled and rumbled with deep thunder. Every so often, a jagged bolt of lightning cracked across the sky, illuminating the sodden countryside, but only for an instant. Then wet darkness choked the night once again.

"Let's go, Grandma," said Beth. "But be careful, okay?"

The old woman nodded. She looked back to her injured brother. "Sam?"

"Just go," he said weakly. "Don't worry about me. I'll be okay." His eyes were troubled, not for himself, but for his sister. "And Cindy?"

"Yes?"

"If you end up having to do what you did when you were nine, then do it. No hesitation, understand?"

In the distance echoed the thunderous report of another shotgun blast. It came from the direction of the forest.

Cindy nodded grimy. "Yes."

The two women looked at each other one last time, then stepped out into the fury of the storm. Together, they ran through the high weeds of the back yard, past a chopping stump near a dilapidated outbuilding, and then into the shadowy trees just beyond.

"Grandma?" Beth asked her. "What did Sam mean back there?"

Lightning flashed, revealing haunted eyes. "I hope to God that you never have to find out," she told her granddaughter.

The winding channel of Green Creek and a quarter-mile of thick woods lay between the Biggs property and the Elder farm. They plunged into the forest and began to pick their way through the close-grown trees, aware that Death in the form of a faceless killer lurked in the darkness, somewhere between them and Josh Elder.

CHAPTER FORTY-THREE

After what seemed like an eternity, Cindy and Beth finally reached the Elder farm.

Beth helped her grandmother up a steep hollow blanketed with leafy kudzu. Then, together, the two began to make their way through the thicket that covered most of the property's acreage. Both were soaked to the skin. The force of the downpour had been relentless at first, but, little by little, the rainfall had settled into a gentle shower as the storm clouds began to move northeastward, away from Bedloe County.

But it was not the weather that concerned them. The thing that was foremost in both their minds was finding Josh Elder alive—that and the menace of the murderer who stalked him. They had heard no other gunshots since leaving the Biggs house, but that did not cause them to let their guard down. They regarded each patch of shadow with suspicion, half expecting the killer to emerge from the gloom and confront them. Beth walked with her head lowered against the rain and her right hand fisted tightly around the butt of the Smith & Wesson in her jacket pocket.

On their way there, both had been silent, immersed in their own troubled thoughts. But both knew what was on the other's mind. They were each trying to determine what had caused Josh to lose control and venture into the storm alone. Neither were psychologists, but, in their own special way, they had shared the terror of the boy's hidden trauma. Privately, each were of the opinion that the first shotgun blast had triggered a response deep within the boy's subconscious mind. Although he seemed to be coping with the loss of his family rather well, secretly he was still very much in denial. The sound of the gunshot had reopened the wound of that horrible night at the old barn and, in turn, sent him running toward his home and the place where he had last seen the members of his family.

By the time they left the thicket, the rain had stopped completely. The clouds above them began to thin and, just beyond them, gleamed the pale orb of the moon. Beth paused and tried her phone again. The signal came in clear and she dialed before she lost it. "An ambulance is on its way to the house but the signal went out before I could tell them where we were," she told her grandmother with a frown.

"Then we're on our own," said Cindy.

Cautiously, they approached the sagging structure of the old barn. As they grew closer, they listened. At first, they heard nothing. Then, from inside the ancient building drifted a sound. A low, mournful weeping. The grievous cries of a child who has been brutally introduced to a very stark and unsympathetic reality.

Slowly, they stepped through the open wall and into the barn. Pale moonlight shown through a hole in the tin roof, casting an eerie glow upon the structure's earthen floor. Josh Elder knelt before the empty tool chest at the far end of the barn. His face was buried in his hands as he sobbed openly and without shame.

"There he is," Cindy whispered to Beth. Looking around, she saw that, other than the three of them, there was no one else there. Satisfied that the boy was alone, she took a step toward him.

Suddenly and completely without warning, the moonlight faded, leaving her in total darkness. But it was not because a

Ronald Kelly

cloud had obscured the moon. Rather it was a change in time that obscured her vision. She felt disoriented and off-kilter for a long moment, unable to see or hear or to even feel the earth beneath her feet. Then, gradually, those sensations returned. But they were not entirely the same as those she had experienced a mere thirty seconds ago.

The storm had returned, or, more precisely, the storm of nearly a week before. Rain pounded on the roof of the tobacco barn and blew through the open wall behind her. The interior of the structure was illuminated by a kerosene lantern that hung from a crooked nail in one of the barn's support beams. It cast a yellow glow upon the area immediately around the wooden tool chest, like a spotlight centered on some horrid and grotesque arena.

Cindy sensed someone next to her. She turned and found Beth standing beside her. The young redhead's gaze was also glued to the circle of light and the activity that took place there.

"We're back again," she told her granddaughter.

"Yes," replied Beth. "But where is Josh?"

"We *are* Josh."

Both realized what point in time they were experiencing — the dreadful moment when Josh Elder had wandered into the barn and discovered the horrible crime that had just been committed there.

Together, they walked toward the tool chest. A dark form knelt before the box, working feverishly at the grisly task of disposing of the Elders' gunshot bodies. The hatchet rose and fell, filling the drafty structure with meaty thuds and the brittle splintering of bone. Beyond the form's left knee, they saw the lifeless face of Gordon Elder staring blindly at them. Then the honed edge of the axe fell again and the face rolled away. Both women gasped loudly and recoiled as lukewarm blood splattered their faces and clothing.

302

The form grew deathly still, suddenly aware of their presence. Slowly, the figure stood and turned around, still holding the bloody hatchet in one hand.

Cindy and Beth stared at the featureless silhouette, waiting. But what happened next was not what they had experienced upon their previous readings. Surprisingly, something entirely different and unexpected took place.

They watched, horrified and amazed, as the single form before them wavered like the shimmering image of a desert mirage. Then, slowly, it *divided*, splitting cleanly in half.

It was at that moment that both women realized why the face of the murderer had not been revealed to them. For the evil that had been responsible for the slaughter of the Elder family had not originated from a single source.

Instead, there had been *two*.

They watched as the pair of forms stood there, motionless at first. One continued to hold the hatchet, while the other bent down and took a sawed-off shotgun from the barn floor. Then, just as Cindy and Beth were certain that the vision would continue, it faded back into blackness again.

"Grandma!" called out Beth's voice. "Where are you?"

"I'm right here, dear," Cindy replied.

Then, abruptly, the roar of the downpour overhead ceased and they were back in the barn again, staring at the weeping form of Josh Elder a few yards away.

Grandmother and granddaughter turned and looked at one another. No words needed to be spoken. Both had sensed the true nature of those two murderous forms.

One had been the tool of the crime, physically committing the gruesome acts. But the other had been the driving force behind the killings. They had manipulated the other like a puppet, giving the order to kill and dismember, like a sadistic general commanding a loyal, but misguided soldier.

CHAPTER FORTY-FOUR

A chill ran through Cindy and, suddenly, she knew that they were no longer alone.

"So, we're back where it all began," said a voice behind her. "Aren't we, Cindy Ann?"

The elderly woman turned and saw two shadowy forms standing in the gloom. One nodded to the other. A double-barreled shotgun was broken open, the spent shells discarded and replaced with fresh ones. Then the breech of the twelve-gauge was closed with a metallic *clack*.

"Yes, Benny," she replied. "Everything always seems to lead back here, doesn't it?"

Cindy and Beth watched as the elder of the two stepped into the moonlight. Ben Arnett smiled at them the way he did when he cheerfully greeted a customer at his downtown drugstore. But the expression of amiable good-naturedness failed to reach his eyes. They sparkled cruelly behind the lenses of his wire-rimmed spectacles, small and shiny like those of a poisonous snake.

"I must admit that I never suspected you," said Cindy.

"No, but your granddaughter did," said the pharmacist. "Or at least she suspected my partner. Or am I mistaken about that, Miss Garrison?"

Beth shook her head, her face starkly pale. "No, you're right. I did suspect that he was involved. But I didn't want to believe it." Sadly, she looked over at Cindy. "I'm sorry, Grandma. I should have told you."

"That's alright, dear," the old woman said softly. She could see the hurt in the girl's eyes. "I understand. Believe me, I do."

"Touching," said Ben. The elderly man was empty-handed, but an object hung through the belt of his britches—a short-handled camp hatchet. The steel head was ruddy with dried blood. "But her feelings were what did you in...all three of you. Tenderness always gets in the way of what is truly important."

Cindy felt her heartbeat slow and a strange calmness settled within her. "So, what's important to you?" she asked. "Fear and pain? Death and misery?"

Arnett chuckled. "All of the above."

She stared at him and saw a man that she did not know, rather than an old and trusted friend. "What the hell happened to you, Benny?"

"That's just it, Cindy Ann," he replied. "Things have changed. I'm not that sickly, cowardly little boy that you grew up with back during the Depression. I haven't been since that day we wandered into this...this *wondrous* place...and found the contents of that tool chest over yonder."

"I don't understand," said Cindy guardedly.

"Oh, but I believe you do," Ben insisted. "Deep down inside, I believe you understand completely." A dreamy, yet sinister look came into his aged eyes. "Before that summer day, I was nothing. Nothing but a skinny, spineless young'un, who was scared of his own shadow. The only nerve I got came from hanging around Chester Martin. When he bullied the kids at school, when he had them down on their bellies, rubbing their faces in the dirt, I saw what *I* wanted to be. I wanted that strength, that power over others. But I was weak. I had the smarts, but I didn't have the nerve or the muscle. So I hung around Chester and, for a while, his cruelty satisfied me. But I lost it that day you got the better of him, that day at school when you twisted his mind and made him see snakes that weren't really there." He spat on the dirt floor with contempt. "I hated you for that, Cindy Ann. God, how I hated you for robbing him of that control that he loved so much. And, in turn, preventing me from sharing in it."

Cindy stared into the pharmacist's face and, beyond the veneer of kindness and respectability, saw the ugly, cancerous soul of a madman. "Benny…"

"No," he said, lifting a hand to silence her. "If you want to hear it, you'll hear it *all*." He licked his lips, then continued. "For a month or so, I was lost. After you knocked Chester off his high horse, I didn't know who I was or what I wanted to feel. I had this need in me, this urge to look upon pain, to witness suffering. And, yes, to even participate in it. I wanted *that* more than anything else. But I didn't have the nerve or the stomach for such. Why, I'd nearly pass out if I skinned my knee or pricked my finger. So my awful need was like a double-edged sword. I cherished the sight of blood, but it also repulsed me.

"Then we went roaming that hot day in July and ended up *here*." He looked around the drafty old barn with a mixture of awe and admiration. "We broke open that tool chest and I looked upon my destiny. I knew it the moment I discovered the beauty of mangled flesh and bone, and smelled the intoxicating stench of raw death. It sickened me, that's true. It made me run out of this barn and puke my living guts up. But it also *inspired* me. While you, Chester, and the Osbornes were crying yourselves to sleep that night, I lay awake in bed and thought of what we had found that day. And I couldn't help but think of how very wonderful the one who had wreaked such havoc must be. In my eyes, he was a god. Around midnight, I dressed and snuck out of my house. I came back to this barn and felt as though I had arrived *home*. The remainder of that night, I slept in the tomb those three boys had occupied for the past few months, reveling in the presence of death. True, it sickened me, but it also comforted me in a way I had never known before."

Tears bloomed in Ben Arnett's eyes, like a man giving his testimony before the congregation of a church. But in his case, the testimony was not spoken out of regret, but out of perverted pride. "As I grew from a boy into a man, my desire to command agony and death threatened to consume me. For years I dreamed of indulging in the act of murder, the way my idol Bully Hanson had, with brutality and without conscience. I hungered to slay with my own two hands, but I couldn't. I was too weak and far too squeamish. I could look upon death, but could not bear to spill blood myself. I looked toward a career in medicine to fulfill my need, but I did not possess the strength or nerve to partake in the taboo glories of the human body. The sight of blood and exposed organs fascinated me to no end, yet I was still unable to indulge in such revelry myself.

"For many years, I was a broken man. Yes, I had success as a pharmacist, a nice home, and a loving family, but none satisfied me. My true love was forbidden, cast aside by my own damnable weakness. Then it changed when my oldest son and his wife were killed in a car crash and their surviving child came to live with me. My eyes were opened. If I could not indulge in my dark passion, then my grandson would. Through him, I would live up to Bully Hanson's potential. I would reign over torment and death the way Bully had so many years before."

Grinning broadly, Ben Arnett turned toward the one behind him. The man remained in the gloom, clutching the shotgun in his manicured hands.

"It took some doing, it took years of training and hard discipline, but eventually he lived up to my expectations. I drove every last bit of weakness from him and forged him into the man he is today." Ben's eyes sparkled insanely. "Isn't he a wonder? He's a true practitioner of life and death, my grandson is. One who is as adept at healing the human body as he is at destroying it."

Ben motioned to the form in the gloom, beckoning for him to emerge from the shadows and take his place at the side of his grandfather and mentor. Beth's heart ached as she looked upon his tall, athletic frame and the able hands that had delivered babies and done delicate, life-saving surgery. Hands that had both held her tenderly and mutilated horribly during the span of a single week.

She found herself hoping that the handsome, young man would not step out of the shadows. That it would turn out to be someone else entirely or perhaps his evil twin, like in one of those corny soap operas. But she knew better than to hope in such a naïve and unrealistic way.

Beth knew, deep down in her heart, that the love of her life was, indeed, the heir of a dark legacy of vileness and depravity. A legacy he had accepted and participated in, even though it was not of his own free will.

CHAPTER FORTY-FIVE

John Arnett stepped into the moonlight, his face a rigid mask that was totally devoid of emotion. But his eyes belied the emotions that he harbored—a tormented mixture of fear, shame, and disgust, as well as rage. Rage and hatred toward the man who had molded him into the monster he now was.

"Kill the boy first," said Ben with a nod.

The doctor hesitated, but for only an instant. Then he started forward, the antique shotgun cradled in his hands.

"No!" screamed Beth. She stepped in front of Josh, her arms outstretched. "You can't, John. I won't let you."

Ben Arnett laughed. "You have no say in the matter," he said, amused. Then his voice grew sterner, harsher. "Kill them both."

John took a couple of steps forward and slowly lifted the twelve-gauge. His eyes blazed with mental anguish.

"John...baby...please, don't," pleaded Beth, her voice cracking.

The man simply stood there for a long moment. Then his thumb rose to the rear of the breech and cocked back the gun's twin hammers, first one and then the other.

Tears trickled down Beth's face. "I love you, John. I really do, with all my heart. And I believe you love me, too."

"Shoot her, John," demanded his grandfather. "Now!"

The young doctor directed the muzzles of the twelve-gauge squarely at the redhead's tearful face. He snaked his forefinger through the case-hardened guard and laid it across one of the double triggers. For a long moment, the shortened barrels of the scattergun trembled. Then, slowly, they lowered.

"I...I can't, Grandpa," he said through clenched teeth. "She loves me."

"You idiot!" snapped Ben. "She's a damn liar, just like all those other bitches. She doesn't love you. She thinks you're worthless, boy. Probably been laughing behind your back, making fun of you." The elderly pharmacist took a couple of steps toward his grandson, frustrated by his hesitancy. "Now do as I said. Shoot her!"

John stood stone still, torn between one love and another. Then he turned and glared at the man who had raised him. "I won't do it. I love her."

Ben's face grew crimson with rage. His eyes widened, seeming to fill the lenses of his glasses. "So you've chosen her over your own flesh and blood, is that it?" He started toward John, his fists clenched. "You bastard! You damn traitor!"

"Stay away," warned his grandson feebly. "Don't come any closer."

The pharmacist ignored him, however. "Well, if you won't do it, then I will!" He wrenched the shotgun from the young man's hands and, for the first time in his life, turned his malevolent desire to kill directly upon another human being. He swung the sawed-off barrels of the shotgun on Beth.

"You were stupid, girl," said Ben. His face turned pale and clammy at the thought of actually committing murder. "And so was your granny. You both should have gone back home after I sent that Martin boy to scare you off."

Beth took a step backward. *Oh God, he's going to kill me! He's really going to kill us all!*

But before he could pull the trigger, John stepped in front of his grandfather, blocking his aim. He grabbed the stubby barrels of the gun in one hand. "Don't, Grandpa," he urged. "Please, just give me—"

Ben Arnett looked as though his world was crumbling. "You lousy sonofabitch! You've betrayed me! Chosen her over me!"

Helplessly, Beth watched as the two men wrestled for a frantic moment, the twelve-gauge trapped between them. Then, suddenly, the gun went off. An ear-splitting boom filled the hull of the old tobacco barn, bouncing off its walls of dry-rotted lumber and rising to the dusty rafters overhead. Then she watched with horror as John fell to his back on the earth of the floor. His eyes stared up at his grandfather with disbelief, while his hands clutched at the ugly crater in the center of his chest.

"John!" wailed Beth. A moment later, she was by his side, holding his head in her lap. She stared down at him, shocked. The color drained from his face as quickly as the blood drained from his body.

"I'm sorry, Beth," he said, tears of remorse welling in his eyes. "I'm so sorry."

As she held him, a steady stream of images flashed through Beth's receptive mind. Deplorable images of a hellish childhood shaped and molded by an oppressive demon of a grandfather. Nights locked in a cold, dark cellar, naked and half-starved. Searing words of mental torment, tearing his confidence and self-esteem, even his individuality, apart bit by bit. And there was physical abuse as well. The constant punishment, the beatings, the awful suffering at the mercy of wire pliers, battery cables, and cigarette butts.

Then came humiliation and submission. Compliance with commands that surpassed the very fabric of human sanity. The stalking in the dead of night, the abductions, the long sessions of torture that had been deceptively masqueraded as surgical practice. And then there was death, both quick and explosive, as well as slow and meticulously cruel. The faces of the victims returned, etched in agony and mortification, the last hope of survival wrung from their mutilated bodies. The stray dogs and cats. The three-year-old child taken from a rest stop off Interstate 40. A teenage girl he had met at a McDonald's in Nashville. Other girls, sweet and smiling—lying whores in his grandfather's eyes. The woman whose tire had gone flat on the lonesome stretch of Highway 70—the one with a back seat full of antiques and the silver pendant around her neck. The middle-aged fisherman bludgeoned and dragged, unconscious, from the edge of Cherokee Lake. Several others: homeless drifters, hitchhikers, pretty runaways with sunken eyes who would do anything for a fix. And then the last of many. The Elders—half-asleep but aware of their fate. Executed for the most horrible of crimes...blasphemy.

"Why, John?" Beth asked, searching his dying eyes. "Why the Elders?"

"They were going to tear this place down," he whispered. "Tear down this horrible place my grandfather considered to be a shrine. That was intolerable to him. He couldn't bear to see it destroyed. So the Elders had to die...to save his temple from falling."

"But that wasn't all, was it?" asked Beth, sensing something dark and evil about the earth beneath her. "There was some other reason."

"Yes," he muttered, the glimmer of light fading from his eyes. "He was afraid that his secret would be uncovered...that *they* would be discovered during the barn's destruction."

"The bodies of those who died here," she finished, feeling an icy coldness deep down in her soul.

"Forgive me, Beth," he rasped, his voice barely audible. "I never wanted to be like him. Never wanted...to be a part of his...evil."

Beth ran a hand lovingly across his forehead. Her tears anointed his face, driving away the awful sadness, bringing a smile.

"You're forgiven."

A moment later, John Arnett was gone.

Ben Arnett stared down at the gun-shot body of his grandson. His eyes burned feverishly, not with horror and regret, but with excitement.

"I did it," he said incredulously. "After all these years, I've finally found the strength.'

It was at that moment that Beth remembered the gun in her jacket pocket. She slipped her hand into her coat and withdrew the .38 revolver. Her hand trembled as she aimed the barrel at him and thumbed back the hammer.

"You fiend!" she sobbed. "You killed him. You killed your own grandson!"

"He betrayed me," Ben told her. "He was no longer family, just a traitor who made a fatal choice."

Beth rose slowly to her feet. "I'll kill you. I swear I'll shoot you down, just like you shot John."

The old man stared at her for a moment, then threw back his head and laughed. "You underestimate me, bitch! You don't realize what I'm capable of. A few minutes ago, I wouldn't have been able to pull the trigger of this gun. But now things are different. Dangerously different."

Before Beth could react, Ben whirled, centering the muzzles of the shotgun on the elderly woman standing nearby. "Throw down that pistol," he warned. "Throw it down or I'll blow her clean in half!"

The redhead stared into his eyes and saw the light of a power-drunk lunatic blazing there. She knew that he was not bluffing. He had overcome his weakness and been transformed into the murderer he had always dreamed of becoming. If she didn't do what he said, he would surely kill her grandmother.

Helplessly, she uncocked the gun's hammer and tossed it to the earth at his feet.

Ben chuckled and kicked the revolver away into the shadows. Then he centered his attention on his former playmate. "You should have never come here, Cindy Ann. You never should have come sticking your nose in things that were none of your business."

The old lady stared back at him. Like her granddaughter, she was aware that the man was on the verge of killing them all, not only to cover his tracks, but simply for the pure pleasure of the act itself. Strangely enough, however, she did not feel frightened. The last time she had felt that way had been when she was a child—on that snowy December night when she had left her hiding place behind the old tool chest and faced Bully Hanson and Claude Darnell.

"Throw down the gun, Benny," she said calmly, taking a step toward him.

Ben simply laughed. He leveled the shotgun's muzzles at her—one chamber empty, the other fully loaded.

Yet she continued. Her face remained grim, but her eyes held an odd expression. A gleam that could only be described as unsettling.

"Throw it down or I'll be forced to stop you," she warned. "The same way I stopped another murderer in this place seventy-seven years ago."

CHAPTER FORTY-SIX

B en Arnett couldn't help but laugh at such a pitiful attempt at mercy. "You always were a stupid bitch, Cindy Ann."

Cindy's face remained impassive. "You've been warned, Ben."

The old man grinned, anticipating the adrenaline rush of his second kill of the night. He steadied the shotgun on the center of Cindy's chest, then prepared to squeeze the trigger.

But before he had the chance to do so, something unexpected happened. Unexpected and completely inexplicable.

The moonlight from the open roof overhead suddenly faded, plunging the interior of the barn into total darkness. He considered going ahead and pulling the trigger, then restrained himself. He wanted to see the old hag when he killed her. And, what was more, he wanted her to see *him* as well.

He waited, listening for the sound of terrified breathing or fleeing footsteps. He heard neither. Nothing except complete silence. Even the boy who knelt at the tool chest had ceased his infernal crying.

Then, gradually, the moonlight returned, shining palely through the hole in the barn roof. When his eyes readjusted to the light, he was surprised to find that Cindy no longer stood eight feet in front of him. In fact, she wasn't there at all. She had completely disappeared.

"Damn!" he cussed. He turned the muzzles of the shogun toward Beth, but the redhead was no longer where she had stood either. And the boy was gone, too. The moonlit earth around the old tool chest was empty and unoccupied.

"What the hell's going on here?" he demanded.

Then, from behind him, came the soft shuffling of footsteps against the dirt floor.

Thinking that they had somehow gotten behind him, Ben Arnett whirled. But he did not fire the last round from the double-barreled shotgun. Stunned, he watched as a dark form emerged from the shadows and revealed itself in the silvery moonlight.

The one who faced him was a tall, burly man dressed in a shirt of checkered flannel, khaki britches, and scuffed leather work boots. His hair was short and blond, his face broad and humorless. And his eyes...his eyes were as cold and gray as a granite tombstone in the dead of winter.

At first, Ben failed to recognize the man. Then it dawned on him. The last time he had seen the big man was when he was nine years old. The day when Sheriff Taylor White and his deputies had escorted the criminal and his accomplice from the Bedloe County courthouse following their conviction for the brutal murders of three teenage boys.

The one who stood before him was the killer he had worshipped since childhood. The cold-blooded murderer known as Bully Hanson.

Humbled by the man's presence, Ben stumbled forward. "It's...it's *you*," he stammered. "It's really you!" Breathlessly, he extended his hand toward the man who had inspired him so many decades ago.

"You weakling!" he rasped. "You have a lot of gall, attempting to carry on my work. You're a sorry, spineless little bastard, Arnett. Forcing your grandson to do all the work, while you stood back and watched, scared of getting your hands dirty!"

"No!" protested Ben. "It wasn't like that."

Bully's breath reached him, hot and repulsive, reeking like sunbaked roadkill. "You have no earthly idea how much pain and destruction I was capable of, how much evil I'd committed during my lifetime. And you thought you could measure up to *my* standards? You ain't worth the dog shit on my shoes, let alone good enough to fill them!"

Ben was stunned by his idol's scathing words. He felt his spirit shrivel up like the dead husk of a spider and that old feeling of inadequacy and weakness return. Then his heart leapt into his throat as Bully Hanson took a step or two closer, until they were standing face to face.

The murderer lifted his hand into view. Clutched in his fist was the twelve-gauge Ben had held scarcely a moment before. Shocked, the pharmacist looked down and found his hands empty.

Ben cried out as Bully jammed the barrels of the shotgun into his open mouth. He shuddered as he felt the cold steel of the muzzles press against his lips and tasted the steely tang of gunmetal against his tongue.

Bully grinned wickedly. "Do you want to experience true death, Arnett? Up close and personal?" The cold, gray stones of his eyes twinkled contemptuously. "Those of us who know how to give it, and give it well, are of a select fraternity. Unfortunately, you were never a member. You were blackballed from the very beginning."

The old man moaned as he heard the crisp clicking of the gun's hammers being cocked and felt the pressure of the muzzles press against the roof of his mouth. Then Bully Hanson unleashed a cold and deadly laugh.

317

The same laugh that Ben himself had uttered dozens of times in the past.

————————

The muffled boom of a shotgun filled the dark structure of the old tobacco barn. The moonlight that had faded behind a stray cloud again returned, casting its pale glow upon the earthen floor.

The thick stench of gun smoke and blood hung heavily in the air. Dazed, Beth walked over and stood next to her grandmother. Together, they stared down at the body at their feet.

Ben Arnett lay on his side, his legs curled stiffly toward his chest. The barrels of the sawed-off shotgun were wedged tightly in his mouth and the fingers of his right hand were pressed firmly against the trigger. The blast had blown away most of his head.

Beth looked over at her grandmother. Cindy continued to stare at the body, her face ashen and stunned.

"Grandma?"

"Yes, dear?"

"Grandma…did *you* do this?" she couldn't help but ask. "Did you make this happen?"

Cindy turned toward her granddaughter. Beth expected to see guilt in her eyes, but it wasn't there. Instead, there was an expression of complete bewilderment…and more than a little fear.

"No," she answered. "I was about to stop him, that's true. But before I could, something *intervened*." She looked around at the shadows that choked the walls and rafters of the old barn. "Something stepped in and prevented me. Something very powerful…and very *evil*."

A feeling of cold dread filled Beth. "You don't think it was—"

Cindy shook her head, looking much older than she had several days ago. "I don't know, dear. And part of me doesn't want to."

Goose bumps covered the redhead, causing her arms and scalp to tingle. "Come on," she said. "Let's get out of this place."

After gently helping Josh up from his place at the tool chest, the three left the ancient building and headed back through the dark thicket, toward the forest and the Biggs property just beyond.

Before entering the woods, Cindy and Beth turned and stared at the sagging structure of the old tobacco barn one last time. They sensed that the old evil was still there. And, deep down inside, both knew that it always would be.

Silently, they turned from that ungodly place and started through the darkness toward home.

EPILOGUE

The phone rang several times before Beth answered it.
"Hello?"

"Yes, is Mrs. Garrison there, please?" asked the voice of a man.

The young woman's suspicions surfaced. Surely it wasn't another reporter calling, trying to dig up more dirt on what had happened in Coleman a month ago. "May I ask who is calling?"

There was a short stretch of silence, then the caller replied. "This is Detective Fred Canton with the Metro Police Department. I really would like to talk to Mrs. Garrison, if it's convenient."

"I'm afraid it's not," Beth told him.

"I don't believe that you understand. This is important."

"Does this concern a case you're working on? One that you would like her to do a reading on?"

The man on the phone seemed hesitant. "Uh...yes, it does."

"I'm sorry," Beth told him. "But she no longer does that type of work. She's retired now."

The man seemed upset. "Since when?"

"Since a month ago."

She could feel his frustration and disappointment through the telephone line. Beth considered the stories she had read in the newspaper that morning. Which crime could it be? The drive-by shooting in the housing projects of East Nashville that had claimed the life of a two-year-old child? Or perhaps the

320

body of the unidentified woman who had been found taped up in an old TV box, naked and stabbed numerous times?

She looked out the living room window. In the front yard, her grandmother was planting flowers around the base of a concrete birdbath. Cindy had said very little since their trip to Bedloe County. She seemed strangely withdrawn and kept mostly to herself. She hadn't even asked Sam about the ongoing investigation of Ben and John Arnett the last time the county sheriff had called. Beth had to call him back herself, just to find out what the state police and the Tennessee Bureau of Investigation had discovered.

And they had discovered plenty. When the earthen floor of the old tobacco barn had been excavated, a total of thirty-six bodies were found. Fourteen had been the remains of small animals, while the other twenty-two had been human in nature. It was suggested that the structure be demolished following the completion of the investigation, but, so far, nothing had been done. The old barn still stood where it had for years...and where it would probably continue to stand for many years to come.

Beth thought of John, of the horrible things he had done, as well as the short time they had shared. She quickly drove him from her mind, before that familiar ache of loss and despair started all over again.

"I'm sorry to hear that," said the voice on the phone.

"Excuse me?" asked Beth, returning her attention to the caller.

"I said I'm sorry to hear that she has retired," said Detective Canton. "She really did a special service for us, and for this city, that's for sure."

Beth was silent for a moment. She considered a decision she had been struggling with for several weeks. Following the review board hearing and her unfair dismissal from Vanderbilt earlier that month, Beth had begun to wonder if her calling in life had been a career in medicine after all. Whether it was a blessing or a curse, she realized that she had been born with a precious gift. One that could no longer be denied.

She hesitated, then spoke into the receiver. "Detective Canton?"

"Yes?"

"My grandmother can no longer help you, but perhaps I can," she said, taking the first step of a long journey. "My name is Beth…"

ABOUT THE AUTHOR

Ronald Kelly was born November 20, 1959, in Nashville, Tennessee, where he was raised a Southern Baptist. He attended Pegram Elementary School and Cheatham County Central High School (both in Ashland City, Tennessee) before starting his writing career.

Ronald Kelly began his writing career in 1986 and quickly sold his first short story, "Breakfast Serial," to *Terror Time Again* magazine. His first novel, *Hindsight* was released by Zebra Books in 1990. His audiobook collection, *Dark Dixie: Tales of Southern Horror*, was on the nominating ballot of the 1992 Grammy Awards for Best Spoken Word or Non-Musical Album. Zebra published seven of Ronald Kelly's novels from 1990 to 1996. Ronald's short fiction work has been published by *Cemetery Dance*, *Borderlands 3*, *Deathrealm*, *Dark at Heart*, *Hot Blood: Seeds of Fear*, and many more. After selling hundreds of thousands of books, the bottom dropped out of the horror market in 1996. So, when Zebra dropped their horror line in October 1996, Ronald Kelly stopped writing for almost ten years and worked various jobs including welder, factory worker, production manager, drugstore manager, and custodian.

In 2006, Ronald Kelly started writing again. Since then, he has written and published several new novels (*Hell Hollow*, *Restless Shadows*, and *The Buzzard Zone*), numerous short story collections, and has become an elder statesman of Southern-Fried Horror in his chosen genre. In 2021, his collection of extreme horror tales, *The Essential Sick Stuff*, won the Splatterpunk Award for Best Collection. He is currently working on The Saga of Dead-Eye, a five-volume horror western series.

Ronald Kelly currently lives in a backwoods hollow in Brush Creek, Tennessee, with his wife and young'uns.

Book List

Novels
Blood Kin
Father's Little Helper (re-released as Twelve Gauge)
Fear (Author's Preferred Edition)
Hell Hollow
Hindsight
Moon of the Werewolf (re-released as Undertaker's Moon)
Pitfall
Restless Shadows
Something Out There (re-released as The Dark'Un)
The Buzzard Zone
The China Doll
The Possession (re-released as Burnt Magnolia)
The Saga of Dead-Eye, Book One: Vampires, Zombies, & Mojo Men
The Saga of Dead-Eye, Book Two: Werewolves, Swamp Critters, & Hellacious Haints
Timber Gray

Novellas
Flesh Welder

Collections
After the Burn
Cumberland Furnace and Other Fear Forged Fables
Dark Dixie
Dark Dixie II
Haunt of Southern-Fried Fear
Irish Gothic: Tales of Celtic Horror
Long Chills
Midnight Tide & Other Seaside Stories

Curious about other Crossroad Press books? Stop by our
website: http://crossroadpress.com
We offer quality writing
in digital, audio, and print formats.

Subscribe to our newsletter on the website homepage and
receive a free eBook.

www.ingramcontent.com/pod-product-compliance
Lightning Source LLC
Chambersburg PA
CBHW051953240626
47153CB00005B/1734